SINFULLY
Ever After

JAYNE FRESINA

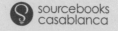

sourcebooks
casablanca

Published by Sourcebooks Casablanca, an imprint of Sourcebooks,
Inc.
P.O. Box 4410, Naperville, Illinois 60567-4410
(630) 961-3900
Fax: (630) 961-2168
www.sourcebooks.com

Printed and bound in Canada.
MBP 10 9 8 7 6 5 4 3 2 1

To Nana

"The more I know of the world, the more I am convinced that I shall never see a man whom I can really love."
—Miss Marianne Dashwood,
Sense and Sensibility

"Who needs a man? Acquire a dog instead."
—Miss Rebecca Boadicea Sherringham,
generally in high dudgeon

One

Was it any surprise, Rebecca thought crossly, that she, at the age of seventeen, already viewed men with such a cynical eye?

She looked again at the words scrawled haphazardly across a scrap of paper.

> *Temporarily light a few shillings. Be an angel and bring Mother's music box, quick as you can.*
>
> Nate

Crumpling the note in her gloved fist, she cursed. "Angel, indeed! If I had a halo, I'd choke you with it, Nathaniel Sherringham."

She peered in through the tavern window. A red blob among several, her brother was identifiable mostly from his familiar, unbound laughter.

How much, she wondered with that awful, sinking pit in her stomach, had he wagered and lost this time? Sometimes she was surprised to find she still had a full head of hair when she woke in the morning, since Nathaniel once tried to pay a debt by offering her abundant bronze locks as payment.

Taking a deep breath, as if it might be the last fresh taste she would ever have, Becky pushed open the door and stepped inside that smoke-filled tavern.

The noise fell away to a surprised murmur as faces turned to observe her through the gray cloud. They couldn't know, of course, that if anyone tried to lay hands upon her, she had an officer's pistol hidden inside her muff and she itched for a chance to use it.

Men! You'll never find a group of women sitting around, drunk, with nothing to do but throw money away and fondle loose persons of the opposite gender, she thought.

"Ah! Here she is!" Nathaniel's drunken shout greeted her as she marched to his table, parting the foggy whorls with brisk, impatient sweeps of one arm. From the lack of focus in her brother's blue eyes and the way he slouched in his chair, she could tell he'd been there for quite some time. Around the table, his opponents were in a similar state of disrepair, all in their cups, all staring at her.

Except for one.

Although Rebecca had meant only to skim the other players with disdain, her scornful gaze tripped to a halt.

In that crowded den of vice, *his* were the only eyes that didn't take obvious note of her arrival. He was too preoccupied by something he kept inside his coat—a small bulge guarded possessively. His winnings, no doubt. But when one of the other men alerted him to the change in their surroundings, he slowly turned his head to where Rebecca stood.

Two dark eyes in a deeply tanned, weather-bitten face met her gaze. As he found her staring back so boldly, he hitched forward, she supposed to get a better look at her. Rebecca did not flinch from studying him—or as much of the man as she could see—in the same way. He was rugged rather than handsome, no more distinguished or dashing than any other fellow about thirty. His hair and eyes were black as a moonless midnight in winter. A daubing of firelight revealed that his nose was slightly crooked and the bridge flattened—no doubt by a well-landed thump, for he looked the sort to attract knuckles and serve plenty of his own. Oh yes, she knew the type.

His chin was square and unshaven, his cheek scarred. The large gray coat he wore must be heavy, but he didn't seem to mind the additional heat. He had claimed the only piece of furniture in the place that was made to keep out drafts—an old-fashioned, high-backed settle chair of the style once found in medieval castles. *And that*, she thought suddenly, *is where he belongs too, in some long ago past of lawless mercenaries and conquering warriors.*

Nathaniel waved a tankard in Rebecca's direction and burped. "This is my sister, a terrible, nagging, ingrate wench. And this"—he swung his arm back again to point at the large slab of trouble across the table—"is Lucky."

No one had ever looked less suited to their name.

Neither had anyone ever looked at Rebecca the way this man did. As if he saw right through her clothes. Right through her skin to where her heart was beating.

Those two coal-black eyes narrowed and his gaze intensified, seeking out her corners, curves, and dips with unwavering, unblinking attention.

"Well? Where is it?" Nathaniel demanded, his chair creaking violently as he twisted around to face her again. "You did bring the music box, like I said in my note?"

She tore her gaze from the other man. "No, I did not. Since it is all we have left of our mother, I certainly will not let you give it away to a stranger. If you were sober, you would not think of it either."

All eyes turned to the strapping fellow across the table. Only his fierce regard remained focused on her.

Meanwhile, Nathaniel's face now matched his uniform. "Damn you, Becky. Don't lecture me. Fetch the music box."

"Fetch it yourself."

He couldn't, though. The chair and table were all that kept her brother semi-upright at that moment.

Raising her voice to address the grim observer in the settle chair, she demanded, "How much does he owe you, sir?"

The lack of response from Lucky's lips brought an ominous weight of silence to the crowded tavern.

His gaze had fallen to her feet and now, as it made its way slowly upward again, Rebecca was forced to recall a time in childhood when Nathaniel, in retaliation for her accidentally burning out the seat on a pair of his breeches, had tried selling her off to a maharajah's nine-year-old son. Of course, she was delivered safely back in time for nursery dinner, but ever since then, Nathaniel had looked for some way to unload his irritating little sister, preferably at profit to himself, and she suspected he wasn't always joking.

Caught in the ruthless grip of this stranger's perusal and with no music box to satisfy his debt, she wondered exactly how inebriated and desperate her brother need be before he offered her up whole again to a willing buyer.

This man wasn't likely to return her in time for tea and crumpets.

Best take the bull by its horns. Problems like this didn't solve themselves, did they?

Raising her voice, she repeated, "How much has my brother lost tonight, sir?"

Still no reply, just that hard stare and a slight flaring of the nostrils.

Becky inquired politely, "Are you hard of hearing?"

The corner of his mouth struggled into a lazy sneer, winched upward with resentful effort. "I don't answer questions from wenches or magistrates."

She sighed. "Well, that's an obstacle, certainly, but not insurmountable. I once reasoned with a sulking orangutan when he stole my best straw bonnet and tried to eat it, so I daresay we'll manage somehow. A fair compromise can always be reached."

The ridges in his brow deepened. "I don't compromise, and I don't discuss business with a bit o' petticoat. When I'm owed a debt, I collect on it."

"Thank you for the fascinating slice of insight into your magnificence. I appreciate knowing where I stand from the start. Now it's my turn."

Stormily silent again, he kept one hand on the lump he guarded against his chest under his coat and leaned back into the creaking slats of the old settle, the winged side of pitted, carved oak casting his face in partial shadow.

"I am not frightened of you, sir," she assured him. "I once stared down a bull that got free of its rope in a crowded souk. I've climbed a banyan tree—barefoot in a monsoon—to rescue a litter of stranded kittens, and I helped a lady give birth in a flood-trapped barouche while the men around me flew into hysteria."

Her brother confirmed all this for the watching crowd with a wry smirk, a hiccup, and a very sloppy shrug.

"And while that air of sinister mystique might impress others," she continued, "I've never found *inscrutable* particularly appealing as a characteristic. But then, I have no patience for riddles. I prefer a direct approach and the minimum of fuss. I don't like too many bows on my bonnets or sugar in my tea, and roses bring me out in a rash." Since he would not move out from behind the winged side again and appeared to be under the misapprehension that their conversation was complete, Rebecca walked up to his chair and, much to the amazement of her audience, pushed aside the crooked table to face him head on. Firelight revealed again the narrowed eyes through which he observed her in mild horror, as if she carried some deadly tropical disease.

"So that's me for you. Now might we proceed? I'm in rather a hurry, if you don't mind. I've got a pair of abandoned breeches to rescue from a stray bathing machine."

One thick, black eyebrow rose slowly, questioning.

"It's a long story and more than I care to bother you with, especially as it's only Tuesday and from the scars on your face, you've got your own gauntlets to run."

His thin lips tightened as he looked around her at Nathaniel, who had almost tumbled out of his chair when she thrust the table aside. Then, finally, another low rumble of thunder emerged from that reluctant mouth. "Run home, freckled wench, and fetch that music box, like your brother here said. Bear in mind, the last soul who tried to cheat me got his teeth knocked down the back of his throat. You wouldn't want that to happen to your brother's fine set, now, would you, Gingersnap?"

If her dander was not already up, it would be when he called her that.

The thunder cracked again, louder this time, for the benefit of his fellow degenerates. "Bloody women, never can follow a simple order. Too busy running the tongue to pay heed to a man's needs. Knew a ladybird once that never shut up, even when we were knocking boots. Put me off me rhythm. Only way to keep her quiet was turning her face down in the pillow. By the time she had breath back to complain about me using the servants' entrance, I'd made me delivery and was out again."

The men all laughed. *Cronies, the lot of them*, Becky thought angrily.

His gaze returned to her. "What? Still here, Gingersnap?"

"The name, *sir*, is Miss Sherringham. You may favor brawn over brains, but surely you can absorb that much."

She heard the rustling of men moving around her, but one warning look and a menacing growl from Lucky halted their advance. "This isn't one of your fancy drawing room parties, Gingersnap. You're on my territory. There are no misses here."

"There is, however, a great deal of cock-and-bull. I'm afraid I've had my fill of that."

"I doubt it. You wouldn't be walking straight if you'd had mine."

Laughter swelled around her again, but she shouted above it. "Since we're dispensing with all polite address, I'll call you Thickheaded Buffoon, shall I?"

"You're getting my bristles up, missy."

"Fancy that. At least you know when you're being insulted—you can't be so very stupid."

"Be careful you don't get on my bad side, young lady."

"Nor you on mine. I can't claim to have knocked out a set of teeth, but I have a mean pinch and a bite that's raised many a tear in a spiteful bully's eye. And I'm not afraid to use them."

His scowl wavered and finally crumpled, relaxing into a bewildered grin. He shifted into a more casual pose but still retained the aura of one holding court over his minions from a throne. Like Caesar, he considered her as if she, Cleopatra, had just been unrolled from a carpet at his feet. "Well now, I've always steered clear of redheads and didn't much like the look of you when you first tipped up." Slowly he rubbed his chin. "But I like a wench with bite. You're growing on me."

"How nice." She smiled with deliberate sweetness. "Perhaps, if you've made sufficient protest at being confronted by a mere woman, we can negotiate and conclude this business to the circumspect and logical satisfaction of all parties."

"Satisfaction? Oh, I'm *sure* we can find satisfaction." His grin widened slowly. "Come sit on my knee."

"I said logical and circumspect."

He squinted. "Not familiar with 'em."

Having seen her brother perform in similar ignorant fashion whenever he felt himself losing a quarrel, Becky remained unmoved by the display and explained sharply, "With *prudence*."

"Damn! Prudence too? I can't take on two wenches tonight." He slid a measuring glance down at his thigh. "Reckon I'd have enough to handle with just you alone, Gingersnap."

More laughter erupted.

"Aye," he added, his voice lower now, tempered just for her. "You're enough for any man, I daresay."

For a moment, she forgot her purpose there. His stare possessed a certain mesmerizing quality. The heat of the tavern must be getting to her, she decided. Of course she knew he was only trying to make her flustered so he could laugh and dismiss her. The idea that Rebecca Boadicea Sherringham could be made to blush was a common misconception among her brother's friends too, when they first met her.

"Mind what you say to my little sister," Nathaniel slurred belatedly from somewhere behind her. "I won't have you insulting the nagging wench. She's my sister and I can insult her. But not you."

Lucky made a sudden lurch forward, his impressive bulk poised as if to seize her.

"St-stay where you are, sir!" Becky gasped in

surprise and swiftly withdrew her pistol from its hiding place. "Don't you dare move. Any of you."

Although she warned all the men there, the pistol was aimed at one in particular. The man in charge.

Amendment: the man who thought he was in charge.

He stared for a moment and then tipped back into his chair again. Amusement gradually warmed his expression, along with something akin to admiration. She hesitated to call it that, because what man would look approvingly on a woman who pointed a gun at his chest?

A madman perhaps.

"What do you find so amusing?" she demanded.

"I was just thinking about the last time I enjoyed the company of a young wench with a fiery temper. Lovely warm pair of apple dumplin's she served up for my pleasure. But I wonder if your fruit wouldn't be even sweeter, being so fresh and untouched." He ran a finger-tip over his smile. "You *are* untouched, eh, Gingersnap?"

"Call me that name once more and I'll shave an inch off both your ears with this pistol."

The man finally lost his grip on a deep, hearty laugh that seemed to take him by surprise. "My ears? Usually other parts of mine get threatened. More vital parts, if you get my drift."

"I assume you refer to the grape and two plums in your breeches? You *would* place greater significance on those soft fruits than you do on anything else."

His eyes gleamed, some of the darkness broken now by dancing light as he studied her face. Each pass of his gaze over her cheek felt like the caress of a rough hand, but one that tried, surprisingly, to be gentle.

"I'm beginning to regret my stay here is only brief." He paused, considering her with his head tipped to one side. "I've avoided these shores for a great many years. A storm at sea forced the captain to make port unexpectedly, but in the morn I'll be off again with the tide."

How strange that he told her that much, explaining himself to a woman, but his words were loosened now, as well as his smile.

"Is there a price on your head?" She wouldn't be surprised.

"Perhaps. Worried for me?"

"No. Why should this matter of your transient nature concern me?" Becky demanded.

"You ain't the sort of wench I can enjoy for a single night's tryst."

"I certainly am not and—"

"I'd want to savor you for longer than that."

She wasn't usually lost for a reply, but this man made her thoughts change course, made her tongue stumble.

"I'd teach you a few things you don't know about men," he added. "You and me—we'd set the bed afire."

He had a brusque honesty, a gruffness she couldn't help but appreciate, even when he made the most improper remarks. After all, she'd warned him that she preferred straightforward conversation, so it would be foolish to complain now that he told her exactly what he was thinking. Not that she needed his words to confirm it. His eyes were eloquent enough.

"I tell you what," he said. "You'll owe me…a kiss."

Becky stared, lips pursed. At that moment, she couldn't answer, because a heavy pulse had begun deep inside her body and taken over all her capacities. It put her blood under unusually excitable pressure.

"One kiss from you," he repeated, "will clear your brother's debt to me."

"That's all?" The words exploded out of her on a wave of startled breath.

"That's *all*, Gin—*Miss* Sherringham." He paused, eyes laughing. "Disappointed?"

She lowered the pistol and glanced over her shoulder to see that Nathaniel had dozed off in his chair.

Lucky didn't move an inch, but an invisible energy was somehow transferred from his body to hers, felt in a ticklish sensation that made the curls at the nape of her neck tremble. "Get on with it then," she snapped. "*Lucky*."

For her, giving a kiss away had less sentimental consequence than losing that music box of her mother's, and as for the matter of a reputation, the antics of her family made it impossible to maintain dignity. Her father's latest escapade, involving a runaway bathing machine, his buttocks, the bracing air, and a shocked, titled gentleman with whom he had a long-running feud, was enough to undo them all.

But that was next on Becky the Bold's list of problems to sort out. "Will you take your payment, sir, or not?"

"Nah. You're too young for me yet. But I can wait. You'll owe me."

She gasped, scornful. "Too young?" The pressure now released, her words escaped at speed like steam from a teakettle. "Too clever for you is more likely."

"No doubt you think you know everything already

at your age," he muttered, shaking his head. "All learned from daft bloody books."

"At least I know prudence is not just a girl's name."

"So says the young maidy who beards the lion in his den with only a pistol in her tender hand."

"I'm a crack shot," she replied proudly. "And there's nothing tender about me. So I've been told." The majority of her companions and relatives growing up were male, and whenever teams were picked for cricket, she was a valuable commodity, treated just like one of the boys.

Lucky's eyes glimmered and then dimmed. "Whoever told you that just didn't know where to find the tender parts. Or what to do for them."

Oh lord, he was trying to make her blush again. Apparently he didn't like to concede defeat, despite the hopelessness of his cause. Stubborn, cocksure fellow!

But Becky's palm, inside her glove, was damp. Her heart bounced and bumped all over the place—as if someone had knocked a collection of drums and cymbals down a staircase.

"You've caught me on a good day, young lady. Impressed me with your pluck." He signaled to the tavern-keeper, who scuttled over at once with pen and inkpot on a tray. Lucky took a playing card from his sleeve and inscribed five words across it. As he blew on the ink, his eyes met hers again, regarding her with that heated stare until she felt slightly melted around her edges. He handed her the card. "Now take your brother and leave. Before I change my mind."

Becky didn't question her reprieve. She tucked

the pistol into her muff and helped Nathaniel to his unsteady feet.

But when she took one last glance at Lucky, she saw, finally, what he kept inside his coat. Above his collar, a small pair of black ears appeared, followed by a scrunched face with large, wide-set eyes that surveyed Becky with interest.

It was a pup nestled against his chest, not a fat purse of money as she'd expected. For a woman who thought she knew all about men, this was a startling discovery.

Catching her curious, bemused eye, he scowled. "I'll find you again, one day," he warned gruffly. "I always collect."

"I quake in my boots at the prospect."

"Aye." That frown cleared again as quickly as it was tried on. He winked suddenly. "So do I."

Nathaniel slurred for her to make haste. Humming drowsily, he stumbled through the tavern ahead of her, probably already forgetting he owed this rescue to his little sister.

Trailing after him, she looked at the playing card and saw it was the knave of hearts. Across it, with a messy scrawl, were penned the words *Gyngersnappe Ohs Lucky Wonne Kisse*.

Well, there are two more things I know about him, she mused. He was an animal lover and a terrible speller— clearly no student of "daft bloody books."

Two

THE WORN, SAGGING WOOD PLANKS MOANED UNDER the force of Lucky Luke Wainwright's tall, lurching weight as he attacked the stairs with a determined but uneven stride, disposing of three steps at once. His dog galloped ahead, skillfully dodging the thrust of his walking cane. Together, man and dog made enough noise and vibration to shake the building.

Somewhere behind them, at the foot of the stairs, a pin-slender clerk still wailed redundantly that he should wait, but Luke had a tendency toward deafness when the words he might have heard did not suit his purpose.

Besides, he did love to make a surprise entrance.

Reaching the top floor, he whacked his walking cane against a door panel and then kicked it open with his bad leg.

"Go on in, Ness. Seize 'em!"

The short, square mutt barked enthusiastically and pounced inside to where three wigged men were seated at paper-strewn desks, none of them having the time to hide.

Luke slammed the door shut behind him, shaking the damp, peeling walls. "Well, gentlemen, I expect you'll want to offer me a brandy, since you're so bleedin' pleased to see me."

They stared, open-mouthed, as he tossed his tattered, broad-brimmed hat for one of them to catch and then dropped into a groaning chair, propping the boot heel of his aching leg up on the nearest desk. One of the men had jumped so abruptly that he lost his wig and the dog instantly captured it in his broad, salivating jaws, shaking his prize like a dead rat.

"I daresay you're shocked. After all," Luke added with a lusty sigh, "'tis not every day a man comes back from the dead, eh?"

"Colonel…Colonel Lucius Wainwright? Could it be?"

"In the flesh. Although most folk call me Lucky Luke these days."

The man gingerly holding his thrown hat exclaimed, "But you're dead."

"Yes, funny that, ain't it? So what have I been up to these last twelve years, you ask? What happened after I was wounded and no longer of use to the Dragoons?"

They didn't ask, of course. He knew they were too busy scrambling to think of what *they'd* been doing in all that time. With the earnings he'd entrusted to them.

"Well, I'll tell you, gentlemen. Since then, I've won and lost several naughty wenches, a damn good pair of boots, and a small fortune on bad wagers. I've traveled from India to Andalusia and from Ireland to the Argentine. Now I'm an old man and it won't be long before I meet my maker. Time then to settle accounts."

The three faces stared at him warily, as if he might be a spectral vision and not a real man at all. He may as well get used to that welcome, he supposed.

"Truth be told, I was disappointed in my last funeral. I mean to make certain the next one is memorable."

"But there was no funeral, Colonel. Not…exactly."

They hadn't had a body to bury, of course. Luke knew he was declared missing and presumed dead. A pair of his boots were discovered in a shack destroyed by cannon fire shortly after his discharge from the army, and since it was assumed he'd been blown completely out of them—it was well known that he never went anywhere without his favorite pair of Hessians— they were sent home to his family in place of a corpse. Luke had chosen to go along with the mistake. After all, he'd never really fit in with his family. They would appreciate not having to put out his fires, and perhaps, he'd thought, he could start anew, build another life. Become someone better without the burden of past sins being known to the people he met.

But he'd discovered that however far a man traveled, he could not escape himself, his conscience, and a heart full of regret. "When I cock up my toes for good, I want it done properly with a few wailing mourners, horses with black plumes, and a good-sized headstone with elegant bloody words carved into it. Something fancy. In Latin." He paused. "Where's that brandy then?"

One of the men belatedly scrambled to retrieve a bottle from a cupboard behind him.

"No glass needed," Luke bellowed, swinging his walking cane up and making them all jump again as he cracked it smartly against the desktop by his foot.

"Now, gentlemen, when I left for India many years ago, I gave you clear instructions for the management of my affairs." He snatched the timidly offered brandy bottle. "Instructions that were ignored, no doubt, once you thought I was never coming back."

One of the men finally gathered wits enough to respond. "We did the best we could with the funds you left, Colonel."

"After you'd taken your fee, I'm sure. Never expecting to see my ugly face again, you felt free to misuse those funds to feather your own blasted nests."

"There were expenses incurred." Another solicitor stood awkwardly, adjusting his wig while eyeing the growling mutt still in possession of his companion's hair. "It took us considerable time and effort to chase down the ladies you intended us to help."

"I don't know how it could," Luke muttered. "I always found 'em readily enough." Or they'd found him. Sweet, amiable women of the loose and lusty variety. There were five in particular of whom he was especially fond, and he'd arranged for each of them to receive financial help when he left.

"But two of them married, Colonel, and—according to your terms—no longer received an annuity. One was arrested for public lewdness and deported, one became a favorite of the prince regent, and lastly, Miss Sally Hitchens took it into her head to travel about the country. She appeared to have restless feet, and not only when performing on the stage. A thief anxious to evade arrest could not have disappeared as often."

Luke sighed heavily and rubbed his forehead where it still felt tight after a night of too much ale. Yes, he knew little Sally Hitchens had something of a wandering gypsy heart, as he did, but he'd hoped the coin he left her would persuade her to settle down, get off the stage, and take care of her baby.

"Where is she now?"

"I'm afraid, Colonel, Miss Hitchens passed away soon after you left for India."

He was grieved, angry, and vexed, all at the same time. After so long abroad, he'd suspected they might not all be waiting for his return, but he hadn't expected every one of them to be gone. Dear, sweet little Sally! Well, he would soon follow her to the afterlife. His dreams recently had been filled with flames and he knew what that meant. Luke's dreams, he was convinced, always held heavy portent.

"So my money went into your pockets and bellies instead, I see!"

There was no immediate reply to that as the accused looked sheepishly around the cluttered room.

"What ho, gentlemen? You must all have been born in the middle of the week as your eyes keep looking both ways for Sunday." He sighed. "Seems these boots had better last me a while yet."

"You are not without funds, Colonel," one of the solicitors ventured. "There is the family business, of course, and your father left a considerable fortune of which you, as the eldest son, would have received the lion's share. There is also the manor house in Buckinghamshire, recently passed on by your great-uncle Phineas Hawke. In compliance with his will, it would have come to you, as the eldest male heir. Since you were presumed deceased, your brother became the sole beneficiary. But you are, now, returned. You are...the rightful heir."

There was a solemn pause as they all pondered the implications.

Truth was, Luke hadn't given a thought to the money when he decided to return from his self-imposed exile. In fact, the Wainwright fortune hanging over his head was one of the reasons why he left the country so long ago and let himself be lost. His only intention now was to set past wrongs to right before he met his end. So he'd set off for England, thinking he'd sort out the details later.

He could almost hear his father's ghost muttering wearily, "Trust you not to think ahead or consider the money, Lucius. You never did have a head for finances." But a great deal of money never made anyone very happy for long, as far as he could see. When he gambled on outrageous wagers, he did it not for the coin but for the thrill.

And there was the fact that the lure of money made people—women, for instance—do very bad things. Suddenly he thought of Dora Woodgrave, a pretty but empty-headed girl who once declared herself deeply in love with his younger brother and then switched her affections—as well as her seductive efforts—to Luke upon realizing that he was the one who would inherit everything.

He could still hear her plaintive voice, "But why would your father not split the fortune equally between his two sons?"

"It is the rule of primogeniture, Dora," he'd told her, "and our dear father is very old-fashioned, very keen to rise up in the hierarchy." She'd looked at him blankly, so he explained further. "It helps to keep a sizeable fortune and an estate together. Land and money are power, so sharing all that's been amassed between siblings would mean weakening the family's power in the next generation." That was how it had been explained to him. He was rather surprised he retained the information long enough to pass it on. But pass it on he did, with catastrophic consequences. At first, when Dora began following him about after that, he was too slow to realize why. He hadn't paid that much attention to her. She was the daughter of his younger brother's tutor, and Luke, home on leave from the army, had too many other irons in his fire when it came to female company. Eventually Dora abandoned all subtlety, threw herself at Luke, and he, in a moment of utter foolishness—probably out of boredom—caught her. He didn't learn until later that his brother had contemplated an engagement to the girl. Of course, Darius was such a shy boy that it took him forever and a day to pluck up courage when it came to women and he never told anyone what he was thinking. "She wouldn't have been right for you," Luke had tried explaining to his brother. But Darius didn't want to hear it, didn't want to believe what sweet, demure little Dora really was.

Luke looked around at the solicitors. "Rather puts the cat among the pigeons for my little brother now that I dug myself out of the grave, doesn't it?"

His dog grumbled, shook the captured wig once more, opened his jaws, and let it fall to the floor. The nervous fellow to whom it belonged bent carefully, reaching for the wig, but the dog poised to pounce, growling. The solicitor hesitated, then thought better of taking the risk and quickly stood upright again. "There is, however," the stout fellow muttered, "a stipulation in your father's will."

"Do tell."

"In order to inherit the Wainwright fortune, you must prove yourself settled down, Colonel, your sins behind you."

Of course. He might have known. His father was the most tightly laced, thoroughly starched old man he'd ever encountered, and his brother Darius came a close second. Two peas in the proverbial pod. Luke was a great frustration to them both because of his carefree attitude, his determination to enjoy all life's vices, and his complete disregard for making money.

"You are an unstoppable force, Lucius," his father once remarked dourly. "I daresay, like all such heedless forces, you will one day meet a solid object that will bring you to a permanent halt."

While young Darius always had his nose in a book, studying every word, Luke preferred learning his lessons from life itself. As a boy, he never paid attention to tutors—in fact he usually drove them to resigning their posts. As soon as he was old enough, he spurned the idea of university and chose the army for his escape. This desire for action over study was mystifying to his father and his brother, and since they would never give up trying to mend him as long as he was within their sights, Luke thought it best to remove himself from their vicinity and save all parties a vast deal of trouble and anguish. Especially after the Dora Woodgrave debacle.

He tapped the brandy bottle on his thigh. "Looks like the old man may finally get his wish then, doesn't it? For here I am, in the flesh, back to settle all accounts before I go to my maker."

"Are you ill, Colonel?" The other men looked bewildered as they surveyed his long form sprawled in—and mostly out of—that chair.

"I may not be in my dotage yet, but everyone has to go sooner or later," he muttered impatiently. "I've had my dress rehearsal and I see where much can be improved for the actual event." And he wasn't going to tell them about his dreams. Folk had a tendency to look at him—at this tall, solid, fierce-looking bulk of a man—and laugh when he told them about his belief in the prophetic quality of dreams.

He clasped the brandy bottle to his chest and waited while the three men before him shiftily exchanged more rolling-eyed glances.

"Out with it!" he bellowed, shaking the cobwebs that hung from the timbers above. "I see there's more to the old man's will, as you stand before me with faces like three spanked arses."

"You must marry, Colonel. A decent woman of good family. Or you get nothing."

Oh, he should have seen that one coming. After a heavy pause, he suddenly tipped back his head and roared with laughter. "In the name of all that's unholy, who the devil would marry me?"

They had no answer to that, for it was an idea too ridiculous for anyone to contemplate. But his dog, excited by the sound of Luke's laughter, resumed the hearty terrorizing of that dropped wig.

Reaching down, he gave the animal's head a quick pat, and as the dog looked up at him, he suddenly remembered another face, similarly gargoyle-like in a way that appealed to his preference for the eccentric and absurd. A tiny, wrinkled face with puffy eyelids and no teeth. "And Sally Hitchens's babe? What became of the child?"

"You did not know, Colonel? Little Sarah has been raised by your brother."

"My brother?" He sat bolt upright, both feet now on the floor. "What the figgy pudding?"

"Miss Sally Hitchens took the child to your brother soon after you left England."

"Why would she do that? My brother knows naught of raising children. He was never a child himself. He was a grim, bookish old man the moment he was born."

Yet again the three solicitors exchanged significant glances.

"*Well?* Spit it out, for the love of hot buttered titties!"

"Miss Hitchens informed your brother that Sarah was *your* child, and therefore a Wainwright."

"Mine?" Luke choked on another swig of brandy and coughed until his eyes felt sore.

Why would Sally not take her child to the real father? The Clarendons' nest was at least as well feathered. Ah, but all the fortune in the world couldn't make up for having Kit Clarendon as a father. Sally knew that, of course.

But why the devil would she choose to blame Luke? Of all the men she might have picked as a father for her babe, he was surely the most unlikely candidate. "Of all the impertinent little—" He wheezed with a sudden burst of laughter. His dog turned its great bulky head to look at him again and twitched its stump of a tail.

"Is this not the case, Colonel? If not, your brother should be informed."

Luke grabbed his cane and pushed himself upright, still chuckling. "Don't you dare." He set down the brandy bottle, grabbed his hat out of the solicitor's trembling hands, and jammed it back on his head. "Of course the child is mine. Why wouldn't she be?" He whistled sharply. "Come, Ness, our business here is concluded. For now."

The dog panted after him at a lumbering but determined gait. A movement much like *his*, so Luke had been told.

Until Ness—short for "Unnecessary"—found him, Luke had never traveled with the same companion for long, but man and dog had been together five years now and looked out for one another. It was simple. Nothing official. Nothing formal or complicated. The way Luke preferred his relationships.

As for the idea of getting a wife to prove he was settled down, he'd sooner abandon himself to Bedlam. Not that he didn't like women. Of course he did. Wenches were bloody good company when they had a mind to be. But a man couldn't dispose of a wife with a few coins and a new petticoat when she became tiresome. Lucky Luke saw himself as a castaway on a deserted island. He had survived there, alone, on his private, uncomplicated paradise for thirty-seven years and he didn't intend to share that space with another human being on any permanent basis. Not even for the little time he had left.

Three

"I could not be happy with a man whose taste did not in every point coincide with my own. He must enter into all my feelings: the same books, the same music must charm us both."

—Marianne Dashwood, *Sense and Sensibility*

Hawcombe Prior, Buckinghamshire, December 1815

"BECKY, YOU REALLY MUST LEARN TO SPEAK ONLY your lines and not everyone else's. It does somewhat distract the audience to watch your lips mirror all the other characters' words."

"Oh, dear, did I do it again?"

"I'm afraid so."

In her anxiety to memorize scenes in the annual Yuletide performance of the amateur players, Rebecca had a habit of learning all her fellow actors' parts too. On the night of the actual performance, her enthusiasm had entirely run away with her again and occasionally caused her to speak for other characters as well as her own, especially when she could not wait for them to recite the line. Now that it was over, she apologized to her friend Justina, author of the play. "I am sorry, Jussy. Surely no one else noticed."

"They were probably too distracted by that Elizabethan beard falling off your face." Justina shrugged easily. "I suppose it wouldn't be the same if the play went perfectly. Rather like life itself. Nothing is ever as much fun when all goes smoothly and the plot is predictable."

Becky sighed. "I had far too many years of unpredictable. I much prefer a nice, steady, predictable life, thank you very much. No more calamities for me. Give me warm slippers by the fire and some embroidery to keep me busy and I want for nothing else."

"Nonsense. You say that, but I am not deceived! There is a constant twinkle of mischief in your eye, Rebecca Sherringham, and no one who loves poetry and romantic novels as much as you could possibly prefer a dull life. Like me, you enjoy a good drama, and don't pretend otherwise. Besides, your embroidery is absolutely awful."

After considering this for a moment, Becky conceded a little to her friend's assessment. "It is true I do enjoy novels. However, when there is drama in real life, at least one person has to remain sensible." She sighed. "And in my family that person is me."

Justina chuckled. "You need a handsome hero to look after *you* for a change, Becky."

"My dear Jussy, you can all go dancing off and find romance. I am quite content reading about it. Novels save me the anguish and trouble of falling in love and all that ensuing upheaval."

"But it's not only about you, Becky. Think of the poor, sad, lost fellow out there, looking to fall in love. A man whose life cannot be complete without you in it."

"He sounds simple-minded, feeble, and possibly a great liability. No, thank you. I'll stick to the company of a book."

"You need a real man. Not a fictional character."

Becky laughed, but it came out as more of a snort. "I'd prefer him to live in the pages. Then I might shut the book whenever I'm tired of him, and if he does something immensely stupid, I can even throw him at a wall."

"But what about those cold nights alone? In bed."

"I prescribe woolen bed socks and warm milk."

"I'm talking about the company of a man."

"What on earth for?"

"Becky!" Justina chuckled. "You are the very limit."

"Someone else for me to clean up after? A dull fellow who doesn't tend his toenails adequately and sheds little hairs all over the place, stealing all the warmth of my quilt and drooling on my pillow when we are obliged to share a bed. All those big… muscles…and sweaty…limbs…" Becky hastily shook her head, cleared her throat, and finished sharply, "No, no. Thick socks and a nip of brandy in one's milk are perfectly prudent solutions to a chilly evening, in my opinion."

"You are a dreadful fibber!"

Becky wrinkled her nose and exclaimed proudly, "Laugh all you like and worry not for me. Be content with *your* handsome hero."

They looked over at Justina's husband. When he caught their eye and responded with a questioning lift of his right eyebrow, they both waved, smiling, as innocent as two young ladies ever could be.

"Poor Wainwright," Becky whispered. "He's still learning how to use his smile, but I believe it's improving, less rusty." And something about it was oddly familiar to her from the start, but she couldn't think why it would be.

"Kindly don't refer to my husband as *poor* anything," Justina exclaimed. "He's not at all poor, because he has me and love."

"I'm sure that enormous fortune helps," said Becky dryly.

"It's not the done thing to talk about money. Who cares about that anyway? Love is far more important."

"I wasn't aware that love had become legal currency, Jussy. I rather think that if you tried to pay bills with it now you might be arrested."

"Oh, you…cynic! One day we will find the perfect man for you. A real man."

"And then who will take care of my father and brother? I am needed at home."

Justina rolled her eyes. "I had better go and thank Joe Haxby for the use of his bellows in the winter storm scene." She began to walk away but then stopped to look back at Becky. "By the way, you can take that beard off now."

"Ha! Most amusing!"

Laughing, Justina dashed back to the makeshift stage and Becky looked for her other friends among the crowd of villagers who came out to watch the play tonight. Some folk had stayed home because of the weather, but many braved the cold to enjoy the festivities. The residents of Hawcombe Prior were, on the whole, a sturdy lot. Becky was one of them now too. She belonged somewhere at last.

Since Major Sherringham retired from the army and brought his family here five years ago, Becky's life had experienced a welcome change for the better. Finally able to make lasting friends, she'd joined the local book society—a small group of village ladies her brother teasingly named "The Book Club Belles"— and settled into life in the quiet countryside.

Her fellow book society members were the closest thing she'd ever had to sisters, but sadly she knew that time would likely part them eventually. The dreaded end had already begun, for in addition to Justina's marriage, two other members of the book society were now engaged. While Justina's elder sister had gone off to London that winter with her fiancé to meet his family, Diana Makepiece, another Book Club Belle, had accepted a tradesman from Manderson and would be married in the summer.

Although some women had good reason for wanting to leave home, Becky was content managing her father's house and living with a degree of independence many unwed young women didn't have. Besides, the more she saw of men—and she had seen a lot of them over the years—the less she found appealing and worthy. The few men brave enough to approach her as suitors were quickly and effectively dispatched, sometimes by the near miss of an archery arrow. A few years ago, to discourage the matchmaking attempts of certain mischievous friends, Becky had written up an extensive list of "Attributes Required in a Husband."

"My future husband," she had announced to her friends at one of their book society meetings, "will possess sandy curls, very fine teeth, good calves, a slender nose, amusing wit, a sunny, open disposition, an informed mind, one or two dimples, and a solid appreciation for poetry. If he can ride and dance well, those will be points in his favor too, naturally. Above all, he must be of sound mind, respectable, dependable, and steadfast."

Her brother, upon hearing about this list, had remarked, "Well done, Sister. That will certainly give you an excuse to remain unwed. You don't want to find a husband and so you make it impossible."

Becky frowned as she thought of Nathaniel. Whenever he made a jest of her spinster status, she retaliated by pointing out that he was just as unlikely to find a suitable partner for himself. Good, honest women gave him a wide berth.

"What the devil would I want with a wife?" Nathaniel had snapped the last time they spoke on the subject.

But Becky knew about his ill-fated proposal to one of the Book Club Belles, a secret he had thought he could keep.

Now, walking toward Becky through the crowd, here came the young woman who had rejected Nathaniel's proposal—the Book Club Belle who also thought she could keep this unhappy secret.

"I'll walk home with you," said Diana Makepiece

as she wrapped a fleece scarf around her slender throat. "Look, it's snowing! How lovely."

Staring at Diana and with the secret of her brother's rejected proposal burning fiercely inside her, Becky was overwhelmed by the sort of teary-eyed sadness that comes when one contemplates great natural beauty and feels humbled. Diana's features often had that effect upon her, especially when candlelight or moonlight touched them in a particular way.

But there was no time to ponder the other girl's unique beauty for long. Hearing her name shouted above the general ruckus, Becky turned.

Mrs. Kenton, the parson's new wife, advanced rapidly in their direction, thrusting people aside, her voice pealing out like church bells. "Don't forget your donated clothing for the workhouse, ladies. I shall be by very early in the morning and taking our parcels to Manderson before the road gets very bad."

They both promised not to forget.

The parson's wife turned her focus upon Becky. "Nothing frivolous, if you please. Plain and sturdy is preferable for those poor souls. Nothing too continental. We don't want to cause offense, do we?"

Somewhat confounded as to why this remark should be addressed directly to her, Becky replied that she would do her best to find garments from her wardrobe with as little chance of offending as possible.

"Because I have seen some of the items drying on your washing line lately, Miss Sherringham, and there is altogether too much lace and flimsy, impractical silk. You would do far better to wear stout wool. There is nothing like it next to the skin. And even those items should not be displayed outside for all to see. A proper young lady dries her intimate apparel by the fire and out of sight."

While enduring this lecture from the parson's wife, Becky felt Diana's startled, curious gaze burning into the side of her face. Oh, the humiliation. Thank goodness Justina wasn't close enough to hear this or she'd never live it down.

Becky had recently become enchanted by an advertisement in a catalog and, on a whim, sent away for some indulgent chemises. She didn't really know what had come over her, but the last thing she wanted was to be ribbed by her friends about this strange fancy, and now she cursed herself for hanging her new items on the washing line. She'd simply assumed that no one would be interested enough in her laundry to hoist themselves higher than the four-foot wall and look over it. She had reckoned, it seemed, without considering Mrs. Kenton's determination to manage every detail of everybody's life.

At last Becky was able to get a word in. "You must excuse us. Diana is expected home promptly by her mama." She took her friend's arm and marched her out of the barn.

"Oh, dear," Diana whispered, "she's now inspecting our washing lines too? Is nothing safe from that woman's criticism?"

Becky imagined Diana and her mother—for whom appearances were paramount—straining their eyes and sitting up late to patch all their worn petticoats, just to save themselves from Mrs. Kenton's judgment.

"Sooner or later," she grumbled, "that dratted

woman will spy one time too many and it will cure her of sticking her nose into other people's business."

"I suppose she means well."

"You suppose wrongly, my dear Diana. She's a meddler who cannot bear for anything to be going on without her in the thick of it. Any good she does is entirely incidental."

Becky had heard Mrs. Kenton loudly refer to her recently as "that unfortunate ginger-haired, brusque creature with the manly stride." To make matters worse, the parson's wife was forever cutting out remedies for the removal of freckles and slipping them into Becky's hand with a sympathetic glance.

"My dear Diana," Becky said briskly, "you have not spoken lately of your fiancé. I do hope he is in health and not seized by this bad cold that has afflicted so many." Ugh. The dullest of subjects, but at least it would distract Diana from what she'd just heard. Nothing was more likely to erase fine lace and impractical silk from a young girl's mind than thoughts of that stale loaf William Shaw, Diana's intended.

While she dearly wished Diana had accepted her brother's marriage proposal, Becky couldn't blame her friend for refusing him and choosing another man instead. Nathaniel was a terrible, vexing handful, and why would any self-respecting woman take that on voluntarily?

No, Nathaniel would remain *her* lot, it seemed. Someone had to look after him, and although she was only a very little girl at the time, Becky remembered promising her mother that she would manage the task. In fact, it was her strongest remaining memory of her mother—of sitting on the edge of her sick bed, the old music box tinkling gently in the background.

She couldn't bear to think of Nathaniel having no one to come home to one day, no one with whom to share his triumphs and troubles. If she could choose a wife for Nathaniel, it would be this calm, levelheaded young woman at her side. But that was a hopeless case now.

Diana spoke softly, "I so rarely mention Mr. Shaw because I know none of you like him much."

Becky bit her lip, looking down at the snow as they walked along. "I'm sure we will grow to like him." But alas, once Diana married and moved to Manderson, they would see her less and less. William Shaw thought himself too good for Hawcombe Prior and was unlikely to encourage his wife's friendships there.

Justina had recently exclaimed in anger, "Diana is only marrying the heinous Shaw because her mama doesn't want her making the same mistake *she* once did by marrying for love instead of money. It fair boils my blood that she would sacrifice herself to that oaf. William Shaw is extremely boring company, dances very badly, has no ear for a tune, and cannot recite a single line of *The Corsair*."

Despite their friend's unconcealed disappointment in her choice, however, Diana would quietly remind the Book Club Belles that security and a steady income were perfectly suitable reasons to marry. Love and passion, as she liked to say, usually lasted only as long as the first set of candles, were long gone by the time a gray hair sprouted, and didn't put food on anyone's table. Since Diana and her mother lived on a threadbare budget, she had wisely chosen a reliable man with a good income first and foremost.

It was very difficult, thought Becky, to love and admire her friend for those qualities of wisdom and rationale while also feeling envy. Even as she yearned to be as ladylike as Diana—to not let every emotion show upon her face, to be cool and unruffled no matter what the circumstance—she couldn't help wishing there was just an occasional uncouth outburst from Diana's elegant lips. Just occasionally. Something to prove she was not perfect after all.

As they crossed the whitened lane toward the narrow path known as "The Bolt," which would take them directly to the Makepieces' cottage, Diana began to sound more cheerful. "Mr. Shaw is joining us for Christmas dinner, and so are the Clarendons."

Becky slipped on a treacherous spot of icy ground and had to grab Diana's sleeve to save herself from a graceless backward tumble. "Your cousins?"

"Yes. They called upon us once before. It was but a brief visit," Diana grinned slyly, "and you *may* not remember them."

Becky frowned, knowing what was sure to come next, for her friends loved to tease her about this!

"I daresay you've forgotten how you rescued my cousin Charles on Raven's Hill. When he twisted his ankle."

As if she might need reminding. Charles Clarendon—quite possibly the most handsome man Becky had ever seen—had been out riding in the midst of a late summer thunderstorm when she encountered him, just after he'd fallen off his horse and was rolling rapidly down the muddy slope, collecting dead leaves. The young man, pale and angry at his misfortune, was convinced his leg was broken. Not knowing what else to do for the desperate fellow, she'd helped him to her own house and shocked a blood-curdling scream out of the cook, Mrs. Jarvis, when she arrived at the kitchen door, soaking wet and partially lifting Charles across her back like a bundle of dirty laundry. Luckily, her brother had once taught her how to carry a wounded comrade in battle—he seemed to think that, considering her capacity for encountering trouble, she might need the knowledge—and Becky had made a passable attempt at it, although Charles Clarendon's feet were never quite off the ground.

Her friends took delight in retelling the story of this "rescue."

"*You're* supposed to be the dainty maiden that sprains her ankle and falls into the hero's clutches, not vice versa!" Justina had exclaimed between chuckles. "Poor Becky! Apparently your ankles are too sturdy."

After that strange, improbable beginning, she and Charles struck up a friendship during the short time he was there, and the Book Club Belles liked to speculate that tomboy Becky was finally ready to fall in love.

He looked the part, as everyone pointed out to her. When she drew up her list of "Attributes Required in a Husband," she might well have been describing Charles Clarendon. He had even kissed her one sunny afternoon, under a perfectly picturesque arch of autumnal tree branches, and after returning home, he sent her a thin volume of Shakespeare's sonnets as a memento.

"The Clarendons are staying as guests of Admiral

Vyne up at Lark Hollow," said Diana as they walked along in the snow, "but they will visit us over the Christmas season. Mama is quite beside herself with anxiety."

"Diana, your mother would give herself an ulcer over an insufficiently boiled egg." Really, there was nothing to fuss about. Even if it wasn't every day that a pleasant, lively young man with fair curls and fine calves came back to visit.

Once word spreads about my new undergarments, Becky thought with amusement, *the romantically inclined Book Club Belles will probably assume Charles Clarendon is to blame for them somehow*. Diana clearly thought that her slip on the ice just now was his fault too. So Becky made a concerted effort to measure her steps to Diana's until her friend stopped on the path and exclaimed, "What's amiss with you? Is there a stone in your boot?"

She sighed, exhaling a billowing cloud of breath into the crisp night air, and then lengthened her steps to their usual unfeminine march.

Four

LUKE STEPPED OUT OF THE MOONLIGHT AS A CLUSTER of villagers hurried by in the snow. No one appeared to notice him until he walked further into the barn and met the astonished gaze of his younger brother, Darius. For the first time in twelve years.

The boy had matured since their last encounter, grown into his ears, which were once on the larger side and earned him the nickname of "Handles." He was now a tall, fine gentleman. A man of consequence too.

Luke grinned. It might not be appropriate to smile so broadly considering the tenor of their last meeting all those years ago and some of the things that were said in the heat of temper—he should be looking repentant, not glad. But he couldn't help it, for he was pleased to see the boy again. More so even than he'd anticipated.

Married life apparently treated his brother admirably.

Darius did turn rather pale and sick-looking, though, when he looked over and recognized Luke standing there, back from the dead.

"*Good God!* Lucius? It can't be." The boy had always refused to call him Lucky or Luke. He was so formal it was something of a surprise that he didn't address his elder brother as "sir."

"Handles!" Luke exclaimed. "I see you've flourished without me."

"When did—? How did—? Christ, I don't—"

"When I heard most of the village was congregated here tonight, I thought I'd come and see for myself. Couldn't quite believe my little brother would sit through a performance of amateur dramatics in an old barn." He chuckled. "Seems you've changed, softened in your old age."

His brother's eyes darkened in that suspicious way—one thing about him that hadn't altered. "I hope you didn't come back to cause trouble, Lucius."

Well, that didn't take long. "Me? Trouble? That's a fine thing to say to your long-lost brother upon his return."

"Yes." Darius hesitated. "You're right, of course. I...I'm sorry. But this is—"

"A shock? Aye, no doubt. Not a pleasant one, eh? You look as queer as Dick's hatband."

"You must come up to the house and—"

"No, no, I won't impose upon you so soon." Luke laid an awkward hand to his brother's shoulder, felt the muscle instinctively stiffen beneath his palm. "I'll come up to the house once you've had a chance to air a bed and warn that pretty young wife of yours. I remember there's a tavern in the village with a room above and that's good enough for me tonight. Just wanted to look in on you. Say hello."

"Nonsense. You must—"

"You'll need time to make sense of old Lucky still being alive." He laughed, attempting to lighten the mood, but it sounded hollow. "Oh, and don't worry about laying on a vast spread just to welcome the wounded old bugger home, eh? Just a slice of plum cake and a cup of chocolate will do me. Nothing fancy. Tell your good lady wife not to concern herself unduly. If there is bacon or smoked kippers to be had, or some stale beer, I'll take it off your hands, but I draw the line at a heavy breakfast. And you know how I hate fuss and fanfare on my own behalf."

"Indeed. Modesty is your middle name. We'll see what scraps we can spare then. Whatever the pig hasn't eaten." Yes, there was a sense of humor in there, somewhere, but it was most often strangled by the boy's iron-willed self-control. Luke was pleased to see this hint of light. Moved by it too. His little brother was thinking quicker on his feet these days. The old, insecure stammer was gone. "You should come up to the manor now, Lucius. In this weather, you can't—"

"Worry not for me, Handles!"

"I would advise you to—"

"I've lasted seven-and-thirty years, little brother, primarily by never listening when anybody starts out a sentence with those words." He grinned again, teeth gritted against the cold air. After one last hasty wave, he moved out of the barn with his usual rapid, ungainly lurch. He knew he'd left his bewildered brother staring after him, probably not at all convinced he hadn't just conversed with a ghost.

But seeing Darius grown up, no more the shy boy, was a startling reminder of the time passed. How much had changed. They might be family, but they were strangers. His brother's life had moved on without Luke in it, and he was a much more worthy recipient of the Wainwright fortune than Luke ever could be.

But he'd seen those eyes quickly flood with dark waters of doubt and distrust almost immediately. Darius looked very much like their father now—at least, how he had looked in a portrait from his early years of marriage. Almost eerily so.

Coming back to life, Luke realized, meant so much more than he had considered when the idea first flickered through his mind. Ah, but as his father would say, was that not typical of Luke's reckless, thoughtless character? His sudden need to repent for old sins was just another selfish idea. As usual, he'd jumped in with both feet and not considered the consequences.

Before he was spotted there, Luke had watched from a distance as his brother chatted with a pretty young woman who must be that newly wedded wife he'd heard about. They looked very happy. The girl with them must be Sally Hitchens's daughter—the one they all thought was his child. No more a child now. Certainly no more a wrinkled bundle with a gargoyle face, he mused. Amazing how that tiny, mottled creature could have grown into a poised young lady.

What could his return do for any of them but cause unwelcome ripples? They managed better without him.

His hand trembled, but he gripped his walking cane

tighter and limped through the snow, retreating into the shadows.

Best let sleeping dogs lie.

A small inner voice scolded him for being a coward, but he knew a reliable way to silence that meddling whisper. A tankard or two of good ale was all he needed to blur the unsightly edges of truth and help Lucky Luke on his wandering way again. He didn't know where, but he'd work out the details later.

❧

In the corner of her eye, a black blob spoiled the otherwise pristine white ground. Becky turned her head, and at the same time, her numb toes stumbled to a halt.

A squat creature sat beside the milestone marker on the village common. It was not quite knee height, and as wide as it was tall. A layer of snow had settled on its ears and wrinkled brow, but its nose did not protrude far enough to collect the same frosting.

She squinted through the falling snow. At first she couldn't be sure the dog was real as it made no movement. Two large black eyes watched her with the same wary regard until, suddenly, it raised its short snout to sniff at the air. The dog lurched forward and down in one motion, burying its ugly, foreshortened face between its paws and letting out a soulful whimper.

There didn't appear to be anyone nearby to claim ownership. Its eyes were just visible above its paws and the snow, but as it watched her approach, there was no movement, not even a warning growl.

"Hello, boy. Who left you here, I wonder?"

The eyes blinked and it seemed as if more folds of saggy skin gathered across its broad brow. Was it possible for a dog to sigh with depression?

Becky took the last few steps with caution, for one could never be sure with a strange dog. A sloppy pink tongue swept out briefly to wet the stubby snout. A very soft whimper emerged, evaporating in the cold air along with a puff of breath.

"You're a sad-looking thing," she exclaimed, glancing around the snowy common again. "Who left you here?"

The dog sat up. Its stomach grumbled and then it whined softly and gazed up at her through drifting snowflakes with the most doleful eyes she'd ever seen.

"You'd better come with me," she said firmly. "You need a good feed and a warm bed. Would you like that, boy? Yes, you would, I'm sure! And a belly tickle too, eh?"

"'Tis kind of you to offer, ma'am, but I'll take a look at your nails before I agree to that last. In my experience, a pleasant tickle too soon becomes a bloody scratch if my mistress hasn't tended to her fingernails. Especially if she has a temper to match the color of her hair."

Spinning around in a swirl of skirt and snowflakes, Becky found a tall, bulky, unkempt fellow standing behind her, leaning on a walking cane. She hadn't heard his approach because of the snowy blanket underfoot, and the dog had not given him away. "Is this your animal? You shouldn't leave him out in the cold on such a night."

He laughed, but there was not much jollity in the sound. "And there I was thinking you extended your offer of hospitality to me. I might have known it was only for the damn dog."

There was something familiar about his voice. Becky squinted through the snow, trying to see his face, but it was only partially visible beneath the wide brim of an oddly shaped hat and behind the tall, upstanding collar of his greatcoat.

"Perhaps you were trying to steal him, eh, missy?" He shrugged snow from his wide shoulders. "Took a fancy to my fine dog and thought to turn his loyalties with promises of heaven."

"Don't be ridiculous. I was not trying to steal your dog."

"Aye, now that I think of it, you have a sly look about you, a devious gleam in those hazel eyes. Never trust a redhead. Up to no good, I'd wager."

"Well, of all the—"

He whistled to the dog. "Come, Ness!"

The animal looked at him but remained seated and licked its snout again.

"Now don't be stubborn. Yonder wench was only leading you on with false promises. What can she give you that I can't?" The man sighed heavily and leaned on his cane with both hands. His breath formed a fat cloud in the air by his collar. "Never believe a woman, Ness. They'll tell us one thing and do another. No, you are like me. The life of a fancy lady's lapdog is no life for you, Ness."

Still the dog did not stand, although a low whimper could be heard as it turned its eyes back to Becky and widened them further, letting them droop at the far corners, adding to the already fierce tug upon her heart. Again its stomach grumbled.

Bending awkwardly and heaving a long, scuffed knapsack over his shoulder, the man muttered, "Come, Ness. We'll be moving on, boy. This place isn't for the likes of us."

The dog's ears twitched and it finally stood on its four short, bowed legs, then ambled wearily toward its master, head lowered in the very image of resignation.

"Wait, sir."

The two stopped and looked back at her.

"Where are you going?" Becky knew she would have a sleepless night in her own warm bed if she let them walk away into the dark.

"Just passing through," he replied gruffly.

"There is a room above the Pig in a Poke tavern."

"The landlord tells me 'tis taken." He paused and she saw a brief gleam of white teeth as he smiled without mirth. "I doubt he wanted the likes of us around. People seldom do. We're not pretty and civilized, me and Ness. I daresay he thought I might steal the plate from over the mantel, while Ness here rutted the eyelashes off his pedigree lapdog bitch." He laughed coldly. "Aye, 'tis best if we move on again, for if there is any trouble near about, it is sure to be blamed on the two of us. It usually is."

"But there is more snow still to fall. Where will you take shelter?"

"We'll find out when we get there. Come, Ness. This is no place for us. I made a mistake." As they began to move slowly through the snow again, she thought she saw the dog limp, just like its master. How bitterly cold its paws must be!

"Oh, for pity's sake!" Becky hurried after them. "You must both come with me for something to eat." Mrs. Jarvis would raise a fuss about feeding a stranger, but what did that matter?

The cook had been with the family three years and always handed in her resignation just before Christmas, only to want her post back again in the new year. Two more strays, therefore, would simply give the lady something else at which to grumble, should Becky fall short.

As the man turned toward her again and his big coat billowed out like black wings, she saw a dilapidated uniform jacket beneath it and then the moonlight hit his face full on.

"But I know you!" she cried.

Slowly his lips turned up at one corner. "I thought you'd forgotten me...Gingersnap."

As if she could! Her heart, surely, had stopped for a moment. Surprise tumbled and flipped through her. Snowflakes whirled around them both, landing on the wide brim of his hat.

I'll find you again, one day.

A spark of excitement lit her up inside and chased away the chill. Here was the first man who had ever looked at her as if she were a grown woman, not one of the lads. "Have you come to claim that debt?"

His dark eyes widened then narrowed again, studying her thoughtfully through the fat, spinning flakes of snow. "Why do you think I'm here, wench? Why would any man come to this place so far from anywhere and so uncharitable to poor strangers?"

His dog's stomach grumbled loudly yet again.

"See, Ness," the man muttered, his gaze fixed upon her face. "I warned you never to believe a woman. Now she's changed her mind about us already. She's afraid."

"Indeed, sir," she assured him firmly, "I have not changed my mind and I am not afraid of you. I've been expecting you for five years."

From beneath the snowy brim of his hat, Luke regarded her in that same cautiously amused manner she remembered. "Five years? Has it been so long?"

"Indeed. You're extremely past due."

He tapped his cane in the snow and glanced briefly, rather shiftily, she thought, over his shoulder then back to her. "And you've been waiting for me all this time?"

"Of course. I keep my promises and I pay my debts."

"That's a first in any woman of my acquaintance," he grumbled.

"Then you need some new acquaintances."

Another layer of snow had formed upon his wide shoulders as he stood there, his breath blown out in gray puffs, eyes squinting fiercely at her from beneath the brim of that unusual hat.

"Well, come along, man," she exclaimed briskly, gesturing that he follow. "I won't bite." It was important to take charge with men and dogs. Necessary to lay down the law from the beginning.

Whoever he was and whatever he thought of women and their promises, Rebecca Sherringham did not renege on hers. Besides, it was only a kiss. And she had to lure him inside out of the cold somehow, didn't she? For his own good and particularly for the sake of his poor dog.

❦

Of all the creatures to run into just when he was about to slip away into the shadows again! That plucky, bronze-haired, pistol-pointing debt marker.

On that snowy evening, she was aglow with light, something around which a weary traveler might warm his hands.

Apparently she thought he was there for her—that he came to claim the kiss she owed. A romantic idea, of course. Typical of a young woman. While he should have amended her mistaken assumption, he felt absolutely no desire to do so. She was rather bossy. Perhaps she'd pull that pistol on him again if he didn't obey her orders and kiss her.

"Don't dally," she shouted over her shoulder. "I get terribly ill-tempered if I don't eat before seven."

"By my salty cockles, we wouldn't want that, would we?"

"Certainly not, sir, if you came for that kiss. Now make haste." She marched on.

Whenever a woman made the error of giving commands to Lucky Luke, it usually meant one of two things: she was a fool, or she was too old to feel in danger from him.

In this case, neither was true.

And oddly enough, on this occasion, he didn't mind being given orders by a woman.

Luke quickly tossed the dog a slice of bacon filched from the tavern kitchen. Ness caught it swiftly and disposed of the morsel with equally efficient speed. Now he picked up his paws and trotted happily alongside his master, stump wagging.

The woman walked onward, leading the way with a forceful stride. Something about her reminded him of Dora Woodgrave. Ah, youth! That must be it. What he wouldn't give to be young again. Or perhaps not. He'd learned a lot of lessons in his younger years and suffered the scars to prove it. Dora was one of those most unhappy lessons.

One of his brother's lessons too.

He sighed heavily, breath forming a mist before his face. He knew he shouldn't follow Gingersnap. He should say goodnight to her, walk on, and never look back.

But she commanded him to follow. And she worried about his dog.

And she had a lovely, well-curved figure.

Uh-oh. See, that is how I always get into trouble, he thought glumly. Hips were his downfall. But then so were a good pair of titties, a high, rounded bottom, and the soft swell of a woman's belly when he kissed it and made her giggle. That hadn't changed since he was fifteen. There was always another pretty woman catching his attention, keeping him moving on from each to the next. The idea of settling with just one seemed patently ridiculous. He could never put his mind to one thing for very long.

"I cannot help but wonder what you are so afraid of, Lucius," his father had observed, "that you need to surround yourself with more than the customary number of females. As if you might one day run out of the commodity."

Suddenly he imagined a stream of angry women's faces at his next funeral. Some would no doubt bring objects to throw at his gravestone. Shoes, candelabra, potatoes. His head had been the target for a fair number of projectiles over the years.

As he watched this kindly, chattering redhead marching ahead of him, he wondered if it was too late to make changes.

Hmm. What would Darius do in this situation?

His brother would probably say, "She does have a mind, you know, Lucius. She's not just a vessel, an object with which to slake your base desires."

Yes, his brother said things like "base desires" a lot, as if they were bad.

Therefore, rather than imagine her sweet nipples in his mouth, or her buttocks warm in his hands, or the delicious little dip beneath her ear where she probably dabbed perfume, Luke considered instead her warm, clever eyes and how they filled with excitement when she thought he was there to find her. He thought of her kindness in taking in two strays. Of her bravery.

What harm would it do to give her that kiss for which she claimed she'd waited so patiently for five years? It was only a kiss.

Five

His savior warned him sternly, "I am well acquainted with rogues and their antics. So don't think to pull the fleece over my eyes, sir. I will give you both food and warm shelter for a while tonight, but don't abuse my hospitality or you'll be sorry."

Again, like the last time they met, she was very keen to let him know she had no time for nonsense, but those golden brown eyes—which she declared could not be deceived—were full of stars, inquisitive and playful. She glanced down at Ness and her lips softened with a half smile.

Luke was sure she took them in purely because of his dog. "Your husband…won't object to company?" Should have asked that before, of course, but he was waylaid by the admiration of her authoritative, extremely captivating walk. Damn it.

He heard a scornful snort. "There is no husband."

That was good news, then. Although perhaps not. The way she said it suggested there might once have been a husband, but he was buried in her backyard, minus his manly tackle, and now feeding the roots of that walnut tree they'd just passed.

Luke followed her into a warm kitchen. Immediately he began to thaw out, snow melting and dripping in glassy beads from his shoulders, the tip of his nose, and the brim of his hat. Ness quickly claimed a spot by the fire, shaking himself thoroughly to spatter the floor with drops of water and then letting out a grateful grunt as he found an empty potato sack on which to curl up beside the coal scuttle.

As she untied the ribbons of her bonnet, he caught her glancing at his walking cane again. "Do take off your wet coat and sit. You must be in need of rest." She cleared a sewing basket from a small stool and then moved it closer to the fire for him.

Why was she so kind to a stranger? What was she up to? Women generally had an ulterior motive, so he'd found. They wanted to go through his pockets while he slept, or they would use his company to make someone jealous, or they hoped to persuade him that they'd been mistreated so he'd fight for them. Or they were bored and looking for a little wicked excitement.

Swinging the leather bag of belongings from his shoulder, Luke overestimated the space in that small kitchen. He knocked into a large Welsh dresser by the wall, shaking all the jugs and platters arrayed there on shelves. Cursing under his breath, he put out his free hand to steady the tilting dresser, and when one silver milk jug tumbled, he had to catch it swiftly in his other hand, dropping his cane in the process. As he set the jug carefully back upon the shelf, he looked over his shoulder and found her studying him—and his fallen walking cane—with great curiosity. Before he could bend and reach for it, she bounced forward, retrieving the stick for him.

"I'm sorry I made you walk at such a pace, sir, but I wanted to get you out of the cold."

"The name is Luke, madam," he muttered, snatching the cane from her hand and gripping it tightly. "But everyone calls me Lucky."

"Of course, I remember. But this time you're on *my* territory and we'll abide by proper manners. So I shall call you *sir* and you may call me Miss Sherringham."

Having removed her coat and bonnet, she slung them hastily on one of the hooks by the door and, in doing so, obscured the small mirror that hung there. She didn't spare a single glance at her reflection in the glass and so was unaware of a dark blot of charcoal smudged between her eyebrows until he pointed it out to her. Then she wiped it with her sleeve.

"Is it gone?" she demanded, tipping her face up for his inspection.

He nodded slowly. "You now have two eyebrows as opposed to the one."

"I was in a play."

"Ah."

"They need me for the male parts because we don't have enough men." She groaned and threw her hands in the air. "*Not enough men.* Ha! There's always too many about, in my opinion, until they're actually needed for something. Then they are nowhere to be found."

Tonight her features were clearer, not semi-obscured by smoke from an ill-tended chimney as they were in that tavern five years ago. The young lady's cheeks had lost the roundness he remembered. They were more sculpted now, tinted a delicate pink from the cold air and framed by dampened twists of copper. Her lips were full, the natural curve sensual, even when she was not smiling. She had the sort of mouth a man might consider flirtatious, coquettish. Until those disdainful, dismissive exclamations about men came out of it to put him in his place.

He gazed at those soft, dusky pink lips, at her full bosom under that flimsy bit of lace and velvet, and her hands—quick, busy hands that would probably feel like the kiss of an angel on his rough, weathered skin.

"Is there something else amiss? My *dear* friends obviously thought it amusing not to let me know about the charcoal, so heaven knows what else you might find."

He scratched his chin slowly. "No. I see nothing else amiss."

"Just the freckles, I suppose." She shrugged. "Not much to be done about those." When she looked up again and discovered him still studying her face, she exclaimed, "I knew a boy once who went cross-eyed from staring. I told him it would happen, but he didn't believe me. Well, the brat soon knew better, I can tell you."

"Witchcraft," he muttered.

"Oh, of course! It's always the woman's fault. Rather than admit a weakness of his own, a man will resort to accusations of witchcraft. *Men!* Good Lord, I have heard every excuse for a man's behavior and never a simple admittance of guilt or an apology. Worthless, the lot of you. Except for my father, of course, who merely can't help himself."

All that because of the one little word he mumbled. A word he hadn't even meant for her to hear. He mentally drew a pen strike through his earlier admiration of her curves and thickly underlined the fact that she talked too bloody much.

If it wasn't so pleasantly warm in that kitchen and his dog hadn't already lain down, he'd turn around and leave. Impertinent, distracting woman. He didn't need a lecture from her.

"What can have upset Mrs. Jarvis tonight?" She was looking at the kitchen table where onions, carrots, cabbage, and potatoes sat in their raw, unpeeled state and then at the empty pot suspended from the iron crane over the fire. A chicken roasted on a dangle spit, but that was the only sign of progress. "Supper should be ready by now."

Quick footsteps, accompanied by a shrill querulous voice, echoed down the passage toward the kitchen. "Of all the ridiculousness I've put up with in this house! I won't have it! No, indeed, I shan't! I'll find a better place, where I'm appreciated."

To his surprise—for the voice had suggested someone much larger—a small, narrow woman appeared in the open doorway. She was already untying the strings of her apron.

"This is the last time I work in a house of eccentrics. I was warned before I came here and I should have listened. One mad old soldier with an aversion to decent clothing, his rakehell son, and a wayward daughter who comes and goes as she pleases at all hours. Acting in plays and wearing breeches, for heaven's sake! Oh, I should have paid heed!"

Luke rubbed his unshaven chin as he surveyed Miss Sherringham and her abundant figure again. The one he shouldn't be noticing.

Breeches, eh? Now that he would have enjoyed seeing.

The cook stabbed a finger in his direction. "What's this? What have you dragged home this time? A filthy beggar. Well, if that isn't the last straw, I don't know what is!"

Gingersnap protested, "This poor man—a wounded old soldier—is hungry and cold. The least we could do is provide him with shelter. Where is your sense of charity?"

Luke winced at her use of the terms "old" and "charity."

"Where the devil did you dig him up?"

Well, that was appropriate, he mused, for he had, after all, just risen from the grave.

"I found him, Mrs. Jarvis, on the common, in the snow."

"Then you can provide for him with your own fair hands—if he doesn't provide for himself first by stealing the contents of the larder the minute your back's turned. I've just handed in my notice to the major, so there!"

Suddenly the angry woman caught sight of Ness, who had lumbered upright from his newly claimed patch by the fire and now plodded across the floor to stand by his master.

"So it's *two* filthy, flea-bitten beasts in my kitchen. I won't stand for this!"

"It's not *your* kitchen, is it," Luke interrupted, "if you've just handed in your notice?"

Gingersnap scowled at him and then tried a concil-
iatory tone with the irate cook. "Mrs. Jarvis, I'm sure
we can set this straight, whatever it is this time. Do
please stay. What shall we do without you?" Such an
entreaty would be hard for him to resist, he thought,
feeling a smile creep over his lips, picturing her splendid shape in breeches again. Oh, he was warmer now,
all right. Nicely thawing.

*For pity's sake, Lucius, you're not here for that!
Remember? Can't you concentrate for one blessed minute?*

"Indeed I shan't stay!" the cook cried. "I warned
the major before. I won't remain in a house where…
appendages…items that should remain covered are
displayed for all to see."

"Mrs. Jarvis, whatever my father has done now—"

"And I won't tend another one of your rescued
beasts." The woman grabbed her hat and coat from
a hook by the door and disappeared in a whirlwind
of mostly incomprehensible grumbles. Luke caught
only one partial sentence. "…scandalous drawers with
a great deal too much lace, left out on the washing
line without a thought for anyone else in this house.
And wages never paid on time. Too much for a God-
fearing widow woman mindful of her reputation."

"Oh, Good Lord," Gingersnap groaned, spinning
about on the spot. "I'd better sort this out. Please
do sit, sir, and rest. I'll return shortly." With that,
she dashed out of the other door and he heard her
steps hurrying away down the passage, but only a
few seconds later, they returned. She peered around
the door. "Oh, by the by, sir, the silver is mostly
Sheffield plate and dented. As for the china, it might

once have been valuable, but it is badly chipped and cracked, the pattern worn away. So if you're looking for something to steal, you're in the wrong house. I suppose you might take the food, but it's raw, as you can see. All this considered, you may as well sit down and wait." She turned to leave again but looked back once more. "And you may inform your dog that we have no pampered pedigree bitch in the house to impregnate." Her speech concluded, she raced off again down the passage.

Ness yawned and trotted back to his crumpled sack. Clearly he had no intention of leaving yet, even if his companion had doubts.

Luke was still thinking about those lacy drawers.

Catching his distorted reflection in the bowed belly of a silver tea urn, Luke examined the sorry state of his grimy, unshaven face. Aye, he certainly looked the part of a penniless beggar. To his rescuer, he was just a crusty, crippled old soldier and one to whom she owed a debt on her brother's behalf. She fluttered and twittered about like a bird. A pretty robin in the snow.

He ought to tell her what really brought him to Hawcombe Prior, that it was quite by chance they'd met again. But she'd be disappointed. Her eyes were shining when she thought he came there to find her. Would it not be ungentlemanly to disappoint her?

Again he asked himself what his very proper brother would do in this position, and he decided Darius would stay silent. When Darius was uncertain, he went quiet and got on with mending his clocks. Both brothers liked to work with their hands in some way. It was one habit they had in common.

Luke looked at the chicken on the dangle spit.

Now that was a bird he knew how to handle.

∽

Her father was in his chair by the dying fire, shoes off and with both big toes sticking through holes in his stockings. A half glass of port balanced precariously on his belly, only two fingers somehow holding it steady around the stem as he snored with a contented symphony of wheezes and rumbles.

"Papa!" Becky hastily grabbed the glass just as he opened his eyes. "What have you done to Mrs. Jarvis?" Evidently the bared toes were part of her trouble, but there must have been more than that, surely.

"I don't know, m'dear. As long as I ain't married her, it can't be that bad."

She set his glass on the sideboard and stepped over his feet to stir up the fire. "She's gone off in one of her terrible huffs and I daresay we won't see her back now until the new year." Rattling the poker among the coals with considerable violence, she added, "You must have insulted her cooking again or said something offensive enough to send her into a mood."

"Is there anything one can say these days that ain't offensive, m'dear?"

"I think, Papa, you are better off saying nothing at all to Mrs. Jarvis." It didn't take much for the cook to find her excuse and walk out, especially this time of year when she liked to go to Manderson and pay an extended visit to her sister's family. Rather than ask for the time off, she preferred to make the major beg for her to come back, of course. That way she could negotiate for a raise in her salary. "But at this moment, our most important concern is my cooking, for I'm afraid you'll have to suffer it for the next few weeks without her."

Her father heaved upright in his chair and laid a hand on her arm while she fluffed the cushion and set it carefully behind his back. "Everything that woman makes is tainted by the flavor of her resentment. I would rather eat a bowl full of your cold and lumpy gravy made with love and good intentions."

"Well, that's all very nice, and fortunate, because that may be what you get to eat tonight." Becky glanced at his exposed toes. "Papa, you had better give me those to darn. Really, you cannot go about with holes like that." She thought again of the parson's wife eyeing their laundry as it dried on the washing line.

"Why not? If anyone should peer in at my window tonight, they will see I have holes, m'dear, and they will know for certain that I have toes, if they were ever in any doubt. And if that upsets 'em, they'd best not see the state of me drawers."

"Papa!"

"I like my clothes comfortable, familiar, and worn-in, Becky. I cannot be doing with new things, as you know. But if you do not wish me to wear my favorite clothes, I can sit here as the Good Lord made me, and then, as I told that surly ingrate Jarvis, she would have complaints of a more serious nature."

"Oh, she certainly would."

"How was the play, m'dear? I wish I could have come out to watch. Blast this cold weather!"

"I will tell you all about it, Papa, when we sit down to dinner. Suffice to say, I managed to speak everyone

else's lines as well as my own. I am always too eager
and impatient."

"But I'm sure you read them very well, m'dear.
Whether they were your lines or not."

"Unfortunately that's not quite the point." While
Becky lit a few more candles so he could see to read
his newspaper, she felt his eyes following her around
the room.

"Dear Becky, I hope life here isn't too dull for you."

"*Dull* for me? Certainly not."

"But you can have few adventures here."

"Thank goodness! I had enough *adventures* by the
time I was seventeen and I did not go seeking any of
those out deliberately. They found me. Now, here in
this place where so very little ever happens to disturb
the tranquility, I can look forward to a peaceful old age."

"I hope not, m'dear." He looked appalled. "One
should never be too old for new adventure."

And this opinion, she thought dourly, *is why someone
in the family has to remain sensible.*

She kissed his brow and left him happily wriggling
his naked toes before the replenished fire.

As Becky neared the kitchen door again, a delicious
aroma tickled her nose. The sound and scent of sizzling
meat made her feet quicken the last few steps. She
pushed the door fully open and stared in amazement.

Her rescued stray—coat, hat, and jacket discarded,
shirtsleeves rolled up—stood at the fire, leaning on his
cane with one hand and stirring something in the pot
with the other. The table behind him was littered with
bones, potato peel, and onion skin. His dog, thirstily
drinking from a bowl of water on the floor, raised

its head to look at her, wagged its stump, and then resumed its noisy slobbering.

"What are you doing?" she demanded.

"Making your supper...before I steal all the silver spoons from the pantry and take off into the night, of course."

It was so utterly unexpected to have help from a man rather than hindrance that she didn't know what to say.

He looked over his shoulder. "Well, don't just stand there undressing me with your eyes. I could make use of another pair of hands. If they're not too dainty for chores."

Dainty, indeed! Undressing him with her eyes! The man had some cheek after the way he'd stared at *her* before.

But Becky was in such a state of shock that she didn't make a single comment of denial to his accusation.

Six

"I DON'T SUPPOSE YOU HAVE ANY SPICES, DO YOU, Gingersnap? Indian saffron? Cumin? Chili?"

She had some familiarity with those things after her years in India, but Mrs. Jarvis would never approve of such as that in her kitchen. She was a "plain" cook and proud of it. "I'm sorry, no. And I told you never to call me that, sir."

"I'll call you what I like until you stop calling me *sir*. The name is Luke, like I told you. *Sir* indeed." He shook his head.

"It is a term of respect that a young woman of my age should use for a fellow of advanced years."

He spared her an exasperated frown, but Becky hid her smile and blinked innocently. She wondered how old he actually was. Despite the walking stick, the man possessed a palpable vitality, raw and uncivilized. Sometimes he had an expression on his face that was almost boyish, but then, if he caught her looking, he made it somber.

"If we must be bloody polite, I suppose I should introduce you to my dog. His name is Unnecessary, but I call him Ness for short. Ness, this here prissy petticoat that you talked into feeding you is Miss Sherringham. Say how do."

The dog raised his snout and gave a low bark.

She laughed. "I remember him when he was a dear little pup and you coddled him in your coat."

"*Coddled?*" he exclaimed, scowling. "I never coddled—I ain't the sort! He was just very small and poorly, 'tis all. Someone had to—" He shook his head and glowered into the cooking pot, stirring harder. "Coddling indeed."

"Well, I beg your pardon for suggesting it." She stooped to pet the dog. "I am honored to meet you, Unnecessary. But what a sad name."

"'Tis a true one." His master sniffed, looking down at them. "He ain't necessary, is he? Just a stupid dog, following me around until he finds better company with more to offer."

The animal barked in apparent agreement and went back to his nap.

Lucky Luke worked with his shirtsleeves rolled up, broad forearms exposed and deeply tanned, suggesting he often worked outdoors and in a state of improper undress. His hands were rough-skinned and large, but the one not clutching his cane was dexterous as it chopped, sliced, flipped, and stirred. Occasionally he paused, tasting from the spoon, then asked her for some other dried herb from the pantry. When their fingers touched by chance, she felt the hard, weathered skin brush against hers. Saw his gaze slip down to her hand, his lips tighten. As if he were angry. As if he thought she caused that frisson deliberately.

"I suppose you were trying to make curry," she said finally and rather stupidly for lack of anything else to say. It was not like her to be lost for conversation, but her evening had taken on an extraordinary, almost—dare she think it—fairy-tale quality. Nothing seemed quite real. Even the snow outside the window contributed to the feeling of still performing in a play. She would not be surprised to look around the corner and see the blacksmith, using his bellows to blow white goose feathers through the air. "Don't you need a recipe?"

"Nah! I'm not good following words on paper. They get all jumbled up in my head. Back to front and inside out. I'm better with my hands."

"Yes, so I can imagine—I mean—so I see."

He gave her a sideways look that resulted in another swift rise of blood temperature. She looked around for something to use as a fan.

"You've been to India then, missy?"

"We traveled a great deal with the army, and my father never liked the idea of leaving me behind. We had no female relatives with whom I could stay." She put her hands behind her back, so he wouldn't keep looking at them. "I went everywhere with my father. When we were in India, I almost married the son of a maharaja."

"Almost?"

She lifted her chin and said primly, "There were too many obstacles in our path. It was an affair that had to end. We were ripped asunder by forces beyond us."

"Sounds painful."

"It was. Very." Forgetting the need to hide her

hands from his heated glances, she picked up a carrot and bit into it.

"What happened? He pulled your hair or broke one of your dolls? Or called you Gingersnap?"

She sighed and her shoulders relaxed as she leaned against the table. "No, my father came and took me home again in time for nursery tea."

"Ah! Fathers! Always in the way." He turned back to the pot. "Now pay attention, Maharani, and you might learn something. I'm a master at the art of cooking."

Oh, she was paying close attention, fascinated in fact. She raised a hand to the back of her neck, where her hair tickled as if he'd touched it with his own busy, agile fingers. "It won't be a proper curry without those spices. I remember my father liked it so hot his forehead would perspire."

"Aye." He grinned at her. "The hotter the better for me too."

She felt his gaze brush her hair, but then he cleared his throat, made his face grave, and quickly looked back at the fire.

"My father likes all the things he's not supposed to have," she muttered.

"We all like that, don't we?"

Becky tucked a fallen spiral of hair behind her ear. "I meant spicy things and rich, sweet desserts. Making my papa follow doctor's orders is an uphill task." She bit her tongue and winced. Why had she told him all that? Surely he wasn't interested in her problems. She'd observed before that he probably had a great many of his own.

"I promise your father will like this stew and it will do him the world of good," he said. "I'm an excellent cook. There will be no complaints."

"No." She glanced at his thick, broad shoulders. "I'm sure there wouldn't be."

"Of course, I don't have everything I need here. We'll have to extemporize. But I'm good at that."

"How modest you are, sir."

He tossed her a quick scowl. "*Gingersnap!*"

"Very well then...Luke. Since you are cooking my dinner, I suppose I can call you that." Perhaps it was the oddity of seeing a man put himself to good use for her that made everything off-kilter and the improper seem perfectly acceptable.

"What happened to your leg?" she asked.

"All wretched villains like me have one of these wounds, you know. We can't join the Scoundrels League without one. Now, where do you keep the salt? And we'll need bread if you have any. Haste, missy! Don't stand about gawping and idle."

How dare he boss her about in her own house? Perhaps, under the circumstances, since he was cooking her dinner, she would ignore it. This once.

Becky strode around the table, hands behind her back again, trying to think of practical matters. "How did you find me here, Lucky Luke?"

There was a pause while he tasted the food again. "Find you?"

"I don't suppose I was easy to trace. We left Brighton five years ago, when my father retired from the army."

"Ah, but I always collect on a debt. Like I told

you." He looked around to find where she'd gone and then shook a wooden spoon at her. "No obstacle gets in my way when I want something. I suspect you have much to learn about men, young lady."

Becky wrinkled her nose and laughed, for the idea of *him* teaching her anything was patently ridiculous. She knew all about men and their ways, having lived twenty-two years with a couple of the most frustrating, ill-behaved males in captivity.

"Something amuses you, madam?"

"That you came all this way just to find me. Had you nothing more important to do?"

"Nah. Not today. I'd put you off long enough. Couldn't leave you pining for me, could I?" He treated her to another of those dark, sinister, sideways glances. "Even bothersome, interfering redheads need a kiss now 'n' then."

"I certainly don't *need* anything of the sort," she declared. "I'm only giving it to you because I promised."

"Hope you know what you're getting into, maidy. It won't be a little kiss like you're used to from your milksop young suitors."

"Full of yourself, aren't you? I'm sure I can manage."

"We'll soon find out, won't we?"

Already too warm, Becky moved away again to fetch bread from the cooler larder.

But her pulse leaped about like a playful rabbit in spring, and she had to go near him again to put plates in the warmer beside the hearth. How could she help looking over and taking another assessment while he was preoccupied?

He was too muscular for a gentleman. Too…large.

There were a few men she knew whom he could probably lift over his head with one arm. She thought of what Justina had said to her that evening—about something to warm her cold nights.

Instantly she closed the door on that image. Slammed it, in fact.

Not that it will help me, she thought. A man his size would simply break the door down if he wanted in. No obstacle, so he said, kept him from what he wanted.

She almost dropped the plates as a little shiver passed through her body and made her catch her breath.

"Like me, you enjoy a good drama, and don't pretend otherwise..." Justina had said to her that evening. "There is a constant twinkie of mischief in your eye, Rebecca Sherringham."

Mischief? Her? As if she had time for it while she was so busy saving everyone else from theirs.

"That's a hefty sigh, maidy," Lucky Luke muttered. "Something troubling you?"

"Nothing troubles me," she assured him firmly, wondering why he was looking at her that way again. He'd assured her there was nothing else stuck to her face, and as far as she knew, all her buttons and hooks were secure.

The plates safely stacked in the warmer, she reached for a cabbage leaf and fanned herself.

"Sure? Nothing ol' Lucky can't take care of for you?"

She swallowed. "Certainly not. I take care of problems for myself."

"Uh-huh. So you do. I'd forgotten."

Thankfully he looked back at his cooking pot, but

Becky was obliged to continue fanning herself with the leaf until it was as wilted as she felt on the inside.

❧

The enticing, rich, succulent fragrance of well-seasoned chicken stew traveled throughout the house, bringing her father to the table that evening without being told. He looked eagerly to see what was in the tureen.

"How clever of you, m'dear," he exclaimed.

"It wasn't me, Papa. Much as I might like to take the credit, the cooking is due to our guest." She still didn't know his last name, she realized. "He came to our rescue this evening."

"As you came to mine, Miss Sherringham." Her handy man was in the open doorway, carrying the bread in his free hand. It appeared as if he'd made some attempt to neaten his appearance before dinner, replacing his uniform jacket, splashing water on his face, and running fingers through his hair.

"This is my father, Major Sherringham."

"Sir, it is an honor to meet you." He bowed then limped forward and looked for somewhere to put the bread.

When Becky whispered that she didn't know his name, he smiled stiffly as if his leg was hurting. "Lucky Luke will do," he said.

She didn't argue but gestured for him to sit, worried about his leg and how long he'd been standing on it while he cooked their supper.

Her father looked with interest at the new arrival. Company was always enjoyed in the house, especially if it was of an informal type, and the more the merrier in his eyes, even if he fell asleep before the guests had departed. Most fathers would be alarmed at their daughter bringing home a stray man, but Major Sherringham placed great trust in his daughter's judgment. This was one of the eccentricities that women like Mrs. Jarvis found so appalling, but Becky thought sheer laziness had much to do with her father's broadminded attitude. Like most men, if he found something he didn't want to do, he claimed it was women's work. He'd hired nannies or ayahs to watch over his daughter as she grew up, while he remained, for the most part, blissfully untroubled by the work of raising his offspring. As long as his familiar comforts remained unaffected, he was happy and thought he had the best children in the world.

"Becky will sort things out," was one of his favorite sayings.

But while his daughter was there to mend things, his son was his companion in breaking them.

He'd been missing Nathaniel's company lately, but tonight he had the chance to share his table with another like-minded man and this made his mood merry, his earlier quarrel with Mrs. Jarvis quickly forgotten.

Lucky Luke settled in at their table, chatting about the army and India, finding two subjects he instantly had in common with the major. His spelling might leave much to be desired, Becky mused, remembering the scrawling blots he'd once penned across a playing card, and she knew he didn't think much of book study, but he had a sharp mind when he chose to use it. He was certainly clever at avoiding direct answers about himself. He navigated around questions like a dancing master around a ballroom.

When her father asked about his wounded leg, Lucky Luke replied with, "I daresay you saw many battles yourself, Major, and suffered more than your share of scratches." Thus her father was led off into one of his long, improbable tales, and once again, there was no explanation for that limp.

Occasionally, Becky got up to refill their glasses or stir the fire, worrying about her father getting a chill. Whenever he was involved in an enthusiastic story— either as a teller or a listener—he had a tendency to lose control of his fork or spoon, which required Becky to give his chin or his cheek the occasional wipe with a napkin.

Throughout dinner, their guest looked at her often, dark eyes squinting through the candlelight, thought- ful, searching, sometimes bemused. Just like the first night they met. Not a part of her, she was quite sure, had been left unstudied.

He was going to kiss her.

Her skin shivered with anticipation until she could barely sit still. There was something proprietary about his gaze, the way it claimed her as surely as an arm around the waist.

After the meal, she left the table and Lucky Luke stayed to talk with her father. Becky found the dog Ness, now with a full belly, snoring happily by the fire, his paws twitching. The scene was peaceful for once with no Mrs. Jarvis angrily crashing her pots and pans about. Snow piled up against the window, and a stronger wind had sprung up to send the flakes spinning and spattering against the glass panes, but it was warm and cozy in that kitchen, and her smile, reflected in the window, was sunny. It was pleasant to hear her father's distant laughter and the low murmur of male voices in the house.

She took three leaves from the pot of mint on the windowsill. If he was going to kiss her, she ought to have sweeter breath. Several other leaves had also been very recently ripped from the stems, she noted. Had he also taken some to be prepared? Smiling, she chewed the mint and resumed wiping down the table.

When Luke came in, she was still cleaning up the kitchen.

"Your father has fallen asleep, Miss Sherringham. I hope I didn't bore him too badly."

"Oh, it's quite normal for my father to drift off midsentence. I'll see him up to bed shortly."

Becky had extinguished the lamps in the kitchen, and now light came only from the fire and the soft glow of the hall sconces through the open door behind him. He cast a great, bulky shadow across the flagged floor, a black, three-legged spider. His eyes were very dark and wary again as he paused there, just inside the kitchen doorway, leaning on his cane.

"Thank you for preparing the dinner," she said. "It would have been cold game pie if you weren't here to share your talents."

"Well, I had to repay your kindness somehow, Miss Sherringham."

He was being very polite now, she noted. His tone changed back and forth, one minute casual and even too familiar, the next formal, distant, as if he couldn't decide what he ought to be. When she'd first met him in Brighton, she'd never imagined that he even knew how to be courteous, but now, seeing him converse civilly with her father, she suspected there were hidden sides to Lucky Luke.

She looked at his scars, his watchful eyes, and then his lips.

I tell you what…you'll owe me a kiss…one kiss. To clear your brother's debt to me.

Becky swallowed hard, tasting the cooling mint on her tongue. She reached into a drawer of the Welsh dresser, fumbled to the very back of it, and brought out the playing card he had once given her. She placed the IOU, writing side up, on the kitchen table.

"I suppose it's time you collected. May as well get it over with." She tried not to look too eager.

He eyed her in his thoughtful, thorough way. "It's not necessary, Miss Sherringham. I've decided to forgive the debt."

Before she could even think to hold it back as a demure young lady should, the surprise burst out of her. "*Not necessary?* After I waited five years for you to show your face again? Oh no, you're not getting away without it. You'll kiss me and you'll do it well. Leaving me with this past due matter unsettled another five years is unacceptable."

The man looked as if he might laugh. He sucked in his cheeks and then rasped fingers over his unshaven chin. "You're determined, then."

"To pay that debt, yes."

"Ah. Just to honor the debt."

"What other reason could there be?"

The dog by the fire snored loudly, paws scratching at the stone floor, chasing rabbits in his dream. The only other sound, apart from the steady thumping of the heartbeat in her ears, was the gentle tapping of snow at the window behind her and the coals in the fire, popping and cracking.

Lucky Luke still hadn't moved.

"Will you come here, or should I go to you?" The length of the table between them was a huge distance suddenly. Then there remained the matter of his limp. Expecting that he walk to her seemed cruel. Becky rushed forward, colliding with Lucky Luke as he moved at the same moment.

But as she came up hard against his chest, she found him, oddly, even taller than estimated. She couldn't reach his mouth, since he wouldn't bend. While her fingers held onto his jacket sleeves, Luke solemnly looked down, considering her lips. Becky, impatient as usual, wondered why ladies spent their lives waiting for men to take the initiative in these matters. In the books she'd read, polite gentlemen always asked first and never kissed more than a hand. It was quite a source of frustration for certain members of the Book Club Belles.

Exactly when, she thought crossly, *was it decided that men should be in charge of these matters?*

Seven

"Kiss me, then," she demanded.

"Where?"

"*Where?* On the lips, of course. Where else?"

Slowly—very slowly—he smiled.

She released her grip on his arms. "I cannot think where else—"

He raised his free hand to the tiny seed pearl buttons that closed the lace above her bodice. Very carefully, his large fingers worked each one free, his dark gaze following their progress. He swept the delicate lace aside to expose skin at the base of her throat.

"You should never have agreed to pay your brother's debt this way, Miss Sherringham. I'm the last man you should ever permit to kiss you."

She gasped, annoyed that he still delayed. Even further irritated by his attempts to teach her about men. "If I didn't already have functioning eyes and ears in my head, I might need the caution. But even if I was the stupidest girl in the world, isn't it rather late to be telling me this now? The debt, sir, was agreed upon."

He ignored that and continued with his warning. And the teasingly slow unbuttoning of her lace. "I'm too old, Miss Sherringham, too damaged, too selfish and set in my ways. Too dangerous for you."

She scoffed. "What makes you so dangerous?" It wasn't as if he could catch her if she ran away and made him chase her around the table, was it? Not that she felt inclined to run anywhere. It was really quite sweet and comical that he thought he had to warn her.

"I'm a sinner with no heart." His fingertips trailed gently over the base of her throat and down across the upper curve of her breast. "No conscience. No soft words and tender feelings. I'd never court you with posies and love letters. I don't dance and I don't know the first thing about poetry."

"Sakes! You don't say!"

"I'm not the faithful kind to sit at your feet and pine."

"Of all this, I am well aware," she exclaimed, tension and anticipation making her sound cross. "Just because I once saw you cuddling a pup inside your coat doesn't mean I'm fooled into thinking you Prince Charming."

He growled. "For the last time, wench, I wasn't cuddling or coddling—"

"This is only one kiss. I'm not expecting courtship from you, sir."

Luke's gaze followed his fingers across her bosom, tracing a light, ticklish pattern over the goose bumps he'd conjured with his touch and his whispers. "So you want nothing more from me? You have no romantic expectations?"

"I am no naive fool! I agreed to pay a debt for my brother and I don't go back on my word."

"Good." His eyelids lowered as he popped the final button free with his rough finger.

Becky tried to swallow but found her throat too dry.

"Because the last thing I need," he added, "is a woman hanging on me. I'm not a man to be trapped, Miss Sherringham. I'm happy alone on my island. Let me be clear. I'm not a marrying man."

It is almost as if he says all this to reassure himself, she mused. "What makes you think I'm a marrying woman?"

"All girls are, of course. You can't help it. 'Tis the way you are made."

"I'm not a *girl*. I'm two-and-twenty. You don't have to worry that I want anything more from a man like you."

"Just to be sure of where we both stand, Miss Sherringham." Lucky Luke bent his head and she felt his warm breath on the bared skin of her breast. "One kiss and no more."

She closed her eyes, barely listening, drawing a deep breath of wonderment as his warm lips made contact with her flesh at last.

Had that wanton groan come from her? Must have. There was no one else to blame for it.

His moist tongue moved aside the lace panel and found the warmth between her breasts. There his lips nestled another kiss. Hungrily, hotly. It continued too long, his rough cheek bristles rubbing against her soft bosom. Heat radiated from the spot his mouth possessed. It tore through her body, beating a route to her most sensitive regions and waking them to a rush of new feelings.

Under her clothing, she felt her nipples tighten, and

her breasts seemed to swell and grow heavy. When he moved against her, his groin brushed her hip.

Nothing floppy there.

His hand swept across the back of her neck, under her hair, and held her firmly, while his mouth moved upward again. Along her throat he came, to the side of her neck, her earlobe, her chin. Finally he found her lips and devoured them, his tongue plunging deeply, greedily. She reached under his arms and clung to his jacket, her fingers gripping tightly, needing something to hold on to since reality had slipped from her grasp tonight.

Finally, when it became necessary to breathe, she pulled free, raising a hand quickly to hold the lace up to her throat. Her skin throbbed. She still felt the gentle imprint of his teeth on her bosom. It was as if he'd branded her skin.

"You're quite an exotic dish, Miss Sherringham. I could eat you whole."

"You'd choke on my bones. They're very hard and pointy."

"They don't look hard and pointy. Nor do they feel it." He ran two fingertips down the side of her neck and she knew he traced her rapid pulse. "You're a very tasty piece." He cleared his throat. "Although I suppose I should be polite and say you're…an interesting woman. A rare beauty."

She laughed uneasily, reaching behind to get her balance against the kitchen table. "You don't have to say all that, for pity's sake. I thought we were being honest with one another."

He frowned. "Not used to compliments, eh?"

"Of course I am. I get compliments all the time," she lied, fumbling with her undone buttons. "Yours isn't the first kiss I ever had. Nor was it the best." It was savage, she decided, having struggled for a word to describe his kiss. How different it was to Charles Clarendon's gentle kiss. This one was demanding, brutish, not at all like the kiss of a gentleman.

It was appalling, really. Later she'd work up more outrage, but at that moment, while this man was still before her, she ought to make the most of it. This sort of thing certainly wouldn't happen to her again.

Lucky Luke laid his hand directly over her left breast, only a rumpled scrap of velvet and lace coming between his hot palm and her pounding heart. Leisurely his fingertips traced the pricking outline of her nipple, teasing and tormenting. Becky regretted not wearing her stays tonight. It wasn't convenient while she had costume changes for the play, and her roles had all been male, as usual, but stays would have provided her with some protection now from sly lips and wandering hands.

"You think me a silly, ignorant, romantic girl who might be swept off her feet," she exclaimed. "Well, you're wrong. I know everything about men like you. I've lived around soldiers all my life."

"Then you ought to know better than to tempt me like this, to let me…" He bent his head and ran the tip of his tongue along her chin while his hand gently caressed her, his finger lightly tracing the little pip that extended now visibly, pushing against the velvet of her bodice. "…between your…"—his mouth had reached her ear—"…yielding lips. To let me in."

He kissed her earlobe and let his thumb play across her nipple once more. A delicious pang of yearning bolted through her like lightning. "Now you're at my mercy."

"You, sir, have a very high opinion of yourself if you think one little kiss would affect *me* at all."

It seemed as if he took this for a gauntlet thrown down, for he moved in again, closer still. He rested his cane against the table to free both hands, and another kiss swiftly followed. This one seemed angry, his lips slanted against hers, taking her breath and her gasp with a rough, unyielding insistence. Becky raised her hands to his shoulders and then lost her fingertips in the midnight darkness of his hair. The front of his shirt and waistcoat moved against her aroused breasts and only exacerbated the situation until she wanted more—much more—than a kiss.

"You still haven't frightened me, Lucky Luke," she managed on a shredded breath. "I begin to think you're all boast and breeches. You'd better kiss me again."

"Again, woman?"

She fought for an excuse. "I haven't decided whether I like it yet. I assume you want to leave a favorable impression or you wouldn't try so hard."

Oh dear, was this that spark of mischief Justina talked about, suddenly coming out of her? *Fine time for it to happen*, she thought crossly. *With a man so very unsuitable*.

"Demanding, ain't you?" He chuckled.

"Extremely. I'm not very good at meek and demure."

"Really?" He paused, looking into her eyes. "I hadn't noticed." And then his lips greedily took hers once more.

❦

Her bright hazel eyes laughed up at him with a challenge; her lips parted and a curling lock of hair tumbled to her shoulders, over his rough fingers.

Very well then. She'd get one more kiss. But not where she expected it.

Luke reached down and gripped her skirt, forcing it quickly upward, petticoats too. She gasped but made no move to stop him. Not a word, just a short, startled sound, as he lifted her swiftly to the edge of the table and pressed her thighs apart.

"Here comes another kiss, Miss Sherringham," he muttered, his voice hoarse. "Let's see if I can impress you with this one."

She had closed her eyes, copper lashes fluttering against her cheeks.

He tightened his hold on her soft thighs, the violence of his lust almost taking over in that moment. Forgetting the pain in his leg for the first time in years, he sank to his knees on the flagged floor.

The delicacy of her skin under his callused palms was like the finest silk, more expensive and luxurious than anything he'd ever touched. For a moment, he was humbled by it. But soon passion claimed him again, taking over any last vestige of restraint. The sheer need to taste her, make her admit that his kiss was the best she'd ever known, was overwhelming.

Although he realized he'd completely neglected to ask himself what his brother Darius would do next, Luke did not stop to amend the situation.

Her scent reminded him of honey. Sweet and sticky, a treat for good behavior. But this woman was a treat for a grown man, and not for one who behaved himself.

❧

Becky trembled as she felt his mouth touch her stockings and garters first and then her skin above them. What he did to her was wicked, sinful, totally unexpected, but it thrilled her from head to toe, even as it shocked her. Oh, she could not stop him, could she? Did she want to?

A resounding *No!* ripped through her.

His lips moved higher, silkily, slyly. His rough, unshaven cheek brushed across her inner thigh.

She opened one eye and looked toward the outside door. What if Mrs. Jarvis should return suddenly? But snow wailed against the window behind her back, and the housekeeper was long gone. In the dining room, her father napped, unaware of his daughter's debauchery. She looked down at the dark, unkempt head between her knees and watched its progress along her inner thigh. Feverish anticipation had taken such possession of her body that she could not move. Everything tightened, throbbed, expecting where he might place that next kiss. Her pulse pounded in a steady, thudding rhythm.

❧

Suddenly he heard Ness growling.

Gingersnap hurriedly tugged on his hair, breathlessly ordering him to stop.

"I haven't finished you off," he groaned, a red mist of desire blurring his sight.

"Oh, I fear you have."

He caught her looking at the kitchen window, as was his dog, but he saw nothing there except a heavy spattering of snowflakes.

Abruptly remembering his cane, Luke reached for it, but in his haste he missed, fumbling fingers knocking it to the floor with a clatter. A wild curse flew out of him as he stumbled against the table.

Miss Sherringham calmly stooped to pick it up again and put the cane into his hand.

"Now the debt is settled," she said.

Glancing over at the window again, he wondered what she'd seen there. Something had brought their passionate interlude to a sharp halt before he reached his target, but apparently she wasn't going to tell him what it was. "Some cunning wenches," he muttered, "would plan such a thing on purpose."

Her eyes widened and sparked. "Plan what?"

"To trap themselves a husband by getting caught like this. Seen…by somebody."

"That remark is hardly worth replying to, but I will say this." She grabbed his hat and thrust it at him. "If I ever wanted to catch a husband, it wouldn't be you, would it? I might not have much in my favor, but I think I might aim a little higher than a gambling gypsy who would do nothing but cause me indigestion. I can assure you I am not desperate for another troublesome man in my life. Don't you think I have enough?"

Luke took a deep breath and studied her calm countenance. His pulse was all over the place as he looked at her standing there with a few strands of hair falling loose and her tiny buttons undone. "I'll be on my way then, Miss Sherringham."

But he didn't move toward the door. He wanted to keep looking at her. And kissing her until she confessed it made her heart speed, the way it did his. Alarmed, he realized this was a new sensation for him. He was usually the one looking for a reason to leave, not an excuse to stay.

Alas, this was not the sort of woman one could keep hold of with the promise of a few presents. His experience of proper young ladies was scant, to say the least. How *did* one keep hold of such a woman as this?

He might like to have this one kneeling at his grave, watering a bouquet of roses with abundant, lovelorn sobs.

Luke eyed her carefully as she adjusted her gown and repinned her hair. Again she didn't refer to the mirror on the wall, relying instead upon his assessment and her own fingers to repair the damage.

"Papa will be sorry you left without saying good-bye," she said.

"Oh, I'm sure he'll understand. Besides, I'm a rogue and a scoundrel of the worst order." He made his face somber. "If he knew where I'd just kissed his daughter—almost on her cherry basket…" *Almost.* Damn it. A feverish need to finish the job rendered him short of breath and words for a moment. He recovered, but stiffly. "He wouldn't want me around if he knew that."

Her reply was a jaunty, "I'm sure that scoundrels association would revoke your membership for cooking my dinner."

They looked at each other for another long moment, Ness waiting patiently at his master's side.

"So," she said with a brisk sigh, "the debt—my

brother's debt to you—is now paid." She'd said that already. Perhaps she was just as blown off her course as he was.

He nodded thoughtfully. "You kept your promise."

"Of course. I told you I always do." She crouched to pet his dog again, blocking their way out. At least, he let that be his excuse for not moving. "I like to keep a clear conscience and I pay our debts in full," she added. "As I try to tell my brother, a responsibility is not nearly so onerous if one attends to it promptly."

He stared at her fingers while she stroked the dog's head and tickled its ears. Any minute now, Ness would roll over and show her his belly, clearly enjoying the attention. He wished it could be as easy for him. "You're a kind and generous woman to have taken us in this evening. Not many would have done so."

She smiled up at him. "It causes fewer wrinkles to be kind than it does to be unkind. And it's easier on the nerves in general."

Luke realized he was wrong about her bearing any resemblance to Dora Woodgrave. She was very different, unselfish and completely without sly, ulterior motives.

Unlike Dora, she had no idea that she was beautiful, had never learned how to use it to her advantage. There was no false modesty in her at all, no vanity. His compliments and his kisses had taken her by surprise, poked a hole in her defenses.

The first time he met her, she had greeted him with a rapid introduction, hammered into the ground like sharply pointed fence posts, meant to keep intruders out. But behind her bravely guarded borders, he had found some insecurity after all, and a little soft spot of vulnerability. Now she held out her hand—not flat for a kiss—but angled on its side, as a man would. "Good-bye, then."

Even as he took her fingers carefully and gave his parting thanks, Luke had a feeling that far from this being the end, they'd just become somehow inescapably bound, twisted up together.

"I suppose I shall forgive you for groping me in that fashion when it was only supposed to be a kiss," she added pertly as their fingers slipped apart again. "The closest I ever came to being manhandled like that was when I rode a crowded mail coach to Jaipur and a very brazen gentleman with a monocle spilled his purse full of coin then formed the impertinent idea that I was sitting on some of it deliberately. Men! Give them an inch and they'll take a yard, as my friend Jussy says."

He shouldn't have given the wench her lips back so soon, he thought wryly. It didn't take her long to recover.

Heaving his leather knapsack over one shoulder, Luke assured her, "What I gave you wasn't a grope, Miss Sherringham. That was a caress, and rather a chaste one too, by this rake's standards."

Her eyebrows rose in high, graceful curves. "Then I should hate to be fully groped by you."

"Would you?" He smiled quite unintentionally. It pulled at his lips before he could curb the urge. "I thought you hadn't decided whether you liked it yet."

She replied coolly, "I have *now*. And I hated it."

"Lesson well learned then, eh? Don't run about like a wanton hussy, kissing strange men." He whistled sharply. "Come, dog. Pick up your lazy paws or I'll leave you behind." He moved by her and through the door while she was still muttering indignantly under her breath about how she didn't need any lessons, particularly from the likes of him.

A few moments later, he and Ness were out in the snow again and heading up the hill.

He didn't feel the cold now. The taste of her sweet skin was warm on his lips, like the remnants of brandy. Just as intoxicating too.

He stopped and looked back at her house. She was a brave wench, and he'd known that since she marched into a crowded tavern and pulled a pistol on him. But she was honorable too—paid debts, tended to responsibilities. Even those that weren't her own.

Fate had dropped this extraordinary woman in his path again for a reason.

Her kiss must have restorative properties, he decided, for it gave Luke Wainwright his courage back.

⊷

On the inside, Becky was not half as calm as she hoped to appear.

She had let a stranger kiss her. On her inner thigh and then on the "cherry basket," as he called it.

Somehow, when it happened, it hadn't seemed quite real.

But the sight of a shocked face at her window had soon brought her back to earth. Mrs. Kenton, the vicar's wife, had indeed spied one time too many, just as Becky predicted earlier that evening.

She couldn't have had a clear view, as she was

barely tall enough to see over the ledge, and snow on the window must have blocked much of the scene. With these hasty reassurances, Becky put her mind to practical matters, knowing she would deal with this problem alone. As she always did.

Time to sweep the hearth, bank the fire for the night, and cover it for safety.

At least that overdue debt was finally paid. She and Lucky Luke would never meet again, and no one else would ever know how Becky the Bold momentarily succumbed to illicit passion with a stranger. A vexing man, a self-confessed villain. The complete opposite of her ideal gentleman.

He'd called her a wanton hussy. Of all the damned cheek!

Satisfied that there was no sign left of his presence in her kitchen, she finally went to bed, but it was a long time before she got to sleep that night. Although Lucky Luke had moved on, her thoughts couldn't.

Where would he go now? Would he and his dog find warm shelter? She might have offered him her brother's room across the hall, but that would hardly be proper.

Proper? She could hear Mrs. Kenton's voice already. *It's a little too late to think of propriety, madam.*

Try as she might, however, she couldn't be in the least sorry about her extraordinary descent into the realms of wanton hussiness. Not tonight, anyway.

Eight

MIDWITCH MANOR WAS QUIET AND MOSTLY IN darkness, except for one Argand lamp in the hall and candles in his brother's study.

"I thought it best for my wife to go to bed," Darius said, passing Luke a glass of brandy. "She was tired after a busy day."

"I look forward to meeting Mrs. Wainwright in the morning." After the tragedy of Dora Woodgrave, he was genuinely glad to find his brother settled and content with a woman. It gave him hope that the damage he caused had not been too deep.

"I thought we'd be seeing you again tonight, Lucius. Although I had no idea when you might arrive."

"You knew the room above the tavern was taken?"

"I know Mr. Bridges has a young maiden daughter, as well as an eye for the cut of a man's coat. He's unlikely to rent a room in his home to a vagrant who looks as if he might have escaped a prison hulk. He was sure to toss you out on your ear before he even heard the name. But you allowed me no chance to tell you that." Darius gave a slight smile. "You're looking the worse for wear these days, Brother."

"Well, I *am* supposed to be dead."

"Yes…quite. I had my housekeeper prepare a cold tray before she left us this evening. It didn't look as if you'd had a good meal in some time."

"Thank you, but I've already eaten tonight. Enjoyed quite a feast, in fact." *To put it mildly*, he thought. She lingered on his lips still.

"I see." Darius's mouth tightened in a hard line and he looked, in that moment, very much like their father: disapproving, suspicious, and accusatory all at once.

"A local lass took pity on me when I couldn't find a room at the inn," Luke explained with a chuckle. "I daresay it was the spirit of the season that inspired her."

Darius scowled. "You will behave yourself in this village, I hope. Good, honest people live here. Not your usual company."

Luke sighed. His younger brother's superior attitude had always chafed, but he was determined to persevere.

He set his glass on the mantel. "I have much to apologize for," he began. "You'll have to give me a moment to get it right. You know words ain't my best talent."

Darius waited, a faint frown creasing his brow.

"When Dora—"

Barely had that name crept out into being than the color drained again from his brother's face. "Certain things should be left behind us," he snapped. "Best forgotten."

"Left to fester? Let me at least tell you what happened."

"What earthly good would that do?"

"We should get it all out in the open, don't you agree?"

"I can't imagine what purpose it would serve to mention *that* matter, beyond dredging up bad memories. I was nineteen at the time and have long since put that behind me. If you came here to be absolved of your sins, you should find a priest. I'm afraid I cannot help you with that." Darius quickly strode around his desk. "We're both grown men now with our own lives to lead, and I'd much rather look to the future, in which there is promise, than wallow in the past, which cannot be changed. Thankfully, in that case." Finally he managed a stiff smile. "In a sense, I should be grateful to you. I could have made a terrible mistake." He sat. "So what are your plans now that you've returned?"

But Luke knew their problems would not be fixed so easily. Even if Darius was willing to forget, Luke *could* not. He leaned on his cane, swaying slightly, wishing he had a better way with words.

"I don't know how much time I've got," he muttered. "I wanted to set things straight."

His brother squinted doubtfully at him from across the desk.

Luke raised a hand to his heart and, with what he felt to be suitably dramatic aplomb, announced, "The end will soon be upon me."

Darius's squint deepened. "You look healthy enough to me, Lucius." He paused and then his eyes widened, the little lines smoothed out. "Don't tell me! Another of your dreams?"

Darius was one who had always sneered at his propensity to believe in the mystical power of dreams. "It was a vision of what will soon come to pass," Luke replied tersely. "There will be flames. Whether that's how I meet my end or where I'm headed, I can't say, but I've dreamed it more than once."

"Lucius, these dreams of yours…have they ever come true?"

"Yes."

"Which?"

"A plentiful number." He couldn't remember which at that moment, but he knew there were several.

"You don't think perhaps it's merely coincidence? Or just an excess of rum pickling your brains? As I recall, you have a tendency to use a wide interpretation when it comes to these visions."

"I cannot help you, little brother, if your mind is so closed to the possibility of a sense beyond the usual five."

"I study facts, Lucius, not fancy. This odd whimsy of yours never fails to amuse me."

"No need to be envious, just because I have a talent you cannot fully comprehend. We can't all be special."

"You certainly are that, Brother."

"Don't hurt yourself admitting it."

How quickly they had fallen into their old sparring. Perhaps things hadn't changed so much after all in the last dozen years. Luke was almost relieved to hear and feel the old, competitive animosity. He knew where he was with that.

Darius cleared his throat. "Are you staying in London with our stepmother?"

"Good God, no. Rather have all my teeth pulled and a hot poker up my backside. Simultaneously."

"But she does know you're alive?"

"Not exactly."

"Not exactly?"

"I paid her a visit." There would be time to explain about that prank later. When Darius was in a more genial mood. "It's a long story." Luke approached the desk slowly. "In any case, I thought you wanted to look forward to the future, so let's discuss that, shall we?"

His brother sat back, eyelids half lowered, hiding whatever went on behind them. "You've spoken to the solicitors, I suppose."

Naturally Darius assumed his return was prompted by the lure of the Wainwright fortune. "Yes. They told me where to find you." He looked around the book-lined room. "You made this old mausoleum into a cozy home. I'm pleasantly surprised. As I recall, the walls were falling down around that ancient miser's ears when we came to see Great-Uncle Phineas. However many years ago that was."

"Almost fourteen."

"Really? So long?"

"I thought you would remember."

Luke rapped knuckles against his scarred brow. "In my advanced years, the memory for numbers gets less sharp."

"And how is your memory for names?" The words fell with ominous heft.

"Names?"

"Sarah, for instance."

"Sarah?"

"She was four when you left us, Lucius. I would never have known of her existence had your mistress—one of them—not brought her to me for safekeeping."

Ah, yes. There it was—the reason for the meaningful tone: the illegitimate child of Sally Hitchens.

"The family solicitors told you that Sarah lives with me?" said Darius.

"They did."

His brother seemed to be waiting for something further, but Luke was still coming to terms with the idea of an inherited daughter—one who was not actually his—and couldn't think of a blessed word to say. He was, after all, a man who lived alone on his island. And happily.

Finally Darius spoke again. "Sarah is a bright girl with a quick mind."

"She doesn't take after me then, does she?"

This was the moment to tell his brother the truth about that little girl, but would he be believed? There was no way to prove she wasn't his, and Darius would assume he was simply trying to avoid the responsibility. If he meant to reform his ways, he must tread carefully in this business, especially since Darius had spent twelve years raising the mite. Besides, what would happen if the truth came out? He wouldn't wish a father like Kit Clarendon on anyone.

"If you have returned to be acquainted with your daughter, Lucius, I hope you take it seriously and do not mean to flit in and out of her life with complete disregard for her feelings or your responsibilities."

"Why would I do that?" he protested.

"It is rather your habit. At least, it has been."

"Well, I'm here for her now." He tapped his cane against the floor. "In the flesh. Just a little older and more worn about the edges. Hopefully I won't disappoint her too much."

"We should be honored you bothered to return at all, I suppose."

"If it won't inconvenience you greatly—and some nuisance is inevitable, of course, since it is, after all, *me*—I would like to stay a while and get to know my family again." Luke reached across the desk and picked up a silver paperweight, tossing it in his hand and then turning it over to study the marks. "Or what's left of them."

"Of course you are welcome to stay as long as you need."

"I should be welcome." He couldn't resist reminding his haughty brother. "Midwitch Manor is, by rights, my house, is it not?" He turned the paperweight over again.

"Phineas left the property to the last surviving male with Hawke blood in his veins, yes."

"Which is now me, disreputable old Lucky Luke Wainwright. The deed to the houses in Mayfair and Bath are now mine too, are they not?" With every word, he watched Darius's eyes narrow another twitch. "And the lion's share of the family business."

"Yes."

"Now that I'm back, I really ought to learn about the roots of my fortune, don't you think? Take a hands-on approach to business."

"You mean to work?"

"What do you suppose I've been doing to keep food and ale in my belly? Sitting on my thumbs and begging for it? Can you see me doing that?"

Darius frowned. "But this is different. Entirely different."

"You mean, I'd have to wear a pompous waistcoat, cut my hair like a dandy, and be polite to people. Preferably not use my fists to end a quarrel?"

"Preferably."

Laughing, Luke exclaimed, "I'll try my best."

Darius began straightening an already tidy pile of books. "What have you been doing to occupy yourself all these years?"

"This and that."

His brother's countenance remained grave. "The last message we had from the army was that you were injured and honorably discharged. For six months, we expected you home, but then we received a parcel containing your boots and a medal instead, with a note that you were believed dead."

"Yes, that was a slight…mishap."

"So since then you've gambled and drunk your way around the world, while it didn't occur to you that some folk might have liked to know where you were and that you still breathed? But perhaps that would have been asking too much of your free spirit." His tone was achingly polite but venturing closer now to the jabs he clearly wanted to use but had forbidden himself. Darius didn't like to lose his temper. He kept to a strict schedule, which any outburst or argument would interrupt and delay. He was the most frustrating, bottled-up, self-tormented boy Luke had ever known.

Leaning forward, Luke reminded his brother, "Did you not just say we should leave the past where it is—or was—and look to the future? In that case, you should not be so keen to suspect me of the worst, Handles."

Darius winced. "Quite."

"Now that I'm back, I could sell some property—this place, for instance—and put a bit of coin back in my pockets. I am rather light at the moment."

Darius reached across the desk and snatched the paperweight from his hand, placing it carefully back atop a neat pile of documents. "You must do what you think best, Lucius. As you say, it is all legally yours now." He paused. "As long as you can fulfill the requirements of our father's will."

"The part about settling down with a bride? Yes, I've been informed of the terms." He nonchalantly swung his cane up and aimed it like a cue at the small silhouette of their father above the mantel. "The shrewd old man pockets his last ball from the grave."

"You are willing to comply?"

"Need the money, don't I?"

His brother's irritable glance once again grazed the front of Luke's grimy and ragged attire. "So I see."

"Now you're wishing I was still dead, eh?"

Darius had no answer for that, but his face kept getting grayer.

"Don't fret, old chap." Luke relented with a chuckle. He shook his head, too weary to continue the pretense. "I don't give a tinker's damn about the money. I haven't come back for any of that. You can have it all. You and that pretty young wife of yours."

Darius stared. "But I can't—"

"What would I want with it?"

"Of course you must take your inheritance now you're returned," Darius insisted firmly. "It is your right, Lucius."

"But I told you, I haven't got long left."

Darius tightened his skeptical lips.

"And can you honestly see me as lord of the manor, Handles?"

"The responsibility might do you some good. What about Sarah? You have her future to think of now."

"I do, don't I?" What the devil was he going to do about that? A daughter. Of all things to find washed up on his island's shore. Well, it wouldn't be the first time he'd taken a stray under his coat, he mused, glancing at Ness who was sprawled by the hearth, already making himself at home. "Worry not, Brother. You know me. I'll work out the—"

"—details later," his brother interrupted with a smirk. "Yes, I remember your modus operandi."

"My what?"

"Your methods. Leap first, blindly into chaos, and put together your reasons and excuses after the fact. As long as you get away with it, all's well in your world."

"Pah." Luke sniffed. "Never did trust a man who speaks Greek."

"Latin."

"Splendid! You can write something for my headstone. The only words I remember aren't fit for ladies' eyes."

"Then I would think they were perfect for your epitaph."

Luke laughed at that, and after a moment, Darius smiled too.

"I daresay it's the part about finding a bride that scares you off," said Darius suddenly, fingers tapping on his leather desktop as he scrutinized his brother's face. "You'd give up your rightful inheritance rather than comply with Father's terms. You've always been deathly afraid of giving your heart to one woman and settling down."

"'Tis not fear. 'Tis good sense. For their sake as well as mine."

"Yes, I used to think I'd rather be alone too. But life's successes, I've found, are so much more fulfilling when you have someone to share them with."

Luke gave a sudden, loud, very wide yawn. "If you don't mind, Handles, you can save the preaching for tomorrow. I'll go to my bed now. It's been a long journey."

Darius's eyes narrowed further and his lips twisted in the faint hint of a smirk, but he merely nodded. "Of course. I'll show you up to a room."

The old Luke would have teased him further, kept up the pretense of being back for his inheritance, but if he was going to make up for past mistakes, he'd have to curb that instinct for mischief. Especially mischief at his brother's expense.

As he undressed for bed later, Luke found, tucked down inside his greatcoat pocket, a large slice of pork pie wrapped in a handkerchief. As he opened the surprise package to share with Ness, he paused. There, in one corner of the linen, was an embroidered letter *R*.

Smiling, he ran his thumb over the silky shape of her initial. Of course, she had no idea that he was still in the village. Expecting never to see him again, she was probably preparing him as one of her amusing anecdotes—like the hat-stealing orangutan and the many-fingered, monocled passenger of a mail coach.

He could imagine her chattering to the next poor fool who leant her an ear.

Once I met a man with a limp and an odd sense of humor, who groped me in my own kitchen, made me a chicken stew, and kissed me in a very peculiar place…

Groaning, he lay back on the bed, his arms cradling his head.

Odd that he hadn't seen her in his dreams. The Sherringham woman clearly had some sort of dangerous hold upon him. She was the one thing he should have avoided, but he'd followed her home like a lost pup and then let her talk him into kissing her.

She was in for a shock when she found out who he was, but he hadn't lied. Just left out a few facts. He *was* a rogue and a scoundrel. About that much he'd tried to warn her.

Nine

THE BOOK CLUB BELLES MET THE NEXT MORNING IN Diana's front parlor. This location was chosen for their meetings primarily because it had a convenient window that overlooked not only part of "the Bolt"—the lane running along the front of this row of cottages—but also a good portion of the High Street, since the Makepieces' gate was situated directly at the point where both thoroughfares joined. Almost everyone in the village was sure to pass that window at least twice a day, and an eager observer could keep track of all business to-ing and fro-ing. As, indeed, Mrs. Makepiece usually did.

Anyone using the Bolt also had to pass that window, but a lot of folk who took the shortcut did so not just to save themselves steps and time, but rather to linger at the tail end of the path where trees had grown to arch overhead and where no one could see what they did. The Bolt was a popular walkway for lovers and those who were, in Mrs. Makepiece's words, "up to no good deed." It had been named for its narrowing shape, but since many who used it did so to dash away and hide from others in the High Street, it was a fitting title in many ways.

Today Becky stood at that parlor window and drearily counted the layers of gray that made up her view. So far there had been no sign of Mrs. Kenton. She must have taken her donated parcels to Manderson early that day and perhaps she was not yet back. Once she was, undoubtedly she would spread the tale of whatever she saw last night through the Sherringhams' kitchen window. Until then, Becky's chance to explain herself was delayed, her nerves in a state of agonizing suspension.

Meanwhile, behind her in the room, Diana poured tea for herself and Lucy Bridges, the tavern-keeper's daughter.

"I do wish we had something stronger," Becky exclaimed with a disheartened sigh, still watching through the window. "Does your mother not have a bottle of sherry somewhere?"

"Really, Rebecca," Diana scolded her. Yes, she was always Rebecca within the walls of that house, for Mrs. Makepiece did not approve of shortening names. She might not be present in the room, but her rules lingered, along with the cloying sweetness of dried rose petals from an overabundance of potpourri. "Sherry at half past ten in the morning? With breakfast?"

"Why not? I don't see what difference the hour makes." After all, last night she'd kissed a strange man in her kitchen, fully aware of the impropriety. Who knew what she might do next? First lacy chemises and now this.

"I wish you would stop pacing before that window,

Rebecca. I'm sure you're wearing a hole in the carpet and Mama has just turned it to hide the faded part."

Becky stopped and folded her arms, but only a moment later she resumed her restless motion.

When she looked at those fragile china teacups on the tray, she wanted to pick one up and throw it at the wall, just to see what the reaction would be. To discover whether Diana Makepiece was capable of expressing any unladylike emotion. She and Justina had often speculated on what it would take for Diana to lose her temper.

"I wonder why Justina is late today," Lucy Bridges exclaimed. "I hope she is not ill. Or Sarah has not caught a chill after the play last night."

"That barn is drafty," Diana agreed. "Next year we really ought to move the play to Midwitch Manor as Mr. Wainwright suggested."

Next year, thought Becky sullenly, *you won't even be here because you'll be married to that wretchedly uninspiring William Shaw.* But she stayed silent, reminding herself that Shaw was the best choice for Diana, the most practical choice, even if he was a dreadful "jaw-me-dead," as Justina called him.

"Sarah Wainwright is a bony little thing," pronounced Lucy. "She eats like a sparrow and claims only a meager appetite." Having no such problem herself, Lucy was already tucking into a toasted, buttered crumpet. "I have made it my mission to see her fill out her clothes by the spring. She has some very lovely frocks, if somewhat plain, but they are utterly spoiled by the lack of a good bosom."

Diana replied primly, "Some ladies have a naturally

elegant, balanced figure, and Sarah Wainwright is perfectly proportioned. One hardly notices...*that*... which is just as it should be."

"I don't think a man would agree with you, Diana." Lucy giggled. "Ask your fiancé."

Becky's gaze suddenly focused on the guilty face reflected back at her in the window and she realized her own bosom was not behaving in its usual calm manner. Lucy's breathy giggles had reminded her of Lucky Luke's fingers exploring. Her breath misted up the window so much that she had to rub it clean again with her sleeve.

Behind her, Diana's voice became another degree sharper. "Lucy, you have spent far too much time around the militia. I certainly would not discuss such a subject with Mr. Shaw." She lowered her voice. "And kindly do not speak of it in this parlor. A lady does not speak of...*bosoms*...while sipping from the best china."

Becky watched desperately for Justina—the only one to whom she could confide her story of Lucky Luke. She couldn't bear Diana's disapproval today, and Lucy couldn't keep a secret even if she was warned that the telling of it would cause every bouncing ringlet to fall from her head. If Justina didn't come soon, Becky feared she might burst her seams and splatter all over Mrs. Makepiece's spotless panes.

The scene through the parlor window was grim. Last night's fragile, fairy-tale snow was now an unprepossessing slurry, mixed with thick brown clots because Mr. Gates had driven his herd along the Bolt not half an hour ago. The romantic scene of the snowy lane from last night was gone—like Lucky Luke, nothing but a memory.

She felt a little like Sleeping Beauty, awoken by a single kiss. But without the beauty part. Or the handsome prince. Or the happily ever after.

At last, she spied a figure hurrying toward them down the High Street in a hooded cloak.

"Here comes Jussy," she cried. "Alone, however. No Sarah."

"Aha!" Lucy speared another crumpet on the toasting fork. "I knew Sarah should not have been out last night in the snow. She is a mere wisp without a bit of good fat on her bones, poor thing! She is probably deathly ill."

A few moments later, Justina burst open the door and dashed into the parlor. Her face flushed, her eyes bright, she exclaimed dramatically, "He is back from the dead!"

The three young women stared at her.

"My husband's elder brother, Colonel Wainwright, is alive and has come home," she added, rushing to the fire to warm her hands. "Oh, blast! I had meant to make you all guess. But I couldn't keep it in."

At once, she was bombarded with questions from all but Becky, who had too much else on her mind and could not care a fig about old Colonel Wainwright's return.

"What is the colonel like?"

"Is he handsome?"

"Is he well-mannered and amiable?"

"Does he mean to stay long in the village?"

Justina handled all the questions with one answer.

"You may see for yourselves tonight, for we are having a party to welcome the colonel. Just a small gathering. You are all invited."

As Justina took her teacup to the sofa, Lucy excitedly and loudly contemplated the possibilities of a new bachelor in the village, while Diana gently urged her to show a little more restraint and less desperation.

"It might not matter to you, Diana," Lucy was saying. "You're engaged. But for the rest of us who remain unattached, it is very good news. Is it not, Rebecca? So few new men ever come here. I sometimes think we might as well live on the moon."

"I'm sure I don't care," Becky snapped. "I wish I *did* live on the moon. At least I could do what I wanted there and the likes of Mrs. Kenton wouldn't be present to spy and lecture me."

In the silence that followed this loud exclamation, she finally looked up from her feet to find them all staring at her.

"What?" she cried. "Why are you all looking at me that way? What have I done? What has that gossiping woman told you?"

Justina frowned slightly and then reminded her, "It's your turn to read."

She'd almost forgotten about *Sense and Sensibility* altogether. Packing her frustrated mood away as best she could, Becky dropped to the sofa with a heavy groan and opened the book to the beginning of a new page, wherein the fictional sisters, Marianne and Elinor Dashwood, had just settled into their new home and met the friend of their neighbors—a gentleman who had been teased regarding his supposed fancy for the younger sister.

In an effort to forget her own troubles, Becky read with spirit.

> "…Colonel Brandon is certainly younger than Mrs. Jennings, but he is old enough to be my father; and if he were ever animated enough to be in love, must have long outlived every sensation of that kind. It is too ridiculous! When is a man to be safe from such wit if age and infirmity will not protect him?"
>
> "Infirmity!" said Elinor. "Do you call Colonel Brandon infirm? I can easily suppose that his age may appear much greater to you than to my mother, but you can hardly deceive yourself as to his having the use of his limbs!"
>
> "Did you not hear him complain of the rheumatism? And is not that the commonest infirmity of declining life?"
>
> "My dearest child," said her mother, laughing, "at this rate you must be in continual terror of my decay; and it must seem to you a miracle that my life has been extended to the advanced age of forty."
>
> "Mama, you are not doing me justice. I know very well that Colonel Brandon is not old enough to make his friends yet apprehensive of losing him in the course of nature. He may live twenty years longer. But thirty-five has nothing to do with matrimony."

&ce;

"Would you like to meet Sir Mortimer Grubbins?" Luke rested both hands on his walking cane, bowed his head, and replied that he would indeed. With his brother watching him so warily, he was on his best behavior, and even the prospect of being introduced to a pig must be met with forbearance.

Sarah smiled pensively—which appeared to be her usual way of smiling—and led him through the orchard, carrying a bucket of scraps from the kitchen.

"Sir Mortimer is a very friendly fellow," she explained, "and extremely intelligent."

This young lady, who thought she was his daughter, certainly had a look of Sally Hitchens about her, but her manners were much more refined. Apparently his brother had raised her well, provided her with excellent governesses, and seen to it that she received every proper instruction. Luke had been told that she was quiet and shy but mature for her age—in that respect, she took after Darius, her guardian for almost a dozen years.

It was the young Mrs. Wainwright's idea that he spend the morning with Sarah, and Luke had agreed, although he didn't believe it would take the entire morning to get to know her. The girl was not quite sixteen. How much, as he'd said to his brother's wife, could there be for him to find out? Mrs. Wainwright had smiled broadly, patted his arm, and hurried off, leaving him to it.

"I'm sure Sir Mortimer is very lucky to be looked after this well," he remarked to Sarah as they neared the large sty beside the orchard. The fence, he noted, needed some fortification. Someone not terribly handy with a hammer had made an effort to bang a few nails into some old door panels, but he could do a better job of it. Behind him, he heard Ness approach with his usual ambling gait, and he looked back to warn the dog. "You be respectful. The pig was here first."

Ness trotted up to the fence, sniffed warily, and then sat, staring between the slats. The pig trotted over, paused, and twitched its moist snout.

"I'm sure they'll soon be good friends," said Sarah, ignoring the low growl coming from Ness and the sultry grunt from her porcine pet. Lowering her voice to a frail whisper, she added, "Best not refer to Sir Mortimer as a *pig*. Not within his hearing. It's impolite, and he is of aristocratic blood."

"I see." Luke nodded solemnly.

She stepped up onto a small, unsteady pile of stones and from there tipped the contents of the scrap bucket into the animal's trough. "Sir Mortimer is an aristocratic boar, a very intelligent soul. When I need to think about something I come out here to talk to him. He always understands and gives excellent advice. If you ever need a listening ear, you could not find a better one. He never interrupts."

Looking around the wintering orchard, Luke thought back to when he and his brother first came here to visit, summoned by Great-Uncle Phineas Hawke, who wanted to see how his estranged sister's grandchildren had "turned out." While they paid their dutiful visit, the gruff old man told the brothers that there was treasure hidden in his house. Darius, showing the usual stiff upper lip, had pretended not to be curious. Luke, at the time, was more interested in finding some ale and skirt at the local tavern than he was in hunting for treasure. But he recalled his great-uncle's words now. *Probably just a story the old devil told in some attempt to get us interested in the property*, he thought.

"Why did you come back, sir?"

He returned his attention to the girl by the pig sty. She swung the empty bucket as she looked up at him with enormous, shining, curious eyes.

"You've stayed away so long. Why come back now?"

He thought she might be a pretty little thing if she smiled more, but living with his stepmother and somber brother, she probably hadn't been given much opportunity to laugh. "I might be of use to you."

"To me?"

"To help you…guide you in some way." Luke didn't know much about fatherhood, but some completely ill-equipped men of his acquaintance had assumed the task and managed tolerably well. If they could do it, why not him?

Luke had no experience of a daughter, yet this girl had none of a father either. Mayhap they could learn together.

She regarded Luke slowly, from head to toe, taking in his grimy coat, his scars, his muddy boots, and all his frayed edges. "I look forward to hearing your advice, sir," she replied with ponderous gravity.

He squared his shoulders. "It might not seem as if I have much to offer, young madam. But I have knowledge to share. Oh, I know you've had the finest governesses money can buy and schoolroom lessons on every subject fit to be taught, Sarah, but I can tell you about life." He would like to do that, he thought suddenly. As with many of his ideas, it came to him in the midst of his sentence and before he'd even thought the details through, but perhaps he *could* be of use to the girl. "Not everything can be learned in the school-room. In fact, most important lessons in life you won't read about in one of those books. I have thirty-seven years of experience to share with you."

She jumped down from the pile of stones, not waiting for his help. "That will be nice, I'm sure, sir."

Like his brother, she was achingly polite.

"There are a great many things a young lady should know," he assured her.

"Sakes! You're not going to tell me about *men*, are you?"

"Men?"

"Isn't that the sort of thing a parent is supposed to lecture me about?"

Luke frowned. "You don't need to know about men yet. Not until you marry."

She reminded him, "I shall be sixteen soon."

"Hmph. Just a child."

"Hardly, Colonel! Some girls my age are married already."

Not on my watch, he thought with an angry sniff. Too many rakes out there, and he should know. Ah yes, now he saw how he could be of use to this girl. "There'll be time enough for all that when you're five-and-twenty. Ten years from now."

"Five-and-twenty?" She pressed her lips together and her eyes grew even larger. "I'll be an old lady then."

"Or even five-and-thirty," he added gruffly, looking away so he wouldn't be tempted to laugh.

Ness growled again at the pig through the fence. Sir Mortimer looked up from his trough and snorted. As the pig swung his hindquarters around and flicked his curled tail, a spatter of mud from the end of it landed on the dog's snub nose.

Luke whistled for Ness. The dog stood, shook his head, took one last, long glare at the pig, and then followed them back toward the house, still grumbling softly, the noise vibrating through the stout folds and flaps of his body with every pad of his large feet across the snowy ground.

Sarah followed, still swinging her bucket. "Were you never curious about me, Colonel, in all these years?"

"Well, I knew you couldn't be…" He paused, gathering his thoughts. "You were better off here under your uncle's care. It would have been selfish of me to intervene, as he was doing such a good job of raising you. Far better than I might have done back then." *That much is true*, he thought, much to his chagrin. He may find his brother an irritating, constipated fellow, but Darius had kept Sarah safe all these years and looked after her, when he could have hidden her away in a ladies' academy somewhere. Instead he had kept her at home, ignoring her illegitimacy, acknowledging her as family. And he had probably managed all this while facing fierce opposition from their stepmother, who cared about few things more than appearances and the opinion of "fine society."

She gazed up at him, unblinking. "Uncle Darius says you were irresponsible, disorganized, reckless"—she counted them off on her fingers—"thoughtless, and unprincipled. He didn't say it to me, but I overheard him tell Aunt Jussy. Is that why you left me behind?"

He struggled for a reply. "I was not prepared for parenthood. I had my own growing up to do."

"And now you are done growing up?"

I'd better be, he mused, starting to perspire under her steady questioning. "Is anyone ever *done*, I wonder?"

She considered for a moment. Then another question burst out of her. "Will you take me to the assemblies in the new year?"

"The assemblies?"

"In the town of Manderson. There will be dances held there in the new year. Aunt Jussy said I may go if you approve. Uncle Darius was going to escort us there, but now he says he can hand that duty over to you and he seemed quite relieved about it."

Luke grimaced, for the word "dances" held no more thrill for him than they did for his brother. "We'll see."

"What happened to your leg?"

"An old wound."

She stopped and looked at him again in that somber way. "You should see Dr. Penny, Aunt Jussy's papa. He lives here in Hawcombe Prior and he's very nice."

"I'm sure he is."

Suddenly Sarah said, "If you mean to share your vast wisdom with me, sir, perhaps you will allow me to help you in return, in whatever small way I can?"

"And just how—?"

"You need a shave and a hair trim, and you definitely need some of my uncle's clean clothes. Also your boots need a polish." While he was still thinking of a response to this curt appraisal, she added firmly, "The ladies of Hawcombe Prior are quite particular. You wouldn't want to disappoint them, would you?"

He didn't give a damn what the ladies of Hawcombe Prior thought of him. It was on the tip of his tongue to tell her that, but he found his mouth unable to form those words. Not with this girl gazing up at him, with her big hopeful eyes and tentative smile. This little girl who thought he was her father.

"There's a barber in the village," she added, "although he's really the cobbler. And if you have a bad tooth, he will pull it for you too."

"Now that's what I call convenient."

Sarah looked down at the dog. "We'll have to do something about you too, won't we, poor Ness? I think a bath is in order."

The animal whimpered and turned his eyes upward to Luke. He knew the feeling. Baths and haircuts? There began the path to an honest man's—and an honest dog's—ruin. Women were devious creatures, always wanting to try and drown a fellow in scented water or cut him with scissors. Apparently even at fifteen, they nursed this desire to change a fellow and mold him into a doll.

"Because if you are to be *my* father," said Sarah solemnly, "I should like you to look decent and respectable at least, Colonel. We may not have a great deal to work with, but we can make the most of it."

What the devil had he got himself into?

Ten

Colonel Brandon was very much in love with Marianne Dashwood. She rather suspected it to be so, on the very first evening of their being together, from his listening so attentively while she sang to them…

"But he talked of flannel waistcoats," said Marianne; "and with me a flannel waistcoat is invariably connected with aches, cramps, rheumatisms, and every species of ailment that can afflict the old…"

—*Sense and Sensibility*

WHEN BECKY PASSED THROUGH THE ENTRANCE OF Midwitch Manor with her father that evening, she did not have much on her mind beyond finding a chance to talk to Jussy alone. Her friend had been in too much haste to leave and get back to her guest after the book society meeting, so she still hadn't been able to share her secret and was, by that evening, a piece of dry kindling waiting for a spark.

It was not likely to be a party of many amusements, for it was not all young people. The miserable Mrs.

Makepiece would be in attendance to cast her haughty eyes over the new arrival, and Jussy had also invited her parents, Doctor and Mrs. Penny. So all things considered, it was bound to be a rather dull evening with everybody on their "best," most unnatural behavior. But since Colonel Wainwright, the guest of honor, was an old man of seven-and-thirty, Becky supposed it made sense to invite people of his own generation. Then he would have someone to talk to and would not feel completely out of place.

"I look forward to meeting the fellow," her father exclaimed as they gave up their coats in the hall. "I have heard much of Colonel Wainwright's bravery in the field." Although Becky thought he ought to stay by his fire on such a cold evening, the major had refused to be left out. While there was the prospect of meeting such an interesting new acquaintance, a foot of snow could not keep him indoors.

Becky looked at him doubtfully. "When have you heard anything about the colonel?" The black sheep of the Wainwright family had rarely been mentioned in her presence.

"It was well known in military circles, m'dear, and Mr. Wainwright has told me a great deal about his brother too. I daresay he would tell other people, if they ever listened to the man. But you young girls all make too much noise and poor Mr. Wainwright keeps his thoughts to himself unless they are encouraged out. Even then, one has to be sitting very close to hear them, for he tends to speak mostly when he has the least chance of being heard."

"Well, I hope the colonel lives up to your

expectations, Papa, and that you will make a new friend. Now, do not drink too much eggnog, and if there are mince pies, Papa, do not—"

"My dear girl, let us enjoy ourselves tonight and not fear the malevolent intentions of mince pies. You may fight them off me if I become overwhelmed. Oh, I smell cinnamon…and oranges."

Unlike her father, Becky had not the slightest hope that the long-lost colonel would be interesting company beyond the novelty of a man returned from the grave. She already had a picture of him in her mind—a short, sturdy, balding fellow with a ruddy, weathered face and possibly a monocle. Oddly enough, she also pictured him as having disproportionately small feet. Where she got that from, she couldn't say, but her imagination sometimes worked above and beyond the call of duty.

The colonel would, doubtless, be one of those loud, garrulous old soldiers who liked to boast about long-past victories—while he stood before them, balancing his large, barrel-like form on those tiny feet. They entered the drawing room and were immediately surrounded by an embrace of warmth and candlelight. Midwitch Manor, not too long ago a dark, eerie place, dusty and littered with cobwebs, was in the process of being transformed into a comfortable home by the new owners. The Wainwrights hadn't chased the old ghosts away, so Justina liked to say, but they were learning to live with them in harmony.

Glancing around the drawing room, Becky saw that she and her father were the last to arrive. Miss Sarah Wainwright played at the pianoforte with Lucy sitting

beside her to turn the music, although she never per-
formed the service at the right moment, being either
too slow or too fast—distracted by a hangnail, or the
lace on her sleeve, or whatever plate of delicacies
passed her line of sight. Sarah's frustration was duly
taken out on the keys.

The Pennys—Justina's parents—sat by the fire with
Mr. Kenton, the parson, who lectured them on the
evils of too much jollity during the Yuletide season.
Diana, her mother, and Mrs. Kenton were clustered
around a tall, dark stranger who had his back to the
door, keeping them all so fascinated by his conversation that no one even looked over to see who had
entered the room.

There did not appear to be any man present with
outrageously dainty feet.

Only Justina, the hostess of this hastily assembled
gathering, noticed the new arrivals and dashed forward
to welcome them. "Thank goodness you're finally
here," she exclaimed, glowing with excitement.
"How could you not have told me your news, you
wretched woman?"

"My news?"

Justina grabbed her hand. "Don't try that innocent
countenance with me! I knew this morning that you
had something on your mind—you were so distracted
and fidgety—but I could never have guessed. I always
assumed that you and Charles Clarendon…but I
suppose you thought it most amusing to hide your
engagement to my brother-in-law. And after all that
you said to me yesterday about romance and how you
prefer to read it than to live it yourself!"

Before Becky could get her stunned tongue in motion, she was hauled across the room, a glass of punch thrust into her hand, and congratulations showered upon her.

Hearing his name called, the tall fellow surrounded by awed ladies turned slowly. Only then did she spy his walking cane. And two dark eyes filled to the brim with sinister heat.

Becky felt the carpet sliding away under her slippers. She almost spilled her punch.

The long-lost Colonel Wainwright bowed his head. "You came at last, Miss Sherringham. Now you can help answer all your friends' questions, for they have many. You mischievously kept our impending marriage a secret, it seems."

She could only stare with her mouth open, until Lucky Luke whispered at her to close it.

"You're a sly thing!" Mrs. Kenton exclaimed in a tone of false jollity. "Fancy not speaking a word of it to any of us. There I was, thinking you a wayward creature indeed to be entertaining a strange man alone in your kitchen last night. I was prepared to chastise you soundly, until Colonel Wainwright explained the circumstances."

"But I—"

"Miss Sherringham must have been too modest to tell you all of how she ensnared me from the moment we met in Brighton," said Lucky Luke. "Is that not so, my dear?"

She could hardly breathe. Her stays were pulled too tight.

"Now I have come to make good on my promise," he said, "and we are to be married."

Somehow she found words and a tongue to make them. "Dear God, you *are* a madman!"

He laughed loudly, grabbed her free hand, and grazed the gloved tips of her struggling fingers with his teeth. "I did not mean to embarrass you, my dear. Not before your friends. But you should have warned them. I had no idea you'd kept our engagement a secret."

Everything she thought she knew about him was blown apart, and then the pieces fluttered back to earth, fitting back together in a new way. Lucky Luke had let her think he came there just for her, to collect that stupid debt. Oh, he must have laughed heartily at her expense, especially when she said she'd waited for him to come seeking her out. But he had not come there for her at all. It was nothing more than a coincidence and he had probably never thought of her in five years. She drank her punch in one gulp, and Mrs. Makepiece, in her peripheral vision, clutched the cameo brooch she wore on a velvet ribbon around her throat.

"Thirsty?" the colonel asked, unsmiling. "May I get you another?"

"No, thank you. I had better keep *my* wits intact."

The lying villain is "Lucky" indeed, she thought. *Lucky I didn't have that officer's pistol in my hand just then.*

Everyone else was standing about rather awkwardly, not certain what to say. Then Justina cried, "I am overjoyed for you," and embraced her with such violence that Becky was almost swept off her feet. "We shall now be sisters-in-law!"

She rigidly bore her friend's tight squeeze, glaring over her head at the man who was supposed to be dead.

He'd combed his hair tonight, shaved too, hiding behind a neater facade. He must have borrowed clothes from his brother, for the sleeves of his evening jacket were a little short and his discomfort was evident, as if he could not relax his arms at his sides.

But his dark eyes remained the same, consuming her inch by inch. Each time his smirking, self-satisfied lips disappeared behind the edge of a punch cup, they might as well be planting another kiss upon her thigh, for the resulting interruption to her pulse beat was identical.

Be calm. She'd once chased a pickpocket for half a mile through a busy souk and wrestled him successfully to the ground; she'd survived a sinking rowboat on the Nile and lived through the bite on her ankle from a poisonous snake.

Rebecca Boadicea Sherringham was not a woman to be vanquished.

She would take stock of the situation and then assess the best course of action.

Firstly, Lucky Luke could not seriously be contemplating marriage. Last night he'd warned her most adamantly that he was not a marrying man. But now he did this out of a foolish idea of having compromised her reputation.

Secondly, had she not told him already that she handled her own problems?

"I'm sorry," Becky announced to the gathered ladies, "but there has been a mistake. I am not going to marry the colonel. What you saw last night, Mrs. Kenton, was this man...fixing my boot lace."

The woman's eyes widened. "Boot lace?"

There followed a short, awkward silence, and then

Lucky Luke laughed. "My dear, you are the very limit. Stop teasing your friends."

Justina looked forlornly at her but could not quite keep the twinkle of mischief out of her eyes, while Diana demurely lowered her lashes and gracefully raised a fan to hide her mouth. The colonel laughed even louder and then seized her by the arm, steering her quickly off to a corner of the drawing room.

"Let me get you another glass of punch, my sweet."

❦

"Boot lace? *Boot lace?* That was the best you could come up with?"

"Marginally better than a hasty engagement, don't you think?" she snapped up at him, eyes firing angry hot sparks. "I had only moments to find an excuse and you had almost a full day, since you were privy to certain facts unknown to me, *Colonel!*"

She was getting herself all agitated, Luke observed calmly, noting the quivering pearls in her ears, the heightened color spreading over the pleasant curves of her bosom, and the empty punch cup swinging wildly from her fingers.

"This is all your fault," she muttered.

"I beg to differ. You're the one who insisted I kiss you. I would have left without that. I was trying to be a gentleman and strike the debt."

"A gentleman?" she scoffed. "The debt was *your* idea in the first place, and you said you came here to claim it."

"Well, that—"

"And I did not give you permission to kiss me… in that way."

"Forgive me, but I didn't hear you try to stop me. In fact, as I recall, you rather demanded that I continue."

"What I do in my kitchen is my business. Augusta Kenton's spying is her responsibility. As my father would say, if she chooses to pry into other folks' business, she ought to be prepared for what she might see."

Forget the idea of a pretty woman sprinkling the flowers at his grave with lovelorn sobs, he mused, remembering the image that had come into his mind last night; she'd probably be shouting at his corpse for dying without her permission.

"Now I insist you tell them there is no engagement."

He pressed a hand to his thigh and grimaced. "Ouch. Bloody wound! Takes my breath away sometimes."

She made no sympathetic move toward him but waited, her lips pursed.

"I warned you, Miss Sherringham! I'm the very worst sort of man to let into your life, into your home, but you wouldn't pay heed. Now see what happened, eh? I'm doing this for your own good, young lady."

"Well, don't keep doing it, *old man*. I didn't ask you to. Oh, why did you have to come here? You and your big...*feet*!"

He looked down, puzzled. "My feet?"

She merely shook her head as if it was not worth her breath to explain.

Luke knew they were being watched by the other ladies and gentlemen, who tried to understand what was going on. Her father was the only person not looking; instead the wily major took advantage of the general distraction by refilling his punch cup to the brim and pocketing several mince pies.

Keeping a smile on his face for the benefit of those who watched, Luke addressed her carefully, in a low voice. "What else was I supposed to do when that gimlet-eyed, bacon-faced woman caught us in the act? Within moments of her arrival tonight, she was regaling the entire room with a detailed description of what she saw through your window. She couldn't have painted you any more scarlet had she a brush and a bucket of blood with which to do it. I didn't want to be accused of ruining the reputation of yet another young lady. I had to act, for your sake."

"You needn't have bothered. You, sir, are the very opposite of everything I expect in a husband, and if you think this is your duty now out of some ridiculous, misplaced sense of—"

"It *is* my duty. I mean to do the proper thing. I came home to make amends, not cause more scandal. I've done enough of that in my life."

Looking up into his face, she appeared to consider this for a moment, seeking the truth in every feature, every line and scar. For the first time in his life, he could look a woman in the eye without having to act, a part, because he had not lied to her. She was unique in that sense.

He knew that he had to say something when the parson's wife began telling a story of what she'd seen through the Sherringhams' kitchen window. While his brother watched him with a peregrine's steely eye, Luke had to make a hasty decision. His behavior was once again in danger of bringing scandal to the family, just when he wanted to make recompense. So he acted on the spur of the moment and told them all that he was going to marry Gingersnap. He'd sort out the details later. Of course.

The rich luster of her hazel eyes drew him in, and then he was spinning around, trying to catch the little gold specks of dust that lived there.

"For a military man, you crumpled remarkably quickly under Mrs. Kenton's barrage of cannon fire," she muttered. "No one takes that windbag seriously." Her expression was bold and determined again, just as it was when she confronted him in a tavern five years ago. "Besides, you're much too old for me," she added firmly. "You're nearing forty, for pity's sake. At that age, you are horribly set in your ways and have no business considering marriage for the first time. A bachelor who has avoided it this long is not fit for that sort of companionship and would be better off with a nursemaid. No offense meant."

"Splendid. I'll try not to take any." Luke scowled. "You're much too young for me anyway. And damned noisy. Not to mention quarrelsome and demanding."

Her eyes flared again. "Pardon me for having an opinion."

"You're a woman." He swung his cane and laughed. "You don't need to clutter up your little head with an opinion. That's why we men are here, to make the important decisions. You stick to bonnets and…and…*boot laces*."

She glared, her eyes simmering, the gold dust caught in a desert windstorm. "You're a villain who is not to be trusted. You admitted it freely."

He leaned down to her. "And you're likely to shoot at me one day."

"No doubt you'd give me plenty of reason to do so."

"Ha! You strike me as the sort who wouldn't require much provocation."

"So, as you see," she snapped, "marriage is out of the question between us. Utterly unnecessary and would doubtless end in tragedy for anyone within five miles."

She thought she had it all sewn up, but he wouldn't argue with her any further. As he'd warned her once before, he didn't discuss business with a bit of petticoat. "Just don't think you'll get another kiss like that from me until our wedding night," he muttered.

That silenced the ungrateful wench, mid-stitch. With that, he turned sharply and limped away from her. Perhaps he limped a little worse than normal. Wouldn't hurt to play on her sympathy, would it?

Eleven

BECKY WOULD HAVE GONE HOME AT ONCE, BUT HER father was enjoying himself too much to leave. Again she reminded herself not to fret. No one could force her up the aisle. No one could kidnap her and make her marry the colonel. These were not the dark ages and she was not living in a gothic novel.

She glanced over at Diana Makepiece and thought of what that young lady would do in these circumstances. Diana's feathers were never ruffled, and no matter what happened, she always retained her dignity.

Becky, therefore, would do the same as she set about refuting his horrendous lie.

One by one, the party guests approached to give their opinion on the supposed engagement. Her father, having conversed briefly with the colonel, told her that he thought it was a "very good jape." He already liked Lucky Luke, of course, and thought nothing of this unseemly haste.

"Yes, indeed, Papa, it is a merry jape of the colonel's, but that is all it is. I am not going to marry him."

Still he laughed. "The fellow apologized for not

seeking my permission, m'dear, but goodness, I am only happy to finally have you off my hands, as I told him."

"Papa, there is no engagement."

"But you invited this one to dinner. You did not chase him off with a blunderbuss like the last poor fellow. Surely that is a good sign, m'dear."

"Papa, that was a bow and arrow." She added hastily, "And it was an accident."

The smile did not leave his face or even waver. "We shall have a rum cake and a large party."

Any excuse for a party, she thought grimly. "But you need me. How could I marry anyone and leave you?"

"Good heavens, you must not think of staying just for me. You must go and look after the colonel now, as you have looked after me all these years. I cannot afford to keep you fed and clothed forever, you know." He patted her arm and grinned gleefully. "He seems to like you, and it would be selfish of me to keep you all to myself much longer. You're almost an old maid. I have told him now that he may have you, and I cannot go back on my word. He didn't even ask for a dowry, m'dear. How can I pass up such a bargain?"

She was still soothing her wounds from that when Mrs. Penny, Justina's mother, rushed across the room and exclaimed merrily, "My dear Rebecca, so you have finally caught yourself a man! How clever of you to surprise us all. You've always been rather too strong and opinionated, but I knew there must be a man somewhere for you. One who would not mind your brusque, forward ways. What a relief it must. be for you. I daresay you were anxious not to be left behind as the friends around you are all snapped up."

"Not at all, Mrs. Penny. I am resolved to live a happy, untroubled life as an old maid. And he's not going to stop me."

A moment later, Mrs. Makepiece joined them and shockingly pronounced Colonel Wainwright to be "Quite the gentleman. Very polite and gallant. He impressed me very much. A fine, charming fellow."

Becky stared at the lady. "Are you quite well, madam?"

"Of course." Struggling to permit herself a smile, the usually dour woman added, "I must congratulate you on your conquest, however it came about." She exchanged a knowing glance with Mrs. Penny. "I'm sure you will both know every happiness."

"Although he is much older than she is," the other lady pointed out, discussing Becky as if she weren't standing there before them.

"Still, I daresay he will bring her behavior under a firmer hand," said Mrs. Makepiece. "He doesn't seem the sort to tolerate a wayward bride, and Rebecca has not had much discipline in her life. It will do her good."

"I am *not* engaged to him," Becky exclaimed hotly, "whatever he tells you. It may try the bounds of your belief, but I am not so desperate!" She began to think she *was* dreaming this after all. Or else she was a ghost that no one could see or hear.

Indeed the ladies looked at her blankly as if she hadn't spoken. Then Mrs. Penny, distracted by the arrival of a molded jelly just placed on the sideboard, had the opportunity to boast about the exceptional talents of her daughter's new chef, a man brought from Mr. Wainwright's Mayfair house.

Becky's predicament was temporarily forgotten while the ladies discussed the merits of molded puddings and French chefs.

Next came Darius Wainwright, approaching cautiously to offer his congratulations. Becky tempered her response carefully.

"Thank you, but I fear it was a misunderstanding that led the colonel to think we're engaged."

"Ah." His dark eyes simmered with hidden thoughts. "I might have known. Another of his practical jokes, amusing to no one but himself. What has he done to you?"

"Done to me?" Alarmed, she glanced over at Mrs. Kenton, but the lady was trailing around the room after a limping Lucky Luke, her lips moving all the while, as rapidly as her feet. Her victim looked as if he wished he had something to swat her with. "He has not done anything to me, sir, I assure you."

But Darius Wainwright stared at her, his face mournful as a month of wet wash-day Mondays. He must know the sort of trouble his brother was capable of causing.

Finally came poor little Sarah, expressing such genuine warmth and excitement at the idea of a newfound father *and* stepmother that Becky's heart pinched when she had to let the girl down. *It would be crueler*, she thought, *to lie and pretend all is well.* So she was straightforward as usual. "I'm sorry, Sarah, but I am not marrying the colonel. It was naught but a misunderstanding."

"How could that be? He seems certain."

"Yes, Sarah. I have found that men are never so certain about anything as they are when they cling to a mistaken idea."

"How very odd."

"Men frequently are."

Sarah frowned. "Do women never make mistakes?"

"Occasionally. The difference is that we learn from ours. Men never like to admit they're wrong and therefore they cannot learn from experience. We become more sensible as we mature. Men often become many degrees more juvenile and harebrained."

They both looked over to where Mrs. Kenton had the colonel trapped, commanding his attention with her blithely intrusive questions. She was eager to let him know she had a connection with his family, for she considered herself a close friend of his stepsister, Viscountess Waltham. It was a subject they were all sick of hearing about. When Becky stole a glance at his face, it was clear from Lucky Luke's expression that he was bored of it too, despite the fact that he'd only just met Mrs. Kenton. "Lady Waltham told me you were quite the scoundrel in your youth, Colonel!" The parson's wife shook her finger at him, her loud voice seizing the attention of everyone in the room.

"In my youth, I was many things, madam. I have put those days behind me now. Excuse me." He screwed up his face as if in great pain and took a step away from her.

But he could not escape Mrs. Kenton. She moved with him and almost got swiped across the leg by his cane as he swerved.

Becky remembered how he once claimed never to answer questions from women. No wonder this forced, studied politeness sat upon him tonight with as much ease as his borrowed clothes.

"You fought with the Dragoons, Colonel?" Mrs. Kenton demanded. "In India? Is that so?"

He grunted a reply before swiftly finishing his glass of punch and not giving the slightest encouragement to Mrs. Kenton's conversation—not that she needed any.

Like a lame, frustrated tiger caged in an exhibit, he bided his time, waiting for freedom again, observing his audience with wary eyes and letting out the occasional menacing grumble. Becky didn't believe for a minute that this reform he mentioned was true. Certainly it could not last. They might have dressed him up for display tonight, but the skin of his knuckles was still rough. He could not hide that, and apparently his brother had no gloves to fit him.

Diana now sat at the pianoforte and began to play, her skilled fingers leaping across the keys in a valiant attempt to obscure Mrs. Kenton's voice.

"The colonel says he met you in Brighton, Miss Sherringham," said little Sarah suddenly. "I have been here a month and you never mentioned it."

"I did not know who he was then. Your father kept his identity a secret."

Your father. Her tongue felt thick as it stumbled over those words. Lucky Luke had a daughter, and she was only six years younger than Becky. In another year or two, he could even be a grandfather, for pity's sake. There was another fact exposed like a raw nerve in a tooth.

A man with a daughter that age should not kiss the way he did. Good God. She melted again, just thinking about the way he'd—

"I should rescue the colonel from Mrs. Kenton," said Sarah, still looking confused.

"Yes, I think you had better. His leg seems to be troubling him excessively."

When Sarah called out for Ness, the ugly mutt ambled out from beneath the pianoforte, looking extremely sorry for himself. Like his master, Ness was all dressed up this evening, bathed and combed, a large bow of plaid taffeta decorating his collar.

Sarah took him over to the colonel, where Ness immediately began to sniff and growl at Mrs. Kenton's skirt, becoming so insistent that the lady's conversation kept getting cut off as she turned in circles, protesting with as much merriment as she could maintain. Becky heard the colonel mutter nonchalantly that he thought his dog was interested in her perfume.

"It does smell a little like a Yorkshire hot pot, madam," he added.

Flustered, Mrs. Kenton protested that it was a perfume she distilled herself. "Everybody always wants to know how I make it. It is a perfume much admired."

"My dog certainly appreciates it."

But after a few more wailing protests from the lady, and clearly having amused himself long enough, Lucky Luke whistled sharply and Ness sat back on his haunches, releasing Mrs. Kenton from his lusty attention. The lady beat a rapid retreat, backing away from the dog until she had reached Becky by the sofa.

"Lucius Wainwright may claim to be a changed man, but he was once an utter rake for whom no stone of debauchery was left unturned." She stared hard at Becky. "It would do you a service, young lady, to let you know the trouble you're taking on."

That statement quickly seized the attention of the other women and they gathered around, even those who might like to think gossip beneath them.

"There is scarce a heart, or at least a reputation, between London and Bombay that he has not left shattered. My very particular friend, Viscountess Waltham—who is his stepsister, don't you know—told me that in his heyday, he often kept three young ladies on his arm at once and still that did not stop him from looking for another. His antics quite shamed the family." Although the woman made some attempt at a whisper, it was not as low or as discreet as it might have been. Fortunately Diana's playing of a merry Scots reel was just loud enough to keep their conversation from the ears of anyone across the drawing room. "They say the man kept a *harem*."

Mrs. Makepiece tipped to one side, gripping the back ridge of the sofa as if she needed smelling salts. A scandalized whisper slipped out from between her pale lips. "A harem?"

"Indeed. The more the merrier in his bed, so I hear. Not that it was always in a bed."

Justina had walked over to join the ladies, and she responded crossly to this outrageous remark, "However my brother-in-law once led his life, that is all in the past."

"But they do say leopards never change their

spots," Mrs. Kenton replied, undaunted. She turned to Becky and whispered behind her fan. "I would advise you to be wary, Miss Sherringham. He never married that little girl's mama, you know, and I shouldn't be surprised if there are more by-blows wandering about the country. The man had a shameless aversion to matrimony. Until now."

"Mrs. Kenton, I have already told you that I am not going to marry—"

"That poor child, Sarah," the heedless woman went on. "Lady Waltham told me he did not take responsibility for the babe when she was born. No one would ever have known she existed if the child's strumpet mother had not delivered her into the family's safe-keeping when Lucius went off to India."

Justina had heard all this, despite Mrs. Kenton's attempt at a sly whisper. "Madam, Sarah's mother is not alive to defend herself against unkind gossip and we know nothing about her."

The woman remained unapologetic. "Well, it is fair conjecture. Lucius never pursued proper young ladies, and any decent mother would keep her daughter out of his way."

Becky pressed her lips together, reliving again how he'd kissed her last night. And where. He was a rake, a reckless libertine *with a harem* and at least one illegitimate child. A daughter he'd abandoned.

The pastor's wife was not yet finished with her lurid tale. She fanned her chin rapidly and continued, "He once seduced his brother's sweetheart, you know. Stole her away from under his nose just as bold as you please. Darius never recovered from the betrayal by both his brother and the little slattern involved. Dora Woodgrave, the daughter of his tutor. Darius would have married her, had his brother not come home on leave and ruined her innocence."

Becky felt her friend bristling with anger at her side.

"If my husband is prepared to forgive, madam, then so must we," Justina exclaimed tightly. "My brother-in-law has returned to us a new man, reformed and contrite. Now he is engaged to my friend, and it is even more imperative that we believe in his desire for improvement."

Yet again, Becky tried to correct this misconception. "But I am not going to marry—"

"Of course." The parson's wife partially bowed her head in a gesture of unconvincing meekness. "I only thought to state the facts for Rebecca's sake. As a friend with her best interests at heart, you would surely wish for her to know."

Justina walked away, clearly too annoyed to stay a moment longer and listen to the woman. Becky would have followed, but now Mrs. Kenton cornered her just as she had the colonel earlier. "Lady Waltham also informed me of the provision written by old Mr. Wainwright into his will shortly before his death. But perhaps you are aware of it? The money may be inducement enough for you. It certainly is for your father, it seems."

"I beg your pardon, madam?"

"Lucius cannot inherit a penny of the family fortune unless he marries and settles down. The eldest son's wild ways were always a terrible concern to old Wainwright. I suppose you are a convenient woman for the colonel in that case."

Becky felt her lips part, but no sound came out.

A convenient woman! Then this was nothing to do with concern for her reputation at all. He was merely using her to get his filthy clutches on the Wainwright fortune and disinherit her dear friend's children.

Becky raised a hand to her breast, touching the skin where he had pressed his lips last night in a wicked kiss. At that same moment, she looked over and found him watching her. How could eyes so dark be that hot? Mrs. Kenton's voice buzzed in her ear. "I know you have no mother to advise you, and your father is a lax guardian. Perhaps that is why the colonel picked you out for this scheme, poor thing. I pray you do not think me talking out of turn, as they say, but I would not stand by and see you misused. If you were a daughter of mine, I would want someone to advise you, if I must be absent."

Becky did not want to believe everything the vicar's wife said. She hoped, for her friend's sake—and for young Sarah's—that Lucky Luke *had* returned a changed man. But hoping was as far as she could go. Look how quickly he had almost seduced her last night!

Those eyes were sinful, secretive. Full of debauched thoughts.

At least they were when they looked at *her.*

He smiled at her. Had the gall to smile! The cad. Last night he'd had the audacity to accuse her of trying to trap him, when all the time he was the one scheming for a bride.

"Yorkshire hot pot, indeed!" Mrs. Kenton grumbled under her breath.

Mrs. Penny popped up on Becky's other side and

tapped her on the sleeve. "Whatever Mrs. Kenton's doubts, the colonel is just the man for you, Rebecca, my dear. Snap him up while you can, for there might not be another man to come your way before it is too late and you are past your prime. He surely cannot afford to be too fastidious. Not with his history. He is likely to manage you well enough."

When Becky laughed, it came out rather high and thin. "Thank you, madam, but if the colonel ever thinks to *manage* me, he might end up with two limps instead of one."

Twelve

LIKE SQUIRRELS AROUND A BAG OF NUTS, THE LADIES had gathered by a sofa on the far side of the room. From the many sly glances cast his way, Luke guessed he was the dominant topic of conversation. Sarah was right, he mused; it was a good thing he'd taken her advice and cleaned himself up. Better he not give them any additional ammunition against him, for her sake. She had come to stand at his side, bringing with her the overly rouged, giggling creature who had earlier turned the music while she played.

"Miss Sherringham says she's not going to marry you, Colonel."

"So I heard, Sarah. The lady likes to tease. She is full of wit and vivacity. Quite makes my breeches split with the hilarity."

"She did not look very amused when she said it. And, by the by, I have my mind set upon her for a mother now. I think she will advise me very well."

"Is that so?"

"And she is not one of those vapid, giggling girls with round heels that you used to chase after."

Luke scowled. "Who told you that?"

She put her proud little chin in the air and said smugly, "I have my ears open, Colonel. Just like my eyes. I am quite sure Miss Sherringham will help me to look after you."

"Hmph." The shirt borrowed from his brother was too tight across the shoulders and constricted the movement of his arms, so he began to feel penned in. He groaned softly, leaning on his cane. "She and I must get accustomed to the idea of shackles."

The ladies around the sofa now dispersed, evidently finished pecking at his nuts. Rebecca walked over to the fire with two of the women following, poking her sleeves, talking to her earnestly in voices too low for him to hear above the music.

"You must ask Dr. Penny about your leg," said Sarah. "He is there, by the fire. Let me take you over."

"If it makes you content, Sarah, I will visit the doctor tomorrow. But now let him enjoy the fire and this good company in peace, eh? I'm sure the last thing he wants is to look at my wounds when he's been invited to a party."

"Very well, but you must promise to go tomorrow."

"If you say so."

"Miss Sherringham will agree with me, I'm sure."

"Will she?" He thought Gingersnap was more likely to prefer him hobbled, so he couldn't keep up with her.

Now Sarah's companion—she of the fair ringlets and red cheeks—spoke up. "I can't imagine why she didn't tell us she was engaged. I know I would be bursting to tell if it were my news. We all thought she would never find a man to marry, for she is so very particular in her likes and dislikes. She fired an arrow at the last man who took a fancy to her. Becky claimed it was a mistake and that he merely wandered between her and the target, but we all know differently."

That did not surprise him at all. Lord, he needed more punch, he thought, gazing into his empty cup.

"Soon I will be the only one of us without a husband," Ringlets added. "I lamented, only this morning, how interesting single men hardly ever come here and when they do, they are immediately snapped up. Now the militia are no longer encamped nearby, it feels as if all eligible men have abandoned us. But Becky said she didn't care and would rather live on the moon."

He smirked as he remembered thinking, the first time he met her, that she must have come from there, or a planet nearby. "What do you young ladies find to do with your time in the absence of *interesting* gentlemen?"

Sarah answered, "We don't miss them very much, Colonel. We have a book society."

"Books?" He frowned. That was hardly compensation for the company of men.

"Yes, you know, Colonel. They have pages and open thusly." Sarah demonstrated with her hands, her face perfectly innocent. *Cheeky miss.*

Over by the fire, he heard Rebecca exhale a short chuckle before she turned away again. Apparently she had good hearing. He wouldn't be able to get much past her notice. His frown grew heavier until he began to feel a headache from it. Must be the heat of the room and all those haughty women staring at him, he decided. Christ, he hated these stifling little parties. Tonight he remembered why it had been such a pleasure to let himself be thought dead, to escape society and the need for rigid manners.

Sarah and her friend were now discussing books. Ringlets exclaimed that she would rather enjoy the entertainment provided by real men than the fictional sort. "Sometimes, Colonel Wainwright," she added, "I believe we read too many books."

"Nonsense," said Sarah. "There is no such thing as too many books."

"Well, you wouldn't really know, my dear little Sarah. It is *your* only entertainment. You haven't been to a ball or danced at the assemblies and met any beaus. You haven't known what it is to be adored and flirted with by half a dozen men at once and learned the art of juggling your admirers, keeping them all in love with you. There would not have been so much time to read books then." She looked up at Luke from beneath her long, fair lashes and gave a coy smile, probably induced by too much punch. "Dear little Sarah hasn't experienced enough of the world yet to know the difference between a fictional hero and a live one. Don't you agree, Colonel?"

He considered that for a moment and then replied, "I am glad that she hasn't experienced that side of life yet or learned those particular arts you mention. Sarah is young and has plenty of time for all that."

"Oh."

There was an awkward silence while Luke stared morosely at his punch cup.

Finally Ringlets found another subject. "Do you like to dance, Colonel?"

"No," he growled. "My dancing days are over."

She glanced at his walking cane. "Of course, how silly of me. You mustn't mind me, Colonel. I do sometimes say the most foolish things."

But Sarah exclaimed, "Even if you can't dance a reel, I'm sure you could manage a minuet or a Boulanger, something without too much leaping about."

"I can assure you, Sarah, that wild elephants wouldn't drag me onto a dance floor again."

As the two young ladies now discussed the next, much anticipated Manderson assembly room dance, Luke let his mind wander to something of more interest. Across the room, his reluctant fiancée appeared to be suffering in quiet torment as those two ladies fussed around her. She finally extricated herself from their pokes and clutches to perch beside the parson on the sofa. There she feigned deep absorption in that fellow's conversation, but Luke saw from the clenching of her hands and the tapping of her toes that it took all her willpower to sit still.

At least he was fairly sure she didn't have a weapon on her tonight. Fairly sure. In that dress, there were few places to hide one, he mused. If there was some other bachelor present, he might have thought she dressed that way for him.

Not that he would have been jealous. He'd never been jealous in his life and was too old to start now.

Uh-oh. She'd just looked his way with a frosty glare that shriveled his plums to prunes.

He tapped his cane on the carpet and straightened his shoulders.

What was he waiting for? Hanging back like a

pimply, uncertain youth! So he began a limping course toward her.

Say something charming and slightly naughty, he thought, and then she'd smile and forgive him for hiding his identity from her. Young ladies couldn't have changed that much since he last seduced one out of a surly mood.

Nothing to it.

⁓

The parson, his eyes round behind his spectacles, gravely warned her against coming out in such a thin muslin gown and with nothing warm across her shoulders. She'd already been assured by his wife and by Mrs. Penny that this particular shade of rosy pink should never be worn by a redhead.

"It does you no favors, my dear," Mrs. Kenton had informed her. "With your looks, you must be careful. The eye can only see so much color at once, and that hair of yours is very…bright. It is always in danger of looking brassy."

"Never mind," Becky replied. "With any luck, it will soon be sprouting gray and then I shan't have to worry about looking garish anymore."

The two ladies further advised her that the style of her gown was too low cut in the front, was far too "fancy," exposed too much shoulder for a small drawing room party, and needed a lace tuck to preserve her modesty. It was not the first time the ladies had taken it upon themselves to criticize her form of dress. Because she had no mother, they seemed to think it their responsibility to point out her mistakes. But since they only ever told her what she did wrong when she was already doing it and it was too late to change, their advice was never much use.

As for Mr. Kenton's quiet concern about her gown being too thin and exposing too much shoulder, Becky could little entertain the possibility of catching a cold while Lucky Luke's heated gaze warmed her shoulders. The villain's thumping cane could be heard like a warning overture before he arrived in her side view.

"Ah, Colonel Wainwright," Mr. Kenton exclaimed, quickly forgetting Becky's failure to dress herself appropriately. "We will expect to see you at church this week, of course."

Becky, glancing up at the colonel's startled face, very much doubted anyone had ever expected him at a church.

"Hmmm." The man could barely move his lips to make that sound. Now she knew exactly why Darius Wainwright's expression—that disgruntled, begrudging smile—had so often seemed familiar to her. "That shade of rose matches your maidenly blushes, Miss Sherringham."

Before she could say anything, the parson intervened. "I have already advised Miss Sherringham to dress warmer in such weather. She risks her health by coming out in December in such a thin frock. The good Lord would consider that an act of disdain and disregard for one of His creations."

"Indeed." The colonel dropped his hand to his side. "And His creation is such a pretty one. So very well made."

"I'm sure the good Lord has many other things to do with His time than worry about what I wear."

"On the contrary, Miss Sherringham," said Mr. Kenton. "He watches over all of us, all the time. He is omnipresent."

"Like your wife," she muttered.

"Surely," said the colonel, his voice low, "God would want us to admire His creation. Therefore I, for one, am glad Miss Sherringham is not all covered up."

The parson did not know what to say to that. Neither did Becky.

Lucky Luke added, "What does it say in the Bible, Mr. Kenton? Something about not hiding your light under a bushel?"

"You are a student of the Holy Bible?" Becky sputtered. "I am surprised. I didn't think you read books at all."

"You're mistaken, my dear. I love a good book."

"You once told me you had little time for them. The words 'daft' and 'bloody' were used."

He ignored that. "In fact, Sarah has just invited me to join this...book society thingummy."

Horrified, she exclaimed, "It's all ladies."

"I'll have to be on my best behavior then."

Oh no, he was not invading their club. "Men are not allowed."

She was quite sure the last thing he read was the suit on a pack of cards. Or an IOU. He had claimed that written words looked jumbled to him and he was surely not a man who could be entertained by the quiet study of any book, let alone a romance such as those the Book Club Belles generally acquired.

This love for books is as ephemeral and suspicious as his limp, she thought. She'd noticed that there were times when he seemed to forget about the need for his cane.

But when he found himself cornered by a difficult question, he made much of that pain in his leg to distract people from the fact that he fudged an answer.

It was interesting that his masquerade had fooled Mrs. Makepiece, of all people. That lady was usually wary of gentlemen until they met with her stringent approval, yet only a quarter of an hour in this rogue's company had been enough to impress her. *Fine and gallant*, indeed! Ha, Becky knew better. Mrs. Makepiece didn't know that he preferred his women face down in the pillow. But Becky had not forgotten that story.

According to Mrs. Kenton, there were hundreds of those women. A harem.

Naturally, one could not believe everything the parson's wife said, but Mrs. Kenton's stories about the scoundrel's past simply confirmed Becky's own sound judgment in this case. For once, therefore, as it supported her own cause, she did not instantly dismiss the woman's gossip as nonsense.

When Lucky Luke began to say something else, she sharply cut him off. "I might have let my guard down last night, in a moment of regretful silliness, but I am not an empty-headed girl eager for a gentleman's attention. Some people in this village may think I fretted while all my friends became engaged and married, but I have plenty of other, better things to do. My father and brother need me to take care of them, and I have no time to manage yet another overgrown boy."

She heard the vicar's gasp of surprise at this outburst, but she could not stop herself. "I certainly do not need one who is fifteen years older than me and has an illegitimate daughter, whom he abandoned, escaping his responsibilities to explore the world and seduce more unfortunate women."

"You sound tense." Lucky Luke's voice was so low, so deep, it quaked her to the very core. "Rebecca."

Her name on his tongue was as startling as a public kiss would have been. She stood quickly, pulse thumping. Oh dear, she had forgotten her vow not to lose her temper, to be as calm and unruffled as Diana.

Alas, despite the need to keep her wits intact, her throat was parched and the punch bowl beckoned.

Only three steps later, he was in her way again, moving with remarkable ease suddenly for a wounded man.

"Don't you carry a fan?" he inquired in a louder voice, stopping her mid-stride.

"No. Why?"

"It looked as if you might be in need of one."

She whispered, "Only to slap your face with it."

To her added annoyance, he merely laughed. "That's a fine way to talk to your fiancé. Am I not allowed to admire you?" He laid his fingers on her wrist, not grasping her hand but simply holding his long fingers there, as if he could feel her pulse through her evening glove. A fluttering sensation swept up her arm and then down through her body. Oh yes, she could quite see how Lucius Wainwright had seduced so many. He would have been the dark and dangerous man in the room who few women could resist. The more often a girl was warned against him, the more she would be drawn to the villain's company.

He only had to brush against her, speak her name in that deep tone, and Becky the Bold forgot that she'd meant to walk away from him. His voice, like a rich, sticky toffee sauce, dripped over her body.

"I enjoyed our supper last night," he muttered very low, "although it ended prematurely. I hope we'll finish what we began. Soon. Don't make me wait too long to satisfy my sweet tooth. I might turn wild and ravenous."

Fortunately no one was within hearing distance. The Book Club Belles had gathered around the pianoforte to sing a song while Mrs. Makepiece played for them, and Becky deliberately did not see Justina gesturing to her. Singing Yuletide songs was the last thing she felt like doing with her insides all in a pickle. The music began without her.

Whispering again, she told him, "I see you don't bother acting the gentleman around me. I daresay you know it would be a waste of your time, since I already met the real Lucky Luke. You may be yourself around me."

His smile changed from self-contented cat to confused kitten, newly discovering that balls of wool unravel. "Mayhap that's why I like you. There must be some reason why I couldn't stop myself trailing after you."

"Like me? You know nothing about me."

"But I do. You told me all I needed to know as soon as we met, remember? It was a succinct but thorough introduction. Once we're married, we'll get to know each other even better."

"Kindly stop talking of marriage," she hissed. "I will not be used just to secure your inheritance."

He frowned. "*What?*" His voice boomed, making Mrs. Makepiece play a brief jumble of wrong keys. Everyone looked over at them.

Thirteen

BECKY FORCED A SMILE TO REASSURE THEIR AUDIENCE and then she walked around the annoying fellow so that he must turn away from their view. She waited until the music and singing began again before she whispered hurriedly, "The last thing you want is a woman hanging on you. Those were your words yesterday. I'm sure once you have the certificate signed to show the solicitors, marriage will not curb your behavior in any way. I will not be a party to deceit. Or trapped in marriage with a notorious rake, who only wants to get his hands on the family fortune."

"Your friend is right and you read too many novels."

Head high, she would have left him standing there, but Luke moved closer, blocking her view of the others at the pianoforte, causing her to take a step back until she felt the wall at her shoulder. "Who told you about the terms of my father's will?"

"Aha! Didn't think I'd find out?"

He shook his head. "When I encountered you yesterday, I wasn't planning to stay long. I had made up my mind to move on. Our collision changed all that. This has nothing to do with the will."

"I'm supposed to believe you're a reformed fellow? At the age of seven-and-thirty? Suddenly you want to change? I told you, I'm not a naive girl with eyes wide as barn doors and a mind full of fantasy."

Luke studied her for a moment and then said flatly, "You're angry."

Somehow restraining herself from screaming, she sputtered, "I wonder why?"

He sighed and shook his head. "'Tis best not to tackle a woman in conversation when her temper is up. I should know better. I had forgotten that."

"If you really don't know why I might be angry—"

"What have I done to you? Saved you from scandal by announcing our engagement. Yes, I can quite see the cruelty, the villainy!" His eyes were jet black now, staring hard into hers. "Apparently that vast experience of the male gender—a matter of which you boasted to me last night—does not include them ever thinking of your reputation."

She gritted her teeth and hissed softly, "Just for a moment, Colonel, let us bypass your true reason for marrying and look at my reason for *not* doing so."

His brow wrinkled. His lips tightened. He leaned on his cane as if she made his leg hurt worse.

"If I ever marry, Colonel, it will be to a man of my choosing, not one who suddenly decides, after a lifetime of avoiding marriage, that he wants a wife. And then assumes the first convenient woman he sets his sights on will agree." The very idea of being cornered into this made her skin itch, and yet if she dared scratch herself in public, the likes of Mrs. Makepiece would never recover. "I sincerely doubt I will ever need another man in my life, least of all one who thinks he can master me. Even as he lies with every word out of his mouth."

"I did not lie to you."

Again, Becky would have moved around him, but he put up his arm suddenly, pretending to draw her attention to a landscape painting on the wall. Slyly he leaned even closer, his cane effectively trapping her there with him.

"I warned you what I am," he growled. "But you still wanted a kiss from me. You insisted upon it. Now look what you did."

It was true, he had not lied about what he was. Only *who* he was. Perhaps, now she knew the truth, she was angry with herself for succumbing, almost as much as she was with him for not telling her his name. For letting her think he had come there just for her. She should have known better. That must account for some of these wild emotions careening about inside her.

He caught her fingers and held them. "The last thing I ever had in mind to be was a decently married man, Gingersnap. *I* ought to be angry with *you*."

"Oh, be angry with my *cherry basket*"—the words sizzled hotly off her tongue—"as that seems to have caused you all the trouble. Blame that." But she hadn't snatched her hand away. The strength and size of his fingers made her hand feel small-boned, delicate. Ladylike for once.

He gave her a wicked half grin. Swaying, he propped one shoulder to the wall, his pose shockingly casual for a genteel drawing room party. "Very well," he whispered. "Let me be angry with that. Slip away with me into the hall right now and I'll see the naughty thing well chastised. I can help you release some of that pent-up mischief held within it." He caressed her gloved wrist with his fingertips and she knew he felt her rapid pulse.

This was very, very bad. Her nipples were beginning to ache and that heaviness had returned to her body. The heightened awareness that made every nerve ending tingle. His grin made it worse. He must have seen her glance over at the door, as if she actually considered his suggestion. Becky knew she had to get away and quickly before she was lost, enthralled by that wicked grin. Tempted by this sinner, like too many victims before her.

"So much for your attempt at reform," she sputtered. "While I wish you well with your struggle, I suspect respectability will soon prove too great an adjustment for Lucky Luke, even with a vast fortune at stake. Standing in this drawing room for an hour has already made you long to leave it."

"How do you know?"

"Because the first time I met you, in that hot, smoky little tavern, you wore a heavy coat, impervious to the heat. Tonight, however, there is a bead of sweat, Colonel, slowly trickling down your temple." She retrieved her hand from his and pointed at the offending drop. He looked at the white tip of her gloved finger as if he might bite it, and Becky quickly put her hand down. "You have adjusted your neckcloth enough times that it looks as if your dog brawled with it, and your lips are pressed so tightly together with resentment that your nostrils must work extra hard to take in air. Oh…there goes another bead of sweat making its course over the wrinkles of your surly frown."

"All these words are making my head ache. Do you mean to say that you think me incapable of change? I thought you prided yourself, Gingersnap, on getting to the point?"

"Very well. I am convinced the effort of being a gentleman will cause your large, thick head to fall off."

"Smug, aren't you?"

"We can make a wager on it, if you like."

His eyes gleamed, immediately interested. "Gambling? Tsk, tsk. Accepting such a challenge will surely mean I have lost already."

"Are you *afraid*, Lucky Luke?"

His lips twitched. "Me? Never. I'm just like you."

Sighing heavily, she turned away, but he stopped her again with a hasty whisper that brushed the curls at the nape of her neck.

"Double or nothing, Gingersnap."

Slowly she turned, raising her gaze to his face again. "Meaning?"

"Give me time to prove I can mend my ways. If I don't, you can call off the engagement and that way still save face. Blame it all on me. I'm used to it."

She licked her dry lips. "Oh, don't try to make me feel sorry for you." *Any minute now*, she thought, *he'll complain about his leg and clutch his cane tighter.*

It was as if she'd known him forever.

The walls of the drawing room seemed to be closing in, candlelight blurring in the sides of her vision. Suddenly she wanted to get out of there probably as much as he did. The heat of the room, so comforting and much appreciated when she first arrived, now felt stifling. She longed for cool air again and space. To turn her face up to stars in the velvety sky and breathe. "And if you do reform?"

"Well, you just claimed that to be impossible." He blinked his dark lashes, trying to look innocent and harmless. Failing at both. Too late for that act with her.

"Then I will give you until the new year." There was no doubt in her mind that he would fail. How many times did she have to tell him that she knew all about men? Suddenly struck with a curious thought, she added, "You would be content with a marriage to a wife won on a wager?" That only showed how little he valued the institute of marriage.

Those dark eyes glimmered down at her. "Love is an unnecessary complication. We can manage without it. You'll enjoy the company of this sinner in bed, nonetheless." His lips bent in a slight smile.

The man had an answer for everything. And every answer left her unsettled, dizzy. Like one of those pale, dainty women who fainted at every opportunity.

How ironic that she'd longed to feel more feminine and this was the man who did it to her. This crude-tongued charlatan.

Becky turned so quickly to get away that she tripped against a chair leg but righted herself and walked across the room with as much grace as she could manage to join her friends at the pianoforte. Yes, indeed, she could see exactly how so many women had fallen around him, for it was very hard to keep one's footing in his presence.

❧

"I hope your intentions toward Miss Sherringham are genuine," Darius muttered, meeting Luke at the punch bowl a few moments later.

"Of course," he replied gruffly before taking a long swig of punch. "Christ, haven't you any brandy? Anything without fruit in it?"

"Miss Sherringham is a friend of my wife's and a very pleasant young woman. Not your usual conquest, as far as I recall."

"That's the damned point, isn't it? I thought you'd be pleased."

After a pause, Darius said, "You met her in Brighton?"

"Yes."

"She's rather young for you."

Luke groaned and scratched the back of his neck, wishing he could get out of his brother's clothes and cool off. "Perhaps." Usually the climate here was too cold for him, since he was used to more tropical places. But tonight, as she had pointed out, he was definitely overheated. Kept thinking about getting her out in the quiet hall and taking a drink of something that would better quench this almighty thirst.

"I hope you appreciate more than her physical attributes, Lucius."

Bloody hell. Anyone would think his brother was seven years his senior instead of junior. "Nah," he snapped. "I'm only in it for the lovely bubbies, ain't I? You know me too well, Handles. There you go. Scuppered me again."

Darius remained grave, watching him closely. "She

told me this marriage idea was a misunderstanding. Why would she say that?"

"A temporary lover's tiff," he muttered. "I expect I looked at her the wrong way or said something I shouldn't. You know how women are. Never quite on the same blasted orbit."

"You're perspiring on my shirt, Lucius. You haven't come back with some fever? Perhaps you should see Dr. Penny."

"It's just these damnable clothes. I'll have to get some new made for myself, won't I?" Irritated, he looked around for something else to talk about. "Bugger, it's hot in here." He saw her with the other young ladies around the pianoforte, singing. "My future bride can't hold a bloody tune, can she?" He winced just as Rebecca caught his eye. She put her prim nose in the air and sang louder.

Ness had wisely scuttled under the sofa.

Witnessing this exchange and his brother's continual perspiring, Darius muttered, "I know you generally disdain any form of advice—and, indeed, pride yourself on having lived thirty-seven years without it—but perhaps you will allow me to caution you in regard to the young ladies of Hawcombe Prior, since I have some experience of them already."

"Why? What's wrong with 'em?"

Darius sighed. "Their *orbits* have a tendency to make one somewhat…vertiginous."

"I can believe that."

"They are very fond of missions."

"Oh?"

"And they read a great many romantic novels."

Fourteen

"It would be a compact of convenience, and the world would be satisfied. In my eyes it would be no marriage at all... To me it would seem only a commercial exchange, in which each wished to be benefited at the expense of the other."

—Marianne Dashwood, *Sense and Sensibility*

"I'M AFRAID THE COLONEL READS LIKE AN OPEN BOOK, Jussy. He's doing this for the inheritance and I refuse to help him uproot you—my dearest friend—and your beloved Wainwright from your home. I would rather end my days an old maid. Which, as Papa pointed out to me yesterday evening, is more than likely my fate."

The two friends stood together, looking at the window display of Hawcombe Prior's one and only shop. It was an emporium that began life as a haberdasher and tea shop in what was really little more than Mr. Porter's front rooms but had since adapted into a treasure chest in which one could find all manner of sundry items without traveling the distance to Manderson.

Justina was purchasing last-minute gifts that day,

and Becky had joined her in hope of finding some new trim to brighten up her best white muslin.

After all, she mused, the Clarendons were coming. One ought to make an effort.

"But the colonel claims he meant to save you from scandal when Mrs. Kenton saw you kissing," said Justina, frowning into the window.

"He *claims* that to be his sole reason, but I know differently."

"He certainly looks at you as if he has many more reasons," Justina replied wryly.

Becky dismissed that with a sniff. She didn't need it pointed out to her that the man had a habit of using his eyes as if they were fingers to unfasten hooks and buttons. He must have looked at many other women the same way. "Hmm. I wonder if Mr. Porter has any nice, thick, serviceable shawls. Big ones."

She saw her friend's frown reflected in the window. "And Sarah says that when you met him, you didn't know his name?"

"Let's just say we were not formally introduced."

"Becky, you are being very mysterious, which isn't like you at all."

She groaned, her breath misting the window pane. "We met briefly in Brighton and then again two nights ago. I...I kissed him because he tricked me into it. Unfortunately, Mrs. Kenton saw us. He decided I'd do for a wife, since he needed one to claim his inheritance, and Mrs. Kenton's wretched spying gave him the excuse he needed to try and force me into it. That is all. The entire tangled mess in a nutshell."

Since she'd lain awake again for the second night in

a row, troubled by thoughts of that unworthy fellow, Becky's eyes were heavy from lack of sleep, staring through the glass without seeing a single item on the other side of it.

She added hastily, "Really, Jussy, you could not seriously have imagined the colonel and me together? It would be a most unsuitable match. Quite impossible." She yawned, belatedly covering her mouth with one hand. "Not to be rude, since he is your brother-in-law, but he is dreadfully old and almost as boring as Mr. Kenton. Not to mention just as full of himself, terribly ill-mannered, and with a curiously eccentric sense of humor. I think he might be injured in the brain, as I saw him stand a full five minutes staring into his empty cup last night, and he couldn't remember anyone's name after they were introduced. Poor thing. He probably ought to be heavily sedated and wheeled about in a Bath chair for his own safety."

"I am always confused when a sentence is begun by someone asking me not to feel offended when the words that follow will almost certainly cause that very effect."

"I'm sorry, Jussy," Becky replied briskly, "but I see no reason to sweeten the medicine with sugar water. It only dilutes the strength of the tonic and postpones the cure."

"Well, I admit I *was* a little surprised that you had kept the engagement from me, and I always thought that Charles Clarendon had a better chance of meeting your requirements, but I wanted to believe it when Luke told us that you'd accepted his proposal." Jussy sighed heavily. "How perfect it would be for us to become sisters-in-law!"

Becky chuckled. "I'm sorry, Jussy. As dearly as I love you, I can't marry a man like that."

"But he vows to be a changed man. I suppose the proof of that will be in the pudding, as Mrs. Kenton says."

At mention of that woman's name, Becky groaned, pushing open the shop door and waving her friend on ahead. "She does have plenty to say on the subject of the colonel, to be sure."

"None of it her business. Oh, I do hope he settles down at last, even if it is not with you. It would please my Wainwright to see his brother married."

"But if the colonel marries, he can lay claim to everything that now belongs to your husband and your future children!" On her friend's behalf, Becky was appalled by this terrible injustice.

Justina, however, barely acknowledged the fact that the colonel's return was inconvenient. She had taken him under her wing as another of her missions. "It really doesn't matter to us. My Wainwright is capable of earning his own money and we shall be happy wherever we go. We could live in Dockley's barn and be content. When you fall in love, you will understand."

That sounded altogether too rosy for Becky. When people made statements along the lines of "All we need is each other," it usually meant they weren't practical thinkers or had never known hard times. "If you ask me," she muttered, sullen, "it's very thoughtless of Lucky Luke to come back. He should have stayed away another dozen years and left you both alone."

"You seem to have taken against my poor brother-in-law rather virulently, Rebecca Sherringham! Was his kiss so very bad?"

Becky turned away quickly. "Oh, look, what do you think of this patterned muslin? Goodness, it's expensive."

"Don't change the subject!"

Becky shook her head. "If the prodigal brother's return doesn't matter to you and your blessed Wainwright, then I suppose it can't matter to me either...but don't think you're going to matchmake for the colonel and me. At his age, he would do better to court Diana's mother if he truly needs a wife and isn't very particular."

Although Becky hadn't meant it seriously, rather than laugh, her friend immediately pounced upon the idea. "Now, there is a very good thought indeed. Mrs. Makepiece *was* unusually civil to him last night." Justina inspected a card of lace. "And we must not forget that Diana's mother has scandal in her past too. She once went against her family's wishes to elope with a young man of whom they did not approve. Therefore she has a little streak of rebellion beneath her starched petticoats. Somewhere."

"Surely, at her age, all that is long gone."

"She is only forty. Too wise and stern to tolerate a *young* man, perhaps, but certainly not old enough to resign herself to a lonely bed. When Diana is married, what will she have left to do with herself then? The colonel would give her companionship in old age."

Becky swiped the lace out of her friend's hand to examine it herself. "It is good of you to be so concerned for that prim fusspot's future happiness."

"It would not *all* be for her benefit, of course." Justina admitted with a grin. "Although you would never say it out loud, I know you feel as I do, that Diana should not be allowed to throw herself away on the awful Shaw."

"William Shaw is a very steady, responsible, reliable man and a prudent choice for—"

"Diana is in love with your brother, despite her mama's attempts to prevent it, and when Nathaniel returns, we cannot let her be married to another. It would be a tragedy of immense proportions. Therefore, her dear mama ought to be given some other occupation to take her mind off this course upon which she is set."

Becky marched purposefully around the table of trimmings, restlessly picking up and discarding various items as she went. Justina followed closely, still speculating out loud.

"Why not the colonel? He is almost her age—only three years younger—and he too has a daughter. They have much in common, unlikely as it might seem at first glance. Really it is very clever of you to suggest it."

It is true, Becky thought morosely; he was almost forty. *Forty*. And father to a girl only six years younger than herself. Becky's mind circled those facts until she felt dizzy, bewildered, and annoyed. At least those were the feelings she could name.

Justina continued, "I heard Mrs. Makepeace say she thought his looks darkly appealing. And she even laughed at something he said."

Becky almost pulled a ribbon entirely off its reel, causing Mr. Porter to glare at her from the other side of the shop. She moved along the counter to scowl at some buttons. "I very much doubt he'll do for Mrs. Makepiece. He barely kept his masquerade up for a few hours last night. Once that slips, she'll see he's much too uncivilized to suit her." She could not picture Diana's mother letting him kiss her the way he had kissed Becky. Did not want to picture it.

Why was the idea so horrid? She struggled over the question but could find no answer.

"My mind is made up on the matter," said her friend. "I shall have the colonel married and settled before my sister's wedding in the spring! You'll see, Madam Doubtful!"

Becky knew from past experience that trying to talk Justina out of anything would only make her more determined. Let the mission fail of its own accord, as it surely would.

Eventually, to her relief, Justina moved on to other matters. "Since you've lost Mrs. Jarvis again, you and the major should come to Christmas dinner at the manor this year. I've invited my parents to dine with us too. Monsieur Philippe is cooking an enormous goose and we'll have plum pudding with brandy butter!"

How could she refuse such a gracious invitation? Since Darius Wainwright's fancy London chef had arrived at Midwitch Manor, dinner there was very much the prized invitation to be had. Her father would sulk if she turned it down.

"If you can tolerate the dreary company of Colonel Wainwright," Justina added, turning to assess her reflection in a mirror while holding scarlet plumes to her bonnet. "He will be there too, of course."

Well, that was unfortunate, but why should Lucky Luke Wainwright's menacing intentions keep her from enjoying the festivities of the season and her good friend's company?

"I would have invited Diana and her mama too," Justina added, "but they have those dreadful Oxfordshire snob cousins coming to visit, along with the beastly Shaw. As for Lucy, her father insists she stay at home to help her mama with all her little brothers." She paused. "It is quite rude of the Clarendons to descend upon Diana's mother with such little notice, do you not agree?"

"I think she enjoys the attention."

"But Mrs. Makepiece barely has the room, as you know, and certainly not the housekeeping budget to feed all those extra mouths." She shook her head. "If you ask me, it's very strange that they are coming, traveling about in winter, to see two ladies whose comfort they never consider the rest of the year. Does their father not wish for them to stay with him for Christmas? It is very odd."

Becky studied some mother-of-pearl buttons. "It will give Diana's mother something to boast about all season, in any case."

Quite casually, Justina said, "I suppose you are looking forward to seeing Charles Clarendon again."

"Not particularly. Why?"

"Perhaps because he fits your 'Attributes Required in a Husband' so very well?" Then, as if the idea had just come to her, Justina spun around and cried, "Poor Colonel Wainwright! That is why you will not even consider him now. Because you wait for Charles to declare himself."

Becky tossed the buttons aside and folded her arms, too annoyed now to look at frivolous trimmings. Why was she bothering anyway when she never got anything right about her dress? "Diana told me the Clarendons are staying at Lark Hollow with Admiral Vyne," she muttered. "So they will only visit for a short time. I may not even see Mr. Clarendon while they are here."

Justina huffed. "Oh, he will make sure he's seen. That young man always wants everybody's attention. I've never known such a peacock. He struts about and shows off his fine-feathered tail. As for the sister, she's as interesting as a wet cabbage leaf, and the elder brother slept through church service the last time they came. Despite their grand pedigree, they are certainly an ill-mannered bunch."

Her friend, it seemed, was ready to forgive the formerly deceased Colonel Wainwright for descending upon *her* without notice, yet she looked upon the Clarendons' Yuletide visit to Mrs. Makepiece with less accepting eyes.

Becky would have pointed this inequity out if not for the sudden tinkling of the shop's doorbell, followed by a loud voice. "Looking for cloth for your wedding clothes, eh, Miss Sherringham?"

It was too late to duck away and hide. Mrs. Kenton was in "full boom"—a status they'd secretly assigned to her worst, most annoying moods, after she was heard referring to her husband's rose garden in the same terms. Whether she knew she'd missed out an *l* or whether she thought this was the correct phrase, no one knew, and no one bothered to correct her.

"Not closeted away at your secret society today then, I see?" she bellowed.

The only reason Mrs. Kenton had not joined the Book Club Belles when she first settled there was because she claimed to have no time to read novels—a circumstance for which they were all grateful, and so they did everything in their power to keep her too busy. But as a consequence of not being a member, the meddlesome lady always referred to the book club as if it was some sort of screen for a wicked coven.

She looked at Becky. "I hear that you are without a cook for Christmas. You and the major must come to us." It was never an invitation with Mrs. Kenton; it was always a command.

"Oh, dear! Such a shame, but I must decline. Mrs. Wainwright has invited us to dine at the manor on Christmas Day." Just in the nick of time!

"But I have already decided upon the seating arrangements at the parsonage. With all this business about the colonel, I knew you would be in need of some sound advice, which I, as a close personal friend of his stepsister, am at liberty to give you. And which, no doubt, the colonel's brother would not, since he is tighter with his information than an oyster shell with its pearl."

"I fear I take too much of your advice as it is, madam. I wouldn't want to impose."

"Fret not, Miss Sherringham. Now I am a resident of Hawcombe Prior, I will take my place here and my responsibilities as parson's wife most seriously. You will never find me holding back with guidance and assistance wherever it is needed."

"Well, that's a relief."

"I know that you in particular, about to be a bride, are in want of guidance. Without a mother to lend a hand or a word of wisdom, it must have been very hard all these years. Your father, dear man, was left quite alone to raise you. As I said to Mrs. Penny last evening, 'tis no surprise you can be a little masculine in your deportment and terse in your manner, for you have been surrounded by men all your life. That sharp tongue has a tendency to make you seem discourteous, which I'm sure you do not mean to be."

Before Becky could utter any response, Justina grabbed her arm, exclaimed at how they were late for nothing in particular, and then dragged her friend out of the shop. From the number of people who left her presence in haste, one would think the curate's wife had some inkling of the offense she caused, but apparently she was immune.

"I wish you would let me give her a piece of my mind," Becky muttered as they tripped out into the street. "If someone ever did that, just once, she might not be such an insufferable woman. She cannot be five years older than me, yet for some reason she takes it upon herself to be *motherly*."

"It is Christmas," Justina reminded her in a singsong tone. "Good will to all men. Even to Augusta Kenton."

Becky eyed her dubiously. "You did not think that way last night at the party. I rather imagined you were ready to throttle her."

"The anger passed when I realized she cannot help herself. We are none of us perfect and ought to be forgiving of faults if we too wish to be forgiven."

Fifteen

LUKE LEFT HIS BED EARLY THAT DAY AND IMMEDIATELY got to work on Sir Mortimer's sty. With Ness overseeing the project, he had soon reinforced the fence and built a small, sturdy step from which Sarah could fill the trough without needing to balance precariously on a pile of stones. He had further plans for the refurbishment of Sir Mortimer's sty, but that would do for the present.

His brother had acquired some fine horses for the Midwitch stables, and Luke was admiring them when he heard Sarah calling his name as she came around the gravel drive to seek him out.

Ness instantly took himself into an empty stall and burrowed in the straw, still not yet recovered from the indignity of that large taffeta bow. Luke, unfortunately, was too large to hide.

Framed by crisp morning light, she appeared in the stable doorway. "Good morning, Colonel. Uncle Darius said you wouldn't be up before noon!"

"I'm used to rising early these days. And so are you, it seems." He'd hoped to get away for a few hours

"I think marriage and impending motherhood has made you soft, Mrs. Wainwright." *And overly romantic,* Becky thought.

"Perhaps."

"Have you forgotten how Augusta Milford—as she was then—first came here to set her cap at your Wainwright and was quite determined to get him, along with the assistance of her most particular friend, Viscountess Waltham?"

"That was before she knew he had fallen in love with me. Before even *he* knew it. But eventually she decided lonely Mr. Kenton needed her instead and she made herself extremely useful to him. So you see, everything worked out in the end. For everybody. Don't set your face in that unbecoming frown, Becky. I am inclined not to let anyone annoy me these days. I am too happy and content myself, I suppose. Oh dear, did that sound conceited?"

"A little, but mostly just addled."

"One day you will fall in love and be too happy to let the little things annoy you too."

Becky quirked an eyebrow. "This romantic nonsense again? You are relentless, Mrs. Wainwright."

"You *will* fall in love," her friend repeated firmly and with a gleeful twinkle in her eye. "Then, since you have been so adamantly against the idea, I daresay you will be twice as much in love as anyone ever was. Your passion will entirely run away with you. Blind to all else, you will embrace Mrs. Kenton right here in this street, because you have finally fallen in love and can be happy."

"Or I might be struck about the head with an iron

horseshoe to achieve the same cloudiness of memory and loss of reason." Becky thought that was the more likely scenario.

At that moment, they spied Diana hurrying across the street to join them, so they waited for her.

"Have you seen my mama?" she exclaimed. When they informed her that they had not, she looked away down the street and moaned softly. "I believe she has gone off to Farmer Rooke's to get a ham, for she will not pay a boy to do it. I told her I would go as she cannot carry it all by herself, but she stubbornly refused to let me. She thinks it common and unladylike for me to be seen carrying a ham—and bad for my posture."

Becky was amused, as ever, by Mrs. Makepiece's impoverished version of snobbery. "You could always dress the ham up and carry it like a baby in a basket. Then no one would know."

Diana refused to laugh although the other two did. Instead she retaliated with her own thrust. "Well, you have certainly caused quite a stir with your colonel, Rebecca!"

That stopped Becky's laughter mid-gust. "He is not *my* colonel."

"He insists that you are engaged to him and you say you are not. What are we to make of it?"

"Make of it what you will," Becky replied grandly. "But I can promise you there will be no wedding. Not for him and me." Catching a sly glance exchanged between her friends, she sputtered, "He is as old as your mama, Diana, and I know he suffers the stiff joints familiar to the elderly. I would not be surprised if he wears flannel waistcoats and has one or two wooden teeth."

"What is wrong with flannel? Will[ ] wears flannel."

"Precisely!"

"But why would the colonel make up suc[ ] about being engaged?"

"It was merely a mistake and nothing mor[ ] replied swiftly. "And I will thank you both ne[ ] mention it again."

But Diana and Justina could not stem their laug[ ]

"Tease all you like! Some friends you are."

"Oh Becky, your face yesterday when you saw [ ] at the party! If this *mistake* happened to one of us, y[ ] would be just as amused as we were."

She was forced to admit the truth of this commen[ ] But only to herself.

The idea of practical, determined spinster Becky[ ] marrying the notorious rogue Colonel "Lucky Luke"[ ] Wainwright—a man who did not possess a single item[ ] on her list of Attributes Required—was probably the biggest joke in the village. Let them have their fun; she would keep her dignity and rise above it.

and go riding. Midwitch Manor apparently contained a good-sized park and several acres of woodland that he was keen to explore. After last night's over-heated party and that confining, borrowed shirt, he was eager to let the fresh air brush fingers through his hair again.

"I just took Sir Mortimer Grubbins his breakfast and I saw what you have done," she said.

"I hope it meets with your approval. And his."

She smiled. "We are most impressed. He has the finest sty in the village."

"Good. Well, you had better run inside for your own breakfast, Sarah, 'Tis cold out here."

"But I wanted to remind you about Dr. Penny. You will go and see him for your leg, won't you? Yesterday you promised."

She was persistent as a gnat bite.

"Of course, I shall." He hadn't planned on riding to see the village doctor, but now there was Sarah, looking expectantly up at him. "I shall go directly."

"I'll have one of the grooms prepare the gig. I don't suppose you can ride in a saddle—not with your leg."

She had no idea, of course, that for the past five years he'd earned his living in the saddle, herding cattle and breaking horses in Argentina and Brazil. He was better on horseback than on his own feet, but before he could explain this, she was organizing the gig for his jaunt down to the village.

"You can't get lost," she assured him.

Well, he'd see about that, he mused. He'd quite like to get lost for a few hours and mull over the stubborn temper of a certain troublesome, argumentative redhead.

"The village is really only three lanes," she added, "and Dr. Penny's house is the first on the left as you pass the chestnut trees along Mill Lane. They have an arched gate with the name carved into it, so you cannot miss it."

To Luke's relief, she did not offer to come with him. She had other tasks in mind.

"Shall I organize your garments for the laundry and mending while you are out, Colonel?"

Eager to get off on his ride, he made a hasty murmur of assent, barely giving it any thought. As soon as the gig was ready, Luke struggled into it, set his cane on the floor by his feet, and took the reins.

"Don't go too fast, Colonel," she warned. "The lanes are uneven."

"I shall be the very soul of caution, Sarah."

The springs lurched with an ominous creak and then they were off at a steady trot.

He felt her gaze following him around the carriage drive, but as soon as he had turned the corner and was out of her view, Luke urged the horse faster, enjoying the rapid bump of the small equipage and that glorious sense of flying along with the wind.

In fact, he delighted in the speed so much that as the vessel flew downhill, he almost didn't see the figure crossing the lane up ahead, struggling under the weight of a large ham.

❧

The three friends were still in the High Street when the Wainwrights' gig trotted toward them bearing the colonel and a fraught Mrs. Makepiece squeezed into the small seat beside him, her arms cradling an enormous ham wrapped in cheesecloth.

Justina forgot what she was saying and nudged Becky yet again in the ribs. She whispered, "Look, our lovebirds! In no time at all, I shall achieve my mission, for it has already begun without me."

The roan mare slowed as it drew level with the three young ladies, and the colonel shouted a greeting. He was hatless, Becky noted.

Hatless. Outdoors. In the presence of ladies. And on a winter's day.

"Does the man have no sense of propriety?" she muttered haughtily.

Justina looked askance at this comment but said nothing. Diana, who was more likely the one to make such a remark, had probably not heard. She was too busy trying to compose herself at the sight of her usually dignified mama in considerable disarray and in the company of the wayward, harem-keeping colonel.

He had scarcely halted the vehicle before Mrs. Makepiece was already half out, not waiting for his assistance and plainly anxious not to be seen by too many curious folk. She was ashen, sprigs of hair sticking out from her bonnet rim, hands shakily clutching her heavy, bulky burden.

"I'm afraid there was almost an accident," Colonel Wainwright shouted cheerily. "I very nearly ran this lady over in the lane. Still, no harm done."

No harm done? Mrs. Makepiece looked not only as if she'd seen a ghost but that it had whistled up her petticoats too.

"The colonel insisted he give me a ride to the

village," the woman explained hurriedly, a loosened lock of her usually rigidly bound hair falling across her brow, "although I assured him I was quite all right, just a little shaken." Her words rushed out on an exhale. "I couldn't see where I was going, you see. I tripped."

Becky knew how the woman felt. He clearly had that effect on every female he met.

"You shouldn't be carrying that great heavy ham, madam!" the colonel exclaimed. "You should have got someone else to fetch it for you."

Mrs. Rosalind Makepiece laughed uneasily. "Oh, it is nothing, sir. Goodness, I am stronger than I look." She hugged that ham like a battle shield when her concerned daughter tried to relieve her of it. "But thank you, Colonel. It was very good of you to assist me."

Becky could hardly believe her eyes and ears. The woman was a giddy mess, apparently charmed by the notorious Lucius Wainwright. No one was safe from the danger. Had it been Nathaniel who almost mowed her down in the lane, he would never be forgiven. Diana's mother would have insisted he did it deliberately.

The bell on the shop door behind them tinkled again as it swung open and Mrs. Kenton emerged in such haste that she almost fell to her knees on the path. "Good morning, Colonel Wainwright, Mrs. Makepiece. I thought that was you. Gracious, that is a very large ham, madam! Surely too much just for you and this"—she patted Diana's hand—"terribly thin girl of yours."

"We expect guests, Mrs. Kenton."

"Guests?" The parson's wife sounded annoyed, as if her permission should have been sought.

"My cousins, the Clarendons, from Oxford, and my daughter's fiancé, William Shaw, from Manderson."

Becky glanced up into the gig and found the colonel's gaze pinned to her. He appeared to have forgotten the presence of the other ladies, so intense was his survey of her person, but when he heard the name of Mrs. Makepiece's guests, an odd look came over his countenance, a tightening of all his features until they looked very grim and pained. He scratched his chin with gloveless fingers, looking away down the high street, apparently lost in thought.

Gloveless. Hatless. So lacking in all the manners expected of a gentleman, she mused. He would never carry this transformation off and win his wager.

"Well, thank you again, Colonel," Diana's mother managed, still short of breath as she backed toward the shop door.

"Are you sure I can't take you the rest of the way to your house?"

"No, no. I have some last-minute items to purchase here."

Mrs. Kenton followed the woman and her daughter—and her ham—back into the shop, needling her for information about her expected guests and probably giving more unwanted advice about how to lay her table. The two other young women were left on the path beside the gig.

"Would you pretty pigeons be in need of a ride?"

"There is not room for both of us," Justina responded instantly, "and I still have a few errands before I go back to the manor."

Becky stepped aside. "I can walk home. It's only across the common."

"I'm going that way. 'Tis no trouble to take you."

Suddenly Justina gave her a shove toward the gig and whispered in her ear, "Now is your chance to heartily recommend Mrs. M. Don't let me down."

The colonel reached for her arm and before she knew what was happening, Becky was hoisted up like a netted pike and crammed into the small seat beside him.

&

She clutched his coat sleeve. "Slow down!" she cried, her face pale, her gaze fastened on the curve ahead.

"What's the matter? I thought you were fearless."

"I'd like to get home in one piece, Colonel. Must you draw attention to us by racing this way?"

"Good lord, woman, enjoy yourself. Take off your bonnet. Feel the wind in your hair."

"Why would I do that?" She looked at him as if he'd suggested she remove more than her hat.

Luke finally slowed the horse, but not for the sake of caution—only for the sake of keeping her company a while longer. "I thought you'd prefer the speed. You seemed the reckless sort when I first met you."

"I can't imagine what gave you that impression."

"Can you not?" he muttered dryly. "When you confronted me in that crowded tavern and pointed a pistol at my chest, I took you for a daring, brave lass. Reckless, spirited. A woman who preferred a gallop to a gentle trot."

"Well, you were wrong. I am never reckless. I am the most sensible of people."

He cleared his throat. "Keep telling yourself that, Rebecca. You don't fool me any more than I can fool you."

Luke felt her stern gaze studying the side of his face, but he stared ahead as they rounded the next bend at a more civilized trot.

"What happened to *your* hat today?" she asked. "Isn't your head cold?"

"Sarah burned it. She said nothing could be done with it. Fortunately, she has not yet given up on the rest of me." Suddenly he realized he'd just given the girl permission to go through his things. Hopefully he'd have some garments left intact when he returned.

The woman beside him exhaled a sigh that misted in the cold air. "Poor Sarah. I'm sure you were a great shock to her." Although they moved at a slower pace now, her hand remained on his sleeve, a small, light weight, gripping the material of his old coat.

Luke felt an odd sensation in his chest. It wasn't unpleasant at all, just different. He stole a quick sideways glance at her and realized how nice it was to see her again today. Not only that, but he'd woken early that day, motivated by the thought that she was only a short distance away and he would surely see her again soon. Funny, that. He'd never looked forward so eagerly before to seeing a particular woman, never felt his pulse quicken in anticipation of being in her company.

He cleared his throat. "Sarah is very eager to help my transformation. See, I have someone on my side. Someone wants me to succeed."

"She certainly has her work cut out for her."

"Wants to help me get a wife, doesn't she? Has her heart set on you for a stepmother. For some reason."

She made a small sound of anguish and turned her head away, hiding her face behind the edge of her bonnet.

Luke persevered. "You know, a mature man of experience, like me, has more to offer a woman like yourself than one of those fumbling pretty boys. I can give you a damn good—"

"Yes, thank you, Colonel. Should I require servicing like a brood mare, I'll let you know."

He glanced at the quivering rim of her bonnet and added slyly, "I was going to say *supper*. I can make you an excellent chicken stew, can't I? You'll never go hungry with me, Gingersnap."

She shook her head and muttered something indecipherable.

Apparently she hadn't noticed that they were passing her father's house and heading for the old stone bridge over the stream. Luke urged the horse to pick up its pace again before she might realize. "I don't know why you keep squeaking and whining about the idea of marrying me, woman."

"*Squeaking* and *whining*?"

"Worse than a privy door in a gale," he exclaimed gruffly, trying not to laugh. "If you're so sensible as you like to think, you'd leap at the chance to marry me."

"And how, in God's name, do you reach that conclusion?"

"At the age of two-and-twenty, a rational wench with so few prospects should be considering a comfortable home and the practical advantages of marriage to ol' Lucky Luke. I hope you're not waiting for some grand love. I suppose that's it, eh? All that chatter about not being a naive girl and having no expectations of romance…all that was a lie. My brother warned me about the Book Club Belles."

She turned to look at him again, holding the back of her bonnet with one hand. Her eyes gleamed brightly with sparks. "I. Have. No. Romantic. Expectations."

"There you go again. See what I mean? Squeaking and whining like a rusty hinge."

She groaned. He switched the reins to one hand so he could pat her knee. "Don't you worry, Gingersnap, Lucky Luke is here to rescue you."

Only now did she realize they were on the turnpike road and moving at a smarter pace, away from the village and uphill. She must have had a lot on her mind to not notice their direction until that moment, he mused.

"Colonel Wainwright, kindly turn this horse around."

"Why? What have you got to dash home to that's more in need than me? Like you said to your cook, I'm a wounded old soldier and the least you could do is keep me company a while." The wheels rattled along, the small equipage shaking as he gave the horse its head. "You can show me the sights," he yelled above the noise of merry, clattering hooves. "I see there's another hill up ahead, and from there you can tell me all about your neighbors. Fill me in on the important facts I should know. Aren't you proud of your village?"

She glared at him. "You are truly ready to settle down here in sleepy Hawcombe Prior?"

"Why not?"

"You will be bored and restless in a matter of days."

"Bored of you? Don't hold yourself in very high regard, do you?"

"In many respects, Colonel, you are just like my idiotic brother. He too escaped marriage for years and then finally asked the one woman too clever for him. Well, *Lucky*, you too have chosen to pursue the wrong woman, because you will not wear me down or charm me. I have scant patience for fools."

"Me neither. Best hold on even tighter, Romantic Rebecca. We're going over a bump."

He was very much enjoying her warm curves crammed in beside him in that little seat, her hand on his arm. But now, of course, she let go of his sleeve, because he brought it to her attention. Luke sped up again and she clung to the edge of the seat instead of to him, staring ahead with a face like a thundercloud.

"What's that place backing onto the river?" He pointed to a small farmhouse with a snow-capped thatched roof and two dormer windows peeping out. He'd noticed it the night he arrived because it was the one place with no smoke blowing from its chimney or candles lit on that cold evening.

"That's Willow Tree Farm. One of my father's tenants died there recently and it stands empty."

"Looks a good place."

"Although it's pretty on the outside, it needs a great deal of work on the inside. Not many would want to take that on."

Luke wondered why the major did not pay for those repairs himself since he was the landlord, but fearing that would give her something else about which to be angry and insulted, he changed the subject. He slowed the horse again to a gentle trot. "Tell me how your father came to settle here. He said something about the village holding fond memories for him of your mother?"

Reluctantly, her lips snapped open to reply, "My mother was born on a dairy farm near here at Hawcombe Mallow, a hamlet on the other side of that hill. My father met her when he was encamped at Manderson. After they married, she never came back here, although he says she often talked of visiting one day." Then, as if she thought she'd told him too much or sounded too wistful, she added peevishly, "I don't remember, of course. I was only a very little girl when she died."

"I'm sorry." He thought of his own mother's death and how that sorrow had darkened his childhood. Sometimes he wondered if his life might have turned out differently had his mother lived longer to keep him in line. When she died, his father and brother had hidden their sadness away, and since Luke had no one else with whom to share his tears, he'd let his anguish and grief out in other ways.

"I suppose he felt closer to her again by bringing us here, to where they met." She wiped a hand quickly across her cheek. "I'm glad he brought us here. It's very quiet and mostly peaceful. A welcome change of pace after so many years of traveling."

Evidently she needs someone to look after her, he thought. The young lass had been doing all the looking after ever since her mama died, as far as he could see. But the sudden glitter of potential tears was gone already, that glimpse of vulnerability swiftly masked again.

Luke struggled for something else to say. He'd never bothered to converse at length with a woman, but this was all part of his reform. So he tried not to think too much about the soft parts of her that were made for man's enjoyment, and he concentrated instead on the vexing components inside her head. It was a challenge to keep his thoughts steady, to be sure, especially with her body in such close proximity.

"You're not the only one with reservations about this marriage you know," he muttered, teasing to see if he could get a smile from her sulky lips. He'd know where he was then; if he could make her laugh, he'd be on solid ground. "You should try being sweeter to me or I'll go off the idea."

She turned her head again, one hand still holding her bonnet, her eyes wide, cheeks pink. "Please *do* go off it!" There was a pause and then she added, "You ought to consider someone like Mrs. Makepiece instead." The words had rushed out of her fiercely.

"Makepiece? The woman with the ham?"

He went over another bump and she grabbed his arm again. "She'd suit you better than I would."

He squinted, pretending to consider it. "She's on the thin side. I like my wenches with a bit more flesh on 'em. Something round and soft and warm to welcome a man home of an evening." He grinned slyly. "Don't want to be ruttin' with a wench who might snap in two, do I?"

She shook her head, sighing in disgust.

"I still don't know what you have to be cross about, woman. I'm doing you a favor with this marriage."

"Of all the rotten cheek! You will let me out of this gig at once! I told you I'm not interested in being part of your act. I will not be responsible for uprooting my dear friends from their home so you can claim your inheritance. And my father and brother need me."

"Listen, missy, I may be an old man in your eyes, but I'll be a rich old man when I get what's coming to me." He laughed and quickened their speed again. "Perhaps that's what you thought about when you trapped me in your kitchen just as that nosy warbler happened by. Hmm? Very convenient, eh?"

"Why would I... I didn't even know who you were, you dreadful man!"

"Don't get yourself all puffed up and irate. Calm your titties, I told you I'll marry you. We'll make the best of it. Somehow."

Sixteen

As they raced along the road, she tried wresting the reins from his hands, to take control of the horse, yelling at him that he would kill them both with his reckless driving.

"Enjoy yourself for once, woman," he shouted, tugging the reins away from her and laughing. "Don't you ever have fun?"

"Fun?" she cried. "I have had it several times but found that the jollities invariably conclude with someone's eye being poked out or a terrible case of indigestion."

He made a disapproving clicking sound with his tongue. "You're a young woman, for pity's sake! You should be enjoying yourself, not fussing over your father and brother as if they're your children!"

"I do no such thing!"

They were racing along now, struggling over control of the reins.

"You're hiding from life, missy. Hiding behind your father and brother. Hiding from your true self and your own passions."

"If you don't stop this horse at once, I'll—"

"Trust me, for pity's sake! I know how to drive a horse and gig. I've raced many times. Do you think I'd put you in danger?"

But she wasn't listening. She was still stuck on something else he'd said. "Hiding, indeed! At least I don't run away from my troubles! I don't run away for a dozen years when life gets challenging!"

Her words did not quite sink in all at once, for Luke was partially distracted by a lock of hair caught across her lips and the warmth of her gloved hands on his bare knuckles.

Fortunately, he heard a warning rumble and retrieved the presence of mind to swerve rapidly. The larger vessel coming around a bend at reckless speed made no move to avoid them, but Luke smartly veered to the verge.

The small gig bumped hard over the verge. Disaster was narrowly averted, but the right wheel groaned and buckled, leaving them tilted at a treacherous angle over the ditch.

"Now look what you've done!" Rebecca cried, her bonnet dislodged, her body half hanging out of the seat. Even as she shouted, a wheel strut snapped, dropping her side of the gig another few inches.

Luke jumped down and then stopped to recall his injury. Feeling her furious gaze fastened upon him, he grabbed his cane and limped around the back of the damaged gig to help her out. "If you hadn't been fighting me, we wouldn't have ended up like this. Let that be a lesson to you."

With her bonnet, she was still swiping at his shoulders and hands—and anything she could reach—resisting his attempts to help her down, when the larger vehicle stopped just a short way on and one of the passengers looked out to observe the scene of the broken gig and the yelling woman.

"Is that Miss Sherringham's voice I hear? Miss Rebecca Sherringham?"

She finally stopped beating him with her hat and looked over at the very smart black coach.

Luke also looked.

A young man in shiny boots stepped down and trotted over, grinning. "I thought I recognized that pretty hair. Miss Sherringham, how lovely it is to see you again."

Back at the carriage, a woman peered out. "Who is that, Charles?"

Meanwhile, Rebecca's demeanor changed at once. She stopped cursing at Luke. This time, when he raised his arms again to help her down, she did not resist. But he might as well be a stable lad helping the lady of the house down after her afternoon jaunt. She stepped on his foot and didn't even apologize.

"Mr. Clarendon, isn't it?" She smiled, turning to face the other man, wiping that stray lock of hair from her cheek and giving the new arrival a curtsy. Luke's hands and presence were dismissed from her person in the same moment.

"Miss Sherringham," the young man exclaimed again, removing his hat and bowing smartly. "What good fortune!"

"Good fortune?" Luke snapped. "Aye...that we weren't bloody killed."

"Really, Colonel," she interjected coolly over her

shoulder, "your language! We were as much to blame, I'm sure."

His language? She dared say that after the barrage of insults she'd just rained upon him?

Luke's good foot throbbed where she'd trodden on it. In fact, there was more feeling in his entire body now than there had been in years, and this time it was not a pleasant sensation. He scowled at the other man. At first he'd been slow to recognize that well-chiseled face, but hearing the name was like another jolt in the bouncy gig.

The lad might only have been ten or so when Luke last saw him and he would never remember Luke, but that deceptively angelic face was unmistakably Clarendon. He must now be close in age to Miss Sherringham, Luke realized dourly. She would have been about ten too back then. Thus, he was reminded again of her dreadful, unsuitable youthfulness.

"We are on our way to visit our cousin," the boy chirped, not in the least put out by Luke's remark and focusing on Rebecca. "Since your vehicle is damaged, you must allow us to take you home."

"Oh…" She glanced at the snapped struts of the wheel beside them. "Well, I…" Now her gaze lifted and caught Luke's. "Mr. Clarendon, may I introduce Colonel Wainwright."

"Good morning, Colonel. We can take both of you, of course. I'm sure we can find room." The young man had a merry, never-fading grin that made Luke's jaw hurt and his foot throb even harder.

"That's very kind of you," she replied.

"You can tie the horse to the back of our carriage and we'll—"

"No," Luke interrupted, terse. "I'll fix this."

Rebecca swung fully around to glare at him. "Don't be foolish. Look at those clouds. It's going to rain."

Foolish? He wrenched open his lips just enough to tell her, "You go on with him then. I'll manage. Alone." He didn't need anybody, did he? He was perfectly happy alone on his castaway's island until she and her pert bubbies drifted by. How dare she accuse him of running off and hiding for a dozen years? Ah, yes, now the words she'd shouted at him a few moments ago finally sank fully in. Challenges? What could she know of life's challenges? She was two and bloody twenty, a wench raised by an indulgent, distracted father.

"You'll get wet, Colonel. How will you manage to get back to the manor? You can't..." He caught her anxious glance directed at his walking cane. "You must accept Mr. Clarendon's offer."

"You go on," he repeated, his voice low. "I don't need anything from Mr. Clarendon."

"You're being rude," she whispered. "*Un*gentlemanly!"

He looked over her head at the other man. "It's good of you to offer, but I'll manage here. You take the lady home."

"If you say so, old chap." Charles Clarendon replaced his hat and held out his arm. "Come, Miss Sherringham, before it rains."

After one last frown in Luke's direction, she went with the young man back to the fine coach that waited.

He watched her go as the first spots of hard, cold rain hit his forehead and the sky darkened.

Luke didn't know what he was most angry about. The icy rain, the broken wheel of his brother's gig, or the bloody Clarendons. That family was everywhere, it seemed. Like woodworm and fleas. If the two youngest were out and about, Kit Clarendon, the elder brother, a brutish, indolent drunk, may not be far behind. Did he know about the existence of his daughter, Sarah? In all likelihood, he wouldn't give a farthing. Sally Hitchens, with her strong survivor's instinct, had wisely chosen the Wainwrights instead to raise the little girl.

Luke looked down at his fist, remembering when he used it to decorate Kit Clarendon's face after he found out how the boy had violently forced himself on Sally. Other folk assumed the brawl was caused by jealousy—a spat over one woman. Only the two men, and Sally, ever knew the real reason for Luke's fury. The elegant coach and horses trotted away toward the village, and the freezing rain gathered a sudden burst of energy, falling harder, blown directly in his face by an impish God. The same deity that continually threw these people and coincidences in his path, like challenges, and called them fate.

First came Gingersnap, marching into his life, tipping it all upside down, and then claiming she wanted no part of it. Now the Clarendons.

Could a man not get a moment's peace?

All he wanted was to come back, make his apologies, clear his slate, and have a nice funeral. As he looked down the road again in the direction of the disappearing carriage, he thought of how her face had lit up when she saw that brat Charles Clarendon. His foot still damn well hurt where she stepped on it in her haste to greet the younger man.

He'd only offered to marry her to save her reputation, and she wasn't even grateful about that. These young folk, he sniffed angrily, what did they know about anything?

Luke quickly unharnessed the horse, and once that fancy carriage was out of view, he tucked his cane under one arm, mounted the unsaddled horse, swinging himself up easily, and took off at a wild gallop toward that abandoned farmhouse.

❧

Becky wound the ribbons of her bonnet around her fingers, wishing she'd taken a moment to replace it over her windblown hair before she entered the smart carriage. "Perhaps you had better drop me at the wheelwright's place and I can send Sam Hardacre out there to find him."

"If you wish. I would take you wherever you desire."

Charles Clarendon had not changed. The sun still seemed to touch him, even on a dull, dreary day like this one. He and his sister, Elizabeth, sat across from her as the barouche rumbled steadily toward the village.

Becky's heart was racing, but from the result of her accident in the gig, not from seeing Charles again. It was fortunate that Justina wasn't with her, she thought, for the mischievous woman would instantly think her warm cheeks and thumping heartbeat—surely loud enough for all to hear—were symptoms of that foolish, impractical emotion called love.

She caught Elizabeth eyeing her boots. Alas they

were filthy, and the hem of her gown was ripped and sagging where her toe caught it as she stepped down from the gig. What her hair and face looked like she could only imagine. She hoped no one would ask her why her bonnet appeared to have been trampled by a cow. Oh dear, she had really lost her temper again and beaten the colonel with it in a very unladylike manner. So much for maintaining dignity!

The Clarendons were both so clean, dry, and tidy that her own dishevelment felt multiplied. *This*, she thought sadly, *would never happen to Diana*.

Becky decided there was no point in pretending or trying to ignore her sorry state. "You find me at my worst. What an impression I must make."

Elizabeth said nothing. Charles, with a dashing smile, kindly replied, "Now we are even then, for you must recall that the first time we met, Miss Sherringham, I was in a very bad way, quite covered in mud and drenched to the skin." His eyes twinkled merrily at her. "If not for you, what would I have done?"

She was grateful that he didn't cast scornful eyes on her wretched appearance. Instead he put her at her ease, as a gentleman should.

"This time I can repay the favor," he added. "Every man likes to find a damsel in distress, Miss Sherringham."

"Rather than be the damsel himself," his sister muttered dryly, her cool eyes mildly pained as she assessed the trail of icy slush that Becky had tracked into the carriage.

Elizabeth Clarendon was the sort of woman who never went out of her house unless dressed in the very latest fashion and with her hair carefully primped. Charles too was always elegantly attired, his boots polished, his fair curls artfully tousled just enough to make it seem as if he didn't bother. But in Elizabeth's case, one got the sense that she spent hours bothering about it, that her appearance was a chore she worked at ceaselessly. As a consequence of straining that hard to follow every trend, she quite failed to find any joy in fashion and had no natural style or elegance of her own.

"It was very good of you to bring me home," said Becky, tucking her feet as far under her seat as they would fit.

"We were going this way," said Elizabeth, her voice quiet and weary.

"It was the least we could do," Charles assured her with more warmth. "I must say how well you look, even in disarray, Miss Sherringham," he exclaimed gallantly. "I always feel so much better when I see a pretty face, do I not, Elizabeth?"

His sister screwed up her own features as a tiny sneeze took hold of her entire person. "I'm afraid you do."

He laughed. "I was just saying to Elizabeth how much I hoped to find you still here."

"Where else would *she* be?" his sister remarked, staring blankly out of the other window and dabbing a silk handkerchief to her small, pink nose.

"Why, any number of gentlemen might have swept her away by now, and I would not have been able to enjoy her company again! How devastated I should be to find her gone."

His sister's snide remark was instantly erased from

Becky's mind as she once again basked in the rays of Charles Clarendon's smile. His company was an uplifting burst of sunshine on that grim, cold day.

"You are staying at Lark Hollow, I understand?" she asked. "Mrs. Makepiece was not expecting you until Christmas morning."

Charles nodded and his sister merely looked weary, slowly plucking at the fringe of her shawl with long fingers and keeping her gaze on the passing scenery.

"Admiral Vyne very kindly invited us for a house party," Charles explained. "But we found it all rather... tedious. Elizabeth couldn't wait to see our cousin Diana again, so we decided to call in a few days early."

His sister threw him an odd look—part irritation, part curiosity—which he ignored.

"The admiral is a generous host," he added, beaming. "But it can get a trifle wearing and exhausting, don't you know?"

"Admiral Vyne fills his house with pretty young ladies, the way a spider builds his web," Elizabeth drawled, "and then lurks in wait to catch a—"

"My elder brother is in his element," said Charles, impatiently cutting over the tail end of his sister's sentence. "We could not draw Kit away today, but I'm sure we shall make him join us for dinner with our cousins on Christmas Day."

His sister seemed less sure of that. "If he can tear himself away. I cannot think Kit will find much inducement here." Once more, Becky felt the other woman's critical appraisal sweeping her from head to toe before she turned her dreary eyes to the carriage window. "What can you find to do in this place for entertainment?"

"Oh, you'd be surprised, Miss Clarendon. There is always something going on."

"I'm sure there is," the other woman drawled wearily.

Becky thought desperately for something to recommend her village. "It is a pity you missed our play, but we have a treasure hunt on Christmas Eve. All the members of the book society take part and it is—"

"A treasure hunt?"

"Someone writes out a list of items to be hunted around the village and we are divided into teams to go out and find them. It's quite a thrilling way to spend the evening before Christmas." It wasn't something she particularly enjoyed herself, for riddles were not her favorite amusement, but she would rather take part with her friends than miss out.

They both looked at her—Charles bemused, still smiling, and Elizabeth utterly expressionless. "And for what prize?"

"Nothing but boasting rights, I'm afraid. The honor of winning." Their expressions remained unchanged. "We all meet afterward at my father's house for hot chocolate," she added hastily. "It has become a tradition."

"How lovely," Charles exclaimed. "Don't you think so, Eliza? Hot chocolate, indeed!"

His sister merely sighed and patted her nose once more with the bundled handkerchief.

"Count us in," Charles added, leaning across the carriage like a man imparting urgent information. "We must take part in all your games. I can think of no better way to spend the season than a jolly good hunt."

But his sister's pale eyes held no warmth and

continued to regard Becky above that handkerchief through a watery mist of condescension.

When they arrived in the village, she was let out at the carpenter's shop, where she apprised Sam Hardacre of the accident on the turnpike road. Then, although it was only a short distance around the common from the woodshop to her father's house, Charles Clarendon insisted on taking her in the carriage and dropping her at the gate.

As she stepped down from the fine carriage, assisted by Mr. Clarendon's hand, a number of passing villagers took note. *That will give them something else about which to gossip*, she thought. Perhaps it would distract them from Lucky Luke for a while at least.

She thanked Charles and had just lifted the latch of the garden gate when she noted fresh footprints in the slush along the path. Prints larger than her own. They were almost washed away by the rain, but a few remained clear. Her father must have had a visitor that morning, for he would not have gone out in this bleak weather, surely. She'd given him strict instructions to stay by his fire. And he had no reason to go out in any case. If he needed anything, he knew she would fetch it for him.

Could it be her brother returned for Christmas?

A few moments later, she entered the house in great excitement, expecting to hear Nathaniel's voice, but she found only her father in the parlor, his imagination caught by a story in the newspaper. "Look at this, Becky. A man by the name of Wolfgang von Kempelen has invented a mechanical chess player. An automaton that can beat anyone at the game, so they say. Is that not a remarkable thing indeed?"

She gave the story only a quick glance. "Hmmm. I've no doubt there is a living, breathing man inside it."

"But they say not. They say it is a miracle of science."

"You may depend upon it, Papa, there is some trick behind it. There always is."

He shook his head, pouting. "I am saddened, m'dear, by your failure to appreciate the ingenious marvels of the world. To open your mind to things beyond your experience. Can you not even believe for a little while in magic?"

"You believe in magic if it makes you happy." It did no harm, she mused, as long as he had her there to handle the practical matters. Someone had to keep their feet on the ground.

She thought of Lucky Luke's accusation that she treated her father like her own child. That she "hid" herself from life and used her family as an excuse to do so. Ha! What did he know about families anyway? He'd abandoned his for a dozen years. If he thought he could come along and lecture her like another Mrs. Kenton, he was in for a surprise.

As she tossed another shovel of coals on the fire, Becky watched the sparks spit and sizzle at her feet, remembering what it had felt like to fly recklessly along the road in that gig while he carelessly threw back his head and laughed. That was what marriage would be like to him, she mused darkly.

She still hadn't got her pulse back to its usual pace.

Seventeen

LUKE RETURNED TO THE MANOR SHORTLY BEFORE dinner. He reunited in the stables with Ness, who had apparently enjoyed a warm nap there all afternoon. After giving the horse a good rubdown, he found his brother in the drawing room alone. The ladies were still dressing.

"What happened to you?" Darius exclaimed upon seeing the state of his clothes and wet hair.

"Slight problem with your unsteady gig, Handles. Worry not. The wheelwright came out to fix it." He gave a wry grin. "I would have ordered a bath in my room, but that would be two baths in as many nights and I'm afraid of washing my excess of manliness all off."

"I hope you got some measurements taken for new clothes." Darius eyed his filthy riding boots. "And there is a tack room in which to clean those, you know."

"I didn't want to miss dinner," he replied, limping to the fire with Ness close on his heels. "As far as new clothes, I'll ride to Manderson after Christmas. That's the nearest town, so I hear."

There was a slight pause. "You *are* staying, Lucius? It *is* your intention?"

"Of course." But somehow the idea of getting measured for clothes reminded him of being measured for a coffin. He couldn't face it yet.

"It's just that you seem a little…distracted. And this business with Miss Sherringham…my wife tells me the young lady is adamant that she has not accepted you. Neither does she have any plans to do so in the future."

Ness stretched out by the fender, gave a loud yawn before expelling some unpleasant gas, and then sighed contentedly, twitching his stump just once before closing his eyes again. Sometimes Luke wished he could exchange lives with his dog. It would certainly be less complicated. "Miss Sherringham is confused about what she wants. As often happens with women."

Darius moved rapidly away from the dog's odor and found a sweeter spot by the sideboard. He offered his brother a sherry, and while it was poured, Luke searched for a harmless subject—there seemed to be too few of those between him and his brother. Finally his gaze fell to examining two framed sketches above the mantel, one of Darius and the other of the new Mrs. Wainwright. "Very good likenesses," he said, taking the sherry glass he was offered.

"Sarah drew them. She's quite clever with her sketches and painting."

"So I see. She definitely captured you both."

Darius nodded. "I remember you used to have a talent for portraiture, Lucius. I suppose Sarah got that from you."

"Hmm." Luke waved that off. "I made a few naughty cartoons of some of my least favorite people, that's all." Talking about his supposed daughter made him uneasy.

"When you set your mind to it, you drew very well. And they weren't always done in jest."

He changed the subject, bringing the focus back on his brother. "I must confess, I was surprised to find you married, Handles."

"No doubt." Darius smiled in his careful, reserved way. "It took me by no less surprise."

Amused, Luke asked him how it had come about.

"I really couldn't say," Darius admitted, scratching the side of his nose with one finger—a shy gesture Luke remembered from years ago. "It was happening before I knew it had begun, and then there was no stopping it."

"But you don't regret it—giving up your bachelor status? Your liberty?"

Darius looked perplexed. "Of course not. Why would I?"

"Come, little brother, you always viewed matrimony with the same jaded eye as me."

"Did I? I was hesitant to let unknown, uncertain factors into my life, into my heart, perhaps."

"After what happened with Dora, that is understandable." He didn't look at his brother's face, fearing what he might see there. Darius was silent. "I'm sorry," Luke added quietly. "You didn't want me to mention the name."

As if he hadn't spoken, his brother said, "I might have been cautious, but your reason for avoiding matrimony certainly could not have been the same as mine. I've never known you to use prudence in your life, Lucius."

"I don't think I know a Prudence, do I?"

"Yes, still an amusing joke, despite the cobwebs!" His brother shook his head. "Well, now you have set your sights upon Miss Sherringham. Are you sure you are ready to give up *your* liberty? It is nothing to be lightly undertaken, this matrimony business. I'm sure you have yet to work out those details that you always save until the last minute."

Luke thought of her sitting beside him in the tight space of the gig and how it calmed his spirit, made him content. But then he also thought of her beating at him with her bonnet before walking away on the arm of the Clarendon boy, her demeanor completely changed.

"Miss Sherringham has very strong opinions," his brother continued in a slow, careful tone, "and she is not timid about expressing them. She has an independent spirit and—as my wife tells me—she also keeps a very long list of attributes required in a husband." He paused, felt his waistcoat buttons with a twitchy hand, and then added, "I only say this to warn you, Lucius. As your brother, I feel it incumbent upon me to… I would not like to see you make an ass of yourself by pursuing a woman who has no interest. I know how you can be like a bull in a potter's shop when you have your mind set upon something." Turning away quickly, Darius strode back to the fire, grabbed the poker, and thrust it into the coals, stirring up the flames. Apparently brotherly concern had, for once, outdone the more usual desire to maintain a guarded distance and keep certain thoughts to himself. Had his wife urged him to give this warning?

Now Luke's leg hurt again. He limped to a chair

and sat. It was his turn to avoid a subject. Or, at least, to slip slyly around it, while keeping the matter in his side vision. "I heard there is some connection in this village with the Clarendons."

"The Clarendons?" Darius skillfully flipped a fallen coal back into the fire. *Tidy as ever*, Luke mused.

"Yes. They have relatives here?"

"I believe so." Then he looked over his shoulder. "Of course, you and the elder Clarendon boy—Christopher—got into a brawl." Darius's eyes widened as he remembered. "He threatened to bring suit against you for attacking him. Claimed you cost him a few teeth."

"Did I?" Luke grunted, sitting back in the chair. "Good. It would be just like him to fight back with a lawsuit and his father's money instead of his own fists. Bloody coward."

"Well, I hope you stay away from that sort of trouble now that you're returned."

Luke laughed bitterly. "You don't think I can behave myself either, eh?"

"Remember you have a daughter now who watches your every move and does not deserve the burden of bad gossip caused by a father who cannot control his anger."

How ironic, thought Luke, knocking back the last of his sherry. After a lifetime of avoiding responsibilities, he now assumed one that belonged to someone else—to a man he despised. Meanwhile he'd have to hold his temper if he encountered the careless fraud who was really responsible for her conception and abandonment. Darius was right; Sarah was an innocent and must be protected. He would not want her falling into Kit Clarendon's hands. Luke may not be the ideal father himself, but he'd do a damn sight better than Kit Clarendon.

"Remember how Great-Uncle Phineas claimed there was treasure hidden somewhere on this property?" Luke muttered, staring at his muddy boots as he stretched them out in front of him, resting his heels on the fender.

"Yes, I remember. I'm surprised that you do though."

"Ever find any?"

Darius snorted. "Not the material kind. Is that what you came here for?"

"Just curious. Old houses like this—hidden doors and passages—you never know."

His brother looked amused.

"What? You're telling me you never wondered? Never went hunting for that treasure, Handles?"

"Oh, I found all the treasure I wanted." Darius smiled, looking over at the little portrait of his wife.

Luke exhaled a low huff. His brother's brain was well and truly pickled by love, it seemed. Surprising any emotion ever found a way inside that carefully regulated brain. He swept a speck of dried mud briskly from his thigh. "I was wondering today how our lives might have turned out had our childhood been different."

"In what way? You mean if you had not been so spoiled and doted upon by our mama, that you feel guilty letting another woman into your heart?"

Luke stared, the sherry burning his throat all the way down. "What?"

"You *were* her favorite, Lucius. You could do no wrong in her eyes."

"Ridiculous!" He angrily shifted about in the chair, trying to get his leg comfortable. No doubt his brother got this idiocy from one of those books he studied. "If anyone had a favorite, it was our father. And the sun shone out of your behind as far as he was concerned."

"Nonsense!" Darius scoffed, poking the fire with renewed energy. "I simply did as I was told and studied hard. I didn't cause him any headaches the way you did."

"And I had no hope of pleasing the old man even if I tried, since there was no possible way I could compete with you, Master Perfect."

"At least *he* gave me some attention," Darius exclaimed crossly. "Our mother was always too busy showering you with her adoration to notice me." His voice had now risen to a hitherto unheard of pitch as he swung the poker. "And she was only the first of a long line of females besotted with you, of course. I may as well not have been in the room when you were there. I was inadequate and superfluous in every way."

"You exaggerate!"

"Do I? Remember Annabelle Chawley's coming out? She burst into tears because you didn't go. When Mama pushed me forward to dance with her in your place, the wretched girl took one look at me and cried even harder. She took to her bed for weeks and everyone thought it was my fault. Then there was Lady Rampton, the lusty widow with the beauty mark on her ample cleavage. After you threw her over, she took my first edition of Marlowe's *Massacre at Paris* and threw it from the library window, aiming at your head, whereupon it bounced, landed in the fountain, and was irreparably ruined."

"I offered to pay for the damage."

Shoulders tense, his brother hissed. "It was *priceless*!"

"How could it be priceless? You paid for it. Or Father bought it for you, no doubt. Bloody books!"

Darius continued, "Then came Maria Prestwick, to whom you had me write love letters on your behalf, supposedly because my hand was neater and my spelling legible."

"Don't remember."

"No, of course not. When you went off Miss Prestwick, you decided it would be the height of hilarity to add a few extra words to the letters yourself and then tell her they came from me. She took them to show her mama, who was ready to have me pilloried for the suggestions they contained, even though I didn't know what half of them meant."

"Did she? The minx!"

"I later discovered they were all appallingly misspelled, by the way. But still recognizable as your handiwork, thanks to your manner of writing exactly as you speak."

Luke tapped his boot toe with his cane. "Are we going to relive the past now, then? I thought you didn't want to look back?"

"And let us not forget Miss Jane Ponsonby. Does that name ring any bells, Lucius? She's the young lady who, while in quick pursuit of you, actually pushed me to my hands and knees and trod upon me."

"Well, someone had to help her into the curricle, and the step was broken." Luke shrugged. "I thought you were being your usual dutiful self."

There was a pause. Abruptly Darius leaned his head on his arm as it rested on the mantel. Luke rubbed his hand over one knee, not sure what to say next.

But then he saw that his brother was trembling. Suddenly Darius exploded with a gale of laughter. It was croaky, breathless, echoing around the room, making Ness look up, ears pricked.

"Poor Handles," Luke muttered tentatively. "It must have been hard growing up with a brother like me, eh? Almost as trying as it was for me to put up with your grim, disapproving face."

Darius put the poker back on its hook. "Yes, it bloody well was." Eventually he turned and Luke saw that his brother was pressing his lips together, trying to stop the laughter.

"I was a pain in the arse, eh?"

"You still are."

Luke grinned. "Can't all be as good and clever as you, can we? See, it's for the best that you take the inheritance. You'll make better use of it than me. I'll spend it all on crates of apricots and pet monkeys or something."

"I told you, Lucius, it's rightfully yours. And I won't hear another word about it."

The argument continued in a gentle ebb and flow, but laughter had cleared the air somewhat. When the ladies arrived soon after, they all went in to dinner.

❧

Sarah and his sister-in-law expressed concern that Luke might have caught a cold in the rain that day. He assured them he was fine and never caught colds.

"Just like Darius," Justina exclaimed, eyes shining.

"My dear husband never caught a cold until he came here, did you, darling?"

Darius looked down at his plate and shook his head. She laughed, a gentle, tinkling sound that suggested she had more to tell on that subject but would drop it for now. The newlyweds exchanged a coy glance and Luke winced. There was nothing worse than being in the way when two people were in love. He was happy for his brother, certainly, but did their affection have to be exhibited before him every half hour?

There were two subjects sure to bore Luke to tears at a dinner table; one was that endless and pointless speculation about the weather, which some people seemed to enjoy, and the other was gossip about love affairs—who was courting whom, who flirted with whom, and whose heart was lately broken. Lovers could be the most tiresome dinner companions of all.

Thankfully, his brother understood this. Darius cleared his throat, hid his smile, and said, "Lucius managed to run my gig off the road today, apparently."

"Oh dear," exclaimed his wife. "I hope no one was hurt!"

"Just my pride." He forced a smile. "Lost a wheel up beyond the bridge, on the turnpike road."

"And you had to struggle all the way home, Colonel?" Sarah cried. "It must have been painful for you on foot."

"I rode," he muttered. "Went up and took a look at the empty farmhouse up by the river. Willow Tree Farm, ain't it? Nice place."

"You can ride?" Sarah cried in surprise. "Even with your leg?"

"It locks up once in a while, but I manage."

Darius muttered, "You were driving that gig without caution, I expect. I await the wheelwright's bill with trepidation."

"Did you see Dr. Penny while you were out?" Sarah demanded, staring at him with large, intense eyes. "As you promised?"

Luke thought hastily. "He was not home."

"Really?" said Justina. "My father was in when I called upon him this afternoon."

Damn it all, he'd forgotten the family connection. Of course, he'd had his mind on many other things that day. Primarily Rebecca, and then the arrival of the Clarendons.

Luke stabbed his fish with considerable force, the sudden, violent scraping of fork prongs on china making everyone look up. "They must not have heard the bell when I came to the door," he said gruffly.

Aware of Sarah still staring, he did not turn his head to look at her.

"Well, that is very odd. Perhaps after church tomorrow, I can take you to see my father," said Justina. "If you would like—"

"On a Sunday? And Christmas Eve, no less? Surely he likes to take a day of rest. No, no, this can wait until after Christmas. There is no rush."

No one spoke for a moment. The meal continued in silence until Sarah said, "Don't you want your leg to get better, Colonel? Or perhaps it does not hurt that much after all."

"Sarah! What a thing to say. I'm sure the colonel would like very much not to have that pain after so many years."

Luke made much of finding a bone in his fish and setting it aside on the plate.

"Well, he doesn't seem in much haste to do anything about it. I was curious, that's all." The girl put down her fork and said solemnly, "I was thinking of when I had a fever several years ago…do you remember, Uncle Darius?"

"Of course."

"I got a great deal of attention because of it, and even though I felt simply rotten in the beginning, after a while I rather enjoyed being treated so kindly by everyone. Even the horrible medicine was bearable because Uncle Darius came up to read to me in the evenings and I got all my favorite puddings." She licked her lips. "And it was also a useful affliction because it kept your stepmother from nagging at me all the time about my posture. She couldn't complain about it while I was deathly ill in bed. In fact, everyone had to tiptoe around me. It was so very pleasing that once I was declared well enough to get out of bed again, I felt quite a letdown."

Again there was silence. Until Darius said wryly, "That would explain why the doctor's remedies didn't work as efficiently as they should, Sarah."

"Precisely," the little chit replied, staring hard at Luke again.

He took a piece of boiled potato from his plate and fed it to Ness, who waited patiently under the table at his feet.

"By the by, Colonel, who is *Lucky*?"

Uh-oh. Luke wiped his lips carefully on a napkin. "It was a name some people called me. In my youth."

"Why?"

He sighed, but before he could prepare a reply, his brother said, "Because people claimed he had the luck of the devil."

For now, that seemed to satisfy the inquisitor.

Where had she heard that name, Luke wondered. Perhaps his brother had mentioned it within her hearing before.

"Lucius was asking about the Clarendons," said Darius, looking at his wife. "They are related to your friend Diana, are they not?"

"Yes." She looked a little flustered, glancing at Luke. "Diana's mother was a Clarendon before her marriage. They are visiting for Christmas."

"I saw them on the road today," Luke muttered.

"Oh." His brother's wife asked Sarah to pass the potatoes and then looked at the mantel clock. "Do you think it will snow again tomorrow?"

Eighteen

IT DID NOT SNOW. THE NEXT MORNING HE WAS dragged along, under a chill, bright sky, to Sunday church service, where he sat in the special pew reserved for the residents of Midwitch Manor, with Justina on one side and Sarah on the other. The young girl studied his every move until Luke felt as if he were five again and under the sharply watchful eyes of a nanny.

In the front row of the congregation to his right, he saw the Clarendons with that somber-faced ham woman and her pretty but unhappy daughter.

And there, in another pew, slightly behind them, sat Major Sherringham and Rebecca.

Last night, after supper, his brother's wife had followed him to the billiard room, Ness trotting at her side, to explain what she had not been able to tell him within Sarah's hearing.

"I'm afraid my friend Rebecca is very fond of Mr. Charles Clarendon. He is her very ideal of a perfect gentleman."

He had felt a hard pinch in his chest at this news, but it should not have been any surprise. The two were of similar age. They made an attractive couple. She had certainly greeted Charles in a very warm and welcoming manner, markedly different to the way she was with him.

"I see," had been his reply.

Justina had stopped in the billiard room doorway, her head on one side, and looked annoyed. "Oh no, not you too."

"Me too?"

"Darius always says *I see* like that when he's in a tight spot and doesn't know how to react. When, in fact, he doesn't see at all and he's still trying to make sense of it."

Luke had laughed it off, assuring her that Rebecca was clever enough to make her own choices, but inside he had not felt like laughing. His blood went quite cold at the thought of Gingersnap falling doe-eyed for that shiny, polished young buck. This morning in church, Charles Clarendon, incapable of sitting still for long, continually looked over his shoulder, trying to catch the eye of Miss Sherringham. Each time he did so, a ray of sunlight bounced off the diamond pin in his cravat and seared a painful course directly into Luke's eyes. The young man's sister pretended to ignore everyone, her bored gaze fixed upon a stone pillar while she patted her nose with a kerchief and sighed.

Meanwhile, Rebecca's father had his chin on his chest and appeared to be studying his coat buttons, although he might well be asleep. He had shown no sign of noticing the simpering of Master Clarendon in the front pew. But others did. It was such a pointed and one-way flirtation that the folk crowded into that small church could not fail to notice.

Gingersnap paid dutiful attention to the parson, however, and for the most part, she ignored Clarendon's idiotic and disrespectful antics.

What was she thinking about? Luke wondered, noting a slightly pensive, wistful expression on her face today. If he was sitting with her, he would be holding her hand, squeezing it gently to reassure her.

Luke suddenly noticed Sarah shivering beside him. The small feather on her cap fluttered in a draft through the ancient window behind them. Immediately he whispered at her to change seats with him and he put up his collar against the cold air.

After the service, the villagers poured out through the arched door of the small church, many exclamations of "Merry Christmas" called back and forth. It had been a long time, Luke thought suddenly, since he'd celebrated the Yuletide season in any form. A year ago, he could not have imagined himself here, attending church with his estranged brother and a little girl everyone thought was his daughter.

"He came back from the dead," the villagers whispered.

"Such a shock to his brother."

"And to that little girl, no doubt."

"They say he came to marry the major's daughter, but she won't have him. You know how particular she is."

"These romantic young girls. Too many novels, that's my opinion. I wouldn't turn him away."

He hung back, lurking in the shadows as villagers passed through the door. At last, Rebecca was within reach and he stepped forward, leaning on his cane. Today he was acutely aware of the need to mind his manners. After the disastrous jaunt in his brother's gig yesterday, he didn't want her attacking him with her bonnet again. He'd been heavy-handed in his approach. That would have to change, clearly. She'd shown that she didn't trust him. He would, therefore, have to earn that trust, but if he meant to do so before the new year—as he'd wagered—time was not on his side.

But he wouldn't let her fall victim to more gossip.

And Sarah had her heart set on Miss Sherringham for a stepmother.

Last but not least, he liked Rebecca. He admired her. She was amusing, quick-witted, strong, generous. To have her look up to him, to trust him and hold his hand willingly, would be a prize indeed.

"Miss Sherringham."

She halted, frowning. "Colonel Wainwright."

He was struck by her pretty face again as if he'd never seen it before. "Will you walk with me?"

She seemed confused and nervous, unable to look him in the eye. "I must wait for my father."

"We can wait for him together then."

Despite its searing brightness, the only place where the sun actually had heat today was when it touched her anxious face and her hair. It seemed to produce a halo of mist around her. Probably, he mused, all that angry breath she exhaled when she looked at him.

"I would not wish to detain you, Colonel. Don't wait."

"But I must wait. What else can I do?" If he were

not attempting reform, he would simply hoist the woman over his shoulder and carry her out of the church. Alas, he wasn't allowed to put his hands on her in public, even if he was running out of time.

The woman looked over at the doorway, which was now blocked by a crowded jumble of folk all delayed over their Christmas greetings. Luke took another step closer.

"I must thank you, Miss Sherringham, for sending the carpenter to my aid yesterday."

"Oh."

"It was very thoughtful of you, considering my reckless behavior," he added.

Her eyes narrowed. "Oh?"

Luke wanted to touch the curl of copper that tumbled beside her cheek. The old Lucky wouldn't have hesitated. But today he kept his hands behind his back, away from temptation. "The next time I take you for a drive, I will be more cautious."

Her brows arched high. "The next time?"

"Of course."

"I don't—"

"You must allow me to make it up to you." He paused. "I didn't mean to frighten you."

She drew a sharp breath, her cheeks sucked in, the curl by her face quivering indignantly. "I was not frightened. Fright is a weakness, caused by inexperience and a lack of self-assurance. I, however, was quite certain where we would end up. My concerns were entirely logical and practical—the expense of a broken gig or the endangering of a limb is not something to be sniffed at. If your intention was to frighten me by racing like that, you failed."

"Why would it be my intention to frighten you? I wanted you to trust me."

Apparently this puzzled her. She opened her lips but no reply came out.

"But you think no one is as trustworthy as yourself," he prompted softly.

"Of course I don't think that!"

"Good. Then you won't object to giving me another chance."

With an irritated gasp, she turned, searching back inside the church for her father, but came face to face with Mrs. Penny, who laughed giddily at finding them standing near.

"We shall soon see you two walking down this aisle together, shan't we?"

Rebecca blanched, even her freckles fading. "Don't wait for me," she snapped again at Luke over her shoulder before rushing around Mrs. Penny and disappearing into the church.

Somewhere behind him he heard that unknown voice whisper, "But he's too old for her. Much too old. He ought to know better."

Another said, "With his past scandals…"

"He only came back for the inheritance, of course."

Before the startled Mrs. Penny could speak again, he moved away as fast as he could manage, squeezing through the cluster of villagers until he had left the dim, dank mustiness of the church behind. He was still recovering breath when his sister-in-law found him and led him over to the ham woman, who stood beside the frost-trimmed churchyard wall. "Colonel, I know you have been introduced to Mrs. Makepiece already."

Although he always knew what to say to a lady on his own territory, he had to struggle to find a polite remark while he was all togged up like a show pony in his brother's clothes. He reached for the only thing he knew about her. "I hope you got your ham home safely, madam."

She blinked nervously and gave a strained smile. "I did. Thank you, Colonel."

His sister-in-law jumped in to help. "May I introduce Mr. Charles Clarendon and his sister Elizabeth?" Ah, he hadn't seen who Ham Lady was with until it was too late to avoid them. "This is my brother-in-law, Colonel Lucius Wainwright, formerly of the Light Dragoons and recently returned to us."

"Ah yes, Colonel!" Charles beamed in that stupid way. "We met yesterday on the road. You very nearly ran us off it and into the river." He shook his finger in Luke's face while laughing as if it was the funniest thing that ever happened to anyone.

"I remember the incident differently," he replied tersely.

The idiot boy's sister thrust her cold curiosity at him with eyes like two icy, flint-gray spears. "Your name is familiar. Do we know you?"

"I am sure there are a great many Wainwrights in the world." Preparing to move away, he stopped and looked at them both again. "You mean to stay long in the village?"

"Good Lord, no," said the sister.

"I wish we could stay longer," exclaimed Charles. "But sadly we can never stay with our dear cousins long enough. Always so many other things to drag us away again from this quaintly rustic idyll."

As he felt a trickle of relief running through his veins, Luke thought he heard his sister-in-law exhale a light sigh of the same emotion while she stood at his side.

"It must make quite a change for you here," he muttered.

"My brother delights in the novelty of staying at that little inn by the green," Elizabeth Clarendon explained listlessly, "and I have the pleasure of the spare room in my cousin's tidy little house." She flicked a sly glance at her brother, who ignored it because he had just spied the Sherringhams emerging under the arch of the church door.

Pushing his way by them all, Charles leaped in Rebecca's path. "Allow me to walk you home, Miss Sherringham! I have waited here in the cold to do just that very thing, chilled my feet to the bone. You must introduce me to your father."

He was loud and solidly planted in her path, his gestures extravagant as those of a magician looking to distract his audience while he fleeces their pockets. Several passing folk turned to look as he imposed himself on his prey in this odd manner. But *she* did not seem to mind—if anything, she looked as if she found him amusing, his childish pout endearing. Of course, she didn't like a man who could look after himself; she preferred little boys whose faces she could wipe.

"We will see you later," Justina called out to her.

Becky looked over and her smile faltered when she saw Luke standing there. Then Charles said something else, waving his arms about like a wind-mill, drawing her attention back to him. Soon they had moved on with Clarendon, her father genially nodding to the young man, trying to follow his energetically aimless conversation.

"My brother finds the oddest amusements in the country," Elizabeth commented, her tone droll. "It seems he shares Miss Sherringham's passion for *dead leaves*." Since no one else present seemed to under-stand the reference, her attempt at wit—if that was what it was—fell flat.

"I hope we can amuse you *both* while you are with us," said Ham Lady.

Her guest managed a weak smile that barely existed before it was snuffed. "I'm sure."

There followed an awkward lull in the conversation, for now that Charles had gone off, it seemed as if the remaining ladies had nothing to say to one another, and Luke felt no inclination to speak. He was still watch-ing Rebecca walk away on the other man's arm and suffering a tightening in his chest that made him think he must have eaten his breakfast too fast that morning.

"You were lately visiting with Admiral Vyne at Lark Hollow?" Justina asked eventually. "Does he not have three lovely daughters? I've never met them, but heard much about—"

"Lovely is a matter of taste," Miss Clarendon inter-rupted. "But they *are* very young and lively. And quite without means. His house falls around his ears. One wonders where all his money went."

That would explain why two Clarendons had sought entertainment elsewhere. They liked their comforts. Although what they were doing in the "quaintly rustic idyll" of Hawcombe Prior remained a mystery. *Ham Lady doesn't look as if she has many pennies to rub together either*, thought Luke. She was probably much worse off than the admiral, so what had brought the Clarendons here? He didn't believe, even for a moment, that it had anything to do with family fondness. He didn't like them here.

"Still, our brother, Kit, is a fool for female company such as that provided by the admiral's daughters and his guests," said Elizabeth. "Everyone enjoys Kit. He could not get away. He could not be spared."

Luke suspected her elder brother was also enjoying a few card games with the admiral, trying to win whatever the eccentric old man had left in his coffers. "Charles was impatient to see our cousin," she continued in a dreary tone. "When he gets an idea in his head, it is very difficult to put him off. But those ideas never last long. There is always another coming soon after and then the former is forgotten."

Shortly after this, Darius caught up with them, and since he was not the sort to be at all sociable unless forced, and no one on this occasion wanted to force him, the Wainwright party had an excuse to leave. Luke hurried over to where Sarah was chatting with her friend, the ringleted tavern-keeper's daughter, and steered her quickly off down the path. He didn't want her introduced to the Clarendons.

Walking out to the barouche, Justina put her hand on Luke's arm and confessed, "How glad I am that they don't plan to stay long. The Clarendons are some of the most pretentious people I've ever known."

He sniffed. "They've been here many times before?"

"Only once, a year or two ago. Mrs. Makepiece is anxious to be accepted back in the bosom of her fine family, so for Diana, I am glad that they visit, but I cannot say I like any of them very much."

Luke wondered why she'd been so eager to introduce him to them. "And the dead leaves comment?"

Justina laughed softly, rolling her eyes. "Becky loves to ramble through the autumn leaves, and if the weather is stormy, all the better. Nothing, she assures me, is quite so exhilarating as to shake one's fist at a thunderstorm." She stepped up into the carriage behind Sarah, and Luke followed. "Becky was out one day doing exactly that—in the rain—when she found Charles Clarendon, who had been thrown from his horse and rolled down the hill to be covered in leaves. It would have all been very romantic if it was the other way around, of course, but Becky carried *him* home. I expect that was Elizabeth's meaning." She paused. "Your leg hurts today, Colonel?"

No, he thought, *it isn't my damn leg.*

She leaned closer and whispered, "Keep your chin up, Colonel. She is only one woman. There are plenty more from which to choose." She fluttered her lashes. "Did you not used to say to your brother that there were many daisies in a field and it would be unwise of you to devote yourself to only one?"

Oh, yes, he'd said that many times. But he hadn't met this particular daisy back then.

Darius was the last to enter and he closed the carriage door. As the horses pulled them slowly down the lane away from the church, Luke looked out and saw

Charles Clarendon and Rebecca walking together, her father a few steps behind. The young man made a great fuss about an icy patch in her path and as he guided her around it with a hand on her waist, he glanced over at the passing barouche. His formerly merry countenance sharpened when he saw Luke watching. Those blue eyes narrowed, losing the boyish gleam with which they had shimmered and flirted throughout the church service. There, in that moment, as the strong, mercilessly unflattering winter sun shone in his face, he looked exactly like his brother Kit. They might have been one and the same man.

Across the carriage, Darius was discussing a letter he'd received from their stepmother. "She informed me that Admiral Vyne has some earl's daughter staying at Lark Hollow. It is, so I understand, quite a social coup. Apparently she befriended one of his daughters in London last season and she's been at Lark Hollow for over a month. I shouldn't be at all surprised if that's why the Clarendons came. They are notorious social climbers."

Luke scratched his chin and stared angrily out of the carriage window. *Then why didn't they stay at Lark Hollow? Why leave that place to come here and inconvenience the ham lady and her woebegone daughter?* The more he thought of it, the more suspicious their motives became. He didn't like it.

Someone would have to keep Rebecca out of trouble. Her father clearly wasn't up to the task.

Darius went on, "Stepmother's letter also informed me that she was visited in the small hours recently by my brother's restless and tormented spirit."

The carriage rumbled around a bend, and since he could no longer see Rebecca, Luke sat back in his seat and looked at his brother. "Really? How extraordinary."

"Quite. Apparently this ghastly specter advised her to repent her sins by giving all her jewelry to the poor, eating only bread and gruel, and beating herself twice daily with a willow switch."

Sarah, who had been silent and sulky all morning, now perked up. "Colonel, how wicked of you!"

"Me?" He raised his eyebrows. "What makes you think it is anything to do with me?"

The girl eyed him skeptically.

"Do I look like a ghost to you?" he demanded. "Might I ever be mistaken for a spirit?"

She pursed her lips.

Luke leaned across the seat and whispered, "Of course, there are certain beastly, unholy terrors that might visit a lady in her chamber, in the dead of night, and wail in her ear until she wakes and huddles under the coverlet. Nightmarish visions from the depths of some horrid, dark place that come up to capture naughty, disbelieving, accusing young girls and punish them for their wicked, unfounded assumptions."

Now her gaze lowered to his bad leg and his cane.

"Especially little girls who question their elders about the veracity of their aches and pains." He sat back again, satisfied that he'd put the little mite in her place.

She did not relax her lips, but her eyes narrowed, watching him even more intently than before, until her aunt suddenly exclaimed, "Sarah, did you by chance borrow my silver bracelet with the mother-of-pearl inlay again? I could not find it this morning, and the last time I wore it was at the party on Friday evening."

"No, Aunt Jussy. I would not borrow without asking you."

"I did not think you would, but it is so strange that I cannot find it anywhere." Her husband suggested the clasp may have broken somehow at the party and she conceded the possibility. "I shall search the drawing room when we get home, for it is one of my favorites. Curiously, Diana told me today that her mother has misplaced her cameo choker too since our party."

Sarah volunteered to help her look for the missing items.

Luke looked out of the window, angrily surveying the frosty country lane and those rotting leaves that apparently caused Miss Sherringham and her charming young man such unbridled delight.

Nineteen

"WHAT A GRIM, WEATHERED, UGLY FELLOW THAT Colonel Wainwright is," Charles observed as they negotiated an icy patch on the path.

"He has led a full life," Becky replied thoughtfully. "I suppose that shows on his face."

Charles looked at her. "My cousin tells me you are engaged to him. Or you were. There seems to be some confusion about the facts."

She might have known it wouldn't take long for the rumor to reach his ears at the tavern where he had taken a room. "It was a misunderstanding and nothing more. We are not engaged."

He beamed. "Thank goodness. I could scarce believe…after all, he is so old. Surely, my sweet Miss Sherringham would not tie herself to such a man, thought I."

She waited to help her father around the same treacherous ice and so Charles stopped too. It seemed as if he had forgotten they were not alone, and his eagerness to be introduced to her father had very soon been satisfied with no more than a few hasty sentences.

Once they were on their way again, Charles seized her hand, tucked her arm under his, and resumed his speedy pace until they had outstripped the major by several yards.

"Then I said to myself," he went on, "perhaps Miss Sherringham has made a wise choice. As much as it would wound me deeply to admit. After all, Colonel Wainwright, so my cousin assures me, is a wealthy man of property. In which case it would be selfish of me to expect my lovely and very dear friend to remain unwed. Especially since I, being only a younger son, cannot offer her the same. It would be a good match for her and I cannot begrudge her the opportunity, even if my heart must be broken. I know she would not begrudge me if the situation were reversed."

Again she assured him, wearily, "I do not intend to marry the colonel. Or anyone. The idea of being a wife does not thrill me."

"Then you and I can still enjoy our nature walks together," he replied, his melancholy demeanor instantly vanished.

She smiled at him. Smiling seemed the thing for a lady to do. He paid her great attention, singling her out to walk with her after church, and she knew other village girls would envy her. Lucy Bridges, for one. It was rare for Becky to know what that felt like. She could manage being valued for her aim, her throwing arm, and her bold courage in the face of adversity, but she had yet to be comfortable with flattery of the sort that other women received more frequently and graciously.

Charles went out of his way to walk at her side, be introduced to her father, and make her smile, but she didn't know why he worked so hard at it and just for her.

"You must know," he announced grandly, "that I came here only to see you again, Miss Sherringham. It is for you that I make my sister annoyed. It is for you that I insult the admiral by leaving his house party and his guests."

"Goodness, I would not want you to insult anyone for me."

He laughed. "Of course you would. Lovers are always selfish."

"Lovers?"

"My dear Miss Sherringham, if only I could keep you for my own amusement." His golden lashes fluttered downward briefly and he gave a strange, high laugh. "You must not mind me. I get swept away in the joy of your company. Carried away by my sensibilities. Especially with you, Miss Sherringham."

It was odd that he claimed to be carried away by his feelings, yet he had not written to her more than once or made another effort to see her in fifteen months.

"But perhaps, one day, our friendship can become something more," he added. "Something more intimate."

Surprised, she exclaimed, "Mr. Clarendon, I wonder what you can mean by speaking that way to me." She might expect forward remarks of that nature—and worse—from Lucky Luke, but not from her fine gentleman. It was quite a disappointment.

His eyes shone, unconcerned. "We are friends, are we not?"

"Certainly."

"And I hope we always will be."

"Then why would you infer there might be more between us, when you know there cannot be? You cannot marry where you would choose, as you told me before, and I don't want to marry at all."

He shook his head as if bewildered for a moment. Then he looked at her. "I am flirting with you, Miss Sherringham. Surely you know. It is all quite harmless. I meant nothing untoward by it."

"Oh." Now she felt foolish. She knew about flirting, naturally. It was what ladies and gentlemen did because they had so little else to occupy their time. But she had never indulged in the practice, having too much else to do.

"And you flirt with me, Miss Sherringham," he said. "Don't pretend otherwise!"

Did she? Puzzled, she tried to think what she might have done that could be construed as flirting. She had been told she had lips too ready to mock, and her brother once accused her of having eyes that stared too openly—whatever that meant.

"I say things I should not," he added. "I let myself imagine things that cannot be. You, Miss Sherringham, bring out the worst in me."

She looked away, grieved and frustrated. It seemed she brought out the worst in a lot of men, without knowing how she did it. Just like the errors she made in her clothing choices from time to time, it was done before she knew it.

"But we are friends. I shall be content with that. I cannot expect anything more."

When she remained quiet, he began to talk about the book of sonnets he'd sent her and so their conversation turned to Shakespeare and poetry. Becky was relieved, for she preferred to talk of books than to try that odd sport of flirting.

Poetry was a subject she could never talk about with Lucky Luke. It was doubtful he knew the first think about a rhyming couplet, she mused. He would probably think it was something naughty and indecent.

Thus *he* had crept back into her thoughts even as she tried to keep him out.

She'd fought so hard in church not to look at the colonel, but his presence was too much not to feel. Even if she didn't look at him, her other senses knew he was there. But he was the very worst sort of man, the opposite of everything she'd ever imagined for herself. Somehow she had to get him out of her mind.

She took a deep breath and looked at the charming fellow walking beside her. The well-spoken, well-groomed, and mostly well-behaved gentleman, who loved poetry and dancing.

"Mr. Clarendon," she burst out, "you must come to our book society meeting this evening, before the treasure hunt."

He agreed at once. There was nothing, he said, that he would enjoy more. In fact, he was so enthused about spending that time in her company that Becky set her reservations aside and relaxed again. She was being overly critical of his flirting, she decided. Just because it was still strange to her did not mean it was wrong. Charles Clarendon was a civil young gentleman with playful manners. As he said, flirting was the fashionable thing to do. There was no harm in it.

A certain person had recently shouted at her "*Good*

lord, woman, enjoy yourself. Take off your bonnet. Feel the wind in your hair."

Enjoy herself! As if it was that simple. Perhaps it was for him—a man with no fixed abode and a dog he couldn't even admit he was fond of. Becky was sure she could enjoy herself too if she didn't care about other people and worry about being hurt.

And for pity's sake, she was not going to start thinking about him again!

❧

"I remember last Christmas, at a little hop at the Park, he danced from eight o'clock till four without once sitting down."

"Did he indeed?" cried Marianne, with sparkling eyes, "and with elegance, with spirit?"

"Yes, and he was up again at eight to ride to covert."

"That is what I like; that is what a young man ought to be. Whatever be his pursuits, his eagerness in them should know no moderation and leave him no sense of fatigue."

"Aye, aye, I see how it will be," said Sir John. "I see how it will be. You will be setting your cap at him now and never think of poor Brandon."

"That is an expression, Sir John," said Marianne warmly, "which I particularly dislike. I abhor every commonplace phrase by which wit is intended; and 'setting one's cap at a man,' or 'making a conquest' are the most odious of all…"

As Diana read aloud this conversation from *Sense and Sensibility*, she raised her eyelashes and glanced at

Becky above the top edge of the book. Becky, in turn, looked out of the parlor window and found the lane still just as empty as it was the last time she glanced out, two minutes ago.

"Who do you watch for so avidly?" Justina wanted to know.

"No one," she lied.

Although Charles Clarendon had eagerly accepted her invitation, he was very late, and as each moment ticked by with no sight of him emerging from the tavern, Becky found herself hoping he would *not* come. That might be for the best after all. The awful enemy known as "second thoughts" had come to her many times in the hours since she issued the invitation.

She had told Colonel Wainwright that their meetings were "ladies only." If he heard that Charles Clarendon had been invited, what would he think of her? Guilt, something she rarely had cause to feel, fizzled through her veins.

And what, pray tell, did that matter? She had never looked for *his* approbation. Never sought or wanted it.

It wasn't as if Lucky Luke truly had any interest in books. He had only mentioned invading the book society to annoy her. Or perhaps to impress her? No. Why would he bother with that, when she'd already told him plainly that she could not be charmed and seduced like the women of his harem?

Becky clasped her hands tighter in her lap.

She had watched him with Sarah that morning in church, saw how she listened to the girl with patience, made her change seats on the pew so that she would not be in the draft. Of course, Becky had not let him see that she noticed.

But she could not get his words out of her head. *"You're hiding from life, missy. Hiding behind your father and brother. Hiding from your true self and your own passions."*

How could he know anything about her passions? A proper young lady wasn't even supposed to have any. Other than music, dancing, needlework, and perhaps drawing.

Her mind in a confused pickle this evening, she barely listened as Diana read on.

> *Sir John did not much understand this reproof; but he laughed as heartily as if he did and then replied, "Aye, you will make conquests enough, I dare say, one way or another. Poor Brandon! He is quite smitten already, and he is very well worth setting your cap at, I can tell you, in spite of all this tumbling about and spraining of ankles."*

"I agree with Sir John, and say poor Colonel Brandon," exclaimed Justina when Diana paused to turn the page. "Marianne is being rather unfair to him. I'm sure he's a perfectly delightful gentleman, even if he does not meet all her expectations."

Diana set down the book, leaving it open in her lap. "While I admire Marianne's spirit, she *is* a little too romantically inclined. Marianne, I fear, is bound for disappointment. She expects a gentleman to embody everything heroic at first sight. If they do not instantly meet with her requirements, she doesn't look at them.

Her sister Elinor at least has the sense to see the good in Edward Ferrars."

"Marianne thinks herself so clever, strong, and impervious to mistakes." Justina sighed deeply. "I cannot think who will do for her. If anyone ever will. What do you think, Becky?"

"What do I think?" She twisted around to face the room after spending most of the last half hour looking out of the window, battling with various emotions. "I think that if everyone continues to hint at Marianne and the colonel being a match, it will only separate them further. Marianne is clearly a self-governing spirit, knows what she wants, and will go her own way."

The short silence that followed was broken by Elizabeth Clarendon's loud yawn. She sat by the fire, her dainty feet resting on a little stool, while she leafed nonchalantly through a ladies' magazine. She had no interest in *Sense and Sensibility* as she'd already read it.

Becky couldn't see why Elizabeth had come there. Her brother, at least, seemed to find real pleasure in the countryside. He loved taking long rambles, just as Becky did, and he reveled in hearing all the village gossip, while his sister made no effort to fit in and showed no real interest in anything. The Clarendons and their fine apparel stood out like sore thumbs in that humble village, but Charles had a natural charm and ease that made him liked by most people he met, whereas Elizabeth was too proud and kept herself apart. She was clearly disdainful of her cousins, and as for the other ladies of the Book Club Belles, she could barely bring herself to speak to Justina, and Lucy was simply eyed from the side as if she were a gruesomely squashed hedgehog.

While Diana paused her reading between chapters, Becky said, "I hope we are not boring you, Miss Clarendon. It must be hard to hear us speculate on a story to which you already know the ending."

"Oh, worry not for me," she replied in her lazy drawl. "I am entertained. There is always something amusing to observe in a group of young ladies." She paused, twisting a finger around the fringe of her shawl. "But do tell me about the colonel—Colonel Wainwright, that is. I heard today from the parson's wife that he was presumed dead for the past twelve years and that now he is back, he will inherit a vast fortune. Is that so?"

Becky was not about to be drawn into this conversation, but Justina replied that it was indeed the case.

"And are you or are you not engaged to him, Miss Sherringham?" Elizabeth's eyes glittered spitefully across the room and she licked her lower lip with the tiny pink tip of her tongue. "It seems a most confusing business, and when I heard of it today, I felt very bad that I had not wished you well."

Forced now to answer, Becky replied reluctantly, "It was Colonel Wainwright's idea of a practical joke and Mrs. Kenton likes to perpetuate it." She would tell no one about the wager he'd talked her into on the night of the party. He had just a week now to complete his transformation and convince her that he could be a gentleman. A week. The man was clearly an optimist.

The other woman's eyebrows writhed in bemusement. "Heavens! What a curious thing. He must have a very odd sense of humor, and he does appear very... *earthy*." She broke into an eerie titter that went on too long in the otherwise quiet parlor. "But of course, one can overlook so much when a man is *that* rich."

"But he'll only be rich if he gets married," Lucy chirped. "Otherwise he won't get a penny. That's why he wanted Rebecca."

"Ah." Elizabeth's eyes glistened shrewdly. "That explains so much."

"And she says she won't have him," Lucy added. "So I suppose he'll have to find someone else."

Becky turned her face to the window again, hiding her expression from the other women, but soon after that, Diana got up to close the curtains, complaining of a draft. Becky was then obliged to pay attention to the book, her elbow resting listlessly on the table, her chin in her upturned palm.

❧

That day, after church, Luke had gone out to get some air again, unable to sit still. Darius found him with his shirtsleeves rolled up, mucking out the stables, having already done the same service for the pig sty.

"It is Sunday, Lucius," he exclaimed. "A day of rest."

"It might be a Sunday, Brother, but the beasts don't know it, do they?" Luke gestured with the pitchfork at the pile of fresh manure he was in the midst of shoveling.

"The sooner we find work for you the better, it seems, as you are so restless. In the new year, you must come to London with me and look over the business offices."

"Splendid." The idea of working in an office made him think of those coffin walls closing in again, but he'd promised to make an effort. And there was more on his mind too. As Darius turned to go back inside, Luke shouted for him to stay a moment. Leaning on the pitchfork, he said, "I meant what I said, Handles. I don't want the money or the houses. You and your lady wife can do as you wish with all of it."

Darius frowned. "But you—"

"I'll keep saying it until you believe me." He thrust the pitchfork into a nearby bale of hay. "It seems no one around here trusts a single word I say."

"Perhaps you don't realize exactly how much you're giving up, Lucius."

He wiped one forearm across his brow and sighed. "I didn't come back here for any of that nonsense. You know how I am with money. If you can spare me just a small annuity, to get me on my feet, that'll do me."

"And your plans? Have you made any yet or are you still flying by the seat of your breeches, leaving those elusive *details* for later?"

His brother, of course, always had to have a plan. Everything in neat order. Luke thought for a minute, looking up at the bruised clouds of the winter sky. "My plans rely on Miss Sherringham, I fear."

Darius winced. "Still hoping?"

"I'm not giving this one up, Handles." He winked. "This time I won't be distracted."

His brother sounded bewildered when he said, "After the way she snubbed you in church, I thought you would have moved on to another woman by now."

"I'm stubborn in my old age, ain't I?"

Darius scratched his head. "My wife had suggested you might take an interest in Mrs. Makepiece instead."

He was amused, remembering what Rebecca had said to him in the gig. Clearly the Book Club Belles had come up with this idea between them. "That's kind of Mrs. Wainwright to think of me."

"Well, don't stay out here too long in the cold." His brother had turned to go back inside when Luke stopped him.

"I know she means well, Darius. Your wife has been very kind to me. Very welcoming. I did not expect it. She's made me feel at home."

Darius still looked unsure, puzzled. "You're family, Lucius. *We're* family."

But Luke had never felt as if he belonged anywhere before. It took some getting used to. He wiped his brow on his sleeve. "If you want it made official…since it's Christmas and I have nothing else to give, let the relinquishment of my inheritance be my gift to you both." Luke gave his brother a quick smile. "You just find work for me, keep me busy, and I'll manage."

Darius took a step toward him and then stopped, frowning. "I don't know what to say."

"Then say naught. We don't have to, do we? Too many words are wasted, if you ask me." Actions were what counted to Luke, not words.

Slowly his brother nodded. He looked quietly pleased.

"Not going to start weeping on me, are you?" Luke exclaimed warily.

Darius stood straighter. "Certainly not."

"Thank the Lord for that." He went back to shoveling the manure.

After muttering another warning not to stay out too

long, and not knowing what else to say, it seemed, his brother finally went back inside.

Once Darius was gone, Luke stopped a moment and reached into the pocket of his waistcoat. He'd found a necklace that day while cleaning out Sir Mortimer's bed to put down fresh straw. At first he'd thought about handing it over to Darius, but he was entitled to keep something, surely. Evidently they didn't even know about the necklace. Anyone careless enough to lose such fine jewelry in a pig sty didn't deserve to keep it.

He'd briefly conferred with Sir Mortimer on this matter and received the response of a complaisant grunt, which solidified Luke's decision to keep his find.

That rarely troubled conscience so easily soothed, he slipped the ruby and pearl necklace back in his waistcoat pocket and resumed the work at hand.

A half hour later, Sarah and Ness came out to find him too. "Uncle Darius says you're at a loose end this afternoon and that you need something to occupy you."

"You have something in mind, young lady?"

"I do," she said proudly. "You ought to come to the book society meeting with me."

"Books?" He sniffed.

"Miss Sherringham will be there," she said with an innocent smile, having saved her best card for last.

Twenty

As they reached the end of another chapter, the doorbell rang out and Diana got up to answer it, passing the book to Becky, whose turn it was to read next. Moments later, Diana reentered the room with Sarah Wainwright in tow. And the colonel.

Instantly all the ladies sat up straighter, even Elizabeth, who finally closed her magazine. Becky's pulse quickened. She had expected Charles, and here instead was his opposite. Midnight had come instead of the sun. And now, if Charles arrived, there would be an eclipse. Luke would give her one of those dark looks, and Charles would tease her about that "engagement." Oh, why on earth had she extended an invitation to Mr. Clarendon?

"I hope you don't mind," Sarah exclaimed, "but the colonel was grumpy as a bull with a sore head this afternoon. Uncle Darius said he ought to come out."

"I was told the book club is for ladies only," he mumbled, shooting Becky an apologetic glance, "but Sarah was adamant I should come with her."

He was immediately welcomed by everybody, his

she was quite sure there was a logical explanation, and a devious man behind the deception.

❧

When Ham Lady entered the parlor with a tray, she brought with her a little chilly air and a general quieting. Rather as if she were a schoolmistress and the women thought she had come to punish one of them. But then they saw what she brought, and after a moment of wary silence, bouncy young Ringlets cried, "Lord, we never usually get wine before the hunt!"

Luke had stood as the woman entered, but she set her tray down and urged him to take his seat again. The Madeira bottle chinked against his glass as she poured with an unsteady hand, squinting hard. "I would have brought tea, but my best silver spoons have gone missing. In any case, it is Christmas Eve. No harm in a little celebration. Do have some cake, Colonel. It is my best recipe."

When Ringlets, Ham Lady, and Clarendon's sister all beamed his way at the same time and the room fell silent with anticipation, he actually looked around to see if someone else was standing behind his chair. So many eyelashes fluttered that he felt the breeze on his face.

Now he began to feel uneasy. He thought he'd just heard Rebecca give one of her wry little snorts.

"Thank you, madam." He took the plate of cake and they all stared, waiting for him to try a bite. No one else, it seemed, would get their slice until he'd tried his. Only when he'd swallowed some and pronounced it "delicious" was the rest of it cut and served.

While the others clustered around Mrs. Makepiece

novelty presence breathing new life into the little parlor. The other ladies fussed and flitted around him like hens around a new cockerel. Justina pulled out a dining chair from the table by the window. Diana even lit two extra candles without first running to ask her mother for permission.

The colonel flipped out the tails of his borrowed jacket and perched tentatively on the fragile old chair. "I did not mean to disturb your reading. Please continue." He sat with his bad leg out straight, his cane resting beside it. "Please don't let my presence bother you." Becky caught the sharp edge of a quick, cutting glance in her direction. "Forget I'm here. 'Tis easily done."

Catching a slight odor of manure, Becky glanced at his boots. Mrs. Makepiece was not going to be pleased about *that* on her faded carpets.

Elizabeth Clarendon slid closer to the group, venturing away from her cozy spot, drawn out enough at last to show interest in something other than her own warm feet.

"My brother reminded me, Colonel, that you are one of *the* Wainwrights of Mayfair." As the young woman simpered and fanned herself with that tattered copy of *La Belle Assemblée*, she claimed a new seat between Diana and the colonel—a chair she'd previously declined, exclaiming it to be too hard and narrow and the creaky leg too uncertain to bear her slight weight. Now, apparently, it would do. "I believe you once knew our elder brother, Colonel."

"Really? I don't think so." He snapped it out so quickly, Becky looked at him, just when she'd made up her mind not to.

Elizabeth exclaimed, "Yes, Charles remembered today after church. You knew our brother Christopher. Everyone calls him Kit. He would be about your age perhaps."

"I could not say," he muttered, fidgeting so that the little chair creaked.

Since this line of questioning had gotten her nowhere, Elizabeth found another. "I hear that you were thought lost for many years, Colonel," she went on. "Yet here you are back again to claim your rightful…place in society."

"Whatever place that might be," he grumbled dourly.

Elizabeth fanned herself harder with that magazine. "I do hope you will be joining us this evening for the treasure hunt, Colonel."

"I—"

"Of course, you must," Justina cried. "We need you to make an even number, and my husband flatly refuses to play. He claimed to have some other important errand tonight."

"I will be pleased to join in," he said, not looking at Becky. "But only if I am needed."

Elizabeth was uncharacteristically animated. "You are needed! It's always much more fun to have another man around. I thought I would have to put up with my brother's company since there seems to be a shortage of gentlemen here."

Amusement pricked, Becky watched the formerly icy Miss Clarendon slowly and drippily thawing all over the most unlikely of men.

The colonel smiled in a stiff, unnatural way,

suggesting his breeches were too constricting or he'd swallowed a cricket ball.

Well, good, thought Becky, *let Elizabeth occupy the man, if she wants him*. In any case, he did not smile at Elizabeth the way he did at *her*. Not that it should matter to her at all how he smiled at anyone. What did she care?

Justina had come over to whisper in her ear, "Do you think he came for Mrs. Makepiece? Better her than a Clarendon."

Not waiting for any reply, Justina continued on her way to Sarah, where she apparently had something of great importance to mention about the girl's bonnet.

Suddenly the parlor door was nudged open and Diana's mother came in with a tray of fruit cake, marzipan, and Madeira wine.

"I thought you would like a little Christmas cheer, girls," she said. And then, "Oh, good evening, Colonel Wainwright!"

She almost managed to look startled enough, but she was wearing her best earbobs and had removed her apron—both things she would never have done if her parlor held only females that evening. It was evident she'd heard the colonel's voice.

It occurred to Becky then, with a slightly sick feeling, that perhaps Justina would make a success of her mission and find the colonel another bride to make him settle down. One bride or another.

He had not lost his seductive powers, clearly. They worked in mysterious ways, but that didn't mean she would ever be affected by his magic. Just like that automaton her father had read about in the newspaper,

and her cake, Luke took the opportunity of addressing Rebecca without the others hearing. He moved his chair closer to where she sat and said softly, "I would advise you, Miss Sherringham, to use caution in the presence of Charles Clarendon. He is not all that he appears or that he would no doubt have you think him."

"Really?" she exclaimed under her breath. "You don't mean to tell me that men sometimes lie and deceive, do you, Lucky Luke?"

Might have known she would never pay heed to him. "Don't get your garters in a twist. Unless, of course, you want me to untwist 'em."

"Then say what you came over here to say."

"Master Clarendon is like Willow Tree Farm, that place by the river."

"In what way?"

"Pretty to look at, but needs a lot of work inside."

"What are you two whispering about?" Sarah demanded, coming to stand by his chair.

He groaned inwardly. "How best to manage naughty eavesdropping children," he muttered. "Fetch me another slice of cake, will you?"

Sarah glowered at him, hands on her waist. "What do we say, Colonel?"

"Make haste, damn you, or I'll take a strap to you?"

Still she waited, lips puckered as a cat's backside.

"*Please*," he added eventually.

"That's better!" The girl's eyes gleamed. "And I am not a child." With a hearty sigh, she took his empty plate and walked away to the tray around which the others had converged like gannets.

"Did you come here this evening just to warn me about Mr. Clarendon?" Rebecca whispered sharply.

"Certainly not. I came to see what the ladies of the book society get up to. I told you, I like books. Can't get enough of 'em." He looked at her soft, sensual lips and thought about kissing her again. Right there in that parlor, in full view of her friends. What was he saying? He'd lost track of his thoughts. "Can't...get enough of 'em."

"Here you are, Colonel," Sarah chirped. "Cake."

He took the slice from the girl, and as she turned her back to say something to Ringlets, he slipped it into his coat pocket for Ness. When he caught Rebecca's eye again, she was watching his hands and she had that same thoughtful look he'd seen in church that morning. "Stupid dog will sulk if I don't share," he mumbled.

"Mrs. Makepiece won't appreciate you feeding your dog with her best recipe, Colonel."

"I won't tell her if you don't." He smiled.

"You're fonder of that dog than you admit."

"Fond? *Fond?* We just stumbled over each other is all."

Again the thoughtful look.

"As you and I did, Rebecca."

Abruptly the bell rang out and there was no chance to talk further in private. Another guest had arrived. The younger, potentially even more dangerous version of Kit Clarendon. Luke flexed his fingers slowly and let them rest on his thighs. Rebecca, he noted, was on the edge of her chair already, biting her lip with anxiety, as if she could not wait to greet the other man.

"Ladies, I am late for your book society. Can you ever forgive me?" Charles grinned like an ass at Rebecca, who instantly got up, flushed, dropping her book to the carpet. "At least I am still on time for the hunt," he exclaimed.

So Master Clarendon had also been invited to join the ladies tonight, and there was no doubt as to who had issued the invitation. Yet she had told Luke that men were not permitted in their club. She might as well have punched him in the gut. Or shot him with that officer's pistol.

He looked at her, but she avoided his gaze. Slowly he bent and picked up the book she'd dropped. Then he shifted his chair back to where it had been, needing the distance between them to let his temperature cool.

Clarendon's sister came to his side again, popping up so unexpectedly and unwontedly that he almost jumped out of his shirt. "I do hope we shall be on the same team for the treasure hunt," she whispered in Luke's ear. Her strong perfume swept into his nostrils, thick and suffocating.

By the window, Rebecca and the younger Clarendon were already lost in deep conversation, sharing a private joke perhaps. He couldn't tell; she had her back to him.

Sarah dashed from behind his chair, squeezing between Luke and the Clarendon woman, shouting that she wanted to draw the teams for the treasure hunt.

"Gracious, your little sister is eager, Colonel. She almost dislodged me from my seat."

Luke replied gruffly, "Sarah's my daughter, Miss Clarendon. Not my sister."

"Your *daughter?*"

"So I was informed."

"Oh. I...did not know you were ever married."

"I wasn't."

She paused the flapping of that rolled-up magazine under her chin but then resumed the action at a slower, more graceful pace. "Well, she is certainly a dear little thing."

"Indeed." Luke smirked, wondering how "dear" Sarah would be if the woman knew she was her brother Kit's by-blow.

Again he glanced over at Gingersnap and her gilded companion. They were clearly a couple, lost in each other and isolated from the rest of the participants.

He still held her book in his hands and he turned it over to read the title. *Sins and Sinfully—*

No. He stopped and read again, more carefully.

Sense...Sense and Sensibility. Well, so much for that story, whatever it was about.

All was forgotten now that Charles Clarendon had come. Ham Lady fussed over the new arrival too, pushing a second slice of her dry cake at the shiny fool, while he laughed with crumbs in the corner of his spoiled lips.

Luke flicked through the pages of the book, trying to get his thoughts and feelings in order. They were all new, all unexpected, all painful. He needed a guidebook to follow.

The book fell open on a page and he struggled to read, but the words blurred and swam like tadpoles. He snapped it shut.

"I can tell you how it ends," Clarendon's sister

whispered in his ear. "Save you the trouble of reading. It's a very dull and stupid story."

"I know how it ends. The hero gets the girl and the villain gets his comeuppance."

"Well, yes." She laughed and placed her hand on his arm. "How clever you are, Colonel."

But villains sometimes tried to change. Was it too late for him?

Twenty-one

As Sarah drew each name from her hat and shouted them out with an extraordinary amount of excitement, the couples formed pairs around her, each team handed a list and a basket.

To Becky's horror, her name was called with the colonel's. He had shot her such a bleak, angry look when he saw Charles Clarendon that she felt her heart stop for a moment. It was a look of disappointment and something more. She was certain he would lecture her again as soon as they were alone.

"Your friend looks very grim again tonight," Charles whispered, his eyes laughing. "Is he sick? At his advanced years, he must suffer maladies to which we are yet immune. What do you suppose is the cause of his limp? Does he have a wooden leg?"

"No, he does not have a wooden leg," she replied, tense.

"Something is amiss with my jolly Miss Sherringham tonight. She seems out of sorts. Is it because I was late for the book reading? I see I must make it up to her."

She knew her mood *was* unsettled. And he had

been so keen when she told him about the book society. Yet he had not bothered to come on time, and the scent of hops on his breath told her why he was late leaving the tavern. Luke, on the other hand, had come to the meeting even with no interest in books.

It was not the way it should be and she did not care for surprises.

Charles was paired with Lucy. "Ah, the sweetly amusing and rather giddy Miss Bridges," as he called her. When Elizabeth Clarendon was paired with young Sarah, her face was a picture of disappointment. Justina and Diana were the final couple drawn.

"We will meet at the major's house in one hour," cried Justina. "And the couple with the most items found will be declared the winners."

Lanterns were distributed, and one by one, the couples left the cottage, heading off on their hunt.

"Come on then," Becky muttered peevishly to the colonel, hooking her wicker basket over one arm. "We may as well get on with it."

The colonel, however, was preoccupied thanking Mrs. Makepiece profusely for her cake and hospitality. He lingered so long in the hall that they were the last pair to leave, and she began to think it was deliberate. As Becky finally got him out the door, she exclaimed sourly, "I hope you're not going to lecture me about Charles again."

He looked somber. "No."

They passed through the gate and his silence was heavy; it seemed unnatural to her and yet it shouldn't be. The first time she met him, he greeted her with grumpy, stern silence meant to intimidate her. "Well," she exclaimed briskly, "you were awfully chatty to Diana's mother. Are you trying to seduce her now too?"

"Of course. Can't help myself, can I? Besides, you did recommend her to me."

She stopped on the path. "So you've given up on our wager?"

Rather than a straight answer, he snapped, "You know how men are. Especially men like me. What do *you* think?"

"I think she's perfect for you. I wish you joy."

He smirked. "She told me I reminded her of her dearly departed husband."

Rebecca huffed scornfully. Mrs. Makepiece seldom talked of Diana's ne'er-do-well father, had never before referred to him as "dear" anything. She stopped grinding her teeth and said, "Well, she married for love the first time and look where that got her. She's making her daughter marry for money, so why wouldn't she? I daresay the Wainwright fortune would be inducement enough for her to overlook anything."

"Are you forgetting all this manliness too? I may not be as pretty as young Master Clarendon, but at least in a dimly lit alley, I'd never be mistaken for a woman."

She groaned and thrust the lantern into his hand. "Here, carry this and make yourself useful at least." *Better keep those hands of his occupied*, she thought.

Under that swaying light, she eyed the list of items on the treasure hunt list and immediately became annoyed with Justina's husband for coming up with it.

"A knave? Ha," she turned to Luke, "you can be ours."

"See? I have saved you valuable hunting time already."

Becky read on. "A childhood toy...oh, Lord, I haven't any, and I don't suppose you—"

"You haven't any left from your childhood?"

She shook her head, further irritated. "There was no time for toys and games. I always had too much else to do."

He said nothing to this, but a heavy exhale of breath clouded around his mouth in the crisp evening air. It was dark already and the little blobs of lantern light, leading the other players off on their quest, scattered across the common in all directions. Becky examined her list again.

"A blooming flower?" she exclaimed. "In December?" Exasperated, she read on: "A sign of royal gratitude? Berries that bring peace? A baby bird yet to chirp? How on earth are we supposed to find that? Oh, I hate this stupid game. I wish I'd never agreed to play it."

Lucky Luke calmly passed her the lantern and took the list in exchange. "Let me worry about the list and you carry the lantern. May as well make *yourself* useful at least."

She scowled.

"You're looking at it too literally, Miss Sherringham. But I remember, the first time we encountered each other, you told me you didn't care for riddles. You prefer straightforward answers."

Becky was surprised he remembered that. "Yes," she sullenly replied. "I am excellent at solving problems— but real ones. Not these silly riddles. This is all so pointless, just as Miss Elizabeth Clarendon said. To be running about in the bitter cold for no reason, like children. That is the strangest list ever. I cannot believe Mr. Wainwright compiled it."

"But you play because your friends enjoy it and you want to be a part of the festivities. You want to fit in here. Arrogant Miss Clarendon has no desire to do that, since she views the people here as less than herself, unworthy of her presence."

She flicked another wary glance up at his face, but he was studying the list on the paper, not looking at her.

"Hold the lantern up, please. You're waving it all over the place. My poor, misty old eyes need the light to read."

With a loud huff, she lifted it higher and used both hands to steady it.

"And now you are angry, madam, not at this list, but because you have to play with me instead of Mr. Charles Clarendon. You have been waiting for his return to Hawcombe Prior and that is why you are so anxious to be rid of my wicked attentions."

She gasped. "I have not sat around waiting for him. Who told you that? Justina, I suppose."

Finally his gaze moved from the list to her face. "No. You told me so with your actions. You're very self-conscious, trying hard to be ladylike around him." He cleared his throat. "You don't have to try with me, you know."

For a moment, she was lost in that dark heat again, but Becky was determined not to drown in it. She was a strong swimmer and had learned at a young age when her brother threw her into a lake. "Oh…do get on with the list, Colonel. Diana's mother watches us from her parlor window, no doubt."

So they walked on.

"What do you mean by saying I take the list too literally?" she demanded. "What other way should it be taken?"

He smiled a little. A very little. He seemed saddened suddenly, she thought. Deflated somehow. "A baby bird yet to chirp? Perhaps one not yet born?"

"What are you rattling your teeth about?"

"Do you keep hens, Miss Sherringham?"

"Yes, of course!"

He turned his head to look down at her again and almost got hit in the eye as her lantern swung. "An egg, Miss Sherringham," he explained.

She sniffed. "Oh. I knew that."

Luke chuckled dourly, folding the list and slipping it into his coat pocket. "Since your usually sharp mind is clearly blunted by calf-love for Master Clarendon, I can see I had better solve the riddles tonight. Just try not to knock me out with the lantern."

∼≪≫∼

He was supposed to be behaving himself, so he tried not to look at her too often as she marched at his side, huffing and puffing.

"What about the other things on the list?" Rebecca exclaimed, swinging the lantern on its tall hook again so that it narrowly missed his head and the flame wavered drastically inside the glass. There was a broken pane on one of the four sides and this made the light flicker, constantly on the verge of being extinguished. "What about the childhood toy?"

"Easy. We'll make one." He took a knife from

his pocket. "Just need a good piece of wood. Not too large."

"Sam Hardacre always has scraps thrown out with the sawdust. He keeps it in a barrel in his yard."

"Excellent."

She led him to the carpenter's cottage, where they retrieved a palm-sized piece of scrap wood. Luke set his cane aside and whittled the spare scrap quickly into a horse, much to her evident surprise and reluctant delight. She looked at his hands as if she would not have believed it had she not witnessed his skill with her own two eyes.

"That's two down," he said, placing the horse in her basket.

"Two?"

"I'm the knave, remember? You said so."

She shrugged. "Very well then." They walked on. "I don't suppose you can pluck a blooming flower out of Sam Hardacre's barrel too? Not even the parson's sturdy rose bushes can produce buds in December."

"You surprise me, Miss Sherringham, with your lack of ingenuity. But I suppose a person lost in the throes of passion cannot see beyond the face of their beloved."

"You are determined to annoy me."

He stopped on the path. "The blooming flower is you, of course."

She drew back, her face aghast at the idea. "Me? Don't talk nonsense!"

"The fairest flower in the garden." It was true, he thought suddenly. She had never looked prettier than she did tonight. But she didn't like him admiring her;

it made her flustered and uneasy, so he should not have said that. A proper gent would never make a lady uneasy. He cleared his throat. "Now for the berries that bring peace," he said briskly. "I believe we can find those in my brother's orchard."

"In winter?"

He laughed. "Just follow me, doubter. I know what we're looking for." Luke had a feeling she was merely being difficult because he was her partner. Her enthusiasm for the game had noticeably waned the moment they were paired up.

They walked up a slight hill toward the manor house. Luke became aware of her slowing down for his limp. It meant that she bumped into him occasionally. He didn't mind it at all. Suddenly she said, "Justina mentioned that you mean to work for the family business now you're returned."

Ah! Polite conversation. Another test. "Yes," he said, ducking smartly to miss the swaying lantern once more.

"Are you sure that will suit you?"

"In what way?"

She looked down at the snowy ground. "I cannot quite picture you at a desk like the one Mr. Wainwright has in his study."

"I'll manage."

"But even with your—" She gestured with her free hand at his leg. "Somehow it seems as if you ought to be doing something more active."

"Such as?"

She lifted one shoulder. "I couldn't say, Colonel."

"As you pointed out, I'm an old cripple. What can I do?"

Rebecca gave an impatient sigh that blew a stray copper lock out of her face. "I never called you that."

"Funny, I seem to recall those very words from your lips. Before you demanded that I kiss you." Oops, it was probably not gentlemanly to remind her. Too late.

She bit her lip worriedly. He expected her to shout at him again for that, but she didn't. "Jussy says your brother is pleased to have you back again."

His sister-in-law must have discussed him at length with Rebecca.

Before he could say anything, she blurted, "Is it true that you once stole his sweetheart?"

No point denying it. She liked him to be straightforward. "Yes. An error of my youth. I was home on leave from the army when I met Dora. She was the daughter of my brother's tutor. I didn't know he had feelings for her. Of course he never discussed such matters with me, nor did I encourage him to do so." He grimaced. "I only learned afterward that he was thinking of proposing to the girl."

"And what happened?"

It might feel good to confess to her, he realized. Darius hadn't wanted to hear the full story, but this was his chance to unburden it. He wanted to be honest with this woman. She claimed she wasn't afraid of anything, didn't she?

"Dora was after me for the Wainwright fortune. Not the first or the last woman to try with Lucky Luke. But apparently she'd chased after my brother first, before she realized I was the one who would inherit everything. Poor Darius was swiftly forgotten. Assuming I'd seduced her on purpose, he wouldn't speak to me. My father was the same. They closed ranks against me and I, left on the outside, thought it best that I stay there. Out of the way."

She stared ahead, pensive, her breath puffing out little white clouds. "What about Dora?"

"Oh, she spent her way through my pockets, and when I assured her that I wasn't going back home to make peace with my father just for the sake of the money, she hastily found a better prospect. I'm afraid my army pay did not appeal to her; she had finer tastes than I could afford."

She nodded, her lips sucked inward as she absorbed his story.

"Is there anything else you wish to ask me about?" he prompted. "We have few chances to be alone together. We ought to make the most of this opportunity." He sighed heftily. "I'll let you ask me questions, I suppose. Just this once, mind, woman. Don't make a habit of it."

For a moment, she hesitated and then blurted again, "What about your harem?"

"My *harem*?" He squinted.

"The ladies who habitually followed you about. Mrs. Kenton says there were hundreds of women."

"Hundreds, eh?" He whistled low, shaking his head.

"Is that all you have to say?" she demanded, almost dropping the lantern, getting her temper up again.

He eyed her in bemusement. "There were women in my past, yes. A man's got to find some relief."

"But women are supposed to remain chaste until they marry," she snapped. "The world is unfairly biased against women."

"That ain't my fault too, is it?"

"And what about Sarah's mama?" she demanded.

Now he paused, took a breath. Here he must proceed carefully. If he told her everything, she might tell Charles and that would put little Sarah in danger. Rebecca might not mean to tell, but when her temper was up, she had a tendency to explode with sparks that she couldn't restrain. He'd seen it and felt their heat several times now.

"Sarah's mama was a merry lady and a very good friend. She did not know an easy life. Not the sort of life you and your friends enjoy, Miss Sherringham. She couldn't read or write, but she *was* clever in her own way. And like you," he glanced down at her as she held the swaying lantern and frowned up at him, "she was averse to the idea of marriage. Liked to look after herself."

"Would you have married her then, if she wanted you to?"

"I...do not know what I would have done."

"But Sarah is your child."

What else could he say, with the Clarendons breathing down his neck? For the little girl's sake, he lied. "Yes. She is my daughter."

Rebecca frowned and looked away again. They were now within sight of the manor house gates and there was a twinkling light ahead of them, proving that another couple had got there first, obviously having the same idea as Luke.

"Make haste, Miss Sherringham," he muttered, pointing with his cane. "I don't like to lose!"

Twenty-two

BECKY PUSHED OPEN THE GATE AND LUKE LURCHED after her. "Which direction to the apple trees? We'll find mistletoe growing there, I'm sure."

Now she realized what the clue "*Berries that bring peace*" meant. As he'd teased her earlier, Becky's mind was working at a slow pace that evening, but he was wrong to think Charles the cause. She was consumed with thoughts of *him*, not Charles. Trying to make sense of this man who she thought she understood.

Oh dear—mistletoe—he wouldn't try to kiss her again, would he? He did say they should make the most of this opportunity.

At least his company on the walk had been interesting and informative. When he wasn't trying to show off for her, not trying to use his charm on her, he was quite…tolerable…company, she supposed.

She glanced down at her basket and the little wooden horse he'd made. He was very clever with that knife of his, chiseling the figure of a horse so speedily. Becky suspected he'd done that before and she wondered where, or for whom. She always admired people who were talented with their hands, but he was very casual about it.

They reached the apple trees and there, sure enough, they found mistletoe. He set the basket down and reached up into the branches, using his handy knife to sever a bunch.

"When I was young," he grunted, "there was a bower of mistletoe put up in the servants' hall below stairs."

"I suppose you captured the hapless housemaids beneath it."

"I didn't have to capture them. They hung about under it, just waiting for me to pass." He looked down at her, grinning.

Yes, she could quite imagine it. Not that she wanted to.

He continued, "Each time a kiss was taken, a berry was plucked off the bower. Then, once the berries were all gone, no more kisses could be stolen beneath it." With a deep sigh, he examined the clump of pearly berries he'd cut free. "I always thought it was a very sad sight, that empty bower of mistletoe. Meant all the jollities were over for another year."

Was it the moonlight catching his sad face that made her want to cheer it up? He looked wickedly handsome. Even youthful perhaps. "I very much doubt you waited a full year for more *jollities*," she exclaimed in a whisper.

And that was something else she couldn't explain— the sudden need to whisper. After all, who would hear them, and what did it matter if they did?

But there was another couple somewhere in the orchard, for they'd seen the lantern from a distance.

That must be the reason why she had fallen instinctively to whispering. Let the other couple struggle to find mistletoe among the moonlit trees; she would not let her voice lead them to it.

With the colonel's arms reaching overhead again for more mistletoe, he seemed even taller and she, standing beside him, felt very small, awestruck by his powerful musculature. She had forgotten the faint odor of manure on his boots, for that was overcome by masculine sweat and something else. Lemons and sage? Perhaps Sarah had attempted to douse him in scent before they came out that evening. Poor Sarah. Hers was an uphill task, but she was quite a stubborn little thing.

As he handed the mistletoe down to her, Becky plucked one of the berries from the cluster. "I daresay you want a kiss from me now," she whispered. "The way you used to take them from those housemaids."

Surely that was why he told her the story.

But he looked startled when the berry rolled into his palm from her fingers.

"You may have just one," she added, pert. "It is Christmas, and Jussy assures me it's the season of good will to all men. Even you."

"Even me, eh?"

Becky nodded. Despite the cold air, she was rather hot. And looking up at his mouth was making her hotter.

A sudden gust of wind blew through the broken pane of glass and the lantern flame went out, leaving them in moonlight. Her pulse was speeding recklessly, just as it was when he tickled her palm and raced the gig with her in it. Just as it had when he kissed her before.

"One berry to make *our* peace," she said.

"I would like that. I don't want us to be at war, Rebecca." Whenever he said her first name, it made her throat feel tight, as if something lurked there waiting to fly out. She was rarely called "Rebecca" these days unless she'd done something wrong and had to be reprimanded. Or unless they were being formal in Mrs. Makepiece's house, of course.

"But I'm not going to kiss you again," he said softly.

She thought she'd misheard. Had he not told her that they should make the most of this time alone?

"Like I warned you at the party, Miss Sherringham," he muttered, "you'll get no more kisses like that from me, until our wedding night."

She knew her mouth had fallen open, but if anything came out, she didn't hear it.

"I'm a gentleman now," he added, with just a hint of smugness. "Gentlemen don't kiss young ladies on their lips." His hand moved through the darkness and he pressed a finger to her upper lip, bringing it down to meet the lower. "Proper gentlemen. Like me."

She could taste his skin on her lips. Appalled, she stared through the shifting moonlight as that breeze rattled the branches above them and cast shadows across his face.

"That is what you said you wanted," he reminded her. "A gentleman."

⁓

She could not hide her disappointment. It gleamed gold in those rich brown eyes. Even in the shadows and moonlight, he saw it.

Luke moved his finger from her soft, tempting lips and ran it slowly along her cheek to feel the cool, smooth skin. Except it wasn't cool as he'd expected; it was very warm. He let his knuckles play carefully over it and felt the weight of sheer need in his chest. The need to make her his.

"Damn you," she exclaimed. And just when he thought she would slap his face and run off, instead she launched herself forward, knocking him off balance until his back hit the trunk of the apple tree. She planted her mouth to his. He should have stopped it, but he didn't. Couldn't. It was years since he'd felt this aroused, this much sheer desire for a woman.

She nipped his lower lip with her teeth and then whispered breathlessly, "You like a woman with bite."

Powerless, dazed, he let her kiss him again, savagely. Her tongue swept his, tangled with it, exploring forcefully, impatiently.

Desperate to regain some control, Luke grabbed the curve of her waist. His conscience told him to push her back, to end the kiss. But he wanted every inch of her for himself. So he tugged her closer and let his hands slide downward to grip that delightfully rounded bottom hidden from him under too many layers.

Shouldn't have done that. Didn't stop doing it though. Lucky Luke was back full force, breaking through the "gentlemanly" veneer he'd tried on for her.

Now his erection pushed at her through their clothing and she slid her hand down to it. He shuddered, cupped her bottom harder, almost lifting her off her feet. Already his mind was thinking of where he might lay her down without getting too much dirt on her coat.

Christ, if she didn't protest, in a minute—

Her lips left his and Luke was left gasping for air, his eyes closed.

Don't let her win, the voice of reason shouted in his head. *She's trying to prove you can't be a gentleman. That you are still that sinner, the old Lucky.*

The cunning, slippery wench.

When Luke opened his eyes, she was gone, taking the basket with her.

❧

Running through the moon-dappled orchard, not looking where her feet landed, she tripped over a knotted tree root and fell into another pair of arms.

"There you are! I've been searching for you." Moonlight kissed his golden cherubic curls as he beamed at her. "Now we can finish the game together. Surely that grumpy old captain won't mind swapping partners. I hear one woman is much the same to him as any other."

"Colonel," she corrected breathlessly. "*Colonel*, not captain." Thank goodness he couldn't see inside her to where she was a complete and utter disordered mess. She had just touched the colonel's manhood through his breeches, felt it move and thicken against her exploring hand. She'd kissed him like a madwoman, unable to stop herself.

What was he turning her into?

"Colonel, captain. Six of one, half dozen of the other." Charles laughed merrily.

"Well, no…not at all. It's quite different."

"Ah, who cares? Come on, what have you got in your basket?"

Becky was reluctant to show Charles the contents of the basket and he had to snatch it from her to see. He looked at the wooden horse, picking it up and turning it over in his hand.

"Where did you find this? Is it yours?"

She swallowed and replied as carelessly as possible. "He made it." Taking the basket now seemed selfish. These were things he'd found and made. They did not belong to her. She was a thief, as well as a hussy.

"Very clever, I daresay. The sort of thing a man learns to do when he has idle time on his hands." Charles tossed the wooden horse back into the basket with a flip of his wrist.

"I shouldn't have taken it. Really, it's his. So is the mistletoe. He solved the riddle." She took the basket back from Charles and looked over her shoulder into the dark orchard, wondering where Luke was.

"Lord, I'm cold!" Charles exclaimed. "Let's go back to your father's house at once for that hot chocolate I was promised."

"But we haven't found all the things on the list." In truth, she'd forgotten the weather. She looked down at her basket, forlorn. Lucky Luke had been her knave, and he had said she was his flower.

Foolish man. What a thing to say to her. She was the most unflowerlike woman that ever lived in Hawcombe Prior. Everyone told her she was a tomboy. They put her in breeches to play all the male parts in the play, and when she joined cricket games on the common, no one liked standing up to bat if she was bowling.

"Where is Lucy?" she asked, finally remembering that Charles was supposed to have a partner.

"Oh, I expect the captain has sniffed her out by now. They can finish the hunt together and bore each other instead of us, eh?"

"Colonel," she corrected him again. "Not captain."

She thought of Lucy and her proud bosom possibly distracting Lucky Luke in the moonlight. It did not make her feel any better, despite the fact that she was resolved not to be sorry, not to regret kissing him like that and stealing the things he'd found. A man like Luke would not care about the rules of any game, so why should she?

Luke saw the other woman standing with her lantern, calling out rather feebly for young Master Clarendon. Then he knew at once where his own partner had gone after kissing him and fleeing into the moonlight.

As he limped through the orchard to join the abandoned young lady, he raised his free hand to his mouth and felt for a bite mark. He was surprised she didn't draw blood. She, it seemed, was hungry tonight.

So was he.

Desire shuddered through his body, through his veins like a potent elixir. But somehow he must conquer it, because he was trying to follow the rules for once.

Ringlets-and-Rouge didn't know she'd been

deliberately spurned but assumed she'd simply gotten lost in the dark orchard. Luke, therefore, was her rescuer and she did everything but swoon into his arms.

"Come on, Miss Brook. Let us find our way to the major's house."

"It's *Bridges*," she exclaimed, her delight at being rescued turning quickly to irritation. "Lucy Bridges! Sometimes I think I might as well not be here. No one pays attention to me!"

He laughed softly. "My poor Miss Bridges! Come take this old lame fellow's arm and we will lament together at being mistreated."

She pouted. "I'm quite sure you were never overlooked, Colonel." But she took his arm and they walked on together.

"Tell me about Miss Sherringham and Charles Clarendon."

The young lady was pleased to do so, telling him all about Rebecca's list of attributes required in a husband and how Clarendon fulfilled them all. "I'm quite sure she would marry him had he asked her. Some said it was only a matter of time. But then you came along, of course, Colonel. And now no one knows what to think."

He sighed, for he was suffering much the same bewilderment.

What he really needed to do was get a look at that list of hers.

Twenty-three

THE PLAYERS GATHERED IN MAJOR SHERRINGHAM'S parlor where he had the merry job of judging the results after several glasses of his favorite port had been consumed. Justina and Diana had brought an egg, mistletoe, a childhood doll, the flower from a bonnet, and a knave from a pack of cards. They would have been declared the winners, but then Sarah returned with an unusually disheveled Elizabeth Clarendon and they had all the items on the list.

Much to Luke's alarm, his daughter had completed her treasure trove with something the others had not found—a sign of royal gratitude.

She took it from her basket and set it down before the major with a proud flourish. "My father's medal," she said. "For services to crown and country. I think that fulfills the requirement."

Every face now turned to Luke, most in open amazement.

"I found it in my uncle's desk drawer," Sarah explained, smug. "Which I know is where you told him to keep it. And when I went through your knap-sack, I also found this." She took the last item from her basket and unfolded it. "A knave."

There, laid on the table beside his medal, was the playing card across which he had written, *Gyngersnappe Ohs Lucky Wonne Kisse.*

Now they all looked at it, all read it. He had no idea how many of those present would put the pieces together.

So that was where Sarah had seen the name "Lucky."

He dared not look at Rebecca's face. After their kiss in her kitchen, he'd taken the card with him, kept it with his belongings. Would she mock him for that? Her scorn could be fairly withering.

He grabbed the card and slipped it into his pocket, but the major had already picked up the medal to admire it and the others gathered around to do the same.

"Why, 'tis the sultan's medal," the old man said, turning it over to show the eight-pointed star and crescent moon.

"All a long time ago," Luke muttered.

"You should be proud of it," exclaimed Sarah. "Why hide your medal?"

Because it was not something he wanted to talk about, and he'd asked Darius, upon his return, not to speak of it. His brother had tried to hand the medal over to him, but he didn't want to look at it. He did not want to be rewarded for surviving when many good fellows with loving families at home had died horrifically. The fact that he—a man for whom no one much cared—had lived to be given a medal on a ribbon seemed somehow ridiculous.

"Some paid for these with their lives," was all he could say to the waiting party in the major's parlor.

The fire crackled in the hob grate, and he felt Miss Sherringham's eyes staring. Everyone looked, of course. But he felt her curious gaze the most, and her silence seemed deafening. For the first time in his life, he actually wished for a woman to speak. She did not, however. And what did he want her to say, in any case?

Again the room fell respectfully but awkwardly silent, until Miss Clarendon cried impatiently, "It would seem we have won then, as we have the most items from the list!"

Her brother rubbed his hands together and added cheerily, "Where *is* that hot chocolate we were promised?"

Eventually the major was prompted to declare the Clarendon woman and Sarah winners of the treasure hunt.

Luke took Sarah to one side. "I hope you know that one should not go prying in another man's belongings. Certain things are not your business, young lady."

"Why not? You're my father, which means that everything about you is my business. I know who Gingersnap is and I'm sure they can all guess. Sakes, here comes that awful Miss Clarendon. I tried to lose her a few times in the hedgerows, but she trailed me like a foxhound. Even when I led her through a muddy ditch and she got her boot stuck, I thought she would give up, but no such luck." She tucked a curl behind her ear. "It seems Miss Sherringham had more success at being rid of you. After all the trouble I went to, you let her fall into *his* clutches."

She shook her head. "Tsk, tsk. What am I to do with you?"

He began to suspect that Sarah had more than a little influence over the proceedings of that evening, from the choosing of names out of a bonnet to the writing of those lists. She had inherited her mama's cunning.

As if she read his mind, she laughed. "Oh, don't fuss, Papa!" *Papa.* It was feeling less strange already to hear her say it.

Once the hot chocolate was brought in, Luke edged toward the parlor door and slipped out into the dimly lit hall. Now where would a woman keep such a list as that one Rebecca supposedly maintained of manly attributes? A diary, perhaps? He couldn't negotiate the stairs with his cane without making considerable noise, so he'd start in the kitchen. After all, that was where she'd kept their playing card IOU. Taking a candle in a brass holder from the hall table, he crept along the narrow passage but had only gotten two steps when the parlor door opened and Gingersnap came out.

"Where are you going, Colonel?"

He thought quickly. "Looking for something I thought I left here."

"Oh? What?"

"A fob watch."

"I didn't see you with one." She walked toward him.

"It's gold. Costly. I'd like it back."

"I'll keep an eye out for it, of course."

He backed up. "You're not going to bite me again, are you?"

Her eyebrows arched high. "I haven't made up my mind yet."

"Haven't decided whether you like it yet?" He smiled wryly. "You shouldn't have run away while you had me cornered."

"I didn't have you cornered." She hesitated. "Did I?"

"I was at your mercy."

Apparently this idea pleased her. Her eyes shone with amusement and she bit her lip, possibly remembering the taste of that kiss.

Limping by her, he beat a retreat back to the parlor before either of them might be tempted.

∽

The Clarendon woman took his arm and almost dragged him to a chair by the fire. "What a charming daughter you have, Colonel. So very sweet. I am quite smitten with her already." She hovered over him like a nurse over a patient. "Although she did take me on quite a ramble. Mischievous creature! But I did not let her out of my sight, to be sure. I confess I thought tonight's game would be very trying on my nerves, but my spirits are brightened considerably."

"Are they?"

She barely lowered her voice and said, "Well, there is so little here to keep my interest. There is no culture here, no fashion, but I must go where my brother goes."

"You must?"

"To keep an eye on him, of course! We expect great things from Charles and he cannot be allowed to make a misstep."

When Luke glanced up, he saw the Clarendon woman staring across the room at her brother and Rebecca. "Great things, madam?" The lad looked like any other overprivileged, slack-jawed, weak-chinned, pampered youth to him.

Whatever his sister's plans and ideas, Chinless Charles seemed to have others on his mind.

Luke's mood became darker the longer he sat there.

Knowing the social climbing habits of the Clarendon family, should the grinning idiot not be using his talents on the earl's daughter at Lark Hollow, where he had supposedly been staying? Instead he was here, practicing his skills on Rebecca Sherringham.

Exactly what sort of hunting had Clarendon come here for?

❦

"So the old man is a war hero," Charles whispered. "He's rather tight-lipped about it. How many fellows do you suppose he slaughtered in battle? From what I remember, he has a violent temper—one only had to look at him the wrong way. Almost sent my brother Kit to his maker some years ago. Fighting over a woman."

Since Luke didn't want to talk of his medal, Becky had decided it was wrong for them to do so, but she couldn't stop her ears from hearing. "Which woman?"

"Who could say? He had plenty of them but always kept an eye out for those who belonged to other people. Greedy, arrogant. Thought every woman ought to be his if he took a fancy to her. Kit took exception to that, naturally, and stood up to the bully."

Becky looked over at Luke. He had confessed a great deal to her tonight and seemed almost relieved to do so. Although he'd said nothing about having brawled with Charles's brother, there remained the fact that he did have a very odd look on his face when he heard that Clarendons were expected in the village. There was also the broken nose.

"I do not like the way that fellow watches you," said Charles. "I am quite put out and feel as if I ought to slap the fellow with my glove."

She looked at him askance. "I really don't think that's necessary."

"But I will not have him trying to take you from me. I shall stand up to the boorish oaf."

Becky was bemused. "I wasn't aware that I was yours, Mr. Clarendon." In a gentler tone, she added, "We both know we can only be friends."

Now he looked saddened, but he did not reply.

"Excuse me, I must visit with the other guests." Her father was enjoying himself tonight with a party of young people filling his parlor, but he was already getting a little too rowdy and had twice bellowed at Mrs. Makepiece that she should "cheer up" and loosen her stays. Becky knew she would have to take the wine away from him before he began removing parts of his own clothing.

She was shocked, in fact, to see that Mrs. Makepiece had walked across the village to join them there for the end of the treasure hunt. The lady usually avoided gatherings at the major's house, because she found his manners boorish—and he, knowing this, took delight in being so in front of her. The fact that Major Sherringham was her landlord and yet she viewed his family as inferior to her own must be extremely galling for her. Yet tonight there she was, suffering the major's comments while she discreetly eyed Colonel Wainwright and his medal.

As Becky rose up from the window seat to perform her duties as hostess to her guests and guardian to her wayward father, Charles gripped her hand. "Bored of my company already?"

"Of course not."

"Good, because I have no plans to leave Hawcombe Prior. I am, in truth, growing inordinately fond of the place. And of the delightful young ladies who live here especially."

Becky kept her face composed, remembering that she was resolved to be ladylike. Not to roll her eyes and be scathing. Not to be "forceful" and dismissive in that dreadfully unfeminine manner.

Besides, he held her hand tightly, and if she pulled away, it would be noticeable to others.

"I am very glad you like our village." She looked over at his sister, who was talkative this evening, regaling Lucky Luke with a story about her "wretchedly wearisome" journey along winter roads to get there. If the man heard a word she said, it would be a miracle. Surrounded by ladies, he had his hands on his broad, muscular thighs, fingers splayed and tapping out a slow tattoo, while he glared fiercely across the parlor at her and Charles. "I do not think Elizabeth shares your enthusiasm for Hawcombe Prior. She must be eager to return home to your father in Oxford."

Charles snorted. "She's not in Father's good books either at the moment." He paused and his eyes clouded over, then hardened. "I mean to say, Papa is never in a pleasant mood. It is very hard to make him happy these days. We are better off out of his sight until one of us at least is back in his favor."

She thought how odd his family must be. Never had she been out of her father's favor. "And your elder brother comes here for Christmas dinner tomorrow?" It would be interesting to meet Kit Clarendon again. She could find out more about Luke's past.

"If he can tear himself away from his present company at Lark Hollow."

She caught Luke's eye again and felt the heat rise under her dress when she remembered how she had kissed him in the moonlit orchard. Somehow the kiss hadn't been enough and so she'd bitten him. It was partially frustration, to be sure. But it was mostly lust, and wonder. And something dark, hidden from her.

He was turning her into a sinner. And he was doing that while he himself sought reform. Slyly turning the tables on her.

Suddenly Charles reached over and, while she was lost in her thoughts, he captured a stray lock of hair that trickled down her neck to rest upon her shoulder. "One day you must let me cut a curl of your luscious hair, Miss Sherringham. I am quite besotted with it."

"What would you want it for?"

"So that I have a little of you with me always," he whispered, his gaze lingering on the coil of hair around his finger. "We must exchange trinkets to mark our friendship."

She laughed, brushing his hand away lightly. "Sounds rather silly to me. A piece of hair isn't much use to anybody."

"You must promise me not to flirt with Kit when he

comes," he said, placing his hand over hers on the window seat between them. "I shall explode with jealousy."

She solemnly promised that she had no intention of flirting with anybody. His blue eyes adored and entreated at the same time, fixing her immoveable in their warm rays. Again he paid no attention to the others in the room, his sunny smile for her alone.

But Becky had begun to realize that she preferred the moonlight.

Cognizant of being watched by almost every eye in the parlor, she withdrew her other hand from beneath his and laid it in her lap.

⤬

Charles Clarendon's sister had pulled up a chair to perch at Luke's side again, and for the past ten minutes had regaled him with some story about which he could not possibly care less. She was the sort of wench who complained about everything when she'd never had a true problem in her life. He eyed her for a moment, his irritation with almost everyone and everything in that room mounting rapidly. Suddenly he growled, "You're going to be disappointed, Miss Clarendon."

Her brows delicately curved, matching the arch of her little finger as she sipped her chocolate. "Disappointed? How so?"

"Whatever you've heard about me, I'm not a rich man, so you're wasting your time. I'm no more worth your attention than anyone else in this room, so go and warm your buttocks elsewhere."

Two hot spots of color rose high on her cheeks. "I beg your pardon?"

"That's why you're playing up to me and Sarah,
ain't it?"

Her eyes widened in outrage. "Well, I never in
my life—"

"Spare me the histrionics, woman. I'll save us
both the time and you the effort. I suspect you're
looking for a fellow to keep you in fancy hats and
parasols. But I've nothing to offer a wife except
a good-sized tallywag and a regular ride upon it.
Best take your wares back to Oxford and hawk
'em there."

Well, there went his intentions of keeping a gentlemanly temper.

When she finally slithered away from him, he was
relieved to take a breath without swallowing more of
her ghastly scent.

"What on earth did you say to Miss Clarendon?"
Sarah wanted to know.

"I told her the truth," he replied with an easy shrug.
"I don't think she was used to it. But I prefer a woman
with a straightforward manner." He shot a quick look
over at Rebecca, and that was when he saw Charles
touching her hand.

Bitter resentment seized him so suddenly it left
him breathless.

When Ham Lady approached a few minutes later
with some polite inquiry, he was feeling trapped in
that parlor, tired of the pretense and angry enough to
snap at her, "I heard you married for love, madam.
You should let your daughter do the same."

Her astonishment pinned her to the spot. "I *beg*
your pardon?"

"Money causes naught but misery and she's better off without it."

"My daughter's marriage is my business, Colonel," she snapped.

"It should be *hers*, madam."

Ham Lady looked as if she might require smelling salts.

"Words ain't my talent," he muttered gruffly, "so it's best for me to tell it direct."

Then, remembering there was nothing forcing him to stay and fearing he might proceed to vent with more unsavory truths, he got up with his cane and limped out of the house.

Twenty-four

Marianne began now to perceive that the desperation which had seized her at sixteen and a half, of ever seeing a man who could satisfy her ideas of perfection, had been rash and unjustifiable. Willoughby was all that her fancy had delineated in that unhappy hour...

—*Sense and Sensibility*

"We are merely friends," Becky assured Justina the next day when she and her father arrived for dinner at Midwitch.

"It looked like rather more than that yesterday evening, Becky. He completely held your attention. Everyone is talking of it. I do hope you have your wits about you."

"Charles Clarendon is a very pleasing gentleman, and I shall always think favorably of him." That, she'd decided, would be her formal response to any questions on the matter. "I have always been polite to him, as a lady is supposed to be, have I not? It is only flirting."

Justina looked anxious. "Only flirting? Well, I hope you do not put your heart at risk. Something about him seems false to me. I cannot put my finger on it. You are my dear friend, and I would not see you hurt for all the world."

Again she assured Justina that her heart was safe, and the two women walked through the hall. Before they went in to dinner, Justina wanted to show her something and diverted her through the door into the drawing room.

Her husband had bought her a delightful rosewood writing desk and surprised her with it that morning.

"This is why he could not join the treasure hunt yesterday. He stole away to Manderson to fetch it. Is he not the very best, most clever, and generous of husbands?"

Becky dutifully admired the desk, which was indeed beautiful and a thoughtful gift.

"By the by, have you seen my silver bracelet anywhere, Becky? I am quite broken-hearted to have lost it."

Becky couldn't remember the last time she'd seen her friend's bracelet. "It's very odd, for I heard Diana's mother saying that she's misplaced her cameo choker too—the one that was her grandmama's and is said to be worth a great deal of money. Oh, and the colonel told me he lost a fob watch." And now that she thought of it, the silver milk jug was missing from the dresser shelf in her own kitchen. She wasn't able to find it the night before when she made the hot chocolate after their treasure hunt.

"Oh, well!" Justina sighed sadly. "I daresay these things will come to light eventually. They can't have gone far." Then, as they left the drawing room, she took her friend's hand and said, "The colonel has given his fortune to my Wainwright, you know. Did he tell you?"

Becky was astonished. "Why would he…? Why would he tell me?"

"I just wondered if he had. He said it is his gift to us, because he has nothing else to give."

She shook her head, not sure what to make of it, but suddenly anxious.

They walked back out into the hall and assembled with the others before proceeding into the dining room. Becky took a seat at the Wainwrights' table beside her father, who was very excited about the meal, particularly the plum pudding and brandy butter. He had talked of nothing else all morning.

The colonel did not come in until they were all seated around the table. *He looks rather pale and haggard*, she thought. After murmuring a low, gruff greeting to everyone, he lurched around the table to take his seat between his daughter and his sister-in-law.

What on earth could he mean by giving up his rights? Her heart felt as if an ice-cold fist had closed around it.

Had he decided to leave? Did he give up not only his inheritance but their wager?

There was so much merry conversation that she was unable to make eye contact with him for the first two courses. But she was still very much aware of the man and every movement he made.

He hunched over his food, barely bothering to mumble a reply when anyone attempted to draw him into the conversation. One glance at his bloodshot eyes informed her of the reason. Evidently hot chocolate had not been his only tipple after the treasure hunt.

When Sarah inquired whether he had yet let Dr. Penny examine his leg—a seemingly innocuous question—Luke dropped his knife, rose from his chair, and muttered a very tight, "Excuse me."

With that, he limped rapidly, and at a slightly wayward tilt, to the dining room door. His first attempt at opening it failed due to an unsteady hand that couldn't grip the handle adequately. Then, when he did get it open, he banged his forehead on the edge of it before stumbling out and slamming it behind him. Sarah got up to follow, but her uncle forbade it and told her to finish her dinner. There was a distinct chill left in the air with the colonel's abrupt departure, and after a pause, Justina explained that he was a private man who did not like to discuss his injury.

"Apparently there are many things he doesn't like to discuss," Becky muttered, thinking of the war medal.

"Well, he is among friends and family here, for goodness sake," said Mrs. Penny. "He need not be shy with us."

The colonel did not come back to the table. His empty chair stood empty and forlorn, and then it began to feel accusatory.

Becky excused herself before the cloth was removed and the pudding brought out. She had promised Diana to be at her house within half an hour, just to pay a visit and help entertain her mother's guests—not to eat—but she could not leave Midwitch Manor without talking to Luke today.

She should, at least, wish him a merry Christmas.

A swift examination of the rooms downstairs did not reveal the missing colonel. Eventually finding her way to the kitchen, she located a packet of headache powders, dissolved them in some ginger beer, and took a glass upstairs to look for him. Someone had to check on the fool man, didn't they? He didn't look after himself.

As she ascended the grand staircase, there was a great deal of noise and merriment coming from the dining room below, so she guessed she was not missed. Not yet anyway. Her steps took her along the creaking landing. She would have listened at each door to find his, sure he'd be making some sort of noise inside. But there was no need to go spying at doors.

Something had followed her up the stairs, and as she walked along with the glass of ginger beer, Ness plodded rapidly by her, leading the way directly to a door at the end of the corridor. There the dog sat, staring up at the door handle and then looking back at her, its ears pricked.

She smiled. "Good boy."

He stood, wagged his stump, and looked again at the door, just as it swung open.

There was Luke, in his greatcoat, apparently prepared to go out.

When he saw Becky, his jaw dropped. For a moment, she thought he would slam the door shut again, so she quickened her steps.

"I brought you something for your head."

He stared, one hand gripping the door handle, the other holding his cane. "Why?"

"You do have a headache, don't you? I've taken care of my brother enough to know the signs."

"You shouldn't be up here, Rebecca. It's not"—he rubbed his temple with the handle of his cane—"proper."

"Yes, I know. And you're a gentleman now."

"Precisely."

"They're all below and no one knows I'm here. You're quite safe." She held the glass outstretched toward him. "I wanted to wish you a merry Christmas before I left."

His jaw twitched. He looked at the glass and then at her again. "You're leaving?"

"I promised Diana to join her this afternoon."

Instantly his eyes darkened, even the whites murky. His lips were pressed tight with resentment.

She looked over her shoulder to be sure no one had followed her. "May I come in?"

"What for?" he snapped.

Seeing she would have to take matters into her own hands again, she suddenly stepped forward, ducked under his arm, and walked into his bedchamber, Ness trotting after her.

He slowly turned to see where she'd gone. "I know what you're up to, woman."

"You do?" she asked jauntily. In truth, she didn't even know herself what she was doing. Perhaps he could enlighten her.

Lucky Luke remained in the open doorway. "You're trying to make me lose our wager. Coming up here to tempt me."

Relief swept her so quickly she almost dropped the glass of ginger beer. "Oh, you still mean to win then?"

"I warned you I don't like to lose."

"But I heard about the generous gift you gave your brother."

Luke sighed. He propped one shoulder against the door frame. "And you didn't believe that my intent to marry you was nothing to do with the inheritance terms. So if I didn't want the money, then I must not want you either. Is that it?"

"Yes." Her voice sounded very small and meek suddenly. Not at all like her.

"It's time you started believing and trusting in me then, ain't it?" He gestured for her to leave his room, but instead she set the glass on his mantel and walked around the bed.

"You departed the table very suddenly and left everyone to talk about you. I suppose it makes you feel important to leave us all wondering."

He said nothing.

"Mrs. Penny thinks you are shy, because you won't talk about your leg or your medal. But you are not shy, of course. You just like to be mysterious."

Still not a word. Her eyes suddenly spotted a familiar object on the table beside his bed. *Sense and Sensibility*. He must have been reading it last night, despite his dislike of books.

"You can take that back," he growled. "I don't know how it came to be in my coat pocket."

"Because you picked it up and took it."

He denied it flatly and then muttered, "Can't make head nor tails of it. Take it back to your friends."

She lifted it and held it to her breast. His eyes followed the motion and then he blinked and looked at his feet. "Will you come out of there, Miss Sherringham, before someone comes up here to find you?"

She walked back around the bed but still delayed going to the door. "Your daughter is anxious about your leg because she wants you to take her to the Manderson assemblies, you know. She wants to show you off, poor girl. She wants to dance with her father."

"How do you know?"

"Because I'm a daughter too." She stroked Ness, who had jumped up onto the bed to sit proudly before her. "I don't know what I would do without my father."

Luke's gaze lifted again, to the book she held and then to her face. "A husband doesn't have to take you away from him."

"Well, I'm sure I didn't—"

"A husband can be a help to you. Share your burdens."

This talk made her uneasy, so she left Ness and walked to the fire. It was not in use at that moment, but he had nailed a length of string from the mantel and an apple dangled from the end of it, inches above the ashes of last night's fire. "What's this?"

"A fire-roasted apple. Best midnight snack a man can have. Never had one?"

She shook her head.

"One night, I'll roast you an apple and we'll eat it together."

Like Adam and Eve, she mused. The original sinners. "Would *that* be proper?"

His eyes burned into her across that little distance. "Not until we're married."

He wasn't going to come in and shut the door, she

realized. Determined to resist temptation, he gripped that door handle so tightly that veins stood out on the back of his hand. "I'm going out to feed Sir Mortimer," he said with a strange breeziness. "Want to come?"

She scowled. "Sounds wonderful."

A brief flare of white teeth revealed his amusement at her frustration and then he turned away, whistling for Ness to follow.

Damn the man.

&

"They're having plum pudding and brandy butter," she said as they came out into the daylight. "Don't you want your share?"

He gave her a meaningful look. "I'll have my share later."

What need did he have for puddings when he had Rebecca to look at? He was inordinately pleased that she'd come to find him in his room. Although it was naughty of her, of course, and she knew it. No one had ever brought him headache powders before; they usually left him to sleep it off because they knew how ill-tempered he could get with a sore head.

Rebecca was not afraid, as she would remind him pertly.

When they arrived at Sir Mortimer Grubbins's sty, he was pleased again to see her admiring his improvements. "You've even made him a sign," she cried, looking up at the painted wooden oval hanging over the sty.

"Sarah painted it."

"Yes, I thought the spelling was too good to be yours."

He laughed. His headache was feeling better

already. "I daresay Master Clarendon has a fine hand and gets all his letters 'round the right way."

"Naturally. But it's not always the elegance of the handwriting that matters."

"Oh?" He waited to hear more, but suddenly, as if she thought she'd said something foolish, she forgot the subject and leaned over the new fence to greet Sir Mortimer instead. "This has to be the luckiest pig in Buckinghamshire."

Interrupted by a shout, both looked around to see Charles Clarendon on his horse, peering through the iron scrollwork gates.

"Looks like someone waits for you," Luke muttered. He wasn't going to get upset about it. He didn't like the sour pang of jealousy, he'd discovered, and he couldn't very well give Clarendon a thumping. Not now he was a father and a gentleman. If he wanted Rebecca to trust him, he'd have to earn it.

"I'm sorry you don't like him, but I—"

"His family has a match in mind for him already. Some earl's daughter with fifty thousand pounds. She is at Lark Hollow. His sister made sure to tell me." Blast! He hadn't meant to say all that, for it made him sound jealous, which he was not. Why should he be jealous of that boy?

Now she took umbrage again. "Why should this matter to me?"

"Perhaps I'll ask him what his intentions are, if marriage is not among them."

"You are not my father, Colonel. Even if you are old enough to be him!"

"Old enough to be your father?" He grumbled, "Only if I was an extremely precocious fifteen-year-old."

"I wouldn't put it past you!" Head high, she walked on quickly, almost running as she came to the iron gates.

"Miss Sherringham—Rebecca—wait. Please."

"I'm just having *fun*," she yelled. "You told me I should have some, didn't you?"

❧

Why did he have to try and control her? She was a woman who had enjoyed a fairly independent life, traveling with her father. Under no circumstances would she give all that up to be one of his minions, having to report all her comings and goings to him. Getting as soppy as Justina Wainwright, who couldn't even stay angry at Mrs. Kenton anymore.

Charles helped her up onto the back of his horse. "I was tired of waiting for you and decided to fetch you myself," he said.

When Becky looked back over her shoulder, she saw the colonel standing with one hand on the gate, watching them through the bars. Wind ruffled the dark hair on his hatless head and pushed the tall collar of his coat against his scarred cheek. She turned her face away, determined not to feel that ruthless tug upon her heart again. It was merely indigestion; she was convinced of it.

But then another thought occurred and she looked back once more. He was still watching. Curiously he did not have his cane with him and yet he must have walked very quickly after her along the gravel carriage drive. His tanned, rugged face was lined with agony.

❧

He watched them disappear around the bend, and then he returned to the pig sty and tossed a bucket of Christmas scraps into the beast's trough. As he stood there, getting his angry breath back, the pig nudged a fence slat with his snout until it opened. Ness ambled through the gap and the slat swung shut again. Dog and pig ate happily, side by side, a friendship formed with that mutual appreciation for good food.

If only other unlikely alliances could be so easily and simply founded, he thought sadly.

His leg burned now as if it was on fire, but as she had walked away from him, he'd had no choice but to chase after her, even when he lost his grip on the cane and it fell to the gravel. He needed her to stop, needed to catch her. That had overridden the pain. Now it was back with a vengeance.

She claimed not to want her reputation saved, and Luke had never before tried to save one. Yet he was determined to make this work.

Why? Just because he'd been seen kissing her?

Because Sarah had her heart set on it?

For his brother's approval?

Out of lust?

Or was there another reason?

He'd never spent so much damnable time thinking about a woman. One awkward, curt, untrusting wench.

Last night he'd faltered again, taken another step back from his quest for reform, drowning his frustration in brandy, alone in his room, cursing the finials of his bedposts and anything else that couldn't talk back. Ness had wisely slept under the bed last night, out of sight.

He knew he should not have said anything to her against Clarendon. That would only cause her to turn farther away from him. She took offense at anyone treating her in a concerned way because she was not accustomed to it and had lived twenty-two years with a father who merrily turned a blind eye to the dangers that awaited his lively daughter. It was worrisome that the major had been so ready to hand Rebecca over to him. Would he be so ready and careless with any other unworthy man who came along? Instead of approaching Rebecca, who would only block her stubborn ears, perhaps the best way to handle this was to have a word with her distracted father. The major ought to be made aware of certain issues developing, for he was the one man who had a right to chastise her, the one man she would listen to.

Fun. Yes, he wanted her to have plenty of that. But not with Clarendon, or any other man.

With him.

Twenty-five

BECKY POINTED OUT THE TURNING FOR THE BOLT, AND Charles slowed his horse as they passed under the arch of wintering trees.

"What was the old man babbling to you about? I saw him stumble after you to the gate."

"He wished me a merry Christmas, that's all." She felt quite winded, as if she had a stitch in her side.

Charles drew the horse to a halt, swung his leg over its head, and slipped down to stand on the yellow, trampled, and muddy grass. He held up his arms for her.

"Shouldn't we ride straight to Diana's, if I'm late?"

"I must talk to you first."

She couldn't very well urge his horse onward and leave him behind, so she slid down but avoided his waiting arms. Her own still hugged the copy of *Sense and Sensibility* to her bosom.

"We walked here the last time I came," he said.

"Yes, but the leaves are all gone now." The branches were bare, tangled, and knotted overhead, a few gaps between showing the stark winter sky.

In the summer, it was a lush canopy of emerald and gold. When Charles was last there, it had turned to autumnal colors and he had remarked upon it being just like her hair.

"This is where we kissed," he reminded her, clasping her hand.

"Let's make haste. Diana is waiting."

"You do not want to kiss me today?"

"No. Not today."

He leaned away as if she'd struck him across the face.

"I heard there is an earl's daughter at Lark Hollow and that's why you're here." Why tiptoe around the subject? She didn't have time for his flirting today.

A loud bellow made them both jump, and suddenly the narrow path was filled with cows. Charles swore under his breath as they huddled out of the way to let the herd pass. Mr. Gates brought up the rear and tipped his hat to them, shouting a "Merry Christmas."

Becky was ready to walk on, but Charles gripped her waist and spun her around. "There is always an earl's daughter somewhere. But that is why I enjoy your company. You are so different from all of them."

"You are expected to marry her?"

"Lady Olivia Moncrieff, I suppose you mean. Who told you that?"

She did not want to mention Luke. "I overheard your sister mention something."

Charles scoffed. "Eliza is impatient for either Kit or me to marry money, since she's had no luck. If one of us succeeded in catching a titled heiress, it would take Father's mind off her failures. That's why he sent us off for Christmas; lost his patience with the three of us.

But particularly with Kit, who should have provided an heir long before now."

She sighed and rubbed her arms, feeling the bitter chill of wind blowing hard down that narrow tunnel of trees. *How very mercenary it all is*, she mused darkly—this business of marriage. Yet it might also be called practical. It was the way she'd always forced herself to think, determined not to stray into romantic ideas and thinking herself above all that nonsense.

"You know that I cannot marry *you*," he added.

"Yes."

"Then what does an earl's daughter matter to us?"

He tightened his hold upon her and she feared he meant to take a kiss, but before he could do so, Mrs. Kenton appeared, her face flushed, possibly from too much festive wine. Racing down the Bolt, she saw Charles's arm around her, but she had not seen Rebecca struggling.

That infamous voice rang out in "full boom." "*Miss Sherringham!* I am shocked! You and yet another man. What excuse are you to make for this? Another boot lace?"

Furious, Becky pushed Charles away and ran, with Mrs. Kenton still shouting after her.

Charles found it all vastly amusing and he laughed uproariously, soon following Becky on horseback.

༄

Luke joined the major at the sideboard as the plum pudding was served.

"Ah, you are back with us, Colonel!" The merry

fellow smiled. "Did you take some air? You seemed in need of it."

"Yes." He looked over at the pianoforte where Sarah and Justina were playing a soft, sweet tune together. "Major, I think you ought to ask Charles Clarendon his intentions with your daughter." He kept his voice low. "It may not be my business, but I—"

"Yet you are still concerned for her?"

"I find I cannot be anything else."

The major's eyed widened. "Then you are not such the lost sinner some would paint you, Colonel."

"Hmm." He didn't know about that; he was fairly sure he had once been every bit as bad as people thought.

They listened to the music for a while and then the older man said, "My good lady wife would not have me at first either, but I persisted. Sometimes a feller must persist."

Always interested to hear more about her background, Luke perked up. "Rebecca told me her mother was a local girl. A farmer's daughter."

"Indeed she was." The major closed his eyes, savoring his pudding and his memories. "The most beautiful milkmaid I ever laid eyes upon. Hair the color of sunset. Just like my daughter's." He opened his eyes and they twinkled up at Luke, also like his daughter's. "She fancied herself in love with your great-uncle, in fact."

"*Phineas Hawke?*" *Is the major in his cups already*, Luke wondered. As far as he knew, his great-uncle had never loved anyone or anything as much as himself and his coin.

"Aye, the stinkin' rich feller that lived here in this

manor house. They had an affair one summer, but he could not marry her. His family wanted better for him and they would not accept a farmer's daughter. She was heartbroken, but I took her in and saved her from scandal. At first I believe she was merely grateful to me, thankful that I could take her far away. But I was persistent. I was patient. I cherished that woman with all my heart and she did grow to love me. We had our years of happiness together." He beamed. "So you see, there is always hope when there is love."

Luke found it difficult to imagine haughty old Phineas indulging in a love affair with a farmer's daughter, but he must have been young once, of course. There was a time when Luke did not believe *he* would ever fall in love either.

He stared at the wall over the major's head.

Was that what this was? This anxiety, this yearning, this madness that tormented him? This admiration for something more than a set of bubbies and good teeth? This need to make her his alone? Had he fallen in love?

"On the very day of our wedding, your sly great-uncle had a change of heart. Sent her a pearl and ruby necklace to try and lure her away, but the lass said her mind was made up. She would not even take it out of the box but returned it to him along with a few harsh words. Aye, she had a temper to match that hair."

No surprise there, mused Luke.

"Hawke was reputed to be such a miser with his coin and yet he sent her several presents, including a music box, which is the only thing she never sent back to him. Becky is very fond of that music box."

"I know," he said, remembering.

Darius had walked over to see what they talked about and when he heard about the pearl and ruby necklace, he exclaimed, "That clears up a mystery for us, Major. While my wife and I were sorting through my great-uncle's papers, we found a receipt for just such a necklace from Gray's in Sackville Street. We have never found the item itself, however, and I assumed it was a present for a lady. Although, of course, he never married."

The major insisted that his wife had sent it directly back to Phineas, so where the necklace might be now was unknown.

"Considering the old man's foul temper, I wouldn't be surprised if he buried it in the backyard," muttered Luke, one hand laid against his waistcoat, where he felt the slight bulge of his secret pigsty find.

So now he knew to whom it rightfully belonged.

❧

Becky was still trying to come up with an excuse for arriving breathless and pink-faced in the Makepieces' dining room when Charles entered behind her and told the folk seated around the table that they'd been racing.

"Racing?" Diana's mother frowned in disapproval.

"Yes, indeed. And as you see, the enchanting Miss Sherringham is the victor." He pulled a chair out for Becky and she sat quickly. "You know my sister already, of course, and you will remember Kit, my brother?"

The thick-set gentleman sprawled in a chair across the table gave an indolent sneer in her vague direction.

He was a little wider than the last time he visited, his cheeks fleshier, and perhaps his lank, sandy hair had receded another inch from his forehead. "Miss Sherringham," he drawled, "still entertaining my little brother, eh what?"

Charles sat beside her. "She has been a most excellent guide and shown me all the sights of the village."

"I'm sure she has." Kit leered across the table and Elizabeth tittered slyly into her napkin.

Becky realized that Diana was rather subdued, picking listlessly at her pear poached in wine. "Where is William Shaw?" she exclaimed. "I thought he would be here by now. He has missed dinner."

Diana lifted her eyes, although they were heavy with sadness. "I'm afraid his grandmama's health took a turn for the worse yesterday and Mr. Shaw could not be spared."

Kit Clarendon gave a series of snorts like that of a boar rooting through a trough. "Seems he ain't so keen as you thought, coz. Old lady rich, is she? I daresay the chap has to stay on her good side. You'll always come second in his affections, but the pin money will make up for it."

Diana looked embarrassed and her mother didn't seem to know where to direct her gaze.

Perhaps it was the anger and shame of getting caught by Mrs. Kenton again when this time it was not her fault. Perhaps it was her frustration with Luke for suddenly being concerned with "proper" when it probably hadn't troubled him for thirty-seven years. Or perhaps it was Charles thinking he could kiss her even against her will. Whatever the reason, Becky could not stay quiet and ladylike. "Not everyone's motives are led by coin, Mr. Clarendon. Diana is marrying Mr. Shaw for more than his fortune, which, incidentally, has been earned through his own hard work and not inherited."

Kit's eyes became two wary slits in his puffy face. "Opinionated, hain't you?"

"Yes, I have opinions. I assumed that since you had just expressed yours, I ought to be allowed to express mine. But perhaps if I weren't a female, it wouldn't cause nearly as much concern."

At her side, Charles laughed softly and slid a hand under the table to squeeze her fingers.

"Isn't she delightful, my rebellious, hot-headed lady?"

She pulled her hand from his.

Kit sniffed, still glaring at her through those unattractive, water-logged cracks in his swollen facade.

"I hope the major is in good health today," Diana said politely.

"Yes, thank you."

"And the colonel? He seemed a little out of sorts yesterday evening after the treasure hunt."

At this, Elizabeth Clarendon bunched her napkin in her bony fist and drew it away from her face to snarl, "So he should have been, after that vulgar display. It was shocking that I should be spoken to in such a manner. I have never heard the like of it. So crude!"

"Colonel?" Kit murmured. "Colonel who?"

"Wainwright," his brother replied with a sly laugh. "You know Lucius Wainwright. He cost you a few teeth once."

"A horrid, uncouth fellow," Elizabeth added, shuddering delicately.

"Wainwright, eh?" Kit growled the name. "He was supposed to be dead. So he's nearby, is he? Interesting."

"He has a plain, spiteful little daughter too. Out of wedlock, of course," Elizabeth remarked nastily. "His family seems to think they can hush up the fact that she is illegitimate. They treat her as if she is a normal child and should be welcomed in any drawing room of society. I wonder what they can be thinking to raise her with false expectations. It will only make it harder for the girl to accept her place later in life."

"Her place?" Diana looked astonished. "What can you mean by that?"

"You know very well that she will never be accepted by fine society, and her family is doing the girl an injustice by raising her that way—with music tutors and dancing instructors."

Becky's fury mounted quickly. "Perhaps you think she should be kept in a dark room and fed bread and gruel to make recompense for the sins of her parents?"

"She only needed a very basic education, enough to find her a governess post eventually. Giving her so many opportunities, they have produced a girl educated beyond her needs. She will never make a good marriage, and to raise her as a lady with prospects is a mistake." She smiled in a cool, condescending way that further curdled Becky's blood. "The parson's wife told me today that the girl's mother was a music hall trollop. A slattern with no family and not a penny to her name." She sighed with false concern. "Lucius Wainwright appears to prefer that sort of woman and it's no surprise to me now, as I've seen how he behaves. A decent woman would never put up with it."

Becky would not listen to any more. "Sarah Wainwright is a pleasant girl, well-read, well-behaved, and a talented artist. As for being raised as a lady, madam, she has more natural elegance than some other women of my acquaintance who could not achieve the same sweetness of temper and lady-like demeanor if they were schooled for a hundred years in the subject. Indeed, I have wondered a great deal lately about the definition of 'a lady' and 'a gentleman.' I find myself more confused than ever by their meaning."

There was a pause.

"Well said, Miss Sherringham," cried Charles.

His sister shook her head. "You know that I am right, Charles. And your *friend*, it seems"—she glared hard at Becky—"only champions a female opinion when it is her own."

Mrs. Makepiece was back to her usual stern countenance today, her hair pulled severely back. "There must be something in the air lately," she muttered sourly. "A lot of this…expressing of one's opinions and emotions." Glowering at Diana, who bowed her head and studied her lap, she added, "It is unseemly. If you ask me, those Wainwrights will quite spoil this village."

Her fancy for the colonel had ended the moment he crossed her and stopped being polite. Perhaps he now reminded her a little *too* much of her deceased scapegrace husband.

"A bastard daughter, eh what?" mumbled the elder

brother, who appeared to be a little slow when it came to keeping up with the conversation.

"It is Christmas," Diana ventured meekly. "Let us talk of something more cheerful, shall we?"

～✦～

Kit and Elizabeth Clarendon left the village that day, returning to their host at Lark Hollow, but Charles remained at the Pig in a Poke tavern. Lucy Bridges's father was delighted that his fine guest decided to extend his stay a while longer, and other local men were equally pleased that the young gentleman was still around, as he had won quite a lot of money from them during his visit and they wanted the chance to win it back.

Becky's appreciation of his "harmless" charms had waned considerably since Christmas Day under the arches of the Bolt, but he did apologize to her for his behavior and begged to keep her friendship. Since she did not expect him to stay much longer, Becky accepted his olive branch but kept him at a warier distance.

Mrs. Kenton had soon spread her gossip, suggesting Rebecca was leading two men along in competition. The story of what that woman had witnessed in the Bolt was enlarged upon until it was barely recognizable to Rebecca, who was actually there.

From her bedchamber window early one morning, she saw Luke Wainwright on horseback riding down Mill Lane, with his dog trotting proudly alongside. He sat the horse well, as if he had been born in the saddle. But he did not come to see her.

She stood at the window and wished he might

look up and smile. He did not. The last time they had spoken, she had yelled at him that she was off to have fun, wounded that he did not want to play that day. He would have heard about her and Charles in the Bolt by now and must think that was what she meant by "fun."

It should not be any surprise, therefore, that he rode by their house and did not call in.

Twenty-six

LUKE CALLED ON SAM HARDACRE TO CHECK ON THE gig, which was still being mended. Then he headed for the turnpike road and Raven's Hill. Ness certainly could do with some exercise, for he was growing fat and lazy thanks to Sarah's pampering. The fresh, crisp air could do them both some good.

"What do you think, Ness? Shall we head for Willow Tree Farm?"

The dog gave a confirming bark and skipped ahead, chasing a soggy dead leaf that blew across the lane from the common.

❧

"Oh! Elinor," she cried, "I have such a secret to tell you about Marianne. I am sure she will be married to Mr. Willoughby very soon."

"You have said so," replied Elinor, "almost every day since they first met on High-church Down; and they had not known each other a week, I believe, before you were certain that Marianne

wore his picture round her neck; but it turned out to be only the miniature of our great uncle."

"But indeed this is quite another thing. I am sure they will be married very soon, for he has got a lock of her hair."

Justina paused her reading. "Becky, are you paying attention to this story anymore?"

"Of course." But truth be told, she was no longer very interested in Marianne, who acted so unwisely with Mr. Willoughby and left herself open to speculation.

At first she had liked the character of Willoughby and thought him a good match for lively, spirited Marianne, but there was something about him that she didn't warm to.

"If Marianne has indeed given Willoughby a lock of her hair," pronounced Diana, "she must truly be in love, although I do not think he is half the man Colonel Brandon is. That poor colonel."

Justina had just turned the page to read on. She made a surprised exclamation, "What is this? Why, it looks like...Becky!" Holding the book open, she turned it to show the others. There, on the edge of the page, where there was no printing, someone had sketched a face. It was carefully done, by an observant artist.

Someone whose mind had wandered while they read. Or tried to read.

"It *is* Becky," cried Diana. Then, remembering where they were, she corrected herself. "Rebecca, I mean."

Becky knew who had sketched her image on the page, of course. He had very skilled hands.

Since they were all looking at her, she said

brusquely, "How dreadful to doodle on the page like that. Some people have no appreciation for books."

But when she heard hooves passing, she looked through the parlor window and there he was, riding by, Ness at his side. How fine he looked in the saddle.

Becky leaped up and grabbed her muff from the table. "I must go out. I just remembered...something."

They all protested her sudden haste to leave in the midst of a meeting, but she was determined.

As she passed through Diana's front door, the first spots of rain made themselves felt. She looked to see which way the colonel had gone, but he was nowhere in sight. Her shoulders sagged. She wanted to know why he'd drawn her face on the margin.

"My dear Miss Sherringham, where do you go in such haste? Do you look for me?" Charles Clarendon rolled up before the gate in a brand new curricle, all shiny paint and soft leather. "I was just taking this new beauty out for a jaunt. Will you join me?"

She looked again to search for any sign of the colonel. He had been traveling down the High Street, which meant he could turn down Mill Lane to pass over the bridge or back up Drover's Way toward the manor. But his horse had not been sweating, which suggested he'd only just set off and would not head home yet.

It was raining harder now, but Charles did not seem to mind. *Of course not*, she thought, for that was how they met—both of them wandering about on a rainy day. She decided to go with him, hoping she might see Luke further along the road. The need to speak to that man today was overwhelming. She did not want to go another day waiting for a chance, but he seemed to be avoiding her. He was always out when she called at the manor. While he was on horseback, he was too fast for her to catch on foot, and she did not have the luxury of wheels with which to follow him, since her father had recently, quite inexplicably, decided to sell their old carriage and not replace it.

She must, therefore, rely on Charles to chase the colonel down.

"Let's go over the bridge toward Raven's Hill," she said, climbing up beside Charles.

"What a capital idea! We shall retrace our steps and revisit where we first met."

She gripped her hands together in her muff and stared ahead, not wanting to encourage him into thinking she had romantic intentions about this ride.

The two horses moved smartly forward, manes fluttering in the sharp breeze that had come up with the darkening of clouds overhead. *There is not much shelter on Raven's Hill apart from an old, burned-out shack*, she thought. If they, or the colonel, got caught out there, they would be soaked.

Soon they were traveling along the turnpike road and then they turned up the rough path to Raven's Hill. There, over the crest and down in another valley, were the remnants of the little hamlet where her mother was born and raised. When she married, she traveled far away. Becky often wondered whether her mother had been afraid to leave or excited by the prospect of a new adventure. Becky's life had happened the other way around, of course. She had enjoyed travel and adventure first then settled into a quiet village. She knew which she preferred.

"My darling, Becky." Charles slowed the horses to a walk, heading for the abandoned shack. Wind whipped at the ribbons of her bonnet. "Will you let me have that lock of hair now?"

He could not be serious, surely. Did he think they were living in a novel?

"I thought you were done with this nonsense," she said.

His eyebrows rose, lowered, and rose again. "Nonsense?"

"Mr. Clarendon, we cannot—"

"Just because we cannot be married does not mean we cannot share more than a friendship. I have certain needs, Becky. I desire you. I need you! You are everything I know my wife will not be. Cannot be."

She shifted away from him on the seat. "I sincerely hope you're not suggesting I become your mistress?"

He gave her a quick frown. "But…why else do you suppose I have spent time here with you?"

"I thought you liked our village. And you came to visit your cousins."

"Becky, I came for you. I have battled these last twelve months with my feelings, but they cannot be denied. Father insists I make a good marriage, but there is naught amiss with keeping a dalliance on the side, a sensible woman who can be discreet."

The abandoned stone shepherd's shack was ahead of them now and he steered the horses toward it.

"I knew the moment I saw you that we were destined to be together," he added.

Becky was alarmed. She could never have imagined his thoughts to have traveled so far ahead. His flirtation was nothing she took to heart. It confused her sometimes, but she just assumed that was her own fault for being unfamiliar with the habit.

As he slowed the curricle, she readied her skirt to step down and make a run for it. "I fear, sir, you have made a mistake, a misjudgment of my character, if you think I would be content as any man's mistress."

He was crestfallen, his voice quite desperate. "But you are my *chère amie*."

She leaped down and marched into the shack to shelter from the rain.

With dazed eyes, she looked around the interior, at the bottle of Madeira, the lantern, the tapestry pillows that she recognized from Mrs. Makepiece's parlor. She thought of her friends' faces watching her leave with Charles, all of them no doubt thinking he was the reason for her sudden exit.

"We can read poetry, if you like," he exclaimed, darting by her and throwing out his arms. "And I will write countless sonnets to your auburn hair."

She looked at him, sighed, and tucked her hands in her muff. "Are you in your cups, by chance?"

"No! Well, I had a few at the Pig in a Poke, but I have all my wits about me."

"I beg to differ." She suspected the few wits he had were ready to flee in shame as soon as he was sober again.

Rain had begun to fall, spitting spitefully down upon them through the leaky rafters of the roof.

"Damn this weather!" Charles exclaimed, staring out through the open door to where his horses grazed.

"The leather hood doesn't fit right and the seats won't dry for hours. Well, we may as well stay a while, even if you are being a dreadful, frosty sulk."

She shook her head. What a fool she had been to think he enjoyed her company and conversation. That he enjoyed walking with her. All the time, she was supposed to read between the lines. This, as Mrs. Kenton would say, was the problem with being raised motherless. She *did* need advice. But she didn't like asking for it. Or hearing it.

Walking by him, she passed out into the full onslaught of rain. All she could think about now was the long walk back to the village in the rain.

"Becky!" He grabbed her arm. "We'll stay warm together inside and wait for the storm to pass."

"That roof leaks, Charles," she replied dully.

He had not thought of practical matters like the weather when he prepared this secret little love nest for his "*chère amie*."

He reached for her. It was not really a tussle, but she did pull one way and he the other. To a passing person, it might seem as if he meant to hurt her. Certainly, it must have seemed that way to the irate dog that appeared out of nowhere and launched itself, jaws bared in a menacing growl, at Charles Clarendon's trespassing arm.

The dog's fangs made contact and Charles cursed, kicking out at the animal. He released Becky and she stumbled on the wet, muddy grass.

"Ness," she shouted, recognizing the dog. "Stop, Ness!"

Although the dog had dropped the imagined assailant's sleeve, Charles was enraged, veins popping out on his neck. He kicked out again and grabbed his whip from the curricle, but Becky leaped in his way, defending the growling dog.

"No. He thought I was in danger. Don't hurt him."

"Stand aside and I'll beat the dog. Teach him a lesson!"

"No! Stop it at once, Charles. I cannot abide cruelty."

Ness had run up to paw at her skirt and Becky saw that the dog was bleeding.

"Something has happened," she exclaimed in alarm. "He's never out without his master." Squinting through the hard, driving rain, she looked down the hill and searched the road as far as she could see it in both directions, but there was no sign of Luke. Her heart was in her throat, for she knew then that the dog had run up there looking for help.

Charles was too angry to be sensible. He refused to go looking for the colonel. "I think you care more about a dog than you do about me. Look, he made me bleed!"

There was a slight graze on his wrist between glove and coat cuff. No more than a scratch. "Please, let us take the curricle and look, Charles. He could be hurt down there somewhere."

But again he refused. His face white with anger, he would not let her take the curricle, nor would he leave the doorway of the shack, where the stone lintel kept him partially dry.

She gave up. There was no more time to waste. "Come on, Ness. Show me where he is, boy!"

❧

The two thugs had come out of nowhere—or more specifically, they had ridden up on him from behind as he walked by the river, leading his horse and tossing sticks for Ness. He heard their hooves and had stopped, expecting them to pass. Instead they reined blows down upon him and he fell into the bulrushes. He blacked out.

When next Luke opened his eyes, he had blood in his mouth and his ears were ringing. But there was Ness, padding around his head, licking at his hair. And there were two feet in soaking wet ladies' boots.

"For pity's sake, what have you done now?"

He didn't know if he was wet most from the rain or the river. Or the blood. They must have beaten him further after he fell, and then they rode off, disturbed perhaps by the fierce attack from his faithful mutt. Ness had taken a few blows himself, but he was a tough little bastard.

His head was spinning, and when he tried to raise it, the sensation was much worse. "Go away, wench," he muttered, spitting out blood. She was one of the last people he wanted to see him like this, since her impression of him was so very bad already.

"Oh, don't thank me for coming to help you." She bent over, grabbed him under the shoulders, and tried hauling him out of the bulrushes, but his weight was too much for her.

"Leave it," he groaned. "I'm all right. 'Tis only a bit of a scrape."

"*Bit of a scrape?*"

"I've had worse." He laughed and then winced as that vibration turned to fire scorching in his ribs. "And I daresay it's not the last time," he wheezed. He wouldn't be at all surprised to find that Kit Clarendon had sent those men in retaliation for the well-deserved beating Luke gave him years before. "I think they stole my horse!"

"Men!" exclaimed his Gingersnap. "Good Lord!"

"Could you stop shouting in my ear, please? I hurt enough. And why are you shouting at me? I didn't beat myself about the head, woman."

Eventually she managed to get him sitting up and then she found his cane in the bulrushes, wiped it on her coat, and put it into his hands. By leaning on her and the cane, he was able to get up on his feet again.

Fortunately, they had not stumbled far when the blacksmith happened by with his cart, and he took them back to the village.

"I can't go back to the manor," he gasped out, holding his side. "I don't want Sarah to see this. Or my brother, for that matter."

The woman, for once, did not argue with him, so he knew he must look very bad indeed. She had taken a handkerchief out of her muff and used it to wipe blood and dirt from his face. "You can stay with Papa and me," she said firmly, taking control of the situation just as he suspected she always had done.

Rebecca was remarkably composed in the sight of so much blood. He didn't think she would ever stop impressing him.

She was still wiping his face and it felt very good. Very good. So he kept pointing out more blood for her to find. There was plenty.

Twenty-seven

LUKE WAS SOON INSTALLED IN HER BROTHER'S bedroom, despite a few salty protests about what "people" might think about him staying there.

"Oh, do shut up," she exclaimed. "You don't want to go to the manor, so where else is there? Who else would have you? I'm quite sure no decent soul wants *you* lying around on their furniture. Fortunately, however, I don't have much of a reputation worth saving." She knew that these days many villagers considered her a scarlet woman, because of all the rumors, first about Lucky Luke and then Charles Clarendon. But she had decided it was her turn not to care for once. She'd spent enough years being the one who worried.

Besides, promising to marry someone on a wager, she'd found, did peculiar things to a person, complicated their thoughts and feelings. Even when they were usually sensible and clever.

But now was not the time to think about herself. She had a man to tend and that was one thing she knew she could do. She had the perfect no-nonsense manner, and she was not in the least squeamish.

Therefore she threw herself wholeheartedly into the supervision of Lucky Luke. Someone had to do it.

She pushed him behind the dressing screen in her brother's room. "Don't get blood on the carpet."

Wincing, he lifted his breeches and dangled them in the air. "I know you've been waiting to get these off me, wench."

"Naturally." She snatched up his soiled, torn clothing as he dropped it over the top of the screen. "I'll bring you a nightshirt of my father's, but you'd better wash first. Wait there and I'll bring you some water for the basin."

"Wait here?" he grumbled. "Where else can I go now you've got me naked?"

She smiled archly. That might be one way to keep him under her control. With this mischievous thought in mind, she took his clothes down to the fire to burn them. He'd have to make do with a nightshirt until she and her friends had a proper plan of action to make him stay. For Sarah's sake, of course. No other reason.

But as she took his waistcoat, poised to discard it in the flames, a pearl and ruby necklace tumbled out from an inside pocket. She caught it in her hand, astonished. What was Lucky Luke doing with such an item in his possession? Something he won gambling, perhaps?

She suddenly remembered Justina's missing bracelet, Mrs. Makepiece's lost silver teaspoons, and the silver milk jug she hadn't been able to find. Then she thought of how she caught him sneaking about in her hallway on Christmas Eve. He'd claimed to be looking for a fob watch. One she'd never seen.

Was it possible that Lucky Luke was not only a seducer and a gambler, but also a thief?

❧

Dr. Penny was sent for, and he confirmed that the patient had suffered nothing more than a few bruises and scratches and a nasty cut below his left eye. Nothing broken. Surprisingly. The ruffians must have been disturbed before they could do a more thorough job.

"For a man of seven-and-thirty, sir, you are in remarkably fine condition, despite being beaten like an old rug."

Luke's brother had warned him of Dr. Penny's eccentricities—his love of stuffed creatures. "Perhaps he can do something for you," Darius had muttered dryly. "He once told me he prefers dead patients, so you qualify. Just don't sit still for too long or he might have you stuffed."

Dr. Penny stood at the bedside and scratched his white hair. "But now to the matter of that leg, Colonel. How will you chase after the rapidly moving Miss Sherringham?"

He scowled and replied gruffly that chasing after that wench was certainly not anything he had in mind to do. He knew she was listening outside the door. "My daughter, Sarah, however, has pestered me to have you look at it. I told her you probably would not be able to help, but she insisted."

"I see." The doctor pulled up a chair and sat. "What happened to the bullet when you were shot? It was removed in a military hospital?"

"No," he snapped. "I took it out myself."

The doctor's bushy white brows shook and heaved like the foam on a rocky sea. "You took it out yourself?"

"Made a bit of a mess of it, but where I was, there were no good doctors." He rubbed his bad thigh, because the more he talked of it, the more it hurt. "Besides, I saw how they hacked me about when they took the first one out after Assaye. I thought I'd make as good a job of it myself."

Dr. Penny shook his head gravely. "Ah, the well-meaning amateur. Thus the healing has resulted in adhesions forming, no doubt. These have contributed to stiffness and restricted, contracted muscular movement. If the leg is not properly exercised...tell me, have you tried thermal springs? Such as those in Bath?"

He could think of nothing less appealing than a journey to that favorite watering hole of society.

It must have shown upon his countenance for the doctor chuckled. "I quite agree. I was there once myself and pray there will never be an occasion for me to return. But the natural sulphur will work wonders for you. That, combined with regular massage, will be of tremendous benefit. I suggest you take some time to try the cure. Greater mobility can be restored."

Luke agreed morosely that it was something to consider. Once Sarah heard about it, he knew she would have something new to poke him about. She was already talking about one day taking a trip there to dance in the Upper Rooms and see the sights. Now she had another reason to want her "father" to take her there. The responsibilities of parenthood were onerous, to be sure. She had even suggested he might take her shopping for bonnets.

Dr. Penny left him that day with the genial assertion that he was in good hands.

So there he was, in Nate Sherringham's bed, hiding out while his battered and bruised face healed. He could hear the low voices outside on the landing as Rebecca conferred with the physician, and he suspected grimly that this wench would take advantage of him now, while he was at her mercy.

It would probably be a damn sight worse than what those thugs had done.

❧

To Becky's extreme irritation, he would not tell her what had happened or who was responsible. "'Tis nothing," he kept saying with a breezy sigh. "I've done worse to myself in my sleep."

She would not let him see her laugh, as she was determined to be a strict nurse. No nonsense. Solemn and dignified. Like Mrs. Makepiece.

"Papa, he will have to stay with us until he is recuperated. Just a day or so," she told her father as she prepared a tea tray for the invalid. "We cannot let Sarah see her father this way, can we?"

He agreed at once. "The colonel must stay as long as he needs, m'dear Becky. As long as he needs."

Ness was also welcome, of course, and enjoyed a beef and gravy supper before he went to sleep at the foot of his master's new bed, ready to protect him again as—well, Becky thought, smiling—as *Necessary*, despite his name.

"I hope you know your dog saved you," she told Luke as she carried the tray to his bedside table, lit the candles, and shut the curtains.

"I wasn't dying," he grunted. "I tripped."

"Yes, and bumped, many times, against something hard, but I always suspected you had a toughened skull."

"Well, I would have got up and been perfectly—"

"If not for your dog, you would have lain there in the bulrushes, in the rain, and probably caught pneumonia."

"Don't exaggerate, woman." His dark gaze followed her around the room. "Where did Ness find you, anyway? What were you doing out in the rain so far from the village?"

Ah, now *that* she would rather not tell. "Since you like to keep your secrets," she replied smugly, "I shall keep mine!"

"Hmm." He scowled and his mouth turned down sulkily. "What are *folk* going to say about me staying here in this house?" The emphasis he placed on the word "folk" suggested he had someone in mind.

"It's only a night or two until the worst of the bruising and swelling has gone down," she assured him. "Don't worry, the blacksmith who brought you here has been sworn to secrecy, and my friends and I will look after you here, keep your ugly face from frightening poor Sarah."

"Your friends?" He clenched his hands into fists on the quilt, and from his tone of voice, anyone might think her friends consisted of Torquemada and the Spanish Inquisition.

She wrote notes to Justina and Diana that evening, and the next day, at the meeting of the Book Club Belles, the three of them shared the secret of Lucky Luke's whereabouts. Becky did not tell Lucy, of course, for she could not be relied upon to keep the news from Sarah.

"I shall bring him some of my special broth," Justina whispered as soon as they had a chance to discuss the matter without the youngest two girls hearing.

"And I will take some of my mama's fruit cake," vowed Diana. "He liked it very much, she said."

Becky smoothed her palms over her skirt and said casually, "While he is in our house, I thought we might have the opportunity to help the colonel, in his efforts to reform."

Diana and Justina stared at her.

"It will be a pleasant surprise for Sarah, won't it?" she added.

"For Sarah?" Justina smiled.

"Yes. She would love to have him dance with her at the Manderson assemblies and they open again in another week. We shall have him ready to escort Sarah to the dance."

It would do no harm to clean him up, she thought. Little Sarah had tried, but she could only do so much with a stubborn seed ox like Lucky Luke. It needed some stronger hands, clearly.

The matter of the ruby and pearl necklace she kept to herself, for she had yet to decide what to do about it. Luke had not mentioned the necklace at all, or even asked about his clothes, but he probably assumed they were being cleaned and mended.

Later that afternoon, Justina and Diana brought their offerings to the house as promised.

"I told Sarah that you have gone to Manderson for

a few days to have one of my father's colleagues look at your leg," Justina assured him. "That has made her extremely happy."

He gave a lopsided smile. "Well, that's good. Worth getting a beating for. What else can a father do for his daughter?"

Becky, busy spreading another quilt over the bed, wondered at the perverse side of her nature that made him seem so dreadfully handsome suddenly. Bruised and swollen and with a cut under his eye, his was a face she liked looking at. As he talked about his daughter, that face lit up.

It was difficult to imagine him capable of thievery, but where else could he have come by that necklace?

The next morning, Luke announced his head was feeling much better, he had stopped seeing stars, and he could get out of bed. Dr. Penny had shown them some exercises to get his leg muscles functioning better, and Becky made certain he practiced them, even though he complained and cursed.

"I don't know why my leg matters to you," he muttered. "I suppose you just enjoy seeing me in pain, woman."

She smiled. "It has a certain appeal."

"When all I ever tried to do was make an honest woman of you."

❧

In truth, he had thought he was about to die. When those blows first contacted with the back of his head and sent him to his knees, Luke had assumed this was it, his just deserts after a life of sin.

Damn it! He'd cursed at the air as he went down, because in spite of his intentions, he still wasn't ready yet to go to his maker. He hadn't come up with a suitable phrase for his headstone, and he hadn't given his brother instructions for the horses with plumes.

Now there was Sarah too. She'd been left behind before with no explanation, and he didn't want to do that to her again.

But then his eyes opened and he was not dead. There was the sweet smell of wet earth under his fingernails, as if he really had dug himself out of a grave.

And there was Rebecca and his dog. And life.

He wanted to embrace all of it. Trouble was he still needed one bloody arm for his walking cane. Unless he finally applied himself to doing something about it. For too many years, he'd relied upon that cane. No one expected too much from a lame man, did they? That pain in his thigh was good punishment for his past actions, he thought. Whenever he felt guilt about the way he'd been as a young man, he fell back on his injury. Like twisting a knife in a wound.

Then a redheaded virago named Rebecca marched into his life and suddenly he wanted to be a whole man again. For her.

The doctor had shown her a simple massage for Luke's thigh, and she, a dedicated if somewhat brutal nurse, insisted on trying it out immediately.

Luke clutched the quilt to his chest as she approached with a stern look upon her face and something that looked like goose grease slathered over her hands. "I don't think this is proper."

"I'm quite sure it isn't." She snatched the quilt out

of his fingers, pulled up the nightshirt—one of her father's—and set to work on his stiff muscles.

"Steady on, woman," he yelled. "Have a care!"

"Oh, hush! You should have taken greater care when you were first wounded. Dr. Penny says frequent exercise and massage would have kept the leg from seizing up. I suppose you laid around feeling sorry for yourself, the muscles gave up, and then they were stuck this way. Just as they say that if you pull an ugly face for too long, the wind will change and your expression will be frozen in place."

He snorted. "Astounding how one silly woman can become a medical expert after a five-minute conversation with the local quack—ouch!"

"That was for calling me silly."

"Argh!"

"And that was for calling Dr. Penny a quack."

But a moment later, it was her turn to utter an exclamation when she saw the linen nightshirt lifting over his groin.

"Well, what did you think would happen?" he growled, amused by her shocked face. "You put your hands on me like this and the stiffness moves from one place to another." It was actually growing unbearable, made his voice a little choked and gruff. She was temptation incarnate, even with her prim face determined not to smile. Her hands might be small but they were talented when it came to his aches and pains.

Skilled at giving him as many as they took away.

It hadn't escaped his notice that she wore her most chaste gown today with lace all the way to her throat.

That was, he supposed, to keep him at a distance. Women placed a vast deal of trust in lace, when all it did was entice a man to peer through it. "Why don't you get on this bed with me? I'm feeling remarkably rejuvenated already."

"I thought you were a reformed man."

"I tried that. Didn't like it.

"You tried it for…what was it now? Two days?"

He laughed. "I can't help myself. Not around you."

Rebecca had just trailed her fingertips across the linen that covered his aching shaft. He stared up at her, saw her bite her lip and blink guiltily. "I wish you'd put that away," she muttered.

"Can't. It has its own mind. Just like your hand, eh?"

She shook her head, but he knew she was trying not to laugh.

She was a difficult, stubborn, argumentative wench, completely and utterly different from any other woman he'd ever fancied. He liked talking to her, making her smile and roll her eyes. Yes, his brother would be proud of him, for he admired far more than the shape of her body under that gown.

But it didn't stop him wanting to rip the muslin and lace aside, throw her down on the bed, claim her for his own.

There would never be another woman for him but her. He knew it. She'd know it too soon.

"What are you smirking at?" she demanded.

"Thinking about the clever hands of my nurse."

"They do seem to have surprisingly restorative qualities, never before suspected," she murmured, gazing down at his rising cockerel.

"And there are some things I could do for her in return."

Her face was too honest and open to hide the fact that she was interested.

He raised one arm, placed his hand on her waist. "You could say this old stallion is feeling his oats."

But the doorbell rang before he could elaborate, and she instantly became all business again. "Behave yourself, or I'll fetch you a bridle," she warned sharply, eyeing the twitching mound under his borrowed nightshirt one last lingering moment before dashing out of the room.

Twenty-eight

THE ROGUE HAD A DEVASTATING EFFECT ON HER PULSE and her lungs, she decided, hurrying down the stairs, hot, flushed, and distinctly short of breath. But as she flew by the hall mirror, she glanced over and caught herself smiling.

She hastily wiped that off her face—what was it doing there, anyway?—but the bell was ringing again now, someone tugging on the rope with rude impatience. There was no time to tidy her appearance.

Expecting the visitor to be one of her friends, she was startled, and then alarmed, when she discovered Charles Clarendon on her doorstep. Oh, if only Mrs. Jarvis was back and had gone to open the door. But alas, it was all left up to her, and there she was, perspiring, with her sleeves folded up and a stained apron over her frock. Her mind in some dark, velvety, hot place.

Charles swept off his hat. "Miss Sherringham, might I come in?"

Where were her manners? *Perhaps I left them with this fine fellow on Raven's Hill in the rain*, she thought scornfully. "Of course." She took the visitor through to the front parlor.

At once, he began. "My dear Miss Sherringham, please say you can forgive me. I acted like a cad that day…I should never have let you walk home alone. I have been wracked with guilt ever since."

Wracked with guilt for two days and yet not enough to actually make inquiries and be certain she returned home safely and in one piece.

A loud bang against the ceiling above warned Becky that the patient was out of bed. Charles glanced upward. "What was that?"

"Oh, I was"—she looked down at her apron— "spring cleaning. Moving furniture. I expect something fell over."

The sooner she got him out of the house the better, before there was another crash above stairs or the unpredictable patient decided to come down. In only his nightshirt. So she said, "I forgive you for leaving me to walk home in the rain, Mr. Clarendon. Is there anything else? I'm rather busy, as you see."

He frowned. "Yes. I wanted to let you know I have been called home. To Oxford. My father needs me there." Charles spoke now in rushed, clipped, angry sentences, and his gaze flitted about the parlor, unable to meet her eyes. "I wish I could have stayed longer, but my father will hear no excuse."

"I see. Well, I hope you have a safe journey." She wondered why he made a special visit to tell her when he thought so little of her anyway. Then she found out.

"I wanted to let you know that my brother sent a

gift for your friend, the colonel. He sends the message that he hopes it was appreciated."

A frisson of panic passed over her skin as she worried that he might know Luke was upstairs. If *he* knew, the Book Club Belles had not kept their secret very well.

But with a hard, spiteful gleam in his eye, he added, "By the way, that girl he pretends is his daughter is not anything of the sort, you know."

"Oh?"

"She's Kit's bastard. My brother told me. He said Wainwright always was a fool and easily tricked by the various little slatterns who fell into his lap, but surely even he knows she's not his blood. You can tell him he needn't think to get any money out of us. If that's what his plan is in keeping the girl."

She thought for a moment, all the facts slipping and sliding again, coming up in yet another new way. "I don't believe he ever plans anything, Mr. Clarendon. I understand the colonel tends to fly by the seat of his breeches."

"Don't be taken in. The man is a menace. My brother has three wooden teeth because of him."

"Well, perhaps he deserves them."

There was a pause while he glowered at her.

She held out her hand, offering to say good-bye, even though she wasn't feeling very civil.

His pinched lips snapped open to say, "A lady is supposed to give a gentleman her hand to kiss, not to shake."

"Just as well I'm not a lady."

He screwed up his face. "How very witty." But

when he finally took her hand, he exclaimed, "What on earth is this on your hands? They're all slippery."

"It's…polish. Furniture polish. I was trying to put the shine back in some…old wood."

He wiped his hands furiously on a kerchief. "I'll bid you good day, Miss Sherringham. Perhaps next time I return, you will be prepared to receive my attentions and appreciate them fully. We will discuss the terms again and reach some compromise, I hope."

She could hardly believe her ears. He still thought she would consider his offer to make her his mistress. "To quote a certain gentleman of my acquaintance, sir, I don't compromise."

He squinted and sucked in his cheeks.

"Good day, Mr. Clarendon."

As she showed him out of the house, he was still wiping his hands.

She closed the door behind him and exhaled with relief, knowing she wouldn't have to try anymore.

❧

"What was that chinless brat doing here?" Luke demanded, standing at the window, looking out.

"Get away from there!" She dashed across the room and tugged on his nightshirt sleeve until he stepped out of the light.

"So what if he sees me? Serve him right. Gone home, has he?"

"Yes. Now come away from the—"

She cried out in surprise when he slid an arm around her and pressed her hard against him. "I like the feel of you and the taste of you and the scent of you. I know you like plain talking. Is that good enough for you, madam?"

"Well, isn't that nice?" She laughed, sounding short of breath. "I daresay you'd feel the same about a slab of bacon."

"Perhaps. But I wouldn't want to do to that what I want to do to you. Not everything, anyway." He lowered his mouth to hers while it was open to argue with him again and he kissed her greedily. Her felt her body melting against his, responding to his kiss. "But I can't, of course. Until the wedding night."

She groaned, ducked out of his arms, and walked around the bed. Wiping her hands on her apron, she said briskly, "Since you're up and about and clearly have your bearings back, you may as well come down to dinner tonight. My father will enjoy your company. He has been ill-tempered of late."

"And will you enjoy my company too?"

"I don't know yet."

He laughed. "Still haven't decided yet, eh?"

"Some people like to think things through before they leap in with both feet," she exclaimed.

"Why? The details can always be sorted out later."

Shaking her head, she walked out of the room, shouting over her shoulder that some of her father's clothes were behind the screen for him.

She stood a while outside the door, thinking about Sarah and Kit Clarendon and why Luke would claim a daughter who was not his. Not many men would do that.

Especially not a man who had avoided responsibilities and attachments for so long. Unless he really was ready to change.

It didn't take long for the news to spread that Mr. Charles Clarendon had left, taking himself back to Oxford with his painted curricle bought on the proceeds of winnings at the tavern. When Becky entered Mr. Porter's shop one morning, she heard Mrs. Kenton holding court. "So there goes that young man, pretty sharpish indeed, back to his father, who no doubt got wind of his attentions to the major's daughter and cut that off."

She froze. Apparently a great many people had seen Charles flirting with her and read more into it than she did.

"I always knew his attention was fleeting, but Rebecca Sherringham never listens to anyone. I tried to advise her, but she is so sharp-tongued and knows best. And now the colonel has disappeared too, after paying court to her since before Christmas. Heaven knows where he's gone. In any case, these young girls…"

As her father had always said, one found one's true friends in a time of trouble. The Book Club Belles rallied around, defending Becky against every bad word they overheard. Justina and Diana came to the house every day and helped her fuss over the much recovered colonel.

When Becky told Luke that he had become their mission, his expression of horror and trepidation made them all laugh. And all the more determined.

Justina arranged her husband's barouche to take Luke—wearing more borrowed clothes—into Manderson on the sly, to be measured for those new clothes he badly needed, and as the first assembly dance was fast approaching, it became time to give the colonel a few dancing lessons. In his own words, he had been "out of commission" for more than a dozen years, and the idea of standing up on another dance floor made him want to reach for the brandy bottle.

"I know how to dance," he grumbled. "Our mother paid five shillings and sixpence a lesson for me when I was thirteen. I just didn't take to it and now, with this leg…"

Oh, the leg excuse again.

"Nonsense," Becky replied curtly. "Dr. Penny says the more you use that leg the better. No, you will not skulk around the edge of the dance. You will join in with your daughter and you will not embarrass her by not knowing the steps. If it's been so long since you last blessed a dance floor with your…talents"—the other girls chuckled—"I suggest we get to work."

Thus began his lessons at the hands of the Book Club Belles. Or three of them, at least.

For the next few days, the Sherringhams' back parlor rang with shouts and laughter as the three ladies took delight in pushing him about.

"No, Colonel, turn *right* hand star first and then back with the left!"

"Allemande, Colonel! That means back to back. Oops. Mind the dog!"

Ness ran about barking in confusion when he wasn't burying his face in his paws, apparently overcome with his master's shame.

One day, the other ladies were late and since Becky could not dance with him *and* play the pianoforte, she brought out her mother's music box to accompany them.

"So this is the magical music box." He picked it up and studied it, smiling.

"Don't get it dirty!" She snatched it back and set it down on the sideboard.

He laughed, took her hand, and with the music box tinkling gently beside them, he led her into a dance she did not recognize. "I'll get you dirty instead then." It was too intimate to be proper. *Mrs. Makepiece would never approve*, she thought.

"What are these steps called?"

"Oh, I don't know. Lady Big Bottom's Fancy? Miss Fanny's Frolic?

"You're making it up. This is your excuse to grope me again."

He winked. "No pulling the fleece over your eyes, just as you warned me once."

Luke spun her around the parlor until she felt dizzy, and only later did she realize he hadn't once complained about his leg.

But he did not kiss her today. She was not sure how she felt about that.

Abruptly he dropped down at her feet, and she let out a light squeal, fearing something dreadful had happened. Or else he was trying to get under her skirt again.

"It's Sarah," he hissed wildly from the carpet.

Becky looked out of the window and saw his daughter walking up the back path and heading for the kitchen door. "Don't fret, Colonel. Your face isn't so bad now. The bruises have almost faded."

He looked up at her. "Don't you suppose she'll be curious as to what I'm doing here when I'm supposed to be in Manderson?"

So she rushed him upstairs out of sight and then went into the kitchen to greet the surprise visitor.

"I've brought you a pork pie, Miss Sherringham, as I know you are without a cook at the moment and Monsieur Philippe has been busy."

"That is kind of you, Sarah."

As she reached for the basket, the young girl laid a hand on hers and said solemnly, "Miss Sherringham, although my father has gone away, I want to promise you that he will return. I know he will."

Becky's heart swelled at this simple, innocent faith the girl had in her father. The man she thought was her father.

"He likes you very much, Miss Sherringham. He just doesn't know the proper way to show it, but he can learn, can't he?"

Choked with emotion, Becky felt incapable of reply. So she merely nodded.

"Will you walk with me to the book society meeting this afternoon, Miss Sherringham?"

In truth, Becky had lost interest in Willoughby and Marianne. Their love story could bring her no comfort now, but she may as well get out of the house. Close and extended proximity to Lucky Luke was perhaps not a wise thing to encourage.

❧

From the upstairs window, Luke watched the two young ladies leave for the book club meeting. It was good to see them walking together, hand in hand, these two ladies he cared about the most.

He went downstairs again, now the coast was clear, and expected to find the major sitting by his fire, reading the paper, but the old man was on his way out.

Apparently he went out quite a lot on his own, a fact Luke had discovered since staying at the house. He was surprised by it, for Rebecca spoke of her father as if she thought he spent most of his time in a chair, napping and safely staying out of trouble. She flitted in and out so often herself that the major's absences went unnoticed.

"Just off to catch the mail coach," he said to Luke as he pulled on his coat. "If Becky is home before me, tell her I shall be back for supper, there's a good chap."

Luke and Ness, therefore, were left alone in the house.

It was raining again, tapping lightly at the windows. Standing in the hall, he scratched his chin and realized he was going to have to sit there waiting around for a woman to come back. He didn't like it one bit. What was he supposed to do without her?

Hmm, perhaps he could make good use of his time alone—look for that list of husbandly attributes she supposedly kept. So he went back upstairs and opened the door to her chamber. The sweet but very soft fragrance of violets hovered in the air and drew him further in. He opened her drawers and rummaged among her silky underthings, lifting them to his face, enjoying the buttery softness. She certainly had a lot of lacy pieces, he mused, for a woman who called herself sensible and not at all romantic.

And as he moved aside another folded petticoat, he

found the little wooden horse he'd whittled in haste the night of the treasure hunt. She had kept it.

He couldn't think what that meant. It was just a bit of wood. Luke picked it up and ran his thumb over the small, crudely fashioned figure. So Rebecca had kept something of his. He shouldn't let that thought run away with him, should he?

Lifting the next petticoat, he halted again. There was the ruby and pearl necklace that had completely escaped his mind since she'd found him in the bulrushes.

What the devil was it doing among her things, and why hadn't she mentioned it to him?

He took it, curling it in his large fist. If she found it gone from her drawer, she'd have to ask him about it. Luke grinned and shook his head. Perhaps the wench thought it was stolen.

Knowing her low opinion of him, she had no doubt labeled him a thief now too. But it was interesting that she did not turn him in.

Twenty-nine

"PEOPLE ARE STARTING TO TALK ABOUT ALL THESE missing items," said Diana as she handed around the plate of biscuits. "It is all very strange."

"Yes, and we all know what is being said about it," added Justina.

They all looked at Sarah, who was poking the fire savagely.

"The colonel has a certain reputation," Lucy muttered, "but no one has ever accused him of being a thief before. Even if he has disappeared for the past few days and we don't know where."

Becky sat straighter. "The *colonel?* Who on earth would think him capable of that? It's ridiculous."

Now all eyes swung to her, including those of Sarah.

"I mean to say," she swallowed, "he's made some mistakes in his life, to be sure, but he would not steal. Who says such a thing?"

"Mrs. Kenton, for one." Lucy bit into her biscuit.

"That wretched busybody!" Becky was almost lifted out of her chair in outrage.

"But so many things have gone," Lucy pointed out,

wide-eyed. "Someone must have taken them, and as Mrs. Kenton says, it is sure to be a stranger."

"Well, then," Sarah exclaimed tartly, "it could just as easily have been Mr. Charles Clarendon."

Every gaze swung back the other way now, to Diana. She flushed vermilion.

"He *was* gambling every evening in the tavern," Justina pointed out.

"Oh, stop," Becky cried. "We are becoming worse than Mrs. Kenton with our gossip." She refused to believe that either man was responsible, but she did not know what to think. If Charles Clarendon was accused, it would look badly on Diana. If the colonel was found to be guilty, it would be very unfortunate for Justina and Sarah.

And Becky, the only one of the Belles who knew about the ruby and pearl necklace, was torn in the middle.

Having sat through the rest of the book society meeting with a mind far too distracted to listen, Becky returned home to find a delicious supper laid out, complete with candles lit and wine poured.

Her useful man had been at work again. It still surprised her. Perhaps he never would stop surprising her. *If only it could always be good surprises*, she mused, thinking again about the necklace.

"Your father ate early and took himself off to bed," the colonel told her when she saw that only two places were set. "He seems to have exhausted himself today."

Confused by that—for her father could hardly be exhausted by an afternoon beside the fire—she sat in the chair he pulled out and said, "I will check on him later. Perhaps Dr. Penny should come out to examine him. He has seemed rather distant lately, and his moods are up and down like a rowboat in a storm."

"Did you enjoy the book reading today?" he asked, sitting opposite.

How strange it was, she mused, to sit and eat with him at her table, as if they were an old married couple. "Yes."

"I don't suppose I'll ever be invited back."

She chuckled. "Only if you are needed to scare off Miss Elizabeth Clarendon again."

He smiled. "Always glad to be of service."

Rain pelted hard at the windows. It had not let up all day and only added to her general sense of restlessness. Becky tried to enjoy the food he'd set before her, but even that could not keep her interest for long. She pushed a Brussels sprout around her plate and fidgeted with the stem of her wine glass while gazing at the man before her. He ate with that gusto now familiar to her, his head down and elbows on the table. Not at all mannerly. Yet tonight she felt no desire to correct him.

He eyed her plate. "You're not eating your sprouts."

She cleared her throat and wound her fingers together under the table. "Sarah is a very sweet girl."

"She is."

"You must be very proud of her."

He frowned. "'Tis my brother who raised her."

"But still, she is *your* daughter."

Head on one side, he looked at her through the candles. "Yes."

"And *I* adore her." *Hopefully he will think that a good thing*, she mused.

He did. His eyes glistened in the mellow candlelight. "And she is quite like you."

"Is she?"

"You know…stubborn, likes to get her own way, determined." She paused and dabbed her lips with the napkin. "Possibly cheats at games…"

He laughed. "She is like me, ain't she?"

Oh, she loved to hear that laughter in her house.

"Eat your sprouts," he said.

So Becky picked up her fork again and finished her sprouts.

It was four days since she'd taken him home with her and put him in her brother's bed. Every night when she went to her own room across the narrow landing, she thought of him lying there, sleeping. He was a loud snorer, as her father had observed at breakfast the first morning. But Becky didn't mind the snoring. At least she knew where he was and that he was asleep.

Her reputation, such as it was, would be irreparably ruined if Mrs. Kenton ever got wind of his presence in her house. A bachelor, sleeping across the hall. No one but her father could possibly believe it was innocent. Even *she* couldn't.

With his reputation, why on earth had he not tried her door? She left it bolted, of course, but she'd fully expected him to try. Had lain awake frequently during those past three nights, wondering why Lucky Luke didn't try that notorious luck.

That night, she decided to leave her door unbolted.

✦

Every night, he'd suffered unbearable temptation

before finally getting off to sleep. Then he dreamed heavily of her, waking eventually in a sweat, the quilt bunched under him. What could he do? Her father was at the end of the hall, oblivious, it seemed, to the danger. Evidently the major had too much on his mind. Or he trusted Luke. And his daughter.

That was an awful lot of trust to place on the shoulders of a beautiful young woman and a scoundrel like Lucky Luke.

That night he lay awake again, just as before, staring up at the rafters, listening to Ness snore like a bear at the foot of the bed.

It was still bloody well raining. The earth surely couldn't take much more water. It was sodden already. With dull thoughts about the weather, he hoped to drift off.

Closing his eyes, he let his mind practice those dance steps the Book Club Belles had been teaching him. It was all coming back to him now, but he was still clumsy as an inebriated camel. He'd have to try not to embarrass Sarah too much and then he—

His door clicked.

Or had he imagined it?

Luke opened his eyes, turned his head, stared through the dark.

A flash of white proved there was someone in the doorway, in a nightgown, looking in.

He hitched his torso upright, resting on his elbows. "Rebecca?"

A breath passed and then another. He thought she would close the door again and she did. But not until she'd come into his room with her candle. The door was shut behind her and the bolt slid across. Whatever she had in mind for him, she didn't want to be disturbed.

Barefoot, she approached his bed.

"I waited five years for a kiss from you before," she muttered. "I'm not going to wait another five years for you to come to my bed and ravage me."

Luke had to wait a moment, make sure she was real, not a figment of his lusty imagination.

"Well?" she demanded. "I gave up waiting for you to come to me, so you'd better move over and let me in."

"Or you'll shoot me?"

"Precisely."

Ness wisely leaped off the bed and wriggled under it.

Luke had nothing to protect himself from her.

So he had no choice, did he?

❧

Luke swung his legs off the bed and stood before her, stark naked. It was a good thing he did that once she'd put the candle down or she might have dropped it.

Before she could say anything, he was tugging her nightgown down over her shoulders, not even waiting to properly loosen the laces. He sat on the edge of her brother's bed and pulled her closer as the linen drifted down over her breasts.

He had not said a word, but apparently he approved of this escapade. If the sight of that enormous rearing manhood was anything to take into account.

His lips went directly to her left nipple while his hands tore her nightgown the rest of the way over her hips and then left it to fall to her ankles. Her heart raced as she touched his hair, buried her hands in its darkness, pulled his head closer still to her bosom.

"Rebecca," he groaned as her nipple popped free of his lips. "I told you no more of this until our wedding night."

"You were just being difficult and sulking," she chuckled, clasping his head again, directing his mouth back to her puckered, aching nipple. "As if that has ever bothered you with your other women."

He growled something indecipherable and lifted her astride his lap. His hands slid up and down her spine and she arched like a cat, appreciating his firm strokes.

She ran her fingers over the dark hair of his chest and lower, following the slender line that wandered down over his flat, taut stomach. All that power under her hands. She felt his muscles shifting, affected by the kiss of her fingertips.

How much he wanted her. And she wanted him. It was sheer, red-hot desire. When her hand reached his manhood, he took his mouth from her again and leaned back, resting his palms flat on the bed behind him, his eyes watching her.

"What do you call this?" she asked softly, stroking that fine length and amazed to see it grow ever thicker and taller. "I know men have names for it. All different. What do you call yours?" Becky knew he was the one man she could ask who would tell her. He would not be bashful about it.

One side of his mouth lifted in a half smile. "Tallywag. Todger. Cock. Naughty Nick. Breeches baton. Sausage roll."

She laughed and he glanced nervously at the door. "It is very fine," she whispered, caressing the darkened head. "And what are these called?" Her other hand cupped his sac. It was very warm, surely the size of two goose eggs, she mused.

Abruptly he grabbed her around the waist. The next thing she knew, she was on her back across the bed and he was over her, his cock pressed against her thigh. "Don't play with me, wench."

"Why not?"

"This is no game." He kissed her chin, her throat, her breasts.

She writhed, filled to overflowing with excitement. "Oh, hurry!"

He paused. "More commands, eh?"

"Yes." Becky reached for his cock, but he slid out of her reach and put his mouth to her body again, licking his way down to her belly button, where he kissed her until she laughed again and had to slap a hand over her mouth to keep from waking her father.

"And what do *you* call this?" he whispered hoarsely, slipping further down and kissing her between her thighs.

She bit her lip. "I don't call it anything."

He ran his tongue over her roused flesh and she gasped, lifting her hips.

"Cherry basket," she moaned. "That's what you called it."

"Pussy," he whispered. "Kitty. Muff..."

And then he eagerly devoured her again, as he had done before, but even more urgently until she wanted to scream.

Becky's eyelids drifted shut and she clamped her teeth down hard on her tongue to keep the sounds of her wicked delight from exploding into the room.

His lips and tongue left no part of her neglected.

But just as she melted into the quilt, he stood again and looked down at her. "Better go back to your room, Rebecca."

She objected at once, naturally, but he was determined to resist.

"You want the rest, you'll have to marry me," he said. "This old soldier is a reformed man and he wants a wife this time."

She sat up, frustrated despite the wonderful sensations he'd just sent coursing through her. "You're supposed to be lucky, Luke."

He ran splayed fingers back through his hair and laughed huskily. "I still am. Only my definition of luck has changed. I found you. I want to make sure I keep you, make you happy."

She stared.

"And make you my wife," he added, his voice low, deep, full of yearning.

While she was still speechless, her heart galloping madly, he tucked her back into her nightgown, lifted her in his arms, and carried her back to her bed across the hall. His leg didn't seem to hurt tonight, she realized much later, as she lay alone and stared out at the moonlight.

She must be good for him.

He was savoring her, just as he'd once promised he would.

∽

The next morning when she rose to make breakfast, Becky found that Luke and his dog had gone.

"They must have left very early, m'dear," said her father. "Even before I was up. And you were late rising this morning! Most unusual for you, m'dear."

"But where did he go?"

"Back to the manor, I expect, although I heard him say yesterday he had clothes to collect in Manderson."

Of course, the new garments for which he'd been measured. Tonight was the opening dance at the assemblies. With everything going on last night, she had not thought about dancing. She wasn't thinking much about clothes that day either, but rather about his body without them.

When she went into the back parlor to look for her sewing basket, Becky realized that Lucky Luke was not the only thing missing from the house that day.

Her mama's music box, which she had left on the sideboard yesterday, and in which he'd taken such an interest, was also gone.

The beat of her heart picked up an unsteady pace as she thought of all those things that had gone missing lately and of the chatter at the book society. Pulse galloping, she flew upstairs and tugged open her drawer. The necklace was no longer where she'd left it.

Yes, there was a thief in their midst and she could no longer deny it.

"Papa!" She ran to find him at once. "Papa, the music box is gone."

"It cannot be, m'dear. You must have misplaced it." He tucked his head back behind his newspaper.

She spent the day searching around the house and found a great many more items missing. Her alarm mounted with every moment of discovery.

But she stopped and considered. *Think sensibly, Becky.*

Firstly: Luke was not the sort of man who would steal from her friends.

Secondly: He knew what the music box meant to her.

Thirdly: She trusted him.

She trusted him.

In her heart, she knew Luke was not the man who had taken those things. Just like that, she knew it.

Thirty

THE CLOTHES FIT PERFECTLY. HE HAD TO ADMIT HE didn't look that bad. Just a little stiff. Would look even better without the semifaded bruises, of course, but at least the swelling had gone down and he hadn't lost any teeth.

He had the clothes wrapped and boxed to take back to Midwitch Manor with him. As he left the tailors and limped along the busy Manderson street with Ness at his side, something curious caught his eye in the bowed front window of a pawnbroker's shop. He stopped, took a step back, and looked again in astonishment.

The night of the dance was upon them. Mrs. Makepiece and the Book Club Belles were all traveling in the Wainwrights' barouche, but the colonel had ridden on ahead as he had other business first, it seemed.

"He rides very well, even with his leg," Sarah informed the other ladies proudly, as if they might not have noticed and admired the sight while he rode about the village. "Wait until you see him properly in his new clothes."

"I wonder if the colonel will dance with Mrs. M first," Justina whispered.

No, she smells of pears. "He may not even remember the steps," Becky whispered back, knowing her friend teased her.

"True. Let's hope he's on his best behavior."

They arrived soon after this conversation and stepped out into the chill night air, all laughing and chattering with anticipation for the delights that awaited inside. Even Mrs. Makepiece appeared to be in good spirits, probably because Diana expected to see William Shaw tonight and she could inch them another step closer to a wedding date before his grandmama intervened again.

Stepping carefully to avoid horse muck, Becky walked across the cobbles and made an effort to cheer her spirits. She glanced across the steps to the candlelit coaching inn above which the dances were held and saw a very tall, darkly handsome fellow waiting there in black evening clothes with an ivory cravat.

And a walking cane. A new one with a shiny silver top.

He saw her, raised his hat in one gloved hand, and bowed.

"Papa!" cried Sarah, dashing by them to find the colonel.

He laughed and embraced his daughter, made her twirl for him to admire her dress. Then he whispered something and passed her a small parcel. Sarah came directly over to Becky and handed the wrapped package to her. "My papa wanted to give you this, but he said it wouldn't be proper for a gentleman to give a lady a gift when they aren't formally engaged. So he asked me to give it to you."

It was a lace and ivory fan decorated with tiny silk violets.

Thank goodness, because from that smile on his face, she was going to need it tonight.

Their group moved inside and up the steps to the small vestibule where coats were left and hairstyles anxiously reevaluated. As she'd hoped she would, Becky felt that returning tremor of pleasure at the prospect of dancing again. There was a smell of fresh paint and polish, for the assembly rooms had undergone a transformation in preparation for the new year. All was bright and hopeful.

She flipped open her new fan—the first she had ever owned—and walked into the dance hall with Justina and Mr. Wainwright, feeling ladylike at last. As Luke had told her, she didn't need to try; to him, she was a lady and always had been. But the fan was the finishing touch, the final flourish.

They were soon surrounded by the crowd. It was noisy and very warm, despite the weather outside, but as the music began, the people surged to the edges of the room, clearing space for the dancers.

The colonel took Sarah's hand for the first dance, a minuet, while the Book Club Belles looked on with pride. And a few crossed fingers.

"That is my brother?" Justina's husband declared in astonishment. "What have you ladies done to him?"

Becky too was wondering what they'd done. It was such a transformation that she thought it might take her a while to become accustomed to it. After what had happened on his bed, she was not so sure the "gentlemanly" colonel was a great improvement on the old Lucky Luke. One resisted her while the other never would have thought it necessary. On the other hand, one had purchased a fan for her and the old scoundrel probably would not have done so.

Or would he? Who really knew what he was, who he was, what went on in that mind of his?

She once assumed he looked at her and saw nothing more than a pair of bubbies. Now she knew he saw more than that. He saw all of her.

"Isn't that Charles Clarendon?" Justina cried.

Slowly Becky followed the pointing fan.

"What is he doing here?"

There he was, in satin knee breeches and dark blue coat with dazzling cuff links, hands behind his back, looking around the room with a bright smile. At his side stood a young lady in a very fine silk gown, sprinkled with beads that caught the light each time she made a slight movement or laughed in a soft, lilting voice. She had fair curls piled high on her head and lavish diamonds hanging from both ears. They were standing with a small group of other, well-dressed folk, but it was clear they thought themselves superior to their surroundings.

Charles touched the woman's elbow, steering her a little to one side. She looked up at him and laughed. He leaned over her and whispered through his smiling teeth.

He was supposed to be back in Oxfordshire by now. He was called home directly, he'd said, but there he stood, bold as brass.

The young man must suddenly have seen Becky at the other end of the hall. He blinked, went red, and quickly looked away again.

The Book Club Belles gathered around her. "Should you talk to him? How rude he is not even to say hello, after paying such attention to you before."

She protested. "There was never anything more than friendship between us. I did try to tell you all."

Probably not a good time to mention that he'd asked her to be his mistress. Her friends were angry enough on her behalf when they needn't be. If they truly had a reason, he might not get out of there with all his hair attached. "There is that wretched Charles Clarendon," cried Lucy, running over to the other girls. "He left me in the orchard, in the dark, and then he abandoned you, Becky, to gossip, after letting us all think he would propose."

"I never thought that," she replied. "I didn't want his proposal."

But Lucy was too furious. She had not forgiven him for deserting her at the treasure hunt, and any other sin he might have committed was merely icing on the cake. "He might at least acknowledge that he sees us, but he turned his back. I saw him—there he goes again, turning his shoulder to us."

"Well, perhaps he didn't see us."

"Oh yes, he did!"

Afraid that Lucy would rush up to Charles and possibly punch him in the walnuts, Becky decided it might be best to greet the man politely and get it over with. A lady surely would. Just because he had forgotten his manners, she need not.

Then he must surely acknowledge her friends and stop acting in that stupid way with his nose in the air.

It felt as if everyone in that ballroom was looking at her suddenly, as if they were all whispering behind their fans. Some of the people there perhaps had heard gossip about her. News traveled fast. Particularly when Mrs. Kenton was behind it.

If she was not very much mistaken, the woman standing with Charles had just whispered something to him and glanced back at the contingent from Hawcombe Prior as if they had all brought manure in on their feet. She heard Charles laugh uneasily.

Well then, she would stick up for her friends as they did for her.

She closed her fan, took a deep breath, and walked around the room to where he and the lady stood.

Finally, she was behind him. "Mr. Clarendon. What a surprise to see you here tonight."

She expected a smile, a flutter of those golden lashes, a hasty excuse.

Instead there was a blank, stony-eyed stare.

"Mr. Charles Clarendon," she spoke a little louder, thinking he might not have heard above the music. "How pleasant to see you here again so soon. We thought you back in Oxfordshire."

His companion drew back with a puzzled countenance. Charles lowered his eyelids a half degree. "Do I know you, madam?" he muttered. "Forgive me. I don't recall…"

Becky laughed. "What can be the meaning of this attitude? You were once welcomed by all of us in Hawcombe Prior, and this is how you repay our hospitality?"

Again he stared.

"Charles," his lady spoke softly, "do you know this person?"

Finally he licked his lips and said, "Ah yes, Miss Sherringham, is it not? Now I recall I had the pleasure of making your acquaintance at my cousin's house at Christmas." He bowed his head and made no attempt to introduce her to his companion. And turned his back.

"You would not want to be introduced, my dear," she heard Charles explain to the woman. "She is a dreadful slattern who threw herself at me this winter and made my time in the country utter hell."

Slowly Rebecca turned. But her feet refused to move away. They swiveled around again. "I do hope your new curricle with the pretty and distinctive yellow-painted wheels runs well, Mr. Clarendon, and that you got the hood refitted. I know leather seats can get ruined in rain."

His lady friend snapped her head around to look at him, her earrings swinging wildly as she glared, and a thin vein stood out on her forehead.

Well, that had warned the woman anyway. It was the best she could do.

She might burst out laughing and it would not be seemly, so she quickened her steps, heading for the cool air outside. She needed to look up at the moon and stars, to rid herself of the stifling rules of society that made so many people's lives miserable slavery, because they feared life and living. They feared the unusual, the honest, and dared not follow their true passions.

&

Still concentrating on his steps, Luke had not seen any of the scene playing out at the far end of the hall until he heard the sweep of gasps that came his way like waves crashing against a stony shore.

And then he saw Rebecca dash by with a wobbling lip, a strand of copper hair falling down the side of her neck, agitated color heating her face.

Within a few moments, the news had flooded the hall. Charles Clarendon was engaged to Lady Olivia Moncrieff, an earl's daughter with fifty thousand pounds. Her fastidious father had apparently opposed the match. There had been a quarrel and a falling out. Her father had sent her to Buckinghamshire to get away from the arrogant young buck who courted her, but the young lady was then followed into the country. Now, so the gossip went, it was imperative that they *did* marry.

For the meantime, they were staying in Manderson while her father cooled his temper and came to terms with this unexpected strengthening of his daughter's stubborn will. Lady Olivia had a widowed aunt in Manderson and they had taken refuge with her—a widowed, childless aunt soon to die and leave the young lady a further fortune of ten thousand.

A few folk at the dance exclaimed that they thought Clarendon was almost engaged to a major's daughter from Hawcombe Prior—and was that not her who just ran out of the room? The poor girl looked distraught.

Luke heard it all and then hurried outside to find her.

Afraid he would find a woman prostrate with sobs, he was relieved to find her dry-eyed, observing the moon, his gifted fan clutched in her hands as if someone might dare try to take it from her.

"You forgot your coat," he said, limping up to her with it. "You will catch cold, woman!"

"I am not in the least cold. I was enjoying the bracing air."

"He has hurt you. I shall go inside and beat him to a pulp."

She frowned scornfully. "Oh, Lord! I thought you were at least too old to think of settling the score with your fists, man." Then her scowl was gone and she chuckled throatily. "What on earth makes you think that peacock hurt me? I told you a long time ago that I am not a silly, romantic, naive girl. I did think he was a friend. About that, I was wrong. Hardly enough reason to mash him to a pulp."

Although she resisted, shrugging and pouting like a sulky child, he managed to get the despised coat over her bare shoulders. "I don't want you getting ill."

She looked up at him. "He said his brother sent you a gift, and he hoped you enjoyed it. I'm sure you know what that means."

Naturally, Kit was too cowardly to come back at him alone, man to man, and sent two thugs to do his dirty work while he kept his hands clean. Nervous for Sarah, Luke looked toward the hall again. "Did he say anything else?"

"Only that I was a slattern he barely remembered."

"Good."

She spun around. "*I beg your pardon?*"

"I don't mean about that," he replied hastily. "I mean, that's very bad. Very bad indeed." He pointed toward the door. "Sure you don't want me to go and mash his brains?"

"No." She smiled. "I shall wish for a wife to plague him to the end of his days, though."

"Excellent idea." After a pause, he said, "Do you... will you dance with me, Miss Sherringham?"

Instantly her proud chin went up. "Certainly. I'm here to have fun."

She was breathtaking tonight. He knew of no fancier word for it. Her hair shone like autumn leaves in rain. *Aye, that was quite poetic*, he mused. He'd write it down if he knew how to spell autumn.

"Before we go inside again." He stopped and reached into his jacket. "I have something of yours."

She frowned.

"Well, something of your mother's, actually."

He had wrapped it in a handkerchief—the same one in which she once tied a piece of pie for him and his dog. The letter *R* stood out in the moonlight.

"Open it," he whispered, since she delayed and he was eager to see her reaction.

Thirty-one

NESTLED IN THE HANDKERCHIEF WAS THAT PEARL AND ruby necklace. He took it and put it around her neck, which was, fortunately, bare that evening. "Aren't you going to ask me how I came by it?"

"Should I ask?" She sighed.

"You might be surprised to know that Sir Mortimer Grubbins found it."

She cast him a skeptical glance over her shoulder while he fastened the clasp. "The pig?"

"Please do not refer to him in those terms. He's of aristocratic blood, so Sarah informs me."

"But I don't understand."

"Once upon a time, many years ago, my Great-Uncle Phineas bought this necklace for a certain redheaded farmer's daughter from the little hamlet of Hawcombe Mallow. But she refused his generous gift and threw it back at him like a surly little ingrate. I daresay she was much like you."

Having closed the clasp, he turned her again to face him.

"Whatever Phineas did with it after that, it turned

up in Sir Mortimer's sty. Since my great-uncle liked to say there was treasure buried on the property, I can only assume he buried it and the p—Sir Mortimer dug it up again. In time for me to give it to you."

Bemused, she ran her fingertips over the pearls. Sadness threatened to overwhelm her. On such a moonlit night, looking at something beautiful, she had a tendency to feel this way, of course. Tonight she was staring up at Lucky Luke.

"Now I can dance with you," he said, grinning, "because you finally look as pretty and togged up as me, Gingersnap."

She took his arm again and they walked back into the dance.

Again faces turned to look, and they gasped as she held her head high and let the candlelight dance over her new necklace. She wasn't usually the sort for jewelry, but tonight, because *he* gave it to her, it felt right.

"You've given me a gift," she said to Luke. "That means we're engaged."

"*Engaged?* Lord, no, not again. I was engaged once before to a chestnut filly, but she bolted at the first fence. Can't put myself through that again."

"Colonel Lucius Lucky Wainwright," she exclaimed, "we are damn well engaged and that's all there is to it, so do shut up."

"You're too young for me." He swept her into the dance and grimaced immediately. She suspected the turn was a little too sharp for his leg.

"True," she replied crisply.

"And wayward. You might change your mind again."

She looked at him and smiled. "Then we'd better get shackled as soon as possible, just to be sure neither of us loses our gumption."

∽

Her friends weren't certain they could believe her when she told them that she and Luke were engaged. Again.

"Are you sure this time?" Justina asked worriedly. "I thought you said he was boring and fat-headed."

"I never said that! Oh, for once, please, will my friends believe me?"

Well, they had to believe her when Lucky Luke took her in his arms and kissed her in the midst of the dance floor, didn't they?

"I am in love with you, Miss Sherringham. You have changed everything I once thought was unchangeable about my life. I hope you know I can never let you go. I can never be a day without you for the rest of my life."

If not for a certain spying busybody, we might not have made it, she thought. Suddenly she had an urge to hug Mrs. Kenton.

Jussy was right, after all.

As happiness rippled through her and made her giddy, she longed for everyone to feel the same way. No one should suffer. For so long, she'd stubbornly refused to believe in love and magic, but now it seemed unfair that some people still didn't.

Glancing over at the other folk watching the dance, she saw Diana with her dull fiancé, William Shaw. He had dragged her over to where Charles Clarendon stood and was hedging for an introduction to him and to the very wealthy Lady Olivia Moncrieff.

Poor Diana. Staring at the floor, she looked as if she longed to sink into it; her misery was palpable. Only William Shaw didn't see it.

It is no good, thought Becky. Something would have to be done about Diana's predicament. As Jussy said, their friend must not be allowed to suffer a marriage without love.

And then she reached up to kiss the colonel again, much to his evident surprise and delight.

"If you don't make love to me tonight, I might change my mind and call it off again," she said, her lips brushing his startled mouth. *May as well get straight to the point*, she thought. "So I suggest you take my maidenhead at once."

His eyes lightened a shade and those black brows rose hesitantly.

"What's the matter?" she demanded.

He took her hand, almost crushing it in the strength of his grasp. "Thank God, you're direct. I can't wait any longer."

As the next dance began, he tugged her toward the doors again, this time pausing on the way to let his brother know he was leaving. "Miss Sherringham feels light-headed. I'll take the barouche and send it back for the rest of you. Can you bring my horse and keep an eye on Sarah?"

Darius Wainwright eyed them both curiously. "Of course, but—"

"Can't stop," Luke added. "In a bit of a hurry, Handles."

"So I see, *Lucky*." His brother smiled. "May I suggest *some* caution?"

"No, you certainly may not."

A quarter of an hour later, they were in the barouche, just the two of them, traveling through the moonlight at a steady, rocking pace. A very slow pace, for Luke had instructed the coachman to take his time.

"I feel light as a feather," she whispered as he removed her hair pins, one by one.

"Because tonight and from this moment on, you have no troubles."

"That's impossible. There is always something to worry about. Life would be very dull without the downs to make the ups."

He chuckled. "Very well then, but from now on, we will share those troubles, eh?"

It might be a challenge for me, she thought, *to share my worries*. But she'd try. "As long as you share yours with me."

"Oh, I mean to share my everything with you, Gingersnap," he replied huskily.

❧

Perhaps he should have made her wait until their official wedding night, but he found the idea impossible. Especially when she nibbled at his chin and her hands opened his breeches to explore.

"I want you now," she whispered, licking her way along his jaw. "I can't wait another moment."

What was a rake to do, but oblige the lady?

Still, if she was indeed a maid, he ought to take his time, be gentle. The gladness he felt in his heart was a warm, spreading glow that soon filled every part of him. He even forgot the pain in his leg.

She was his. She was all his.

With one careful hand, he stroked between her thighs and felt her readiness to welcome him in. So soft, so warm. He shuddered. "Rebecca."

She climbed astride his lap, her knees on the seat, her skirt lifted and slippers abandoned. Although he meant to enter her slowly and with care, a sudden bump in the road brought her down sharply on his erection, causing her to cry out. Luke wrapped his arms around her, kissing her, his thighs taut while he restrained himself from the need to drive up into her.

Good God, Lucky Luke had been conquered by a virgin. After all his years of avoiding maidens.

She kissed him. "I love you. But I think…I think you just killed me."

He laughed against her lips. "Then we'll die together. The French call it *le petit mort*."

With his hands holding her bottom, he lifted her slightly, repositioning, and then he lowered her with care.

She gasped, her head flung back, her back arched.

Luke moaned her name again and buried his face between her breasts. He knew he wouldn't last long. Not this first time. Oh, but there would be others. Many, many others.

He began to raise and lower her in his lap in a steady rhythm until her breath grew shallower, quicker. And then she squealed, her teeth clenched, her body tight and hot around him, holding him in with all her power.

This was the sweetest sin he'd ever known.

It seemed fitting that after all their travels, they should finally come together like this, in motion.

There, at last, they both expired, wrapped in each other's arms, neither knowing where one body ended and the other began. Neither caring.

The journey from Manderson to Hawcombe Prior could take as long as half an hour on bad roads, even with fast horses. That night it took them an hour and a half, with several stops along the way to retrieve a lost shoe, a garter, and even a stocking that flew through the window and became hoisted on a tree branch.

But the hour and a half was not wasted. Three times, it was not wasted.

Thirty-two

"...There is something so amiable in the prejudices of a
young mind, that one is sorry to see them give way to the
reception of more general opinions."

—Sense and Sensibility

HE WENT TO SEE HER FATHER THE NEXT DAY, FOR BOTH
of them were keen to marry as soon as the banns
were read.

The major was thrilled to hear the news—once it
was ascertained that Luke had not changed his mind
about wanting a dowry.

"No, Major, I won't ask you for any money." He
placed a box on the table between them and slowly
opened it. "And I won't mention this to your daughter, or where I retrieved it." Carefully he removed her
mother's music box and set it down on the cloth. The
major stared and his eyes reddened, but he was silent.

Luke took a deep breath. "I recovered the other
items too and will see to it that they are returned to
the owners without raising suspicion."

Sinking to his chair, the old man stared at the music box. He placed one gnarled hand upon the lid and patted it, like an old friend. "I had no choice," he muttered. "Bills must be paid. She was a sensible girl and would have understood. I kept this till last, tried to hold on to it. For her."

"Debts?"

"Don't tell Becky. She has so much else to worry about and she always tries to help, to make things right. It really isn't her job, but she won't pay heed."

Slowly Luke nodded. "I am somewhat acquainted with her temperament, but you need not fret. She won't know about this. Just don't take anything else to the pawnbroker, eh?"

His face bewildered, the old man began to weep, crumpling in his chair.

Luke reached into his coat. "I think you and I can do some business while I'm here today and it may help you out of this hole, but next time you're in trouble, come to me."

"To you?"

"Who else would you come to but your son-in-law?"

Thoughtfully, the old chap nodded. He sniffed. "I suppose, since I'm giving you my daughter, I ought to get something in exchange." He was cheering up quickly, looking around for his brandy. "And we really ought to celebrate."

Luke laughed. The major hadn't even heard his plan yet, but he was happy again, his troubles temporarily shifted. Fortunately, the money Luke had earned abroad as a ranch hand, and the sale of his medal, had given him enough to buy those items back from the pawnbroker.

He'd also swallowed his pride to take some money from the Wainwright fortune—just a little—enough to get him set up in his new life. Although he wanted to pay it back over time, his brother wouldn't hear of it and insisted it was a wedding gift.

The Wainwright brothers had finally found a way to lower their barriers, but now, of course, they had something more than blood in common. They'd both fallen in love.

"It has preyed on my mind, Colonel," the major said, "worrying about how I could get those things back before it was noticed they were missing."

As if no one had yet noticed.

"It is a weight off my mind."

"Well, now to your other problem and a more permanent solution," said Luke, thinking they'd better discuss business before the major got too soused. "I understand you have some farmland to sell."

❦

The wedding of Colonel Lucius Wainwright (formerly deceased and of no fixed abode) and Rebecca Sherringham (of India, Egypt, France, and Africa, but most recently of Hawcombe Prior) went off without a single curse, misadventure, quarrel, or stumble. Afterward, there was a small feast held at Midwitch Manor, during which Ness and Sir Mortimer were arguably the best dressed guests thanks to the decorative talents of Miss Sarah Wainwright.

Following the consumption of some suspiciously strong punch and very sweet cake, the newlyweds climbed into a flower-strewn barouche and began their journey to a new beginning. On the other side of the village.

"Why are we stopping here?" Becky demanded, as the wheels rolled to a slow halt in the muddy ruts before the gate of Willow Tree Farm.

"Because this, my darling wife, is our home." He opened the door, stepped down, and then turned to give her his hand. "Sarah and Ness will join us in a week. After our honeymoon."

"We're renting from Papa?"

"No. I bought the place."

Becky followed him down, leaping to miss the worst of the mud, mindful of her lovely bridal gown, over which all her friends had sweated and pricked their fingers for the last three weeks. "We're going to be farmers?"

"Yes. If you approve." He looked at her tentatively. "Do you? I know the place needs work, but I'm handy."

"Oh, I know that." She spun around, her sight blurry with tears. "We can stay here forever?"

"Of course we're staying. Got to look after your father, ain't we?" Luke put his arms around her, and for the first time in her life, Becky could not hold back her tears, but they were tears of joy. And she hid her face in his chest, surreptitiously wiping her nose on his waistcoat. In the guise of a gentleman, he very gallantly pretended not to notice.

❧

Luke had come to Hawcombe Prior quite certain he would soon be in his grave. After all those dreams of expiring in a fire—or heading straight to a very hot afterlife—he'd been sure he hadn't long to live.

But on his wedding night, as he lay surrounded by his new wife's wild, long waves of polished copper and flaming bronze hair, he realized that he *had* seen her in his dreams after all.

Rebecca was the fire that consumed him. Every night in their bed.

Now he could tell his brother that one of Lucky Luke's dreams had finally come true.

❧

Becky polished the music box every day and it took a place of pride on their mantel. Her husband never told her where it had disappeared to, but she found out, of course. There were no secrets in that village.

She soon knew that Luke had retrieved all the items from the pawnbroker in Manderson. That he had done it all without the slightest fuss, just to save her father from worrying.

He might like to think he was a rogue of the worst order, but he had a very soft side of kindness that he did not even seem to know he had. Or he did not like to admit it.

As for Rebecca Wainwright, she might think herself the most levelheaded, reasonable, and judicious young lady in Hawcombe Prior, but she had a saucy, wicked side that very occasionally—much to her husband's enjoyment—could not be restrained.

And so they lived, sinfully ever after.

Colonel Brandon was now as happy, as all those who best loved him believed he deserved to be; in Marianne he was consoled for every past affliction; her regard and her society restored his mind to animation, and his spirits to cheerfulness; and that Marianne found her own happiness in forming his, was equally the persuasion and delight of each observing friend.

—*Sense and Sensibility*

Acknowledgments

Thanks to everyone at Sourcebooks for helping me fulfill a dream, to my friends and family for putting up with me, and of course to the readers, without whom none of this would be worthwhile.

About the Author

Jayne Fresina sprouted up in England, the youngest in a family of four daughters. Entertained by her father's colorful tales of growing up in the countryside and surrounded by opinionated sisters—all with far more exciting lives than hers—she's always had inspiration for her beleaguered heroes and unstoppable heroines. Visit www.jaynefresina.com.